TANZANITE

DR. SANTHUSHEE WAIDYARATHNE

Australia

Dr. Santhushee Waidyarathne
drsanthushee@gmail.com

Santhushee Waidyarathne
ABN 20147589728

Ordering Information:
Quantity sales. Special discounts are available on quantity purchases by corporations, associations, and others. For details, make contact via the email address above.

Tanzanite / Dr. Santhushee Waidyarathne. —1st ed.
ISBN: 978-1-7636248-0-1

Dedicated to:

My dear husband Awantha, thank you for all your encouragement and support during each step of fulfilling my dream.

My loving son Dovin and my amazing daughter Bivonya, thank you for being my sparkling light.

Thank you, Universe, for giving me this incredible journey of life.

Tanzanite

An ocean unrelieved
whirling fathomless ripples
riddles of moonless past
may the beams of stars.
Shells of necklace unheard of
dangling down braided to
untold tales of echo.
Seeking treasures
absence twisted entity.
It is hard to trust until the end.
Wring the grief
struggling for war
Tanzanite is nowhere.

The soul is cherished
walks behind you
simply diversion.
Waves of dreams
fondle the promises
up until passing.
Cease the thoughts
close your eyes
no remaining beyond.
Aware of the blink
between black and bright
uniting among agony and soothe.
Arrest the quiz
knit the swing of nature
yet Tanzanite beside you.

Shells embraced
forgather
bonds twisted
eternal stories of
laugh and tears.
Let it lose
untie the knot
uncover the mystery of nature.
Release the fear to unfold
light on the Tanzanite
you are holding.
Shells of necklace now nowhere.
Yet
Tanzanite Immortal.
Dr. Santhushee Waidyarathne

CHAPTER 1

Kingdom Uttaya ' Terra

The fire is raging red flames with glittering arc lights. A girl in white attire is sitting in the middle of a circle. Her gorgeous face looks like faded jasmine, the tears blubbering down. Her hair danced with the swirling wind. A man carrying himself with a long beard is seated beside the fire. His grey dhoti, wrapped in a faded orange robe, swayed to the side. His eyes remained shut, and the fire started surging together with the murmuring mystery sound of a mantra. The girl raised her face while glancing slightly at the man with a long beard who appeared as the priest.

People gathered around the pit at some distance, chatting with scary faces. The women carried their children tightly while the wind tried to fly away with their clothes. As the mantra grew high-pitched, a tall man stood beside the priest and opened his deep voice, "stay calm, Mitra, we all need you, so stay calm." He said while gazing at her with cloudy eyes filled with unknown fear. He is the prestigious king of Kingdom Uttaya, renowned as Yarush.

Mitra, the princess, turned her blue eyes and shook her head. Then sighed miserably. Beyond the circle, a woman accompanied by another three. They were holding her forcefully. Her eyes were an ocean of tears. She mumbled and raised her hands towards the naked sky, "God protect my child." The clouds diverted the bright blue to black-grey, letting the horrified thundering appear in a flash. The people shouted,

"God have mercy on princess Mitra, don't take her away from us, protect her."

Standing beside the priest, the king held his black stick again to their side and yelled.

"Be quiet," he commanded. His shimmering white gold dhoti and his shoal swing with blow.

His weary face tried to hide his bewilderment; his lips twitched with a white-grey beard. At the same time, His broad shoulders were wetted with sweat. All the folk gathered on an isolated sea cliff with fearful eyes. The flames raged up with orange curls resembling a mother surrounded by hundreds of kids securely twisted in their hands. Billowing sea tried to peep out the fire flames. The wind started whirling and rolling along with rumbling thunder. The rowdy sea waves simultaneously heightened beyond the mysterious gloom. Suddenly, a small boy began to run toward a cliff edge. He is adorable and young; his mother began to yell out loud, "wait, don't run," but the boy was running like a flash, stretching his hands upward and trying to catch something invisible to others. He didn't hear his mother's scream; he repeatedly smiled at someone who followed only his little eyes secretly. Finally, as he was near the cliff, the princess stood up. Suddenly, the thunder groaned. The wind started to howl violently, and the gigantic sea waves slapped on the cliff terrifyingly. The sun has hidden, and the entire sphere is sunk in misty dark gloom. The man cried out,

"Mitra, you should not jump over the circle."

But she instantly jumped and sprinted like an arrow, yet her long, silky cloth swathed around her slim body tangled her toes. She ran, following the way the boy was running as he reached the cliff edge; he stretched his hands to the sky again and smiled at the unknown ghostly gesture. Then he moved his tiny foot for the next step, but Mitra hastily pulled him back. The boy escaped, but Princess Mitra, who could not control her pace, quickly fell down the cliff. The sea waves hurriedly cuddled her delicate body. They dragged her away from the sight. "Mitra, my child," the woman bawled, and the wind started lamenting with devastated souls.

Kingdom Spavitar ' Henaten

Mitra opened her eyes; it was dark, a bit cold, and lying in a comfortable place; she was dismayed and mumbled, "where am I?."

She rolled her eyes around, and its cave ringed with several cressets. A few candles were lit next to her, and she was wearing a different white and gold mix silky dress. Numerous dazzling flowers were placed beneath her bed, close to the candles. She tried to recall how she had fallen from the cliff edge. Unexpectedly, her suffocated, paralysed body fought with wild, heartless sea waves. Then, on the spur of the moment, a singular, gorgeous, colourful giant creature with glimmering fins dragged her inside the water. Afterwards, a thick black concealed her eyes. It was pretty hard to recognise that abrupt cowering hallucination. It was an indeed unheralded nightmare. She tried to step down, but her body felt numb and fainted.

"Welcome back, princess Mitra, my daughter; it took a long; time for me to see you again, my love."

A lady with a soft voice appeared in front of her. She appeared charming. Her glossy brown hair is extended to her feet, and her vivid black eyes twinkle with thick eyebrows. The light of the candles brightened her face. Yet She is calm and embraces her warmly.

"I am queen Mudi, your mother." Mitra presents a curious look at her.

"no," she said.

"I was supposed to die. You are not my mother. I don't know where I am. And.. My head is spinning," she stammered.

The lady quietly sat beside her and then began to pat her head. Her soft fingers slowly ran through Mithras' hair. Mitra shut her eyes for a few seconds. She sensed some magical power transmitting inside her and soothing her gradually. Yet her whole mind was torn with sudden distress,

"Where am I?" she questioned in a hushed tone.

"You are now where you belong, my dear though your soul travels so far," Queen Mudi whispered.

"Why it's travels?" Mitra raised her head.

"Each soul travels for a temporary shell. When the body is broken, it travels to another for a certain period, yet it is not permanent; the soul falsely bonded with that fragile shell." Mudi stopped and glanced at Mitra.

"When the shell broke, unfortunately, the soul had created an attachment with it. Hence, the soul seeks another new shell and makes a bond to carry out the continuation; if no bond, no shell or soul persists, it's all demolished, my dear." Mudi holds Mitra's hand.

"So Why am I here?" Mitra calls out confusedly.

"slow down no need to bother your mind. Let's solve this leisurely princess Mitra. The crown princess of kingdom Spavitar."

"Kingdom Spavitar," Mitra exclaimed.

"But I'm supposed to be the crown princess in kingdom Uttaya," Mitra mumbled.

"Of course," Queen Mudi raised her voice.

"It's your soul is transferring between two frames

and in two worlds." she paused her words and sighed.

"Why is my soul wandering around the two worlds" Mitra cried again. The unresolved silence veiled the atmosphere.

Then, the entrance unlocked at once, and a girl came off." Queen Mudi," she said.

"Mitra might be disturbed and exhausted; we must be patient until she is retrieved from the bafflement."

The girl is wearing a floral gown in pink and white, and her curly hair is endowed with oak leaves. She presented a charming smile with sparkling eyes.

"We have limited time, Pesha, and she should focus on her responsibility." Mudi admitted impatiently.

"No need to press her queen Mudi. Our mother warned not to make trouble. I'll be here and explain everything, trust me," Pesha confirmed.

Queen Mudi nodded and walked out slowly.

Mitra stared at Pesha "who are you?" she inquired confusedly.

"I am Pesha; we knew each other a long time ago."

Mitra raised her eyebrows "what are you?"

"I'm the quiet soul of untied with bonds. I stand alone and hold absolute inner peace; I can appear neutral only your equanimity can power me. I'm the messenger of Godmother Atunura."

"Who is mother Atunura?"

"She is the whole universe, the power of everything around us, whole ruling energy. She is the nature, the creator of all Godmother Atunura."

Pesha muttered in a soft voice.

"I am dismayed, and it's hard to believe am I alive or got rewarded with life after death."

"Well, you may know it shortly anyway. So welcome back to the kingdom of Spavitar princess Mitra," Pesha reacted with a charming smile.

Kingdom Uttaya 'Terra

The storm started disappearing from the gloomy atmosphere, permitting the sky to glimmer with hope. The dusk arrived a bit more to console the wailing shadows. The woman was weeping on the beach, a white silk cloth elaborately draped around her body. Another few women attempt to calm themselves.

"My daughter, I lost her forever," she screamed.

Mitra is lying mutedly on a stage made out of a wooden stick. The candles glittered beneath the pile, and the white Jasmines covered her body. The young girls held the baskets of white Chrysanthemums—the sea coils to kiss the moaning sandy beach. The little girls were building circles of white Chrysanthemums around the wood stack. The colourless chrysanthemums and sea breeze twisted with the snowy mist of the rippling sea and whimpered the sorrowful song to nature.

I saw your cute smile
and
I touched your gentle face.
I hold you.
You were born inside me.
A soul with an enormous heart
hide inside the dark wave.
Naked sky lamenting
while butterflies flee away.
I'm still here waiting for you
to fetch the seashells
feel the scent of misty blossoms
chase the ducklings
listen to the birds' chatter.
So
wake up and grasp me

still

we can drift through this nightmare.

Mitra's mother gazed at her daughter's corpse miserably and wept. Candles were no longer shining, and a scented vapour unfurled throughout.

"My eyes were sinned to see your death before me. I have no strength to bear this pain, come back Mitra come back."

Her wretched heartaches slowed away with the trembling breath. The tall man seated next to her was holding her arm. They settled around the bone fire close to the wooden stack.

"Try to make up your mind, Tara. I'm unaware of what to say, but we have already acknowledged that her destiny could not be changed. God granted her breath when she didn't cry, and it was planned to refund it. But, though we tried to cease it, we were defeated."

King Yarush opened up his bold, deep voice and sighed.

An old man bent close to King Yarush.

"It's a time for the cremation, my lord."

It was Vamu, the most humble, indebted servant of the king. Yarush stood up and grabbed the flambeau. Vamu's words echoed in Yarush's ears; his fingers were shivering. He took a shuddering breath and mustered the entire force to his numbed hands. The mantra commenced, and Yarush gave a miserable glance at Tara. Then he desperately tried to mobilise his feet, but all his mind was abandoned in his past. He remembered Mitra running towards him.

He cuddled, folded her inside his broad shoulders, and slowly kissed her forehead.

"My lord, time is passing," Vamu whispered.

Then, the sound of chanting mantra surging, Yarush hauled his stony limbs to roam around the woody stack. He paused, stared at Mitra, and bent his tall body to touch her lifeless face. Then his watery eyes glanced at the burning flames and brought them out towards the stack.

"No, stop." A harsh voice roared, and Yarush unexpectedly ceased.

Kingdom Spavitar ' Henaten

Mitra woke up struggling with the invisible delusional sensations. Her whole mind is stuck in a misty, perpetual black. Pesha seemed nicely dressed in a shimmering green gown length to her toes, her curly hair encircled by yellow roses. Her curved eyelashes quake vaguely simultaneously with the stunning green eyes.

Her tender hearted tone desists Mitra's awkwardness for a split second.

Her loveable attitude tore her bewilderment unconditionally.

"Come on, let's walk; it might blow away your entire discomfort" She directed Mitra towards the narrow opening; Mitra gradually rose and sauntered outside with Pesha.

A steeping path came across in front of them, entering into a pear-shaped den of shadowy high ceilings, a substantial white Crystal roof with spiny grey protrusions resembling innumerable unicorn horns from the ice. Next, they moved to a somewhat different area with ivory walls and a small underground filled with blue water. The skinned rock floor jagged with countless stewed elongations eroding from the pure cool water. Some stumpy crystalline corals unfurled alone from the ground upwardly with pinkish rounded gagged natural contours, and a few tall crystals stood up like milky mountains.

"What a stunning setting," Mitra whispered, glaring at Pesha.

Mitra felt thrilled with her reawakening emotions,

"It is not water, specks of sapphire," she mumbled. Pesha waded into the water and made it splash throughout the area. Tiny water drops sprinkled on Mitra's face. Mitra smiled delightedly and stepped inside the water, letting it lap around her waist. Her long hair quivered side to side, resembling the browny black clouds surrounded by the deep blue sky.

"Come on, let's walk along this underground creek," Pesha admitted.

They splashed across the flow unhurriedly. "I'm cold," Mitra said. Pesha lends her hand to Mitra, who leaps swiftly onto the flat rock. Their long dresses got drenched in water. Pebbles-like rocks spark with brown lies on both sides of the bank. The way became narrow, reaching the grey conical path with a low ceiling. It was embodied with brown-yellow patched coral and the vastly extended swelling knobs overgrown to the floor. Each knob was separated scantily, identical to a tree stalk with roots. Some of the coral was shining; the cave was cosy and miraculously scented with a fresh fragrance.

Mitra peeped throughout amazingly, the brownish coral trunks demarcated with white curly layers stretching across the ground.

The floor is glittering in ivory with bluish sparkles and resembles a portrait hidden in upper heaven.

"A dream extends beyond the sensors, but why do I feel much familiar with this place" Mitra murmured.

Pesha peered into her face

"Maybe you used to spend quite a lot of time with King Pedro here," Pesha replied.

"Who is king Pedro?"

"He is your father, past king of kingdom Spavitar."

"My father," Mitra exclaimed, twirled her eyes all over the cave and wandered inside quietly. Then, suddenly, she stepped behind and squeezed her head with both hands; her lips dried out, and her body twitched along with her limbs. Pesha handled her tightly.

"Mitra, what happened?" she questioned.

"No," Mitra shrieked." That black viper" she yelled. Mitra's unconscious, powerless body leaned over to Pesha after a while.

Kingdom Uttaya ' Terra

Yarush halted his arms and turned around. "Wait, no cremation," the voice hollered. Some person stood in the distance, glaring at Yarush. He has sharp black eyes, and his grey-coloured, entangled curly hair extends to his shoulders. His moustache twirled upward to catch his ears, with his extensive white head touching his hairy chest. He was draping a milky white cloth with a golden border. He bent and shut his eyes, then unfolded one arm towards the sky while bearing a spear on the other arm. He glimpsed at the pyre, sighed heavily, and arrived closer to the Yarush. Then drew the flambeau from Yarush and flung it to the sky in a flash. He stared at Yarush; the sky turned darker simultaneously with a loud gale. "Oh, It's you," Yarush faltered. People watched the entire scene shockingly ; likewise, someone had created a bizarre spell over them to accept this inexplicable circumstance.

"I have warned you she has born for an exceptional reason," the man wakes his voice. Then, while Yarush looked down, the man moved forward and lifted his spear straight to the thundering sky.

"It's her destiny, the decision of Godmother Atunura," the man exclaimed.

"Yes, I know it is a simply questionable decision; both of us waited for ages to become parents. Finally, she was rewarded to us with an agreement to grant her life back to the one gifted it," Yarush said, wiping out his teary eyes. His frail body swings and knelt towards the man,

"Such an injustice," he cried out.

"What an injustice are you complaining about, king Yarush? Let me explain the empathy of mother Atunura; recall your memory straight away to the fundamental matter you suffered from some years back," the man said calmly. Yarush sighed moan-fully." A lifeless newborn prized with soul," the man said aloud. The people glared at each other with astounding eyeballs.

"Some years back, queen Tara was struggling throughout the extended period to have their child. As a result of Tara's endless praying for mother Atunura, eventually, she was blessed with a baby. Yet, alas, it was merely a breathless body." The man recollected the horrible past.

"Yes, it was me who was unfit to give birth to a lively child; I am the one who is bearing whole misfortune and my all incapability to fulfil the future heir of kingdom Uttaya," Tara revealed in a blunt tone. "Barris," she said, "Glad to greet you after quite a long time." Barris looked kindly at Queen Tara. "It's not about your misfortune; it only matters about breaking the promise you made with Mother Atunura."

"I know I'm guilty about everything. But, I needed to keep my daughter with me as long as possible to protect her." Tara confided.

"As you were aware, she does not belong here, and she was awarded a soul for a particular reason," Barris said roughly.

"I know her funeral defined on her date of birth," Tara's broken voice unfolded.

"That sad day I believed I'm not worthy to carry my life, my whole dreams shattered when I spotted my lifeless newborn. I have ruined my main responsibility, and I got cursed by my in-laws they all blamed for the bad luck I am holding. I wanted to die by poisoning me and releasing Yarush from our entire bonds because I knew he would never leave me though I could not gift him his blood. We loved each other greatly. Nevertheless, I believe in mother Atunura and her energy. I ought to expect my destiny. So I took the poison."

"Why, Tara, why did you want to leave me?" Yarush yelled.

"Yarush, I was cursed by all others and symbolised as the ill-luck for the whole kingdom. My body, my womb not strong enough to bear a lively child." Tara cried.

"Yes, but Mother Atunura prevented her, and she made me convey her message; we met right on that cliff, the Death child revived back with a beautiful spirit. Mitra rebirth on the cliff. But I made one promise with both of you after she reached her youth, and the soul should be returned to its origin. You cannot cease the detachment of the soul." Barris held his words and gave a glance at Tara,

"you promised to me, Tara, that you would never interfere with this, but you arranged all those witchcraft and tried to divert the natures oath."

Harris turned to Yarush,

"You promised you would protect her body inside the sacred cave agreeing with Mother Atunura's order, because it should not be cremated, but now you all are performing the final rites and attempting to destroy her body." Barris yelled.

Yarush gazed at the sky with a sweaty face. "I wanted to end this all; whenever I touched her, I felt I would lose her soon. Hence her every birthday brought some enormous anxiety to me. The bond between us is destined to persist even after her demise. Because I have to protect her powerless body, Tara will be more devastated, and it will suffer her forever and me too. I wanted to find the end of all these things. I'm sorry." Yarush sighed. Barris reached closer to Yarush." Mitra's soul re-joined with the origin in Spavitar, and I took her lifeless body out from the ocean and replaced it on the cliff; it must be secured until the soul returns someday," Barris revealed.

"Princess Mitra of kingdom Spavitar, will she revisit me again." Tara mumbled. Barris came close to her and peered into her eyes. "Queen Tara, you are not misfortune, no command exists that each woman's belly should carry a foetus. We all resemble a tiny spot in this false reflective sphere. We are holding our fragile frames to chase an illusion. Profoundly our birthdate is set with our death. Until then, we made justifications for competing with our wrecking souls along with this ruining human trunk. You are not cursed as you were born for some special duty is directed to you by the universe. You added some extra colour for Mitra's life. You raised her by nurturing the spirit inside her and completed your duty as her mother. Someday you will be prized with her warm-hearted gratitude on behalf of all your earned devotions. So until then, fulfil the rest, protect her body," he explained and presented a pitiful glare at Queen Tara.

The crowd carried powerless Princess Mitra inside the sacred cave. Barris murmured some mantras for extended periods. Then he commanded to close the door. The ocean became calm, along with the gloomy sky. The gale ceased, and a tiny breeze swept away the hidden memories. But a little fellow stood close to the cave holding a yellow rose.

"Princess Mitra you saved me from death let me promote my tribute to you," he whispered and placed the yellow rose on the doorstep. Kingdom Uttaya strived to cease the echo, along with perpetual silence.

CHAPTER 2

Mitra awakened. She was lying on the same bed, a few candles lightning close to her and firewood blazing in the corner of the passage. It brings more warmth while expelling the familiar dark inside. She tried to recall her a few hours back, but befuddlement haunted her, along with the blind remarkable reflection of past symbols. Queen Mudi showed herself in front of her with tearful eyes.

"My poor child," she said.

"Mother," Mitra whispered.

"My memories threatening me, mother, I have no strength to proceed forward" she paused her words and stared at Mudi

"Cuddle me, mother. I have been seeking for a long time," Mitra pleaded.

Mudi rubbed her tears while sobbing and seized her firmly.

"The black viper mother, it was close to me" Mitra's lips twitched with fear; she shut her eyes with a shaking heart.

"We were able to protect you, Mitra; no need to be frightened." Mudi cuddled her and then touched her face with all love.

"It happened in your childhood. You were shocked after your father's death. You stayed unconsciously for many days and your eyes remained shut. We tried to revive you and also protect you from black vipers. Then Mother Atunura, detach your soul and reconnect it with the demise princess of kingdom Uttaya in the world of Terra. It is a parallel human world similar to our planet of Henaten. You both hold the same appearance. And they decided to accept you as Princess Mitra in the kingdom of Uttaya."

"My soul is travelling with two planets," Mitra exclaimed.

"So true, Princess Mitra, you are unique henceforth; you must prove that distinctive reason you are destined." Pesha's words vibrated throughout the cave, and she approached close to Mitra.

"I have little memory of Henaten," Mitra sighed.

"There are two major territories that govern the Henaten, respectively. One is Spavitar and the second is Thebeslon. Spavitar is the principal ruler of the planet Henaten. Because we are much stronger with our spiritual mastery. we directly connected with divinity following nature or the energy of the entire universe." Mudi clarified.

"But except the world of Ovigons, the black vipers," Pesha added.

"During the extended period, Spavitar and the Thebeslon maintained a satisfying mutual relationship. Thebeslon agreed to the whole decisions made by Spavitar, following the other small kingdoms around. All leaders respected each other and ruled their territories peacefully."

Mudi stood up and sighed with tired eyes.

"Unfortunately, the Ovigons neither welcomed this quiet, amiable habit. All black vipers desired was to end it and ruin each other lives with three poisons." Pesha muttered.

What are those three poisons? Mitra questioned.

"Avaricious, hatred together with imprudence." Pesha answered.

"They released their evil spirits, and they born in here contemporary with absolute humans of Henaten. They empower their souls with three poisons to torture the whole sphere and split entire harmony. They ruined our all understanding with Thebeslon and others. They divided our planet undoubtedly." Pesha slowly knelt beneath Mitra and grasped her hand.

"Mitra, it's only you and King Darev eligible to recover this catastrophe. Only you two are capable of protecting the Henaten from Ovigons and wipe out the poisonous spirits." Pesha pleaded.

"Darev, I'm quite familiar with that name," Mitra whispered.

"He was your childhood friend," Mudi responded.

"And now he is ruling the kingdom Thebeslon, he surrendered all other territories, and he stands whole leading Henaten except us."

"Why?" Mitra questioned the disturbing attitude.

"It's a long story, Mitra," Mudi added.

"Mitra, unleash your emotions restrained your centre mind join with the whole energy of the universe or else with the nature. Mother Atunura will explain you each thing. Listen to her and let her resolve this tangled puzzle created around you. she will connect your senses straight to your heart.

Goddess of nature and universe has no obligation of words to communicate merely to enter your heart. Let her in Mitra. Close your eyes and join with her. Talk to her, Mitra," Pesha murmured repeatedly.

Mitra shut her eyes and felt her spirit drifting throughout for some noteless justification. Mudi and Pesha moved out of the den. Mitra sensed her eyes abandoned in some visions. Mother Atunura grasped her hand to roam among them.

Kingdom Thebeslon ' Henaten

The kingdom of Thebeslon is an enchanted paradise shrouded in the glorious ocean. The upper part of the island border engaged directly with the state of Spavitar. And the other domains encircled Spavitar and Thebeslon. They are all ringed with Spavitar and Thebeslon by narrow landed passages. Those routes elongated from each kingdom, linking them precisely with kingdoms Spavitar and Thebeslon. These landlines with steeply banked curves resemble greenery stalks on the cerulean ocean. The silvery seawater wrapped around the Thebeslon, and several rivers keeled down rhythmically over a rocky cliff, designing sparkling, unbroken falls. Some are slender and lengthy, and some are bulky and notable. The seashore is remarkable in fine shingles extending vastly along round sandy grounds. The fragmented water layers of cascades create thin, lacy mist veils throughout the sphere, resembling snowy Alyssum flower bunches wafting away from the upper heaven. The vast mountains emerged from the centre of the land, covered with bluish greenery. The flourished forests are green emeralds, and cold, delicate wind swirled up and down to whisper secrets to the falling leaves. The field between the mountains was replenished with bright-scented blossoms. The giant oak trees stand mutedly with long trunks. Some massive, aged tree trunks wearing the crown of morning mist resemble aged Emperors of divine territory. The dainty ripple of darting streamlet flows against the sheer slope and assembles inside the radiant down pools, recreating the astounding portrayal of nature.

King Amenmose ruled the kingdom Thebeslon. He is tall and sturdy, with curly grey hair and blue eyes. His straightforward personality, concurrently with his gracious spirit, raises the kingdom's prosperity daily. He was spending a reputable life with Queen Rene. She is a gorgeous woman both inwardly and outwardly. Her sparkling, delightful, remarkable black eyes reflect her enormous golden heart. The castle is sighted at the top of the highest mountain. It was a splendid palace coupled with extraordinary supremacy. The king and Queen owned three children, one son and two daughters.

Prince Leo is the elder son, Princess Lamila is the second daughter, and the third one is Princess Hatra. Prince Leo is talented and good-hearted. However, he is a bit arrogant because he loses his patience quickly. Lamila is quiet and less talkative but attractive. She has mysterious black eyes, and she enjoys significantly being alone with herself. The youngest daughter, Princess Hatra, is the unruliest character because she made crowded disputes with the king and Queen. Queen Hatra has a short body frame, fair skin tone, and excellent light brown eyes. Her red wavy hair extended above the shoulders. Her smile is not straight, and her teeth are a bit large, but she appears to be quite gracious and innocent. Her oval-shaped face is simply unpredictable. Queen Rene has worried about Princess Hatra from the onset. She addressed her as a "sneaky kitten" because Rene felt her eyes were not vivid but doubtful. Rene saw the darkness of Hatra's complicated mind following her rude manners. It made Rene more anxious because Hatra owned the crown after King Amenmose. According to the law of Henaten, the youngest of the family is eligible to bear the crown.

Hatra constantly fought with her sister and brother. She hid their toys while playing and lied to Queen Rene on uncountable occasions. In addition, she cheated in games almost all the time.

Leo considered tolerating her sisters and being concerned about them as his responsibility. Therefore, he usually ignores Hatra's misdeeds. However, Lamila's situation differed from Hatra's as Lamila's annoyance surged daily. Lamila shut off her emotions, bounded with Hatra and tried to build a distance between them. Hatra used to lie to fulfil her underlying agendas. It created bountiful inconvenience to her parents and siblings, even for her maids. Her unstable mind could not concentrate on learning; hence, her teachers continually disappointed her. Her messy habits invariably disturbed the maids. She teased them when they rearranged her sloppy living sites.

Hatra loves to be admired by others often. Therefore, she frequently gets disturbed when somebody snatches her fame away from her. One day, she pushed her friend into the middle of a deep hole full of thorns. Hatra hated that girl because she was more innocent, talented and charming than herself. The poor girl cried out with wounded legs. While others attempted to rescue the girl, Hatra kept herself sobbing sadly. Her dramatic nature convinced her that she was very troubled by her friend. Simultaneously, she secretly scowled at the girl with fiery eyes. The girl was shocked by wholly following Hatra's silent threat and kept mute.

Time slides along, and Hatra comes close to the teenager. Her sly behaviour grows higher each day. Queen Rene became more irascible when she heard about Hatra's embellished stories. Rene wept with Amenmose on numerous occasions concerning Hatra's misbehaviour. Yet it is all tangled knotty riddle.

Gradually, Hatra's grown body commenced pursuing the attention of the Males. She was outfitted with a tight, red-coloured gown with a deep plunged neckline. She kept her wavy black hair loosely, letting it waggle slowly along her broad hips. Though her face was not pretty, her flirtatious eyes scrutinised each corner with each step.

She kept her eyes restless at night with her burning trunk and shivering lips. She decorated her bare body with red jewellery and spent hours in front of the mirror. Then, she sighed when she realised that nobody had been expressing romance towards herself. Lamila's marriage added extreme fidgety to Hatra. She secretly started to drink red wine each night. Her steaming soul wailed unconditionally for her unresolved desires. When midnight arrives, her naked body lies desperately on the floor. Her breast goes up and down together with her each rapid breath. Her half-shut eyes drizzled in red wine. The wine could not satisfy her hunger for desire; hence, she enclosed her isolated shadow at the bottom of the intoxication. When the morning sun peeps throughout, she towed her powerless body out of her chamber and wiped her sleepy, rosy eyes.

Hatra made her all visits to the royal tutor regularly and pretended to be the humblest student of all. She attracted the tutor with her charming, kind words. Yet she hated the tutor and her entire lessons. As the future Queen, Hatra had to acquire quite a bit of mastery over each entity related to ruling the kingdom. Unfortunately, her numb, crazy intellect never let her commit her obligation.

One day, Hatra was gone for a walk with her friend Maleeka, and eventually, they came close to the river bank. While relaxing on the riverside, her eyes capture a man who stretches on the flattery rock. Hatra observed him closely. He is middle in height and might be five or six years older than her. His nicely combed hair curves backwards at the end and slightly drops on the forehead. His black-brown eyes shine straight with her view. Hatra presented a light smirk and shook her head off. His broad shoulders, brawny arms, and arrogant, sharp stare fizzle out her whole heart. He is tan, powerfully formed, well-built, and shined with daylight. The wind howls among them to resolve their flaming emotions. Hatra felt her heart pounding as she squeezed it tightly and curled her neck slightly. His eyes sparked deep inside her spirit and blazed her up to her caged desires. She stood abruptly; her entire soul was yearning to destroy all-mighty fences. She stared at him with half-closed eyes, hair danced with the breeze.

The man could not pull his eyes away from her; Hatra slowly moved her limbs in the middle of the river. She shut her eyes to picture his gestures in her mind. While the river circled, she pleaded to alleviate her soul from icy cold water. The mysterious superiority of water engorged the natural lines of her blooming body. The water trickled down from her soaked-up long gown. Her grown breasts and broad hips marked the presence of female art. The sun was shadowed by unknown clouds, inviting a grey mist to veil around the river. Hatra's numb ears did not touch her friend's loud buzzer. The frigid sprinkle concurrently with that unknown gesture's eyes abandoned her unconditional soul and arrested her somewhere beyond the arc. She shuddered when contemporary with lapping water passed her waist. In a flash, she tugged away from the strong arm. Her face stroked with his warm exhales. His mighty hands were bearing Hatra. She spotted her shape in his vision; it was familiar with her patterns. The water dribbled from her red hair, and her arms fastened around his neck. It was he who was touching her for the first time. She closed her eyes to conceal this ecstatic momentum. Finally, the man made her lie down on the floor. Hatra found it hard to release her soul from that magical delirium, and she mumbled, "thank you." The man opened up with a deep, bold voice. His body leaned over her, and his eyes peered at her face. It was filled with kindness.

"Princess are you alright?" he asked.

"Ya, who are you?" she questioned back.

"I'm Hatop; my father is a retired soldier, and I'm too worked for the King." He answered.

"Thanks, Hatop," Hatra faltered.

Her friend Maleeka approached, and she cuddled her while shouting out.

Hatra was taken back to the palace with the help of the servants. Queen Rene was sitting next to the Hatra's bed with teary eyes. Even though Hatra was her most troublesome child, Queen Rene felt worried. Hatra weakened with constant fever for a few days and feebly stretched down on the bed. Although Queen Rene cared for her all the time, Hatra cured slowly. She kept pondering almost all the time. One day, she commanded her maid to fill the room with black and red roses to puff her lungs with the fragrance of freshly bloomed roses. Because the arrival of Hatop diverted her life wholly. Her mouth remained shut, and she showed herself with extreme calmness. Her sorrowful eyes repeated his name, "Hatop." She commenced writing her first letter of love to Hatop with jerking fingers. Deep inside, pleaded for his warmth. Only she sought his endless love. Her lips trembled, and her muscles twitched when she memorised his handsome frame. She cuddled to his broad shoulders in her dreams and slowly mumbled, "Hatop, I want to be you mine forever."

One day, Maleeka visited Hatra "you made me frightened that day Hatra luckily that man was there," she said. "I wish if he was not there, Maleeka," Hatra was expelled woefully.

"What's the matter, Hatra" Maleeka questioned curiously. "He killed my soul and stabbed to my heart. I feel I'm merely a lifeless corpse without him. I'm isolated in haunted darkness. I'm sensing the absolute pain of near death. My eyes, my entire spirit imploring for his unconditional love."

"What are you talking about? Are you out of your mind?" Maleeka asked Hatra astonishingly. Her fingers tightly grabbed Hatra's arm. "I'm in love with him," Hatra whispered and shut her eyes. A few tears dropped and wetted her cheeks.

"But Hatra, he is a son of a retired soldier, he is an ordinary village man; how can you involve yourself with a man like that. You ought to be the future Queen of Thebeslon," Maleeka spoke confusedly.

"I can throw away my crown if he loves me Maleeka; please hand over my letter to him. You are the only person I am trusting," Hatra begged. Maleeka stepped backwards with a shocked face.

"What?" She shouted. "You are ruining everything, Hatra," Maleeka sighed heavily.

"You can do it for me, can't you?" Hatra questioned.

"But Hatra," Maleeka hesitated. Hatra grasped her shoulders.

"Maleeka, I have no life without him." Hatra beseeched her and stretched the letter" Maleeka sighed speechlessly and walked away. Hatra tumbled down on the bed and sighed contentedly.

Love is an excitement of glorious and magically spellbinding mistakes. Unfortunately, it is an acceptable fault that guides someone through their bountiful attachments. Those attachments are followed by misery and anxiety. Yet nobody can defend this marvellous creation of nature. Which was designed to conserve its own continuity. A torturing ambush encircled over sentiments to prison mankind inside the conclusive cage. Profoundly, it's an illusion of endless war. Yet, it is an incredibly hypnotising fantasy. Free of all attachment, it resembles silent water with no ripples. Utterly quelled with no storms and no boundaries. Nevertheless, the honey bee must be attracted by the flower, or it should pertain to it. Because it is the eternal law of living.

....

Hatop took the letter and was wondering about the following steps. It's not the first letter of love he has been touched. Though he is not the visitor of the journey of the relationships, the matters engaged with the present moment abandoned him in a confused argument. He had to end his uncountable short-term love stories due to the burden of his family.

He accepted that he had some enticement towards Hatra, but as a training soldier of a middle-class household, how could it become possible with a crown princess. However, he determined to scratch out this luck lottery, or it might be a terrible death. The two sides of the coin are on different images. He smirked to himself and folded the letter.

Hatra felt absolutely relieved when Hatop replied to her about meeting her up. She was excited with all, looking forward to being his beloved eternity. So Hatra rambled with Hatop in all her imaginary delusions. She thoroughly believed that Hatop would love her more than everyone else. Hatra has never acquired the attention of her parents since childhood. When she asked for the toys from King and Queen, she was habitually gifted with Leo and Lamila's used toys. Hatra denied that madly, her face dimmed with sadness. Eventually, her grief turned into hatred.

As a consequence of that, she began to hate her siblings. Leo was admired by Queen Rene and Lamila and was mainly admired by the king. Yet all they attempt to teach her is merely her responsibilities and the extreme heaviness of the crown. Neither of them poured her their pure-hearted affection related to Hatra. They forgot to peer inside her heart; they never devoted their time to cuddling her. Instead, Hatra's isolated mind tended her to speak unstoppably, letting herself hide out her interior bareness.

She needed to snatch others' senses around her for a second.

She hated her brother and sister for accomplishing her idea to hurt her parents. Queen Rene was almost always distressed about Hatra's disobedience and misbehaviour, which she ignored to capture the reality of Hatra's reactions. Even though Hatra's was blessed with a world of Ovigons, she grew up with humans. Therefore, her deep core constantly rotates among the two spaces. Hatra desired to be her parents' most special child, but would they accept her, or were they secretly grieving to have a daughter like her? They never recall questioning her about her approvals and not ever prized her.

Their ignorance guided Hatra to choose the Ovigons' world and be a part of it. However, the slight warmth of love can divert the blood-sucker to a God, or else negligence followed by rejection can be translated from God to evil.

Hatra could not share her sentiments with Rene as Lamila achieves; when the castle was placed for royal functions, Lamila was always gifted with her most liked attire. Because Rene considered Lamila's enjoyment all the time. But this never happened with Hatra. When Hatra entered the party, Rene's smile swiftly vanished. She bends her head with a gloomy face and bears a big rock on her top. However, when Leo appeared himself, Rene's uneasiness faded away. Her eyes started to sparkle up like seven stars in the sky. She

delighted and introduced him to everyone: "Here comes my handsome man."
While Rene grasped Leo's fingers, Amenmose's hand wrapped around Lamila's shoulder. They all laughed together, bounding to each other. Hatra
watched them lonely behind the corner and silently wiped her tears. She
tightly handled her red wine and then gritted her teeth.

Nevertheless, her painful emotions were kicked away by the rage. Her
eyes replenished with flames, and her nature found much serenity and pro-
tection by her own blessing of anger. But, on the other hand, the Ovigons
inside her are powered up with hatred. Unfortunately, her own blood created
it inside her.

One evening, Hatra was staring outside from her balcony. One bloomed
red rose rested on her palm. She removed each rose petal and fantasised
about Hatop. She closed her eyes to imagine him. She heard a giggle of
women. Hatra opened her eyes and carefully watched beyond the balcony.
She spotted Lamila and Queen Rene walking in the garden, holding their
hands together happily. Lamila recently visited to see her mother. Hatra quietly moved inside and sat on her bed. She breathed rapidly, then sighed. Hatra
removed the final rose petal and threw it away

"No. he would love me more than everyone, I can become his most important person," she confirmed.

"Mother never attached with me likewise she does with Lamila and Leo,
who am I? Why was I born here?"

Hatra murmured sadly, then lay on the bed gazing at the roof. The tears
ran across her cheeks.

Soon after, she fell asleep. Suddenly, she woke up a few hours later, and
it was almost the middle of the night. She heard someone calling her name.
A dark shadow was standing near the terrace, peeking inside. Hatra raised to
watch it more clearly, yet that unknown gesture was sighted as the blotted
image. A violent hissing sound touched her ears, and she peeped around with
fearful eyes.

"You were born to fulfil the duties of Ovigons," the dark shadow said.

"Who are you?"

"I am you, and your soul is my possession, I can resolve your sadness. My
witchcraft can accomplish your wish."

"Nobody for me in this palace. I am so alone." Hatra sighed.

"You were not their wish, but you belong to Ovigons, and your entire heart pleased Orana."

"Orana," Hatra pronounced.

"You are a perfect and lovely princess. Your parents are so nasty as it seemed. I can feel your desperation, but I appreciate you. The shadow stretched her arms towards Hatra.

"Princess, I think the bond of love between the parents and children should be persisted unless another new life might not invite their globe." The shadow floated inside Hatra, and she felt some intense enchanting energy hanging out with her. Hence, she stared at the shadow without moving.

"Though they gave birth to you similar to your brother and sister, neither attached with you. But I think this bond among them and you should be smitten with bottom of your heart regardless of the difference between each other. But what a pity they ignored you."

"They hurt me each second each minute criticised for everything neither want to talk to my heart."

"You suffered whole this life aren't you princess?" The shadow patted Hatra's head smoothly.

"You grieved because you except the joy. Because all the bonds are naturally designed to gift both rejoice and misery. Profoundly it will weaken you and stuck your soul in an endless voyage."

"I am yearning for that contentment I want someone who stands with me only for myself, someone who lives for the sake of my soul."

"I will be with you and stand for you if you seize me, inside you," the shadow whispered.

"Believe me, princess, I can fulfil your dreams. He will be with you forever. Try to reach him and grab his love do whatever He commands you. And protect me."

"Why am I protecting you?" Hatra questioned, confused.

"Protect me from the positive souls about to reside at Henaten, these souls who are possess with the blessings of mother Atunura. They will destroy Ovigons and me."

"No" Hatra shouted.

"We have to fight against these souls and tear down them away from the world of Ovigons. The black vipers will be the superior power of the Henaten" Orana grasped Hatra tightly.

"It's your duty, princess, and I will follow you each step."

"I promised," the shadow laughed aloud, and Hatra felt some mighty force veiling around her, suddenly drowning in a thick black.

CHAPTER 3

I t was a special day, Princess Hatra. She waited until the sun had gone down. Then the night rises contemporary with her anxious heart. When midnight arrived, the castle sunk into a deep sleep. Hatra quietly hid inside the red cloak. Hatop familiarity with the palace surroundings loses her fear about their meeting. She carefully escaped the guards and secretly trotted to the secret tunnel in the Palace's backyard. The passage directly enters the sea beach. Hatra entered the tunnel, which was narrow and dark. While shivering with fear, her limbs hesitantly mobilised. She halted briefly and then placed her hand on her chest. She gasped to breathe while her eyes remained closed.

"No, I must go to meet him," she mumbled with trembling lips. A few minutes passed, and Hatra took a deep breath. Then she moved her slightly shaken legs.

Hatra ran along the tunnel like a whirlwind, letting her uncontrollable speed eventually make her fall down. Then, finally, she raised her head and sighed with pleasure. Her sweaty forehead felt the coldness of the indulging sea breeze. Suddenly, a rough, brawny arm stretched solemnly towards her. A hand for herself. Hatra glanced at her heartfelt fluttering with strange, soothing bundles of emotions. Her hidden desire knotted with some shiny eyes fixed at her, and he is not another; it's Hatop. So Hatra shuddered with the muted mouth.

She stared at him and surrendered herself in the deep hole of unknown excitement. Even though Hatra's hand is firmly grabbed by Hatop, neither exhilaration nor warmth is exhibited in his eyes. He spoke roughly. He is unfamiliar with the romantic honey words as a soldier, yet all war and battlefields thrill him.

Along with little moonlight, the lonely gloaming shore triggers her to curl up in his arms and roam inside their delirium of colourful designs. Her heart yearns to murmur the poems of love with him. So Hatra rambled with Hatop silently and tried to smile at him shyly. Yet Hatop slowly released Hatra's hand and made his steps faster than her. Neither romance was exhibited from his face and eyes, and his mouth remained shut all the way through. Hatra peeked around while walking, her entire heart filled with unknown fear of Hatop's puzzled behaviour. Suddenly, Hatra increased her pace to catch his quick steps, and then she paused her legs in front of Hatop, obstructing his way. She smiled innocently and stretched some white roses towards him; she plucked them from the palace garden and carefully placed them in her pocket of the long gown on behalf of Hatop. He glanced at Hatra, then at the roses and smirked weirdly, "walk fast, princess, it's getting late," he said roughly. Hatra put the flowers back in her pocket and sighed bitterly. While Hatop moved his limbs, Hatra gazed at him with confused eyes.

Neither mental satisfaction contented him because his entire soul was pleased with the physical perception. The burden of his weighty life filled with thousands of fights pushed his nature to pursue all lust instead of love. He never bothered about sweet, loveable words. Because it was somewhat difficult for him to touch the woman's heart. He believed that women should always walk after him, and he used all his rights to kick them out whenever he needed to, following his stoned heart, which never relied on romance.

He walked towards the isolated rocky den at the shore's end. His quick steps discomfort her, and she fell on the sand many times. Hatra felt overtired with painful legs. Hence, she stopped her walk and panted for a while. But he didn't notice it at all. At the same time, Hatra peeks at the den, shivering in the frozen cold. The sea waves saluted her toes hesitantly. The gloom veiled all over the cave, and the grey clouds shaded the moon, permitting the burning souls to fulfil their desires.

Hatop directed her inside the den and unexpectedly embraced her tightly, ripping off the dark shadows. She gazed at him speechlessly, allowing her entire heart to sink into his eyes; his stormy sighs and lips played on Hatra's face. Then, finally, he harshly kissed her; though his crudeness stirred up her pain, she begged to sense the ecstasy throughout the agony; likewise, the drought earth endured the blazing sun until the deluge.

It was merely lust that overflowed throughout, not the feeling of affection. And it replenished our whole desired hearts. Hatra forcibly struggled inside the Hatop's muscular contour when he grabbed her waist and seized her tightly. His deep exhales stroke her face, and then his lips are enclosed in her neck and far. Gradually, Hatra's aroused emotions imprisoned in his rhythm. He pulled out her long gown vigorously. Hatra showed her unrobed body before him without being awkward and hesitant. He slowly made her lay down beneath him to hunt her all secret desires. Her delicate body crowded with his disobeyed nibbles. His firing eyes drowned in lust, neither spewed with sensual peace. Hatra moaned to undergo this heartening, frenzied pain. She slithered inside him to pursue his warm murmur of "I love you," yet he impatiently denied it whole. He came over to her body and slashed her stretched attires.

Hatra screamed out loud when his strength arrested her deep inner; his superiority stoned her. Her nails drew artistic patterns all over his muscular frame. Her elated moaning faded with the windy sea gale. They abundantly healed the triumph of bodily attachments rather than emotional devotion. Yet their weary souls were relieved along with the befuddlement and repeatedly surrendered to endless desires. The ocean sings songs with misty night. The white roses lay solemnly in the corner of the den, hiding inside Hatra's gown. But it's hard to find freshly bloomed flowers among the broken petals.

Afterwards, the den appeared to be much more familiar to them. They shared countless moments of escaping themselves inside it. They showered their enormous, ardent desires each night without a doubt. Hatra consented to whole lifeless cave rocks to reveal her hidden passions by disrobing herself in front of them. Neither noticed except the rowdy sea waves that chased far distant sands. Hatra's deep inside, perpetually yearned to have romantic moments with Hatop. She dreamed of talking with him endlessly under the shadows of dusk. Her heart craved to tell him all the hidden secrets and much needed to know about him and his life. She wished he would open up to her someday. Hatra hoped to wander with him, tangling their hands among the soft sea waves. Yet, all the times they met, Hatop pulled her directly into the dark den. He removed her gown impatiently. He never remembered asking her permission beforehand. He used her to please himself, considering her whole body as his own asset.

A few months passed leisurely, and Hatra covertly played her all sneaky visits to Hatop. But one misty morning, Hatra felt giddy; she spent her whole day lying on the bed. She lost her appetite, and some sour taste in her mouth made her terribly unwell. Suddenly, some alarming senses stabbed her head, reminded her of something inaccurate, and burned each muscle. She felt her entire body; her whole veins were numb. She locked her door silently, then dropped to the armchair and breathed rapidly as her pale face wrinkled with unknown fear. Her heart banged. "disaster," she mumbled unsoundly with trembling lips and commenced to sob.

Hatra spent a few days hiding inside her chamber. Rene visited her several times. She lay feebly on the bed. Rene's innocent eyes were incapable of capturing Hatra's secret sickness. She commanded the maids to heed Hatra consciously and serve her favourite meals. The Palace was busy and excited with Prince Leo's wedding arrangements; Leo was soon about to marry a royal princess. Hence, Queen Rene had to spend considerable time on all the chores related to the ceremony.

Hatra kept pondering for many nights, and eventually, she met up with Hatop that gloomy night. Hatra rode back to him alone.

Hatop waited for many days, bearing all doubts about her unexpected absence. Then, finally, he eagerly hauled her inside the cave when he spotted her. While his restless lips wandered around her blanched face, half nude powerless trunk, the most ruinous words spilt out. It abruptly ceased Hatop and shaken the den.

"How dare you?" Hatop groaned.

"It's all your fault. Do you want to see my corpse?" He faltered.

"This is a disaster, Hatra," he exclaimed, shook her shoulders strenuously, and pushed her away.

"All this happened because of you, so be ready to blot it out forever from your body," he said nastily. Hatra knelt beneath him and began to cry. Hatop bent against the rock wall and knocked it with his fist. He pressed his head to the rocky surface and moved it from side to side. After a few minutes, he sighed quietly. He began to smoke while glancing at the thick night. The heavy smoke emitted from his mouth.

"We have a secret journey tomorrow morning; you must come with me," he commanded.

Hatra raised and wiped her cheeks.

....

When Sun rays wiped out the darkness, Hatra appeared outside. While everyone snuggled in bed, Hatra silently escaped, returning to the shore. Her faint heart fluttered like a leaf. The one satisfied with her entire body exhibiting affection now throws all the hideous consequences to her account. The cold sweat above her forehead drooped down, tensing out each frozen blood vessel. She sauntered behind the Hatop and slightly glimpsed the shadowy woods. The colossal tree stalks wrapped with thick, gloomy mist glared at Hatra, resembling the isolated tombs of a scary graveyard. Hatra shut her eyes, expecting that Hatop would hold her hand, but he paced along the way quietly. Hatra drew her legs with frightened eyes and silently wiped her tears.

Gradually, they reached the tiny shady house in the end corner of the wilderness. It stands with a tottering structure and dark, narrow walls among the mysterious, gloomy black silhouette that haunted the house. Hatop tapped the door and called "Marisa" in a calm voice.

An aged woman with whitened grey hair was visible to them. She has eagle eyes and a pointed nose. She is unpleasant and looks horrible in her frowsy black, yellow dress. Hatra looked suspiciously at Hatop because she had never known about such an unusual place inside the forest. The woman invited Hatra to walk inside the house with her. Hatra instantly looked at Hatop's eyes. Hatop nodded and winked his eyes to Hatra to proceed with Marisa. Yet, the appearance of the filthy, older adult, very similar to an evil witch, hauled Hatra's legs to turn back hesitantly. She clung to Hatop's neck, whimpering with all frightened and cuddled him tightly.

Hatop pushed her away mercilessly,

"Go and expel that nuisance out of your body on behalf of my life," he growled aloud. She stepped forward swiftly with an uncontrollable, anguished, bursting heart wiping down her wet cheeks.

Hatra headed to the dingy, narrow room, which was not very spacious and shuttered with smoky stained walls. A small bed is low and covered with an old pillow and a raggy quilt. The woman made her stretch down on the bed; she was holding a feather with a sharp point matched with a knitting needle. It glides lower inside, extending far down to throwing up insufferable pain. Hatra screeched with agony, yet dark woods seemed familiar with that sound. The blood spilt out following a terrible, deadly pain. It was highly torturing rather than the gleeful pleasure she sensed when Hatop's magnetic male power flooded her deep inside. The slaughtered unborn, soaked in pure red flesh, blow away from the womb. The voiceless cry of delicate humans is not sensible because the pleasure of their intimation is much more delighted than that of suppressed life. Their thrilled giggles drowned in the suffocating pain of a rejected visitor who was temporarily accommodated in her body. The unborn succumbed soundlessly.

He might probably beg for his last breath, but no one listened.

The fear of knowing about death and feeling about it is not as fascinating as the romantic tales. Poor, vulnerable remnants are buried secretly deep in the dark jungle.

Hatra's frail body fell down the way. Her pale face and eyes dimmed with pain. Hatop swiftly put up her body in his strong arms. As they returned to the hidden tunnel, Maleeka stood alone for Hatra's aid. She secretly took Hatra back to the castle. Nobody noticed.

Hatra stayed long, extended days inside her room. She was extremely feeble. Rene worried about Hatra's sickness but didn't know anything, and Hatra pretended it was a typical ailment. Hence, Rene bothered Hatra to concentrate on her meals. Hatra's pale face and eyes alarmed Rene. She spent countless sleepless nights beside her. King Amenmose secretly attended to Hatra while she was resting on the bed. He softly kissed her forehead and walked away without disturbing her sleep.

Meanwhile, Hatop partied with his gang; they smoked and finished several cider containers. It relieved him from Hatra's absence concurrently with his over-exhilarated freedom.

The days passed in an unexpected rhythm. Lamila gave birth to a baby girl. Rene and Amenmose were pleased immensely as newly promoted grandparents. Hatra is completely recovered; she spent a reasonable time inside her chamber, lonely. Rene forced Hatra to visit Lamila; her heart thumped when Hatra spotted the baby girl. She touched the baby's rosy cheeks and held the small body close to her chest.

The new arrival of Lamila's daughter repainted her awful memory of her evacuation that brutally killed blood. Her whole sphere shattered into pieces. Somehow, she didn't feel gleeful, bubbly emotions while her physique dealt with Hatop. She remained half dead. It satisfied Hatop more than ever because he got all his consent to fulfil his lustful enthusiasm. Therefore, Hatop ignored her and convinced himself she would gradually engage in intimacy following that unexpected incident. The cute smile of Lamila's baby girl devastated Hatra's absolute mental peace. But with time, as her guilt grew up in her deep heart and tended her outer core to chase after some physical pleasure over and over from Hatop, her sudden arousal feelings astounded him. Though she denied accepting her guilt, she wanted to get rid of it when it haunted her.

Hatra suddenly grabbed Hatop's half-finished rum pot and emptied them all. Hatra cackles out loud, surrounded by numerous finished bowls all over the cave. She ripped her clothes and twirled around the body. Her desires paced up in a high pitch twisted with the deep intoxication. Her unveiled body ascended over to Hatop to satisfy her blazing fire inside. It lasted through many cold nights. When the sun sprinkles out, Instead of escaping to the castle, her undraped slumber body hangs on with Hatop in the cave. Her staggering body was often unable to walk; hence, she clutched to Hatop firmly. She kissed him madly and chuckled out loud. Her guilt invariably ruined her dignity and pride without any confession.

Hatra flees again from the Palace to the cave the day after Leo's wedding. She was planning to ride back to the castle promptly. Yet her drunken state made her sleep inside the cave until the dawn expired. The King and Queen panicked when they knew that the Hatra had disappeared. They command their guards to search for the princess. A man informed the guards about an isolated cave at the end of the shore. Eventually, all the people gathered around the cave with upsurged curiosity. They saw a couple inside the cave clinching to each other; their stripped clothes decorated the cave with numerous emptied rum pots. They arrested Hatop and then Princess Hatra, who seemed unconsciously carried to the castle. Hatra's powerless body lay on the bed, and they kept her inside her room under full supervision. Queen Rene hit her head against the hard wall and wailed loudly; she could not stand that massive disgrace. While crying, she made all her valuables fall on the floor, her most precious traditional jewellery protected secretly inside the highly secured boxes smashed on the bottom. The weeping and cracking sounds drummed around the castle. All glitters fade away with Rene's blotted eyes.

Meanwhile, King Amenmose stuck himself in a private room, puffed out in total disappointment, and expelled his hidden tears. His heart pounded with his exhausted mind. As he held his left chest shortly, a throbbing pain triggered him unbearable. "All ruined," he mumbled feebly to himself with shutting eyes, then lost his balance and tumbled down. His breathless body remained solemnly on the floor, leaving his soul privileged in enormous peace. The legendary crown flopped from his head.

....

Sometimes, life holds its unprecedented attitude. Nevertheless, nature concedes that what is equitable is the audacity to follow a chosen rhythm. King Amenmose's sudden death disoriented the kingdom. Everyone blamed Princess Hatra because of her misdemeanour. Queen Rene refused to talk with Hatra; hence, she was forbidden to participate in her father's final rites, and Hatra stuck herself inside her space. Honestly, her disrupted heart worried about Hatop. Her deep soul bothered on behalf of Hatop rather than all the misdeeds for which she was liable. Her vicious nature and self-oriented emotions confidentially discern all the way to release Hatop from jail. She felt secretly glad about the King's unexpected demise, but outwardly, she wept immensely and showed others she was repenting for her guilt. Each day, she visited the prison behind closed doors to see Hatop. His weary expressions burnt Hatra's core spirit, and she sobbed night and day.

Time healed all the wounded selves, leaving only a scar reserved. Ivory bouquets decorated King Amenmose's grave. Meanwhile, bright peony buds bloomed around Hatra and Hatop. Even though the kingdom didn't welcome Hatra, following numerous disputes, she crowned herself as Queen Hatra. She got all her authority in a short amount of time. Her mind tickled in an over-rejoicing. Rene refuses to stay in the Palace and moves with Leo. Hatra cried, shedding all tears in front of others, pulling her mother's hand and pleading not to leave the castle. Yet her inner mind was elated with this golden fortune. She captivated others' pitiful eyes with her dramatic performance. After a few days, Hatop was released and Promoted to a higher position instead of a trainee soldier. Eventually, he became the most reputable loving husband of Queen Hatra following a grand, spectacular wedding ceremony. Finally, the whole kingdom and Palace were authorised by the new Queen.

Hatra attained all her attempts to attract people to Thebeslon. She opened all the doors for poor people to touch more gold coins in their hands And granted new clothing and delicious meals to an unlimited crowd. Impoverished, helpless men and women were predominantly caught under the sympathy of the Queen. Sometimes, old, filthy, smeary beggars were invited inside the mansion; the Queen cleaned and fed them in her hands. Everybody praised Queen Hatra; even a single sand drop in Thebeslon respected her name. At the same time, whirling dried leaves covered King Amenmose's grave. Queen Hatra is a name renowned and glittered in the entire atmosphere of the kingdom. Majorly, Hatra was pursuing prestige. All she wants is to recreate a good heart among the folk.

Yet frankly, she hates the virtuous people and denies well-behaved, obedient women of her same age: only the cruelty, anger and covetous in her mind. Profoundly low, needy, destitute people reminded Hatra of her inherited power and wealth. Their raggy garments contrasted with Hatra's enriched glamorous attire. Their poverty upgraded Hatra's self-pride. Hatra was veiling up her reality from the fame of self-admiration. From the bottom of herself, she was ever so high-spirited with the dissimilarity between herself and the others. The vanity and ego shrouded her immensely. "Long live the Queen" was sung throughout, driving Hatra to sink into her success. While depositing all apologetic memories in an enclosed stoned box, her steamy body increasingly invaded Hatop's warmth. They lay out many more sleepless nights chasing their unsatisfied hunger. Eventually, they were utterly blessed after Hatra got pregnant with Joser.

Unlike in the past, Hatop's mind is over-excited about the Hatra's pregnancy. His bright eyes sparkled with the dream of having a most handsome, strong, healthy son undifferentiated from him. He was meticulous about Hatra's health, relaxation, and joy. He used to ramble along the seaside many more evenings, holding Hatra's hand gently. His one arm is enclosed around Hatra's shoulder, letting her body comfortably lean on his side.

"Our son will be the most renowned King of Thebeslon, and he will rule the entire Henaten," he whispered to Hatra with a high-spirited chuckle. His mind was thoroughly exhilarated by how well he would be privileged as the prideful father of the future emperor. While gazing at the delusional, charming red colour horizon, he giggled with Hatra.

The months passed rapidly, and Hatra's belly grew more prominent and noticeable. She seemed healthy and weighted. Her eyes glimmered with gladness. Hatop advised the royal carer and the maids to always keep an eye on her well-being. Hatra waddled in the palace garden, watching the ' beautiful blossoms; Hatop was always beside her. One evening, Hatra whimpered with unknown pain. Hatop briskly held her by his strong arms and took her inside the chamber. He waited outside impatiently until the royal carer attended to her. After midnight, the whole Palace delighted with the first cry of the new prince.

....

Prince Joser was born, and the entire kingdom was thrilled with the exclusive publication. The most healthy, cherished newborn snuggled on the feathery mattress. The fragrance of orange, yellow and white daffodils enhanced the sight of a cosy, spacious bedroom. The new curtains quivered in a soft breeze to warmly welcome the newcomer. Hatop held Joser more cautiously and kissed his chubby cheeks. "My son, my blood," he muttered, his ocean of love overflowing. Hatra glanced at them, bearing a satisfied smile. Leo, Lamila

Whole royal families gathered around the Hatra to share this precious moment. Joser became the most loved and blissful child of Thebeslon as his bright giggles echoed far beyond the castle.

Hatra encountered the most valuable period of life while restoring her dignity among her siblings. She was crowded with her responsibilities as a queen and a mother, unlike Hatop, who luxuriated in the Palace by entertaining himself with his newly welcomed most affluent mates. He sneaks onto the bed at midnight. Then, he yelled to Hatra and the maids to take the Joser away from the room as he needed to sleep peacefully. Hatra silently wiped her tears, gazing out the window while Hatop snoozed loudly. When the morning arrived, Hatop woke up and started showing grumpy moods. He yelled at the maids and Hatra for delaying his tea or breakfast. Mostly, it's a taste that is not acceptable to his tongue.

He blamed Hatra for disrespecting him and neglecting her duties as a wife. They had many arguments, usually in the mornings, which extended until noon. Sometimes, Hatra got slapped, but she hid her frustrations in her glorious royal attire, and her wet eyes always seemed to shine with the prestigious crown.

Queen Rene returned to the castle on behalf of her most adored grandson. Rene grabbed all the powers to look after Joser, and Hatra got some relief; she pursued back to Hatop. Yet, in her life, cycling between her dilemma sometimes and many more moments, controversies began to pile up in their sphere. First, Hatop's reckless behaviour frustrated Hatra; the freedom he was chasing for himself increased the space between them. Then, unexpectedly, everything exploded with Hatra's second pregnancy. Hatop refused to accept their second child, believing only Joser would be the future King of Thebeslon. Finally, however, after multiple disputes, Hatra obeyed Hatop.

Ultimately, she consented to drive back to Marisa, the gloomy, dark end of the woods. Once again, a voiceless unborn is deliberately hidden from the breath. But unlike in the past, Hatra dreadfully dropped into unwell; she became unconscious with sickness. Her body lay on the bed feebly, her cold, blanched face frightened Rene. When the royal carer visited off for the sake of Hatra, the awful truth spilt out. Rene clenched her teeth with endless anger and cursed Hatop. Fortunately, after several efforts, Hatra recovered and was advised not to involve herself again in that kind of matter because it would probably be hard to save her life. Simply, It would kill her. Yet she survived, letting another wounded scar secretly reside inside her.

CHAPTER 4

The time flew away, letting Joser grow older and more vigorous. Then, the time slowly reaches to celebrate his sixth birthday, and the entire palace is turned over by his mischievous. His energetic body ran throughout the castle.

"Grandma, Grandma, come and catch me," he shouted aloud while giggling. Hatra cuddled Joser's grown body; Hatop patted Joser's blond hair over his little eyes. As he got tickled by both parents, colourful chuckles filled the atmosphere. Joser walked on the seaside many evenings, holding his parents' hands. Hatra sighed serenely while glimpsing at Hatop.

Spring starts with the greenery shoots they roamed around the Kingdom merrily with Joser. The other nations invited them to enhance their mutual relations with each territory. Hatop purely handled all these, and Hatra fulfilled his commands. While Hatra and Hatop had a wonderful time isolated on a magnificent island, their rising emotions streamed together with the dazzling stars of the splendid night. Hatop's lips ran through her deep neck, letting Hatra's wavy hair wrap around Hatop's fingers. She hid inside him; her eyes sparkled like shiny pebbles. After a certain distance, they eventually returned to their natural rhythm of life. Hatra fluttered her wings over the moon; she felt much overjoyed with Hatop's unexpected romance wandering around her,

"He might have changed himself because of Joser, so he would love me more than in the past. So I can be his worthy person besides Joser," Hatra thought silently. She stood in front of the mirror and smiled at her own image, which was visible.

"My unilluminated past will be wiped forever; hence there would be no nightmarish vision of the future" Hatra sighed with relief. Though the future is decided to appear as a mystery, Hatra blindly trusts it.

A few months later, Hatra looked skinny; her body became thin and fee-ble. Her large eyes looked and blanched. Finally, one morning, she fainted with her powerless body. A reason discovered was her sudden illness, a stormy gale blown out with the scary thunder: enormous, large clouds subse-quently crashed the Hatra's life.

"I have told you all the time, I don't need any kids except Joser, he is my one and only son, and there's no one eligible for the crown; only Joser will bear it," Hatop yelled out loud and slammed the door. Hatra slowly sat on the bed and lamented. Hatop wandered the room anxiously, halted beside the window and breathed heavily. Suddenly, Hatra stood up and moved her steps towards him. She stood before him and glanced straight at his eyes. Hatra placed her hand on her belly, tears wetting her pale cheeks.

"But Hatop, the one inside my womb... It's our child too and your blood."

Hatra stuttered. Hatop pushed her frail body against the wall and seized her tightly.

"Shut up, you idiot woman, I have told you, and I'm telling you repeatedly, I'm not interested in having any more children from you" he threatened her with blazing eyes. He released her harshly and hit the flower pot next to him. The sound of the broken pot shuddered Hatra; she began to sob silently. Ha-top footed near the door and opened it. Then he turned his head towards Hatra,

"Get ready to back to Marisa tomorrow," he expelled in a hushed tone.

Hatra shook her head; her lips trembled, and the cold sweat covered her forehead; she abruptly moved forward and grabbed Hatop's arm

"Hatop, please, it would kill me; I have no strength to face it anymore."

Hatra pleaded to him. Hatop released his arms from her and then forcibly pushed her away, letting her fall. Then, he squeezed her neck with both his hands while leaning on her body. Hatra gasped.

"I don't care if you want this worthless matter; you can spend the rest of your life with it. So if you choose it over to me," Hatop stopped his words and looked directly at Hatra. She remained stared at him fearfully.

"I will be out from your life forever with Joser," he blurted out, freed his hands, and moved back to the door to leave, but Unexpected appearance dis-turbed him. Rene entered the chamber hastily. Hatop gritted his teeth and frowned at Hatra, bursting in rage, then suddenly he jumped back towards her violently, yet she hurriedly sneaked behind the closet; she shivered in fear.

Rene pulled from Hatop's hand. While he rolled his eyes to capture Hatra. Rene stopped him and held him gently with both hands.

"No, my dear son Hatop, have mercy on her I beg you on behalf of my daughter. If it happened once again, she would die; last time they said a miracle protected her. I cannot let my daughter's corpse in front of my eyes. Trust me, Hatop, I'll take care of the child in her womb; I will put up with all the responsibility related to that issue. I swore to you." Rene spoke out in a stilly, kind voice. Her tears dropped on Hatop's cold fingers.

A gloomy silence shrouded the enclosure, and Hatra quietly crept out. Hatop glanced at Rene's wretched gesture; her words diverted his mind momentarily. Then, Hatra began to weep loudly; Hatop yanked Hatra from her hair beside him in a flash. His senses went mad with uncontrolled annoyance. Hatra bawled and struggled to escape from him.

"bloody bitch you ruined everything," he groaned violently and slapped across her face. Hatra fell with an unexpected blow, and Rene screamed with shock. Hatop footed outside vaguely. The door slammed out loud. Rene cuddled Hatra and patted her head softly. Hatra sobbed continually and folded inside her mother's warmth.

"Hatra, Is that your devoted love that committed all your own. I wonder how it suffers you and how it's destroyed your entire life slowly."

She paused her words and touched Hatra's belly,

"It suffers this poor soul about to be born and those who murdered soundlessly. I'm pleased about your father because he is more fortunate than me."

Rene muttered in a cracked tone. Then sighed sadly.

Hatra wept alone many nights, yet Hatop didn't return to talk to her. He ignored her totally,

"I might be the unluckiest woman out in this world; therefore, happiness is quite far away from me" she mumbled.

Meanwhile, the nature of Thebeslon was exhausted by the massive storm. The dark clouds gathered around the palace, and the loaded sky burst into quakes and dribble showers. Joser smiled merrily, playing with tiny drops of rain. Rene gazed at the weeping sky with darkened eyes; her heart was much weighty than the tumbling raindrops. Swollen rivers ran throughout the village. Hatra, a heart overfilled with sorrows, her eyes found restless with unstoppable tears. Hatop refused to talk or meet her as he silently shifted to an isolated room far from Hatra. He didn't even sit to dine with her, too. All his meals were served directly in his room. Only Joser is allowed to meet him. The separation from Hatop drained Hatra's whole energy; she sobbed on the bed. Often, she sat on the floor in front of Hatop's chamber, lamenting alone. But the door never opened for her. Hence, she cried each day woefully and walked away after spending a long time there.

One night, Hatop was doddering to his room, and his eyes slightly opened; they seemed as red as the rowdy sun; he was blindly drunk. Hatra was waiting for him; she madly ran towards him and clung to his neck as she spotted him. But Hatop recklessly pushed her away. Hatra supported herself by holding the wall beside her. She glanced at Hatop with watery eyes. Hatop opened the door and hurriedly moved his legs inside. Hatra vaguely knelt towards him and grabbed him on the leg. Both hands were concealed tightly around it.

Hatop tried to kick her away; however, Hatra gradually slipped inside his space. The whole night existed with their shrieks and massive arguments. Hatra was slapped and beaten by Hatop. Finally, she left his chamber, leaning over to a maid. Her face was reddish and swollen, and the blood came out of her cracked lips. She is too weak to cry. The sudden divergence of Hatra and Hatop, followed by massive arguments, frightened the Joser. Even though they were involved with inevitable disagreements before this circumstance, it lasted for a short period, yet the entire situation thrives doubtfully. Joser felt very distressed about his mother, who was becoming skinny and had a light face. He didn't feel joyous about the baby growing inside her belly.

Though Granny has told him about a new brother he can play with, Joser doesn't feel any warm welcome towards this little guy. Instead, Joser began to hate the unborn child despite being loved and accepting his sibling when his ears touched his mother's silent sobbing. He cuddled Hatra and wiped her tears with his little fingers. Then glimpsed at her growing belly and frowned. The one inside is the reason which is invariably guilty and responsible for all these struggles. Some delusional reflection veiled around his little soul.

Queen Hatra was enormously traumatised because of her deep affection smitten with Hatop. Therefore, she was racked with his pain following her incapability to release her heart solidly fixed on him. It might be love, a desire, agony or irreversible misery. She wished to give birth to the child in her womb because she was afraid of dying soon. Otherwise, this awful foetus could easily be dabbed out from her. While her whole heart lamented on behalf of the Hatop, neither did she care for the unborn. Her past expectancy related to Joser appeared as much healthier and more energetic. Yet presently, she skipped most of the meals. She was purposefully absent-minded about the newcomer and constantly worried about the days she spent with Hatop, their intimate moments, and how he heeded Hatra when she was expecting Joser. But this worthless matter destroyed everything and detached them ruthlessly.

Hatra pays out considerably more sleepless nights. The dark circles clustered around her eyes while dragging her thin limbs; she frequently felt down. She rambled slowly on the sea sand and gasped for fresh air. The two maids always supported her frail body. She grieved for the past; recalls flashed in the whole atmosphere. The moments she spent with Hatop, his affection and warmth expressed even for a split second, survived her for thousands of years. Hatra's deep insight strenuously endeavours to secure the bonds she loves; she cannot accept the theory of uncertainty that the entire world obeys; hence, she fights hard against the natural phenomenon and becomes an insane victim. Profoundly, she was chasing the impermanent contentment which gifted her with endless torment. In contrast, her soul attempts to load the pure solace through it yet is merely twisted with misery and fear. Nevertheless, she clustered her whole strength to revive the visionless bonds; she is idiotically wandering around her life.

Meanwhile, Hatop did not commit his precious time to visit her as he was chained by the heavy smoke and rum from night to dawn. Hatra lay on her bed staring at the roof, her grown belly slightly visible. Rene sat beside her feed unhurriedly and wiped her wet cheeks. Hatra's fantasised expectations dimmed with suspicion and desperation, yet her cracked, wretched soul flew solemnly far beyond the horizon. This might be the hidden truth of an exhausting life tangled with attachments.

Several months passed, and the new visitors' arrival date gradually came closer. The royal carer advised Hatra to be comfortable with adequate rest and promptly served meals. Each royal maid carried out their routine duties secretly, worried about the tragic situation related to Queen Hatra. Nobody seems to show many greetings to the unborn guest. There was no sound of preparing cosy rooms with soft layers; neither was the closet replenished with fresh linen. A rejected visitant is unknowingly invited to be born in an environment where his breath is utterly unwelcome, a dramatic injustice created by nature or cold-blooded humanity. This confounded theory was never amenable.

One windy night, Hatra again appeared inside Hatop's space. Unfortunately, he was gazing outside through the window and mistakenly kept his door open. Subsequently, a heavy whitish smoke blew out from his lips.

"Hatop," Queen Hatra's feeble voice broke the silence.

"What on earth are you doing here?" Hatop turned over while throwing out his smoke pipe away.

"Hatop, I have no strength to tolerate this anymore. I wish I would rather die better. I'm suffocating." She halted her words and lamented, then shifted a few steps closer to him. While Hatop silently stared at her, she swiftly grabbed his hand and placed it on her grown belly.

"Hatop, this carries your blood together with mine, your child Hatop, our child same as Joser, please accept him Hatop, I beg you. We can rebuild all these Hatop believe me, and we will have the most precious life with our little kids. Don't let it ruin, Hatop." Hatra cried out.

"No, Hatra, this is not my blood and not my child" Hatop ceased the words and peeped straight into her face.

"I have one and only son. He is Joser and no one else," He muttered in a firm sound. His words pierced and ripped Hatra's entire heart; she slowly released his hand with a shocking gape.

"Hatop, are you insane? How could you talk like this? I? devoted my entire life only to you. You have known it from the beginning, and forever each moment I have only spent with you. My body, my whole soul only belongs to you.

You are the only person allowed. Would you please not bring such a dishon-
our between us, Hatop? Don't disgrace me."

Hatra shakes Hatop from his broad shoulders and yelled out loud.

"I don't care, Queen Hatra, I have told you more clearly, and I'm telling
you that the child inside your womb is not mine. I would never accept it. Now
for God's sake, get lost and leave me alone," he growled harshly, pushed her
out, and eagerly shut the door. It slammed out loud, letting the rocky walls
shatter, too; the whole surroundings drowned in perpetual silence. Hatra
plopped on the ground; she closed her ears with both hands. Hatop's words
repeatedly vibrated around her. Her eyes enlarged and emptied with tears. It
was midnight, and the entire castle was shrouded in peaceful sleep. The
whole of nature muted cryptically. Hatra heard someone whisper, and then a
hissing sound filled her ears. A strong wind whirled around Hatra. She sensed
that something was holding her tightly; hence, she slowly shut her eyes.

"Queen Hatra, do what he ordered to you, kill it and wipe it out of the
Henaten. The one who reside your womb is a son of the nature. He will be a
threat to Ovigons. Therefore you must destroy it and protect the black vipers." The wind disappeared, and Queen Hatra opened her eyes and slowly
stood up.

Hatra secretly covered herself with a black robe and drifted off the palace.
She walked through the hidden tunnel and across the sands, her limbs aching
and her heart whacked. Though she was afraid, her soul was veiled by the
mysterious nightmare; hence, she determined not to turn back until she
reached the actual location. She stepped among the dark woods, but neither
worry captured her because Hatop's sharp words haunted her with his
gloomy shadow. She paused her legs and grasped the tree trunk to puff up
her tired lungs. Again, she commenced the journey and dragged her legs,
mustering her whole strength to reach the far end of the woods before dawn.

Her legs eventually brought her in front of the entrance of the past slaughtering house.

"Marisa" Hatra screamed in a high tone, then tapped the door loudly. Her
short, shallow breaths overspread around. While one hand tightly fitted on
her spine, she lost her balance with the shooting pain radiating from her

backwards. She bent down, supporting her against the fragmented grey wall. The door unlocked suddenly, and the older woman bawled in a shrilled voice.

"Your Majesty, what happened? What brings your here alone."

Marisa hurriedly grabs Hatra and holds her. Hatra leaned onto her, gasping for a breath. Her heart pounds vaguely.

"Marisa, for goodness' sake, expelled this matter out of my womb; I want to blot it out from my whole spirit. I'm not afraid to destroy it, please," Hatra cried in a feeble voice. Her lips shivered.

"Your majesty, forgive me; this seems so bad." Marisa trembled and peeped around, but no other gesture was seen except by Queen Hatra. Marisa slowly lugged Hatar's frail body inside a low-ceilinged, ugly, dingy enclosure. Marisa's eyes wandered for a space to make Hatra lay down. Instead, a stretched-out half-broken rustic wooden bed on the side, numerous cobwebs effortlessly decorated it. A dusty plush blanket covers the thin, miserable, filthy mattress.

Marisa slowly settled Hatra on a shapeless armchair, which was narrow and uncomfortable. Hatra howled out loud unexpectedly. Some clear water wetted the stained ground.

"My God, your majesty, it is about to come; what am I supposed to do inside this poor old shack" Marisa cried out shockingly.

Then she swiftly looked around; a plain, dusty, coarse carpet was extended beneath the bed. It was a dirty shag decorated with tiny, dried bloodstains.

"Forgive me, your Majesty," Marisa whispered to Hatra and made her lie on the shabby rug. Hatra's weary voice trembled in the dark, shuttered sphere.

"It has already emerged out, your Majesty," Marisa says; a feeble cry unfolded through the peeling, stingy walls. One innocent soul was lucky enough to open his eyes in that dreadful cemetery, and the scary executioners' hands rewarded his life. Hatra shut her eyes, whimpering. Marisa carried the little one; her fingers jerked, and she glanced at him; her lips twitched. Her heart halted for a second. For the first time in her life, she holds a breathing newborn. Marisa stared at the poor soul with wetted eyes. Suddenly, heavy footsteps began to haunt outside. Several armed men gathered around the house with Lord Hatop. He tapped the door hard, Marisa groaned, then panted, kicking the door impatiently. Marisa cautiously settled the newborn beside Hatra and hurried to move out. In a flash, Hatop became visible in front of her. She stepped back and bowed her head timidly.

"Why she is on the floor, she should be on the bed," he roared.

"The bed is almost very old partially broken and unstable, barely supportable, Lord Hatop," she responded calmly. Marisa returns to the infant and wraps him wretchedly from plain threadbare linen. She comfortably rests the baby on the filthy, ragged blanket covering the lumpy old mattress. A musty smell, together with fresh blood, touched Hatop's nose.

"It's a boy," Marisa murmured.

A feather-light, tiny creature peeked out his glittering, shiny blue eyes. He is beautiful, with a bright face resembling a blossom from the brown, stinky, smelly, muddy stream!. Prince Armion was born; Hatop knelt beneath the bed and sighed woefully. All his wars arrested him in his cursed soul. Yet he was unaware of the absolute truth of life. Or, neither promoting any attempt to demolish the vicious cycle of the dark, he chose something beyond the present.

Prince Armion and Queen Hatra shifted back to the castle.

The maids and guards were startled by the message and expressed their warm welcome when they spotted Prince Armion. Queen Rene's high-pitched commands and shallow rapid breaths excrete her outraging emotions of the entire circumstance. She ignored Hatop and ultimately denied him but pretended as usual in front of visitors. Yet, her lonely eyes filled with unknown fear and misery, she kissed little Armion with over-spilt love and touched his innocent face. Hatra gradually healed and became healthy as in earlier days. Hatop sneaked inside his isolated area and never remarked himself visible to others. Armion kept down with Hatra; she ordered the maids to keep him with her every second. Armion's birth inclined her to new hope. She softly touched his bright cheeks while kissing his forehead. He cried round the clock both day and night. The royal carer advised Hatra to heed him carefully because he is feeble and not as healthy and active as Prince Joser. He cried many times to fill up his little tummy repeatedly. One morning, Joser visited to see his very first new brother.

"Oh Granny, look at him; he is very much similar to a tiny mouse who has felled from the roof," he exclaimed with his enlarged, bubbly eyes. Then he slowly leaned his little body close to Hatra's cosy mattress and patted Armion's little nose. Armion rolled his shimmering blue eyes around.

"He is rather small to play with me, mother; I thought you would have brought a larger and stronger one than him. He is so small, isn't he, Granny?" Joser questioned. Hatra's face dimmed with Joser's immature words.

"Oh, that's no wonder mother, you carried a very tiny tummy because you didn't eat food. But I think Aunt Nora will get a huge one. I saw her tummy was much bigger than yours. So, mother, I can play with that one," Joser added. Hatra shook her head and gazed at Armion. Rene grasped softly Joser's little fingers "come on, little man, let's go out. Your brother is too sleepy now." Joser agreed with Rene, kissed Hatra's face, and ran out.

Little Joser talks directly strike Hatra's intellectual, recalling the negligence she committed regarding Armion. She sighed sadly and shut her eyes with unexpected devastation. After a few days, Hatra, bit by bit, deviated from her routines; while fulfilling her responsibilities as a Queen, she solely inclined her attention towards Armion. Hatra sows the seeds of highly bounded, self-obsessed affection concerning Armion. She protected him and kept him attached to her ferociously. Profoundly, she wanted to conceal the actual discrimination that had happened around Armion.

On the other hand, his eligibility as future king helped Hatra build a bold bond. She ensured that she would not release the Armion away from her. Hence, she initially enchanted him and grabbed his trust and confidence towards her. Meanwhile, Hatra utterly resisted Hatop. Though they had the same endless struggles, Hatra seemed to overcome herself. She preferred to glitter her name and fame forever as the most devoted and noticeably honoured mother of future king Armion. Hence, she encircled Armion inside her mindlessly. She gradually ignored Joser because comparing the tales about the two brothers made her guilty. While Rene was comforting Joser uninterruptedly, Hatra did not remark on her presence on his behalf. Joser, who is growing older, is silently aggrieved about his mother's sudden transformation after his brothers' arrival. Therefore, his little mind overflowed with jealous thoughts about Armion. He utterly believed that his little brother detached himself from his mother.

Consequently, he neither sensed affection close to Armion, yet the tragic hatred miserably replaced it. Hatop's mysterious behaviour never sacrifices himself to replace Joser's heart with love and make his little mind more contented. However, that bitter truth about Armion survived quietly in his sphere. All this eventually leads to Joser growing up with an extraordinarily stubborn and deceitful attitude. His insensitive, self-oriented behaviour got worse with bad, rude manners. Hatra's deepest affection was smitten with Joser more than the Armion. It has no boundaries and vows. As time lapses, Hatra begins believing that Armion is much more indebted to herself because of all the dedication and suffering she underwent." I suffered so much to grant your life Armion, I dedicated my life I lose your father because I choose you, each second of my life I am spending with you, I'm heeding you more than Joser, It's all my pure affection towards you. don't ever leave me Armion. You have no right to do so. I would be the worthiest person of your life no one else can replace it. You have to stay with me forever and you must be grateful to your mother's commitments."

Hatra murmured, touching Armion's cheeks.

"Our bond is perfectly permanent, Armion. I'm holding your string all the time. We are bounded. No one can separate us" She confirmed.

Her complicated, superficial, egocentric nature created numerous controversies in their lives.

CHAPTER 5

Armion grew slowly, and he was relatively stepped behind from his age. He constantly cried and often denied his food. His frail body habitually depended on whatever illness. Unlike Joser, Armion kept up himself, totally inactive and not very energetic. He sat alone, neither word expelled from his mouth, as he was utterly muted. His sparkling eyes were worried with some unknown misery. He only cuddled Hatra and spent considerable time with Rene. He was frightened, so he stepped back and hid behind Hatra when someone attempted to touch him. Some days, he cried continuously and, shut his eyes tightly and screamed. He even hates the night and dark, gloomy chambers. He spent much time gazing at the sky abundant with bright blue and white clouds. Nobody was allowed to touch his toys except Hatra, and Joser often denied playing with him. Armion prefers to be isolated rather than hang around the crowd. Sometimes, he becomes significantly crossed and grumpy about unknown matters. Each night, he awakens frightened by some awful nightmare. Some days, he smashed all the goods inside his room. His strange and peculiar behaviour persistently bothered Hatra. Rene embraced Armion; her wholehearted love poured towards him, and she kindly kissed his little hands.

"My poor Armion, you were too delicate to combat that dreadful past, but it's all over now. Understand your life gifted to you by nature, my dear." Rene silently whispered to him.

Hatra tried crowded remedies to cure Armion, but all were found in vain. He became more and more anxious and strange. All his incapability's, bonded with his inappropriate nature, enormously frustrated the entire mansion. When Hatra glimpsed at Armion momentarily, his watery blue eyes cracked her heart. That horrendous reality ceaselessly punished Hatra. More and many times, she sadly wiped her endless tears. But no one sighted except her mother, Rene.

Even though Hatra and Hatop haul their marriage, the constant beat of their unresolved troubles fills the castle. Hatop never changed his room, even a few years after Armion's birth. From the early stages, Hatra played her Queen role outwardly; Hatop was the clear-headed mind which ruled the kingdom entirely. However, his evil routines gradually made the nation unsecured and lose its sereneness. The wealthy and impoverished residents must grant their central part to the palace. Hatop's unethical laws and his own deceitful mentality concerning coins and valuables prevailed insatiably. In addition to wealth, he chased superiority. He made mastery plans to surrender other small kingdoms under his power. The numerous wars were controlled by Lord Hatop interminably. Even though Thebeslon is progressively empowered, the nation has to deal with a bounty of miseries. The gold, silver, gems, gold coins, and all these values belonging to other kingdoms were perfectly snatched by Lord Hatop and his soldiers. The civilians of corresponding territories were brought to Thebeslon for slavery. Hatop was thrilled regarding all his victories following his loaded prosperity. His ego invariably clashes with Queen Hatra. Her born, high-graded royal blood and all the prestige she carries often made him unsettled. Therefore, he created continuous arguments with Hatra. He fights with her for not fulfilling her tasks as his wife. He made Hatra work as his maid rather than a Queen or wife. Queen Hatra had to make his tea, prepare his meals and even do his laundry under his commands. Though their splendid palace was abundant with royal maids, Queen Hatra carried a specific role as Hatop's maid. Her depressing expressions, with all unhappiness, healed and upgraded his vanity. He blamed her, and neither rewarded appreciation except she got slapped by him for a small mistake. Hatra tolerated all these because she immensely feared losing him. Honestly, she loved him for a mysterious reason. Besides, Hatra feared the blame and shame she would have to confront after breaking her marriage. Honestly, she is not intelligent and skilled enough to run out the Thebeslon without his aid.

Hatra's total despondency and complete desolation made her extremely attached to Armion. She felt Armion was the only motive for this miserable life journey. Hence, she sobbed with him each night,

"Armion, my dear son, you are my most precious that got gifted to me; never leave your mother alone, promise me that you will protect me forever."

Armion hugged her with his tiny hands. The mother and son pretended to stand together to heal their wounded souls. But, apparently, Armion's bitter reality was blotted out by Hatra's overflowing tears.

....

Nonetheless, the kingdom Thebeslon evolved to become highly dominant. Another influential region named Spavitar held a unique, impressive authority. It is a magnificent island embodied with multiple crystal caves. The whole territory possesses unprecedented elegance and bears extraordinary worth due to its Crystals and gems. Queen Roura ruled the Spavitar, renowned for her different surprising spiritual skills. People in Spavitar are far from other civilians, most live according to their spiritual values. They are highly independent, and no visitors can touch the strange numinous beauty of this nation's landmarks. Profoundly, no one can conquer with their unique superiority. The most prestigious states with mighty war sovereignty became vulnerable when they arrived at the kingdom of Spavitar. Because Spavitar is noticeable to other greedy leaders who crave its hidden treasures. Queen Roura and the royal family are virtuous; hence, they governed the kingdom equalled. Frankly, poverty is unfamiliar to Spavitar. The prosperity overspilt far and wide. People in Spavitar proudly fulfilled both physically and emotionally. Lord Hatop has bountiful pains regarding this exceptional nation because it is the hardly approachable goal. Many of his attempts were unconditionally destroyed. Therefore, Hatop considered applying his unethical indirect strategy to catch up with it. He secretly aimed at the demolition of Spavitar and Queen Roura. Some neighbourhood rulers had ravenous appetites related to Spavitar and joined Hatop.

Eventually, Hatop was pleased with other kingdoms who stood with him to chase their ultimate goal. The most powerful rulers of those regions were honourably invited by Lord Hatop to Kingdom Thebeslon to enhance their warm-hearted relationships. Lord Hatop organised a grand occasion to welcome those royal visitors. Queen Hatra was commanded to join the event with him. Unfortunately, Armion seemed terribly unsettled that day. He was utterly agitated and wailing. Queen Hatra tried to console Armion, but it was difficult to leave him. All his maids and even Rene found it remarkably challenging to settle him.

He pulled Hatra's hand and didn't let her step out. Finally, Hatra decided to participate in the occasion with Armion. Hatop furrowed his eyebrows with the presence of Armion and scowled at Hatra secretly. Armion turned his head around the hall. Then Hatra introduced him to other respectable royal guests. They all greeted Crown Prince Armion more attentively. Sadly, Armion wasn't satisfied with their greeting. He instantly stepped back when they tried to pat him. Their hollow-hearted manners and foxy looks were poorly accepted by Armion. He became more distressed and commenced blubbering. He shouted loudly, grabbed the objects at an approachable distance, and threw them over. All Hatra's efforts were not capable of controlling him. The visitors were startled by his nature; all these tantrums were not suited to his age. Armion pulled the tablecloth, letting all glasses and dishes be broken into pieces. All the cracking noise abruptly paused his crying, and then he began to cackle in a flash. He laughed uninterruptedly. At once, he drew back another tablecloth again, letting another bundle break into portions. The visitors stared at each other. Hatop felt naked among all. Armion's laughter made his blood boil. He shivered in enraged and rolled his blazing eyes immediately to Queen Hatra. She instantly hauled Armion towards the exit, but suddenly, Armion bit her hand harshly. Hatra screamed in pain. Indeed, she was bleeding. Armion was utterly confused and shocked when he realised he had hurt his mother. He swiftly sat on the floor and began to yell while rocking his body rapidly. Hatop tried to seize him, and then he started to roll over the ground, screaming loudly. After a span, with the aid of the numerous palace maids, Armion was taken off. The whole occasion ended up in a mess. Hatop pulled his hair, groaning and hitting the wall nearby; he locked his room with blazing anger. He was totally baffled by the disgrace. He fastened his eyes, all his headaches with throbbing pain; he wrapped his hands around his head and screamed, "he destroyed me, he destroyed me."

Hatra was sitting on her bed, shaking in fear, following a massive struggle to put Armion asleep. A maid covered her wound carefully. But, honestly, Hatra didn't sense the pain; she was utterly distressed about the incident. Suddenly, Hatop entered the room, his firing reddish eyes quivering with each muscle Hatra, afraid of, halted her breath. Her lips dried. Hatop jumped towards her madly, pulled her forcibly from her hair, and slapped her face. Hatra twirled around with an unexpected attack and plopped on the floor.

"You witch, your crazy son disrobed me in front of everyone. Look how he ruined me totally. I have told you many times to kill that monster, but you gave birth to that filthy mindless coward; he is not my blood or my son either. Have you ever thought, how is your brainless dumb going to bear this prestigious crown" Hatop bawled

"Forgive him, Hatop; it was all my fault he is innocent and immature"

Hatra mumbled with bleeding lips. Hatop furiously grasped Hatra from her neck.

"You still trying to cover up his all wrongdoings; you better die before him, bloody witch." Hatop rigidly pushed his fingers on her neck. Hatra screeched out loud.

"Hatop, stop all enough" Rene swiftly leapt between them. Hatop released his hands. While Hatra gasped to breathe, Rene slowly approached Hatop with a blazing stare.

"Who is crazy Hatop is that Armion. I wonder why you could not recall the things before his birth. He was much close to being slaughtered, then fortunately survived, yet he was immensely tormented. Honestly, what you can expect from him Hatop, a healthy, intelligent son like Joser. You destroyed Armion. You utterly ruined that poor innocent soul. Obviously, he ought to be silly mindless dumb because he lonely bears all the sins that both of you are responsible for. It's not that poor kid; both of you embarrassed him and ruined him."

Rene spilt out the bitter truth angrily.

"Enough, old woman, I don't want to listen to your sermons," Hatop yelled.

"I am Queen Rene; who are you? Soldier Hatop," Rene questioned, peeking inside his eyes.

"Remember Queen Rene, your crackbrained daughter will not be capable of running this kingdom without me. It will be demolished." Hatop smirks.

"It's already torn down; you spoiled the whole pride of kingdom Thebeslon. King Amenmose never steals from the poor citizens, and he was not a double-dealer. He was truthful and respected the whole of humanity. You smashed his entire sacrifice, his vision for a wealthy, prosperous nation."

Rene's words vibrated around. Hatop grinned, and unexpectedly, he laughed loudly. Hatra stood utterly baffled. Finally, Rene presented a furious glare at Hatop.

"It's not me, Queen Rene, your daughter, ruined his visions; both of you dreamed about the prosperous kingdom while your most precious daughter, the crown princess, selected me as her dream. What a tragedy, so I easily succeeded in my goal, and now I am Lord Hatop. I know all these sad stories are quite hard   to accept, but we all have to endure it somehow."

He muttered. Hatra swiftly turned around, and Rene kept speechless. Hatra shut her ears with both hands.

"No, this is not true," she cried. Her lips flinched. She felt past shadows spinning around her. Then she immediately turned back. Hatop stepped forward to move out. Hatra impeded his way; she breathed vaguely, her forehead covered with sweat, her wounded lips swollen, and her face turned red; her eyes resembled a flare of a burning heart. The tears ran through her slapped cheeks. She came close to Hatop and tugged his collar from her one hand. Her whole body shuddered, and her eyeballs swivelled around the Hatop's face. He was staring at her like a sculpture.

"Is that true Hatop, Is it mean that you never loved me, and you used me merely to accomplish your bloody target" Hatra grunted.

"Is that mean that you have no emotions about me, or you had nothing with me except this all royal status and fame you have achieved?" Hatra yelled.

"Answer me, Hatop," she mumbled. Hatra stretched her hand towards him; a sharp, pointed knife was placed directly to his neck.

"You initiated our game of love, Queen Hatra; I never chased after you. I felt we arrived at the end presently. I cannot say I didn't love you because you brought your whole heart to me, and you granted your entire life for me; I was unable to return back to you either," Hatop opened up in a broken voice.

"You lied to me, Hatop, you cheated me," Hatra shouted.

"I never cheated on you, Queen Hatra. Even though all these honey-words and romance are not quite pallier with me, I accepted you and Joser into my life. But I would never ever accept that silly lunatic. He is not my son, and he is not my blood. Our relationship does not exist until you are attached to that insane dumb." Hatop angrily threw out his words.

"so the reason for all these matters that you are rejecting me is sole because of Armion," Hatra questioned.

"Yes, I cannot accept him," he replied silently.

Hatra slowly moved out the knife; she rested her hands on him and turned around; she moaned quietly. A few seconds passed. Hatra broke the silence.

"you were right, Hatop; he is not your son. A cold-blooded, heartless man like you can never become his father" She stepped forward and confronted him.

"He is the son of nature, not yours," she wailed in agony; her whole body trembled, and she clenched the knife.

"Hatra stops this nonsense, for God's sake; this is enough; put away that knife," Rene cried. Hatra gave an unbroken chortle, and the tears burst from her eyes. Hatop was gazing at her; he was absolutely dazed.

"I'm the one who should be cursed; I destroyed everything," she murmurs. Then, she takes the knife straight away and quickly cuts both wrists.

"No," Rene hollered. Hatra's unconscious body tumbles down onto Hatop's arms as the blood spurts. Rene's outcry shakes the stony bars. A strange gloom again surrenders the palace.

....

Hatra lay on the bed many days; her eyes remained while the castle was highly unquiet. Finally, following numerous wakeful disturbed nights together with massive efforts, Queen Hatra received her life back. Hatop was expressionless; he spent his chamber wholly isolated. He was beside Hatra when she opened her eyes. Their eyes met accidentally, yet she immediately turned away her head to escape his sight.

Hatop felt some stabbing grief; he moved out hesitantly, locked himself inside his room, and constantly queried about her well-being with the maids. Then, after a Few Days, he stepped again inside her space. But Joser was standing close to the entrance. He held a long stick in one hand. Then, as Hatop was about to rush inside, Joser stretched his rod towards him.

"You cannot see my mother; you hurt her. If you step inside, I will hit you."

Joser spoke out to him in an irritable voice. Hatop paused his legs at once. He was pretty baffled by his son's unusual words. He felt rather queer.

Then Rene came closer to them, "Joser" she frowned, then took his stick.

"Joser, don't ever talk to your father that way; behave yourself," Rene said roughly. Joser slowly slipped away. Hatop walked inside doubtfully. Suddenly, his limbs are immobilised. His heart paced uncontrollably; it was Armion sleeping beside Hatra. Both of them snuggled to each other. Hatra's face seemed much more peaceful with Armion. Then, in a flash, Hatop vanished his sympathy on behalf of Hatra. His eyeballs again blazed in a fire.

"She is happy to be with him, not with me," he mumbled and violently punched the wall with his fist. Then, he drifted back to his place.

It was pretty inexplicable why Hatop hates Armion. He was born into a middle-class family. He has two brothers and one sister. His father was outwardly calm, but he was rigid and impassive. It was hard to say his parents shared a good relationship. They lived their tedious life journey and were satisfied with their duties soundlessly. His father devoted his life as a royal soldier, and his exhausted mother struggled to put up with children from dawn tonight. Hatop's 'father spends leisure time with his mates because the house is stuffed with children's booms. However, they stayed as a family and occasionally cursed each other. Hatop's elder brother is calm and he is intelligent. When he arrived in adolescence, he left the family, overpassing his responsibilities as the firstborn. Hatop carried the whole burden of the family after his father's unexpected illness. Neither appreciated him, and each one considered it his own responsibility. His mother grabbed every coin he earned. His youngest brother was his mother's favourite. He is more mischievous, joyful and attractive than Hatop. The mother, his sister, praised the youngest. Hence, this youngest is always rewarded with full family blessings, love and compassion.

Hatop's muted mouth, grumpy look, and rude attitude, smitten with an awful temper, killed their interrelationships. Nevertheless, Hatop accomplished his duties as a soldier flawlessly. It satisfied him and expanded his dignity by appearing as a recognised royal employee among poor, feeble people. His conversations were sometimes harsh; he misapplied his potency to gain additional recognition from society. Hatop also followed a resistant manner toward women. Yet the women always captured his elegant impression and handsome, powerfully built physique. They were all effortlessly enchanted by his lustful glowing eyes and thick eyebrows following his sharp nose and wavy hair. He smiled rarely and chatted in a bold, gruff voice, which enhanced his presence. He had a peculiar thought regarding women. Habitually, he condemned the women and never peeped at the interior emotions of any woman.

Only touches the outward figure. Instead of making romance, Hatop was pleased to make a distance with them. That distance, he invariably overruled his authority over them. He satisfied his quench by arresting the one who loved him beneath his well-built body. Hatop wanted to be more noticeable as a dominant relevant to females than the tender-hearted fancier. He desired them to make out begging below him; their tears thrilled him more than smiles. He was glad to consistently see their sad, fearful face throughout the relationship. Hence, he considered it an honour; it misguided his soul that they respectably treated him, so he repeatedly hurt them. It was merely a temporary pleasure he attained to recover his wounded heart. But it entirely disappeared when he captured his mother pampering his youngest brother. Hatop was sustainedly criticised by his sister for unknown reasons and even repeatedly neglected by his mother. He did not receive any gratitude from them. He got ignored, and nobody bothered about him. His isolated, fractured spirit tends to expel his continuous strains in extraordinary ways. He dreamed of becoming the most reputable and influential person in the kingdom. It was speculated that wealth and power could alleviate the deserted places of his worthless life. He is soundlessly convinced that it is the only way to become his family members most appreciable and notable person.

Many women were intolerable with him soon and left him. But his mean-spirited nature never worried about losing them. Hatra was the one who brought all the fortune beneath to his feet. Profoundly, she was his lady luck. Her enormous affection, extreme obedience and devotion flooded him. It startled Hatop immensely. Instead of expelling his fellow sentiment, he tortured her, disregarded her and then criticised her. His self-centred mind gradually built up with egotism. Hatop's traumatic and discriminated heartfelt calm to watch the real suffering Hatra holds on his behalf. Ultimately, he thoroughly succeeded in seeing the crown princess knelt beside him, pleading for his sacred love.

CHAPTER 6

Hatop looked out the window; a heavy rain poured down, and the gloomy shadows shrouded the sky. The cold breeze touched his face. He smoked heavily to get rid of his regretful emotions. He spent a lot of time with Joser the last few days. Joser found a bit settled with Hatop after an extended period. Before Armion's arrival, Hatop shared plenty of joyful moments with Joser. Hatop used to tickle Joser in the morning,

"My crown prince, my lazy little son, time to wake up' Joser crept inside the bedcover to escape from him. But Hatop quickly pulled him out and tickled him without stopping. So, while Joser's adorable giggles unfurled throughout the palace, Hatra peacefully watched the deep fondness of father and son.

"Come on, my prince, clap on my back," he shouted cheerfully to Joser. When Joser clung to his back, he made twirls and hopped, letting Joser laugh uninterruptedly. These sweet moments flashed inside Hatop's remembrance, and he sighed sorrowfully.

"Why did you bring Armion among us, Hatra "he silently mumbled. He recognised the Armion as the most repulsive grey outline who tore their serenity. Same as his little brother, who separated him from his mother. Hatop's memories are all of the transformations that had played around his mother after his brother's birth. Hatop's mother pointed only to her most precious younger son. His father, elder brother and sister were all spellbound by him. His mother secretly reserved the youngest's best portion of every delicious meal. That little monster grabbed all the presents that their father used to bring. However, Hatop constantly fought with him. Therefore, endless struggles were placed at home, and finally, Hatop was harshly whipped by his mother. She cuddled her youngest son and nuzzled his head while throwing all the blame directly at Hatop. Then, she began to praise his little brother's innocence. Nobody seemed kind enough to wipe Hatop's tears nor let him wrap himself in their warmth. He used to cry inside the dark, broken shelter close to the house. A separate area filled with some giant trees. An insignificant shade of grown bushes around. Hatop wailed, begged God to take back his little brother's life, and prayed for his quick death. Yet, his eyes neither spilt out with tears when time flew nor replaced with a bad temper. He recognised no sympathy. All that anger and hatred bloomed inside him. One gloomy evening, Hatop was sitting in that shelter. He got whipped by his mother after a fight with his little brother. He cried, lonely, gazing at the dark shadows wandering around. Suddenly, a strong wind started. The trees wavered side to side, and a horrible hissing sound broke the silence. Hatop raised him and watched all over with terrifying eyes. A black mist began twirling around him at once, and some solid enchanting power dragged him inside it. Hatop felt a pitchy dark enclose his eyes. He was unable to speak because his voice did not come out.

"My dear Hatop," someone called him.

"Listen to me, Orana protects you all the time. Forget your heart and obey your brain. Do not ever follow your heart. Kill it and revive your brain." An image of a woman surrounded by numerous black vipers spoke with him. The vipers have blazing, scary, ruddy eyes, spilling blood out of their fearsome mouths. Hatop gasped. The woman patted him.

"I consider you as my son Hatop, and I will bring true success beneath to you. But you have to follow my commands and respect me. Then the world of black vipers will remove all the obstacles in your life. They can destroy all your enemies."

"Orana forever resides in you, Hatop, and your soul is bound with Ovigons," the voice echoed all over and vanished.

After a while, Hatop opened his eyes. He raised and looked around, yet nobody was visible to his eyes.

"Orana," he whispered silently.

The Ovigons slowly arrested his miserable, broken, shattered soul; eventually, they turned delicate humans into cold-blooded black vipers.

When Hatra announced their first unborn before marriage, he quickly recalled his mother's image, carrying his little brother in her belly. Hence, he planned to wipe out his blood from Hatra's womb. At the end of the visit to

Marisa's place, Hatop felt delighted in his deep heart. Likewise, he threw his little brother out of his mother's tummy. But, as he is aware, King Amenmose's good heart and empathy would never ill-treat him, and there is no way to hurt Hatra and their unborn. Therefore, Hatop was insanely followed by his evil mind, and Hatra obeyed him.

Eventually, Hatop's destiny performed all the miracles around him. He became the most prestigious person in the kingdom. But it was not the vastly foremost reason to him to be exalted. Though his little brother was lucky enough to grab his mother's whole love, his life was miserable. All his misguided, heedless behaviour ravaged him. Hatop's little brother became a strong drinker, always drunk as a skunk. His wasted body seemed to drop down on the way home many times. His wife flees out with another secret lover. He was ashamed and constantly blamed by Hatop's elder brother and sister. His mother cursed him for all the disgrace that he was liable for.

Eventually, Hatop became the most honourable and essential individual in the family. All his prosperity and fame accomplished his life. Hatop made all the comforts to his parents until their death. His little brother pleaded to satisfy his starving. Hatop silently smirks while throwing plenty of coins towards that wretched unlucky fellow who lived alone and roamed in a blind mind. Neither worried about that fruitless life. A few months after Hatop's mother's demise, his younger brother's powerless body was found hanged inside that old shelter. Though he died very young, his appearance was similar to that of a filthy aged pauper. Hatop organised a grand funeral on behalf of his little brother. He showed that he was downhearted about his beloved brothers' unexpected departure. But that evening, he poured wine with Hatra, and they spent their most magnificent night ever. They both got drowned with their unmasked firing desires. Hatop met his peace after a long time, and it became immensely rejoiced with Joser's visit. Hatop confirmed to himself that Joser would be their one and only child.

Because his wounds, heart, and terrified mind falsely persuaded that having many kids would repeatedly create the same situation, even for Joser. Hence, he hated having children after Joser. He dreamed of seeing Joser as the King of the Thebeslon. But Armon's unexpected birth slashed his fantasy and rebuilt his hidden wounds, leading him to save Joser from Armion. Hatop started to deny Armion. Likewise, he rejected his little brother. Therefore, he is convinced that Armions does not belong to his blood. All his thoughts and deep affection revolved around Joser. Hatop quietly kissed Joser's forehead, closely sleeping next to him.

....

Hatra recovers slowly. Both hands healed, but her heart, broken into pieces, never healed. It's pretty unapproachable to seek a remedy to cure her injured spirit. She sat on the comfortable chair, cuddling Armion, sitting on her lap. Hatra's, both hands wrapped around him. Hatra looked pale and weak, and her body turned scrawnier; her eyes appeared enlarged with dark blue circles. His lips stayed muted along with her whacked soul. She gazed at the roof while her maid sponged her body and switched herself into another outfit. At night, her eyes are not reachable for a nap. She got exhausted with prolonged restless eyes. She secretly drank rum the whole night. It relieved her; she felt her traumatised mind harmonised with each sip. Yet her power-less trunk was found not tolerable with this harmful habit. Rene got mad and bawled her out as she began to vomit each daylight. Hatra lay on the floor, covered her entire dress with vomit, and giggled with half-shut eyes. Suddenly, she stretched her hand and attempted to stand up, but she plopped below and started wailing alone. Finally, after some time, she yelled out. Rene watched her daughter's pathetic situation with a broken heart. It was unbearable; Rene sobbed while sitting beside Hatra's unconscious wasted body.

The door opened slowly. Hatop entered inside. Rene hurriedly raised her head. Hatop calmly reached to Hatra and tried to lift her.

"No," Rene growled.

"Get out, Hatop," she cried. Hatop footed his leg backwards, then glanced at Rene.

"She is my wife, queen Rene. I ought to help her," he muttered.

"Help, are you going to help her, Hatop" Rene repeated his words and grinned. Then, unexpectedly, Rene grabbed Hatop from his collar.

"You are a foxy soldier who destroyed my daughter; open up your evil eyes and watch how she suffers. You ruined her life and used her to accomplish your cunning plans. So, what you up to now, prove all that true love." Rene groaned.

Hatop released himself from Rene and turned away his head.

"It is so hard to find answers, Queen Rene; all things seem to be rather complicated; I cannot accept this situation either; it hurts me a lot too. However, I'm not ready to bear this whole guilty alone. Because I got invited from your daughter to be her very first lover." Hatop halted his words and looked at Hatra.

"Our story had a colourful beginning Queen Rene however, this is the dark ending," he sighed heavily. Rene stepped forward and directly peeped inside Hatop's eyes.

"I want to wipe out your dark shadow completely from my daughters' life, soldier Hatop. For the sake of God, leave my daughter and exit from this kingdom too." Rene threatened him, and the tears ran through her pale face.

Hatop was speechless; he stared at Queen Rene and quickly moved out. Rene knelt beside Hatra and sobbed alone.

....

A few days expired, and Hatop stuck himself inside the room. He spent hours smoking his pipe while Hatra snuggled inside her bed. Her maid watched her all the time more carefully. One morning, Leo visited the castle, and Rene wept with Leo for a long time. Leo listened to her mother's whole heartache and tried to relieve her. He was infuriated about Hatop as his voice trembled with unrest emotions. But when he met up with Hatra, he quieted his annoyed feelings; he cuddled her heartily and opened up his warm, kind voice to comfort Hatra's decayed soul. Lastly, he went to face Hatop as Leo stepped inward. The smoke filled the entire area. Leo looked thoughtfully at Hatop, but Hatop instantly shifted his eyeballs away.

"I don't want to give any explanations to you, Leo, and you better leave," Hatop said harshly.

"I'm not here to listen to your explanation either," Leo answered madly.

"Then what brings you here? "Hatop queried.

"Look, Hatop, I accepted. My sister took the first move to initiate the relationship between you two. Maybe her destiny mistreated her. Somehow, she exists in a critical circumstance presently. It's fairly difficult to watch her agony." Leo paused.

"Me too," Hatop added in a busted tone.

Leo walked a few steps close to Hatop and stood before him.

"I'm not aware of what you realise, yet I might not be able to control my hands if she tried to lose her life again. And none of us will be capable of spotting her corpse and enduring such a catastrophic condition." Leo ceased his words and tried to control his resentment.

"so if it happened further," Leo growled and grasped Hatop's neck tightly. The flames fired through his eyes, and his body shivered angrily.

"Lord Hatop, keep this in your mind. If you are responsible for such a tragedy, my hands will be responsible for your last breath. So beware, don't let your fate vanish. I can do anything on behalf of my little sister," he threatened. Hatop gasped with a sweaty forehead. Leo vigorously pushed away Hatop and left. Hatop stood alone in front of the chamber like a statue, then hauled his body inside, slamming the door loudly.

Hatop sat on his chair nearby with a disoriented face. He kept pondering until midnight, sneaking inside Hatra's room. Hatra was stretching on the bed. He quietly sat Close to her. Then, I leaned toward her. But Hatra rolled the other side and ignored him.

"Hatra, we need to talk," Hatop implored her in a cracked voice.

"Hatra, I'm not aware of the final destination of our journey. Maybe I'm not a suitable person for you. We have to solve these tangles, I'm not begging you for your love, and I don't want to apologise to you. But it would be much better if I could release myself from you, simply for your sake. After that, no more worries will suffer you." Hatop sighed.

Hatra turned her eyes straight to his face, and her eyes appeared tired and pale.

"You never talked to me, Hatop; I followed your commands each day if not, you slapped me," she murmured.

"it might be the way I show up, my love Hatra; I have nothing aware about all those glamour and tender-hearted love," Hatop said.

"Truly, Hatop, it is a venom rather than the love spewing from your heart. It trapped me. I got deeply enchanted by it. And your all charming appearance made me more attached to you. Your venom veiled my whole body. It got arrested in my heart, emotions, each muscle and even my blood. It, and killed me out wholly. Yet, I was unable to escape. I got addicted. It might be my bad luck because I'm completely dependent on it. It's a terrifying obsession. However, it is my rest. I look through for my harmony from that deadly venom Hatop. Forgive me; I'm helpless and cannot protect myself from that because I'm in love. I accepted, and I will accept your way of loving" She stopped and gazed into his eyes.

Hatop was wordless; he gazed at her, and then she seized his hands.

"Hatop, please don't leave me. I want to be with you until my death," she whispered. Hatop forcefully released his hands from her and escaped from the room.

"Hatop, don't go," Hatra cried. That frail, broken voice pierced his heart, vibrating around his ears. Then, finally, he shut the chamber door, tumbled on his bed, and tightly fastened his eyes. But Hatra's whole words and her sad image haunted me throughout the night.

The next day, Hatra woke up late. Rene arrived at her room with Armion.

The maid was serving breakfast to Hatra. She ate slowly, and Armion sat beside her. Hatra kissed his cute face and smiled.

"You are the only reason for me to have faith in this useless life; you are a gift to me, my son," Hatra mumbled and cuddled Armion and pressed her cheeks on Armion's forehead. Then, unexpectedly, one of Hatra's maids rushed inside the chamber. She looked around hesitantly.

"Your Majesty," she said.

"What's up, Dora" Rene questioned.

"Lord Hatop is about to leave the palace; he ordered the guards to get ready his horse," Dora answered.

"What!" Hatra yelled and jumped out of bed. She placed one hand on the chest and gasped.

"Hatra, let him do whatever he wants; there should be an end for all these," Rene shouted.

"Mother, I want him; he is the father of my both sons. I don't want to split up my family," Hatra cried confusedly.

"No, mother, I promised to myself that I would be with him forever. Though he ripped me into pieces, I needed to be with him. So I accepted, and I'm accepting that terror into my life, mother," she sputtered, and tears filled her eyes.

"Your Majesty, Lord Hatop is taking Prince Joser with him," Dora added.

"What?" Rene was shocked.

"No way," Hatra mumbled. Then, she swiftly carried Armion into her hands and dashed out of the mansion; she ran straight towards the main entrance. She spotted Hatop standing beside his horse while holding Joser with one arm.

"Hatop," Hatra cried out loud. She kept Armion down.

"Armion, my dear, please sit on here until I go down and talk to your father," she quickly settled Armion on top of the stone stairway and instantly moved down.

"Hatop, please wait," she screamed again. Hatop briskly turned around his head with Hatra's voice.

"Mother," Joser shouted out when he spotted Hatra. Hatop hurriedly took Joser into his arms and moved to climb up on the horse.

"Hatop, wait, please don't leave us." Hatra came close to him with wet cheeks. Her untied hair looked messy without combed; still, her pale face looked tattered. Hatra sat upon her knee beneath Hatop and grabbed his leg.

"Hatop, please don't leave us alone. Would you please take Armion and me with you? Please don't abandon us here. If we cannot live together, we all can die. So let's die together, Hatop. Let's die," Hatra sobbed.

Then she raised her head, and the tears dropped down silently.

"Please have mercy on me, Hatop," she pleaded while glimpsing at him. The most dominant, renowned queen of Thebeslon is arguing to protect her family. Her devastated soul wailed in perpetual fear. Though she is wearing a precious crown around her head, a desperate mother hides her deep inside. A weary soul of an exhausted wife begging for sympathy from her husband or a single drop of affection.

Nevertheless, in the splendid mansion next to her, she is tortured by unresolved grief. The gold coins, valuable jewellery, and opulent attire appeared bare next to her fractured heart. Her isolated, muted aches overflowed as tears, like the woman in a poor, filthy shelter with a raggy old dress. Though the royal blood separated Queen Hatra from the ordinary women, their inexplicable, mysterious life stories share the equivalent rhythm of a mother and a wife.

Hatop silently glanced at Queen Hatra, who was wailing nearby. Maybe her everlasting tears melted rowdy heart for a split second.

"Hatra," he slowly murmurs. He bends and raises her, his strong arms huddled around her shoulders. Their eyes met each other after a long time. Hatra leaned to his broad chest as she continuously sobbed, her hands resting on Hatop's neck. They embraced each other. Joser slowly crept inside the middle of them. While three of them held in one's arms, poor Armion sat atop the rocky stairway. His apathetic face invariably remained calm. He quietly played his role, resembling the unwelcomed visitor who tumbled down among them without notice. Perhaps the majority role that he will fate to play throughout his life.

The family reunited again. Joser was highly excited about the entirety. Through Joser's agreeing with Hatop to leave the castle, he got abundantly worried about moving apart from Hatra. But he has a strong bond with Hatop. On the other hand, Hatra consumed exceeded time with Armion. When Joser noticed Armion always twisted with Hatra, he was burning vastly from anger. Thus, he quickly determined to exit with Hatop. In some way, all the pains sorted considerably, Joser's giggles between the Hatra and Hatop. Rene hastily grabbed Armion's hand and guided him inside the castle.

Hatra's life revolved back to regular life. She marked herself as the reputable Queen of Thebeslon. Ultimately, the kingdom ruled according to the Hatop's ethics. Armion used to lay out his days with Rene; he sat on her lap, and all his ears got closed from her amazing stories. Armion spoke relatively minor, but he was clever enough to comprehend many things. Because Armion has an excellent memory, he giggled while Rene tickled him. He was frightened of darkness and became irritated at night. He often cries from disturbed sleep, so he walks up and cuddles inside Rene at night. some days, he whimpered whole throughout the night.

"My dear son granny is with you; you are safe no need to worry," Rene consoled him.

Joser permanently joined Hatra and Hatop for their long travels. But Hatop refused to take Armion with them all the time. Therefore, Armion used to hang around with Rene all day. Rene and Armion roamed all over the kingdom. Occasionally, they spent their hours inside the woods. Armion holds sympathetic emotions; therefore, he shows favour toward trees. He collected flowers from his tiny hands and then blew the summer balls. However, Armion didn't hurt any small creature because his silent soul respected the whole world. Rene addressed his pure, simple heart. She believes that Armion is shocked because of the past pains he had to face before his birth. Hence, she trusted Armion would wipe out all the wounded memories and shine as the crown prince.

"I know you, my son, I believe you, and you are much more capable than everyone. Someday you will remark yourself," she whispered while gazing at his innocent eyes. Armion eagerly wrapped both his hands around Rene and chuckled. Though they created a deep bond, Armion is very attached to his mother. Hatra feared losing her twist with Armion. Somehow, she yearned to keep Armion under her controllable surroundings, yet she pleased him with delicious sweets and enchanting toys. Sometimes, Armion received gifts from Hatra. She persuaded him she was particularly concerned and loved him more than Joser. Poor Armion's broken, fragile soul always relied upon and believed his mother. His spirit gleams when it's touched with undiminished adoration. He secretly endured his broken soul with great fortitude.

CHAPTER 7

Time flew away, and Armion grew up. His entire behaviour gradually changed with his age. Hence, everybody commenced to praise him. While the lighted beams remarked his life wiping out the dreadful past, He shined like a white lotus popped out from the filthy mud. Armion learnt a whole lot intently and became the most genius. And his talks were meaningful and generous. His unbelievable intelligence and good heart made all sparkle around him. Even his tutor was stunned by his incredible skills. He overpassed the Joser and made himself the most outstanding person. The revelations about Armion mastering many martial arts at a very young age astonished Hatop. People wondered about his talents; nobody could defeat him with sword fighting. Hatop was admired numerous times because of Armion's incredible cleverness. Finally, he introduced Armion as his son.

"Armion is my most loveable youngest son," he boasted. Rene presented a sneering smile when she heard Hatop's painted sweet words.

Armion bonded with trees and felt much chained with green leafy trunks. He never wanted to cut any of the trees in the kingdom, so Armion made small cottages on top of the vast trees and consumed his days inside them. He never enjoyed hunting and was opposed to hurting others. Instead of killing, he constantly struggles to save the creatures. He healed birds with broken wings, saved the rabbit from the hunters' traps, and cured fractured deer. Joser has a cold relationship with Armion because he is profoundly incompetent compared to his brother, but he has uncountable friends than Armion. Hence, he was massively famous among royal companions. Even though everybody was amazed by Armion's intelligence, they rejected him. Clearly, they hesitated to accept his marvellous spirit filled with genuine humanity. Joser never wanted to play with his brother; therefore, he deliberately disregarded him and never invited him to join. Honestly, Joser's conflicts with his rising enviousness about Armion. Joser always wanted to grab Hatra's attentiveness simply by expelling Armion away. He secretly cursed Armion each day for snatching away his lovely mother. Armion, who does not acknowledge all these old stories, thoroughly believed that Joser would accept him someday. Thus, Armion unfolded his warm heart towards his brother.

Nevertheless, Joser walked away. Armion sadly sighed miserably, "Brother." He secretly wiped his tears when he spotted Joser playing with Leo and Lamila's children. Isolated, Armion climbed his treehouse and passed his days. Eventually, he started to make sculptures. His artistic mind guided him to make incredible statues. Gradually, he separated from the outer world and tried to find his own contentment alone. He shares his emotions with Rene, and she teaches him everything. They planted flowers together. Sometimes, they made sweets together. Armion rested his head on Rene's lap and listened to her past stories on the night. Her fingers ran around her hair. He sensed her undivided pure, an enormous love.

"Granny, don't leave me," he whispered. Rene kissed his forehead softly.

Joser's styles are absolutely much similar to Hatop's. He has enticed brown eyes, curly hair, and a solid body; the entire portrayal is enchanted. However, though he has soft, charming expressions, his stoned, rough nature is filled with cruelty. He has an everlasting craving to assemble wealth, and his deceitful manners, followed by mock sympathy, fulfilled him. He hunted animals with his royal mates, poor creatures whose yelping for last breath pleased himself. Hence, he spent many evenings inside the woods with his playmates. However, Armion does not ever agree with Joser's' heartless deeds. Thus, he secretly released the animals caught in Joser's' trap.

Consequently, Joser used to argue with Armion relentlessly. When Joser complains about all these to Hatop, he conveys all his pity on behalf of Joser. He blames Armion for making useless disputes with his brother. Armion cried, lonely, bearing all the frustration. He always tried to be attached to his one and only brother.

"Brother Joser, they are poor lively creatures, they also fixed to their lives like ourselves. They feel pain and fear to die, keep empathy on them," he explained to Joser kindly.

"You are a silly jerk Armion, don't interfere with my thing; please do stay away" Joser frowned. Armion wept with his grandmother, immensely hurt because Joser ignored him. Rene Patted Armion's head gently,

"Armion, instead of search about others try to discover about you," Rene muttered. Armion whirled his teary eyes.

Joser and his mates covertly pulled Armion's tree cottage down and flattened his splendid sculptures one day. Armion sobbed many sleepless nights with a wounded heart. Hatra reassured him that she would advise Joser not to create unwanted misdemeanours. But her mouth remained calm before Joser; she embraced him while enjoying his well-built physique.

"My handsome elder son," she mumbled proudly. She totally forgot the Armion's innocent, sad eyes in front of Joser. However, gradually, Armion discovered he should divert his way far from Joser. He realised Joser and himself had a massive space that had not been replenished. Joser never greets him as his own brother. Armion cares about Hatop and respects him as his father. However, whenever an incident happens, Hatop is deeply worried about Joser. He didn't bother about Armion; neither word was expelled out of his mouth for the sake of Armion.

Nonetheless, he sometimes quarrelled with Leo, Lamila, and Nora when Joser was hurt by their children. However, Hatra exhibits her deep-hearted affection and recreates herself beside Armion. She would never involve herself in blaming others for distressing Armion. Instead, she artfully painted a different drama and misguided Armion from her crafty words.

One evening, Armion roamed among the forests. Suddenly, he spotted a large black viper swallowing itself. He realised he could not save that starving, violent viper, which was too dangerous to get closer. So he returned back and cuddled inside Rene's warm hands.

"I wonder how that viper swallows himself Granny, it was swallowing its own tail, and I'm unable to save that poor creature either," he mutters in a broken voice.

"it's the nature Armion," Rene replied.

"Why?"

"Sometimes nurtured your own viper inside the cage of your soul. You released it from the cage when, that viper grew well with your egocentric mind.

Though you heed it and you built it by your own that violent viper chase after you because its ultimate goal is to destroy its own creator. Indeed, that viper is our ego. You made it and after all, you get trouble to save yourself from that horrendous scary viper."

"So how we escape from that viper granny?"

Then forget yourself self, Armion. Demolish the entire attachment with you. Let each thing be rested in its own space. You can gain nothing from possessing, yet you will obtain everything from losing it."

"So what will happen to the viper granny?"

"There is no viper survive without the creator," Rene uttered.

"I wonder why someone's cruelty harms others, granny."

"sometimes nature steel the innocent life to power the cruelty. Sometimes it's a tangle Though the heartlessness wins for the moment nothing is persists. Whole decided by the nature." Rene added.

"What a puzzle Granny." he sighed.

"Life is a mysterious journey, Armion. Death is a temporary halt. If your heart is filled with insatiable hatred and stupidity. It can create your own viper to swallow you up to your last breath, so beware of your emotions. Respect morality because we are stepping towards our death each second." Rene explained slowly; Armion raised his head.

"What's the meaning of all these granny," he asked.

"There's hard find the meaning of whole entity, it all what we recreated inside, from what you perceived from your senses. Whole this revolving between the past and future. Yet, we are after the unusual illusion. A dream we built with our useless trunks. Whole is devastating. That's the profound veracity." Rene peeped inside to Armion.

"beware of your thoughts my son, death might be much soothing than the living or it might be the worst if you were unable to judge the real value of existence. Soul is much precious, only the hardships can light up your liberation."

Rene explained and sighed.

"Granny why all of them rejecting me" Armion questioned in a shattered tone. Rene shook her head and smiled, holding both his arms.

"They rejected you because you are the most valuable."

She replied calmly.

"Listen Armion, though it was too harsh, endure it mutedly, don't struggle against it because it's all in vein, reject the acceptance from the outer world. Face the absolute truth. Because the theory of uncertainty shrouded all through the life."

Armion stood up silently.

"Armion, we two have a small excursion tomorrow, I hope you wake up early," Rene said with a chuckle. Armion smiled and walked out.

The next day dawned. Rene disguised herself as an ordinary woman. Then she ordered Armion to dress like an ordinary village person. They roamed through the kingdom and reached the filthy, poor shack. Armion spotted a poor man and the woman lying on the floor. He sat beside them and held them kindly. While Queen Rene cooked delicious meals, Armion bathed them and cleaned that shack. The villagers were unable to recognise them with their ordinary clothes. Armion played with some youngsters. He felt contented and satisfied with the whole.

"Try to heal your wounded heart by healing aid-fewer poor souls. Strength up your empathy rather than the sympathy. Work for the others selflessly and light up your spirit, my son."

Armion smiled with sparkling eyes.

"Armion forget this worthless torso, it's merely a temporary lodging."

Rene muttered while lighting some scented candles all around her room.

"Recognise these human feelings, Armion and you can become the king of their heart." she said in a hushed tone. Armion glanced at the candle glow.

"This candle glints and sways with the howling breeze, granny like our lives, nevertheless I promise to you. I will rebuild the kingdom once and end their agonies." Rene presented a delighted smile, looking at Armion's innocent eyes.

....

A few days passed leisurely; one gloomy sunset, Rene unexpectedly fell down while walking in the mansion garden. Rene remained unconscious for many days. It was hard to find the exact reason. Yet, she became unwell and frail daily. Finally, she opened her eyes after many days and talked with

Armion. He spent all his past days beside her. Finally, Rene lay on the bed, inactive with her aching, feeble body.

"I think my time is over now, my son," she mumbled lowly.

"No granny, don't speak about your death please it's too early for it," Armion grabbed both hands.

"I all be all alone here granny nobody for me," he sobbed.

"You are expecting too much from others my son. So don't expect love and dignity for yourself. Neither will granted you all these. Demolish your bonds Armion, observe about your soul, wipe out your both painful and elated emotion then eventually you will be touched with your own harmony," she mumbled.

"Granny, please tell me the truth of all these. why am I always feeling that I do not belong here" Armion questioned.

"You were an unwanted visitor here, my son," she said.

"An unwanted visitor," Armion repeated.

"Hatop never desired to have another child after Joser, he denied you. Hence your mother was exhausted in that critical time. They have destroyed their two unborn children earlier. So if they followed it again your mother would probably lose her life. Therefore she gave birth to you. And I forced them to do so," Rene said Armion sighed woefully.

"I opened my eyes with this rejection, or else it may be the desire of nature," He admitted in a broken voice.

"You have to fulfil my dreams Armion, you visited here to complete King Amenmose's unfinished duty. You are owed to me, so it's all your responsibility. And you are most eligible for that matter." Rene smiled, staring at Armion.

Armion rested his head next to her,

"stay with me Granny, don't leave me," he commenced moaning quietly.

Hatra attended Rene several times and chose a new maid to look after her. Laicha, a middle-aged widow who is kind and generous, is dedicated to her chores. She was bothered about Armion and cared for him too. Hatra worried a little about Rene and shed crocodile tears while kissing Rene. But deep inside welcomes Rene's last rights soon. Hatra was living peacefully with Hatop; hence, she was keen to secure it. But Rene and Hatop had cold debates about Hatop's truth-less behaviour. Rene insulted Hatop repeatedly and criticised his wolfish style of ruling the kingdom. Hatra got into endless trouble because of Rene, and they fought. Hence, Hatop expelled his anger throughout Hatra. Hatra secretly considered if her mother's death would smooth their lives rather than her stay with them. She desired to spark her entire fantasy with Hatop.

Laicha spent all the time with Rene contentedly. She comforted and cared for Rene each day. One day, Rene called Laicha,

"Laicha take care of my crown prince Armion after my death," Rene requested her.

"Your Majesty, I will fulfil your hope forever, I promise you," Laicha muttered, wiping her tears. Leo and Lamila constantly visited to see Rene. Leo yearned to take his mother back to his place, but Rene refused to leave Armion.

"I want to die here, watching my dear Armion's innocent eyes. That is my last wish." Rene confirmed. Meanwhile, Hatop organised a massive party for fellow kingdom royal guests. Unfortunately, that evening, Rene got seriously ill. She implored Hatra to hold on the following hours with her.

"I'm spending my last few hours, Hatra. Please do stay with me. I want you to sit beside me before my last breath," Rene whispered with eyes filled with tears.

Hatra turned her head away and rolled her eyes,

"I'm so sorry, mother. I can't reject that function. As you are aware, all about my duties as Queen. We will have enough time, Mother, won't we? I think it is too early to discuss your death. You are my beloved mother, and you should be long lived." Hatra kissed Rene slyly, and her falsely kind voice touched the Laisha's ears', and she looked away unhappily. Rene closed her eyes sadly to stop her tears. Armion argued with Hatra and pleaded with her to stay, but Hatra denied it. Armion walked back to Rene desperately.

"Armion, take me to the garden, my son I want to have some fresh air," Rene requested. Armion held her into his mighty arms and settled her on a garden bench. Rene stretched some tiny box towards Armion.

"Open it up," she said.

"What is this granny?" Armion asked with curiosity.

"It's a gift for you, Armion," Rene replied.

Armion unlocked the box unhurriedly. It's a necklace accompanied by a large crystal pendant.

"It is Tanzanite," and she wore it around Armion's neck.

"Armion I have to tell you a story about me," Rene muttered softly.

"I'm ready to listen to it, granny" Armion grabbed her one hand and peeked inside her.

"I'm not born here, Armion. I was born in Spavitar."

Armion raised his eyebrows with shocked eyes.

"Spavitar," he repeated.

"I do not own any royal family. I had a little family in Spavitar. My father's death followed an animal attack.

And soon after, my mother passed away after giving birth to my little sister. I held her in my hands and promised to look after her, but unfortunately, she joined my parents a few days later. They all left; It's me alone; I cried a lot, yet nothing remade." Rene halted and moaned.

"People recognised me as someone holding a bit of terrible bad luck; hence most of them rejected me, and, some pitied me, I raised alone, the woods feed me, the streams quenched my thirst. But, mother nature accepted me wholeheartedly."

"I am so sorry to hear all these granny" Armion grabbed Rene's hands.

"One day I was roaming among the woods, and I heard someone is crying for help. I flew near the river where's the sound coming through"

"Suddenly, I sighted a little girl in the middle of the river. She is drowning and crying for help. I jumped into the river without thinking twice. I only wanted to save her life. Somehow I was returned to the shore. She was cuddled inside me and shivering with cold. I remembered my little baby sister, who passed away. So whole the memories unexpectedly filled my mind."

Rene paused.

"My name is Roura, she said to me," Rene sobbed.

"I felt that God has gifted me back my little sister. I took her to my place happily, suddenly that evening kings guards gathered around my tiny shack. They took the little Roura and me directly to the castle. I was astonished, Roura refused to lose my hand she hold me tightly. We felt much attached to each other. And with all amazed I came to know that Roura is the crown

Princess of Spavitar, and I'm the one who rescued her life" Rene stopped her words and coughed. Armion patted her chest.

"Granny, you should take some rest now, you must be tired," Armion said sadly.

"No my son, I know I'm having quite short time, and all of them waiting for me but you should aware all these let me speak," Rene implored.

"Because of my bravery, the King and Queen adopted me as their daughter. And also, Princess Roura didn't let me go back. She wanted to be with me all the time.

For some unknown reason, we shared a deep-hearted bond. As a royal princess, I stepped inside the castle, and my destiny turned in the opposite direction. I learnt all the things hard. The king and Queen loved and cared for me as their own daughter. Besides all, I was happy because I had a family and a home. Roura and I became the most affectionate sisters. We didn't have any secret."

"Queen Roura, mother of King Pedro," Armion mumbled.

"At that time, Kingdom Spavitar and Thebeslon were ruled peacefully. There were no disputes and clashes between them. Everything went well. The crown prince of Thebeslon once visited our castle" Rene halted her story, and a beautiful smile emerged on her face.

"Your grandfather and I fell in love with each other and we got married," Rene's eyes glittered with shine.

"Before I leave, Spavitar, Roura and I embraced each other it was challenging to make separate from ourselves. She gifted me this Tanzanite, and it's a true reflection of our love and our relationship as sisters. I protected it my whole life." Rene sighed and touched the Tanzanite.

"I frequently visited Spavitar with your grandfather, but Hatra's whole stubbornly behaviour diverted our fate. Everything ended at once." Rene sighed heavy-heartedly.

"when Hatop, your father, started to interfere with all the ruling matter, he grabbed each thing under his arm using your mother. He demolished Thebeslon and commenced all the wars against Spavitar and destroyed all our bonds. I was incapable of facing Roura. Your mother was never sensible about things, and she blindly trusted Hatop. Neither of them was aware of my past story, and I didn't need to share it with them either. I secretly cried because I'm powerless" The tears filled her eyes.

"Roura died unexpectedly; after some time, Hatop commenced his secret missions against Spavitar. I heard Roura got poisoned. Some said she died after an attack by the black viper. Nonetheless, Nobody is aware about the exact explanation of her death. It remained as unresolved mystery," Rene breathed out sadly.

"A mystery; how could it happen" Armion questioned in confusion.

"I can still memorise our beautiful past and I was unable to see her for the last time. She departed from me forever." Rene wept; Armion tried to console her.

"I can't blame your mother, Armion; honestly, I could not recognise herself; I never tried to touch up her emotions. Instead of being tied up with her heart, I was frustrated about her mischief. That frustration created a huge space between us. Thus she slipped out of my hands and got separated from us. She built her own world yet eventually got ruined in front of my eyes. I am too responsible for that catastrophe." Rene muttered in a regretful sound.

"Why don't you gifted this Tanzanite to my mother granny, because she is your daughter and I think this necklace is more suitable for her." Armion questioned slowly.

"Your mother's eyes are not vivid, those eyes frightened me all the time. This should be gifted to someone holding a golden heart; it's not Joser either, eligible for; it is only you, Armion, and I'm aware of you from the beginning; you are absolutely different from the others. You are the most eligible person to hold the crown. I believe you, Armion, you can rebuild our kingdom and establish our whole good heart with Spavitar." Rene smiled and wiped her wet cheeks.

Armion touched the Tanzanite,

"I will fulfil your dream Granny, with all my courage." Armion promised, gazing at her eyes.

The dusk veiled over, and the moon hid inside the gloomy clouds. Rene shivered with the cold breeze. Armion took Rene into his hands and carried her back to the castle. Rene lay on the bed and breathed feebly. While her whole body trembled slightly, Laicha massaged her feet quickly.

"Laicha," Rene mumbled, assembling her whole strength.

"I want to see Hatra; please bring her here," she stammered. Rene coughed while Armion grabbed her fingers and kept his head beside her. He lamented aloud.

Meanwhile, Laicha reached the door of the Hall, where the function was placed. It was almost midnight. Laicha looked around hesitantly; she was anxious to find Queen Hatra. She looked around impatiently and finally determined to step inside the Hall immediately. But suddenly, the door opened. Lord Hatop appeared, and Laicha walked a few steps forward hurriedly. But her legs halted when she sighted Hatra. The Queen leaned to Hatop, her entire trunk wobbled side to side. She wrapped both her hands around Hatop's neck and giggled. Her eyes were red and slightly closed. Hatop hauled the wasted Queen hurriedly inside their chamber. Laicha stayed a few moments with shocked eyes, then dragged herself back to Rene. She realised that the Hatra was not conscious at all.

"How can she merry herself when her mother struggles for last breath on her death bed" she mumbled.

Laicha stepped inside the Rene's chamber with all devastated minds. The room bears a tiny light glow; all candles were soon blotted. Armion was sobbing alone, embracing Rene's deceased body. Rene lay peacefully on the bed with tightly shut eyes. Laicha knelt down beside her. "I'm sorry, Queen Rene, forgive me," she whispered, then closed her eyes to break the unstoppable tears.

CHAPTER 8

The sun rose, and Hatra's loud bawling shook the whole mansion. Each seemed downhearted with the demise of the most humble and admirable past royal Queen. Hatra cried without a stop and fainted for numerous moments. Then, next to King Amenmose's grave, they buried Queen Rene.

"My mother, please don't leave me alone" Hatra's mournful outcry burst tears in all others. Consequently, they all showed their sympathy towards Queen Hatra. Laicha stared at Hatra's fickle dramatic reactions with astonished eyes. She wondered about Hatra's erratic personality in dual copies. After the funeral, Hatop sighed with relief.

"My biggest headache is over now. Hereafter, I can govern every aspect of Thebeslon peacefully, and there will be no interruptions," he said.

Hatra wiped her tears as soon as she returned to her chamber. She lay on the bed leisurely and let her maid Betty massage her feet. After having evening tea, she had a warm bath. She floated on the blue water relaxedly. When she entered the room, Hatop was sipping a glass of wine.

"The night is still, young lord Hatop," Hatra whispered; her eyes were overflowing with arousing emotions. She stood behind and leaned towards him, resting both hands around his waist. Hatop swiftly turned around, dragged her vigorously, and squeezed her tightly into his arms. His eyes scrutinised her sheer dress, then smirked lasciviously and finished his glass. His eyes blazed with lust. He slowly drew his thumb finger along her semi-nude breast, and she sensed tickling numbness throughout her body. Then his fingers slanted the wine bottle unhurriedly and spilt it all over, letting her body soaked. Hatra drowned in exploded emotions and pushed him away, breathing heavily and standing against the wall. Hatop approached her, allowing their bodies and lips to clutch together profoundly. They shared their breath while they felt the thunder of their soaring heartbeat. She tasted his rowdy lips, and her fingers slowly released his clothes. And Hatop quietly carried her to the bed.

"I want to taste my wine Queen Hatra," he said roughly. His lips, ran around Hatra's burning body, and then he ripped her thin gown into pieces. Hatra concealed and pushed down by his force. However, his sharp teeth signed sincerely inside her smooth skin. Moreover, she endured it, hiding her soul twisting with that endless ardour of rhythm.

Hatra's entire body seemed to be in pain, and Hatop's amativeness was flooded. But that pain and agony emptied her senses from the memories related to Queen Rene. While her inner heart questioned her negligence, she outwardly gruntled her awakened hunger. Since that magical bizarre demolished all her sins, she had committed to suffering her mother. Ultimately, she came together with the rhythm of fascination, which is much more impressive than her sored trunk. Hatop rapidly exhaled while moving on her body. Hatra closed her eyes and whimpered gleefully.

In the morning, Hatra sat at the breakfast table. She looked wearisome, with swollen red eyes. Though her stomach fits with her rising appetite, she withheld eating before Armion. She began to lament again. He glanced at her with a worried face. Then he pushed his plate to the side and approached her.

"Mother, please don't cry" he implored while kissing her head.

"Armion, that night, if I didn't participate in that function, your father would smash me into pieces. I begged him because I wanted to stay with my mother at her last moment. But he disturbed me, and I became so worried. I sobbed secretly, thinking about her each second. The party didn't make me any joy at all. I stayed alone suffering from a terrible headache. Finally, I fainted, and your father carried me back to the room. I missed my beloved mother. I wished to kiss her last time, but Hatra faltered and cried aloud."

Poor Armion trusted Hatra's all lies. He cuddled and comforted her.

"Armion, I feel dizzy and uncomfortable again. I need to go back to my room." She mumbled in a feeble voice.

Then she leaned to him unsteadily, and Armion directed her way; he made her lie on the bed cautiously.

"Mother, please think about yourself and particularly about your health. I lost my granny. So I can't let you leave me too. I can't live alone mother. There's no one for me in this world except you." Armion sighed.

"Death is so far for me my son I will live long with your whole love," Hatra muttered while patting his head quietly.

The palace seems to be reviving back after Rene's death. Armion made himself busy practising with the sword.

When the sword briskly passes around him, he can dilute his sore heart for a split second. Each day, he remembered the things he learned from his grandmother. Queen Rene was an excellent sword fighter. She taught Armion the very first steps of Marital Arts.

Armion gazed at the stars some nights, lonely, recalling whole memories.

Meanwhile, Joser was found extremely busy with an important event. Routinely, he was nowhere inside the castle during the daytime but quietly returned at night. Hatop felt suspicious about Joser's behaviour. So his eagle eyes secretly inspect Joser. Deeply, his mind is abundant with massive dreams related to Joser. Hatop has already proposed Joser to a crown princess of a fellow kingdom. Though he didn't grant his consent to it, Hatop arranged all actions according to his choice. Soon, he learned that Joser had a relationship with an ordinary young woman. Hatop burnt with anger, and he became furious with that message.

Gaika, a farmer's elder daughter, silently snatches Joser's heart away. Though she was not very graceful, Joser fascinated her for unknown reasons. Gaika was attracted by Joser's captivating appearance. They spent their most isolated romantic meetings deep inside the forest. They snuggled to each other in the hidden caves. Joser found it hard to release himself from Gaika; therefore, more and more, he entangled her.

After their father's unexpected loss, Gaika's family was down in the flames of poverty. Joser aided them in every way. Lucy, Gaika's mother, greeted Joser with all honour. Gaika's little sister enjoyed the sweets that Joser brought from the castle. Joser is courageous, and he is not very devoted to his parents. He chased for his liberty and independence on every occasion. He is passionate about assembling money and has succeeded with it concurrently. He gathered great wealth around him separately. He often planned to settle his life outside the castle. Though Hatra and Hatop adored him from the bottom of their heart, his emotions didn't tie firmly with them. But he stuck around Gaika's beating heart.

Hatop madly waited for Joser one night; when Joser's shadow touched the castle door, Hatop jumped in front of him and slapped Joser harshly.

"You ruined me, I was planning to gain success to your life, but you wasted everything," Hatop groaned.

"Joser, listen to this carefully. You must be ready to marry the crown princess of the Kingdom Temos, and that would be the end of all these nasty events." He said furiously.

Joser walked away with a muted mouth, rubbing his aching face. Hatra followed him quietly.

"I can't forget her mother," he said sadly, looking at her face.

"I know your heart my son. Stay calm until your father gets rid his anger. Be patient, I'm always by your side," she confirmed.

But the very next day, Joser met Gaika again. Gaika sobbed after she heard the whole incident. They were alone inside the deserted dark mountain cave. Joser leaned over to her unveiled body as Gaika turned to the other side and twirled her eyes upward.

"If you finish our whole bond to fulfil your father's wish to marry that crown princess, I will quit my life. Death is better than losing you." Gaika uttered while peeping inside Joser's face.

"You can succeed his wish over my dead body." Joser raised his eyebrows, all dazed with her broken voice.

"No, Gaika," he shouted and ceased her bare shoulders tightly.

"Let me solve all in a good way Gaika trust me," he whispered and kissed her madly.

Gaika never attempts to discover that she genuinely loves Prince Joser. Her mother, Lucy, perfectly advised her to win his heart. On the other hand, Gaika fantasised about becoming a Queen, and she visualised it all in her dreams. First, she craves to have dignity and an elegant, fancy life. Secondly, she needed to promote a comfortable and restful life for her sister and mother. Hence, she found that enchanting Joser's heart was the most suitable way to approach her ambition. However, Gaika was fortunate to earn Prince

Joser's love for herself. And then she twined around in his muscular body. She never hesitated to be alone with him and got drowned in their desires. Merely for the sake of their love and to achieve her wish. However, later, Joser commenced yearning for her love and warmth and deeply twisted inside her.

....

Hatop spent his days with an agitated mind. The sleep couldn't reach his eyes. He knew Joser would never detach himself from Gaika; therefore, Hatop became increasingly hopeless. Finally, he shut his eyes, but a violent hissing sound unexpectedly disturbed him. As he opened his eyes, some black cloud veiled around him. He sighted a giant black viper with ruddy eyes.

"Orana," he whispered.

"Lord Hatop, the reason you are bothering is worthless. You cannot change Joser's fate. Because it is planned already." The viper talked.

"He is my most loving elder son Orana. I had many dreams about him." Hatop said downheartedly.

"Forget him Lord Hatop, you have to think about prince Armion he is the worthiest. He was born in a highly auspicious time. He has his born luck to rule entire Henaten."

"Yes he is the future king, but" Hatop sighed.

"No, you never believed him Lord Hatop, you always underestimated him."

"I had enough reasons to do so Orana."

"Lord Hatop, before he accomplishes his journey, we have to get him under our power. If we lose him, he will be a danger to whole black vipers."

"How?"

"He has all born energy for that; therefore, we have to use my witchcraft to make him obedient to us."

"Witchcraft," Hatop smirks.

"Lord Hatop, if he follow his principles, that would be our end, so we must trap his soul by my enchantment. We have to put in negative energy to hold and keep him under control"

"Orana, I am worried about Joser," Hatop growled.

"Listen we have to do nothing with prince Joser let him marry Gaika. Because he is belonging of Ovigons."

"You make me more annoying," Hatop groaned

"Lord Hatop you must visit to my place before everything get in to more trouble. I am expecting you and Queen Hatra in dark woods."

"I am not concerned about your magic, Orana," Hatop shouted aloud.

"What happened, Hatop? Are you alright?" Hatra shakes him. Hatop saw a bright light, rubbed his eyes, and looked around. It was almost morning. Hatra was sitting beside him.

"I didn't wake you up because you were sleeping tightly anyway. Shall we have some tea?" Hatra asked him kindly while resting her arms on his shoulders.

"Yes," he replied with all confusion and scratched his head.

Joser married Gaika privately and planned to leave Lamila's place. Hatra supported Joser in all his plans without exception. Moreover, she added her hearty blessings towards Gaika. She respected Gaika's bravery and was satisfied with the similarity between Gaika's love story and herself.

"Gaika committed herself to Joser like I devoted my entirety to Hatop," she thought blindly. On top of that, she hated the well-mannered crown princess of the kingdom, Temos, who was affluent, talented and virtuous. Indeed, Hatra's egoist mind hesitates to welcome her to the kingdom. On the contrary, she firmly believed It would obliterate her self-honour.

Secondly, she denied the gap of righteousness between herself and the crown princess. Hatra's selfish heart empathetically seeks someone who is beneath herself. So the Gaika, the daughter of a wretched widow, ideally matched her principles. So, she secretly arranged everything with Lamila to comfort the lovers until Hatop wiped out his anger. Hatop became downhearted, and his soul cracked into pieces. He worried alone and smashed all the things around him.

"I lost my son; he ruined my dreams," Hatop cried madly.

Hatra consoled him while showing her broken heart about Joser. Then she wiped her tears in front of him and sobbed.

Neither man in the village can speak about Gaika and Prince Joser. They feared him because they knew the cruel misdeeds responsible for Joser's' thugs. Joser dominates the people brought to Thebeslon as the prisoners from the fellow surrendered kingdoms. The poor, miserable humans worked day to night to earn massive profits for Prince Joser. Though Joser has a charming appearance, his heart has no place for mercy. Therefore, nobody ever rumoured or let out any unpleasant words to Gaika or her family. Instead, they recalled the memories of the distressed labourer who spoke against Prince Joser regarding his unethical values. That poor guy's powerless body was next to the muddy swamp. Some said it might be the attack of a poisonous snake, yet nobody knows the absolute truth. People rumoured about a black viper adopted by Joser. But nobody seeks the evidence. But the wealthiest people of the village did not ever delay the portions they required to gift to Prince Joser.

Prince Joser has already built a vast, magnificent palace in Thebeslon, near the main castle. He designed the mansion according to the Gaika's needs. He wished to settle his life there with Gaika and her family. Hatop kept himself in his room for a few months, disheartened.

Nonetheless, Hatra delightfully followed her routines. Ultimately, Hatop agreed to hold a small wedding ceremony for Joser and Gaika. Hatra invited them to return, but Hatop did not show up. Gaika's wedding was a simple occasion rather than a royal ceremony. The noble guests were not invited; only the family members joined the event. Gaika's eyes dimmed with the heart-rending mind, and she sighed sadly. Though Queen Hatra spoke with her warmly, Lord Hatop ignored her completely. Hatop denied inviting Gaika to stay with them. Instead, he refused to greet Gaika as his daughter-in-law. Armion never let himself interfere with all these conflicts. He kept himself quiet, but he welcomed Gaika kindly. Therefore, Gaika called him" My little brother." Gaika and Joser spent a luxurious life in their mansion. Every day, their wealth rose; they were bound by their lavish lifestyles regardless of right or wrong.

After Joser's' separation, Hatop's lifestyle seems quite unlike it. He felt apprehensive about everything and fought with Hatra for silly reasons. He blamed the maids impatiently. However, to tolerate his troublesome, lousy temper. He fired some of his guards for an unworthy matter. At night, he wandered around the terrace alone with his smoke pipe. His perplexed mind found it simply hard to catch some rest. One morning, after having a big argument with Queen Hatra, Hatop anxiously walked to the garden. The garden covers uncountable trees. It was planted by Armion and Queen Rene, and heed those with much love. After Rene's demise, Prince Armion consumed his time in this garden. He spent many hours among the trees rather than in his room.

"What the hell" Hatop growled.

"Is this a garden or a jungle?" he questioned out loud.

Truthfully, Hatop has not once passed the time with lively green trees. He was never attracted to blooming flowers; instead of enjoying the beauty, he wanted to pluck them and keep them only with him. His ruthless heart never seems to be elated with green leafy saplings. He preferred to stick around with his royal mates while wasting his time laughing at their dirty jokes. The materialised artificial, which can promote physical pleasure, satisfied him rather than the silent, solemn trees.

The soundless murmur of rustling leaves irritated him. The fragrance of the freshly emitting breath tingled his nose. He commenced sneezing uncomfortably.

"It's killing me, I feel this whole castle surrounded with thick nasty wood," He groaned.

"Or else this might be another curse of that wicked woman who recently died," he mumbled and drew his legs back to the inside.

That afternoon, Armion re-entered the castle after spending much time beside the beach. Once he stepped into the garden, he was utterly dumbfounded. He screamed out loud. His trees were cut and pulled out, and many naked trunks stood like tombs in a deserted graveyard. The entire garden became visible as bare ground.

Armion was shocked; he stood with a speechless mouth; he pulled his stoned legs back to his chamber. The tears ran through his eyes. As he entered the room, Laicha appeared in front of him with a worried face.

"Lord Hatop commanded to clear out the garden, your highness," she said slowly. Armion swiftly walked to Hatop's room. He opened the door vaguely, letting the door hit on the edge of the stone wall loudly. Hatop looked confused by the sudden arrival of the Armion.

"What do you want? What do you expect by hurting me? What pleasure you gain through my tears. All those trees not might be worthy to you than the money and gold but for me it was my life. You destroyed my life father and it's not the trees you pull down it's my life, my breath. You destroyed me." He shouted desperately. Hatop stared at him with startled eyes. Hatra quickly jumped between them.

"Armion, my son, don't get angry. Stay calm it's just your father ordered to clean the garden It was quite bushy and crowded." Hatra explained softly.

"I don't need your explanations mother" Armion left the room immediately. The door slammed again loudly.

Armion blew outside the castle, drove his horse close to the woods, and peeked around. Afterwards, he halted his horse in a particular place and disguised himself as an ordinary village man. He rushed between the trees and proceeded towards the river in the woods. Then he stopped himself and sighed. Finally, his ears caught someone's sweet, charming voice.

"How did you hurt little bird? Isn't it painful"

Armion closely observed everywhere; he spotted a young woman below the oak tree holding a bird. There was a basket by the side of her. Armion covered himself, hiding beneath the shady tree and watched her face more clearly. Armion's heart flickered for a while. She is of medium height, sparkling bright eyes, and her beautiful face shines with golden skin. Her soft, silky hair, length to her waist, slightly swings. She was wearing a simple gown and an apron. The few birds gathered close to her; she might have been feeding them. Armion became incompetent to move his eyes away from her sight. She is stunning, and some magnetic power forces Armion to talk with her.

"A gorgeous daisy flower I have ever seen; it's truly attractive," he whispers slowly. Then, he stepped forward and appeared in front of her.

"What's wrong with the bird sister? Any problem? Armion questioned kindly. The girl was stunned by his unexpected arrival. She looked at him with shocked eyes and then stepped backwards. Armion got utterly dazed with her entire impressive outward form. Her face, eyes and her smile abandoned him beyond the clouds.

"Nothing wrong brother. This bird cannot fly because of its wounded wing," she explained unhurriedly. Armion looked around, but his eyes tangled with her. She quietly hands the bird to Armion. He fought to pause his thumping heart.

"No worries, I can cure him; I will take it with me. He might be able to fly when his wing healed." Armion spoke slowly and watched her lovely face while talking.

"All right then" The girl quickly turned back and took the basket. She gave him a tiny smile and raised her footsteps.

"wait," Armion interrupted her.

"You found the bird, it might seek for you after he got cured, so what if he wanted to meet you again. I mean to say goodbye." Armion's foot bit forward, letting himself closer to her. The girl looked at his eyes suspiciously and wrinkled her forehead.

"Who are you?" she asked hesitantly.

"You may know me some day," Armion whispered.

"But this poor bird wants to know whole about you to show his gratitude," he said smoothly. Then he slowly peeked into the girls' eyes; they gazed at each other for seconds. The girl awkwardly shifted her eyes away, then pulled her legs to move, and instantly, she turned back,

"If he wants, he can find it by its own," she shortly replied, then escaped from sight. Armion watched her until her shadow hid inside the forest. The river meandered according to its rhythm. Armion knelt, and a wonderful smile emerged after a long time.

"A golden daisy flower," he mumbled. The little bird chirps twirls its little head and then hops beside him. He kindly holds it in his hand.

"You will heal your wing soon but I might find a way to bring myself back to the present sense." A bright chuckle burst out of his lips.

Armion returned to the castle with the evening dusk. Hatra waited for him anxiously. As he popped in, she grasped his hand.

"Mother, I'm too tired" he pulled away from his hand back and quitted herself. He wanted to avoid her long, tiring conversations. His heartfelt fluttering While staring at the night sky, he recalled her eyes, smile, sweet voice, and long wavy hair shaking with light wind. The sleep was hard to touch his eyes. He wandered across the balcony and puffed out. Armion shook his head from side to side. He sat beside his daisy pots. Then, he moves his fingers smoothly over the flowers, "why am I so unbridled this is quite strange, she is haunting around me," he questioned himself.

The following day, Armion woke up; he ordered Laicha to feed the bird and watch it closely.

Then, he rode the horse close to the woods and changed his clothes. He waited near the river for several hours, yet nobody appeared before him. Hence, he arrived back with a weary heart. Afterwards, he repeatedly visited the river and waited for extended hours, but she was invisible. The bird healed. He stared at the bird while recalling her sweet memories again and again.

"My eyes are sore by waiting for her. Can you find her on my behalf?" Armion mumbled while watching the little bird.

The bird healed its wing, and Armion returned it to his world. He released the bird; it soared up to the blue sky. Armion gazed at it alone. Then, he stepped back to the castle with all his isolated soul.

CHAPTER 9

A rmion spent a few days inside the castle, and his fingers moved swiftly around the sculptures he had built recently, "your eyes." He mumbled. And then he sighed again as he stared at the sculpture." I want to recreate you in front of me, yet my hands found quite numb until I can sense you wholeheartedly." He whispered.

"Who are you? My mind so unquiet because of you, I wonder why I couldn't find you." He spoke to himself in a hushed tone. Then, at once, he stood up and footed near his horse and drove it again to the woods. Prince Armion halted the horse and disguised himself as an ordinary village man. His legs drew him close to a cottage he visited with Queen Rene. A poor older woman lived there alone. He spotted the old granny sitting in the front yard and a young woman standing beside her and combing her hair. Armion quickly covered himself with a huge tree trunk and watched them curiously.

"Is it tasty granny do you like it?"

Armion vaguely raised his head with that astonishing voice. His heart was delighted when he identified the gesture as a young woman. It was her standing next to that old granny. Armions eyes delighted with her sight, and he stepped backwards and stayed silent. The young woman bent slightly, and the old granny slowly grabbed her hands tightly.

"My dear, you bathed me, washed my clothes and cooked delicious food for me. I'm so grateful to you for your kindness. My blessings will carry with you each day."

Granny kissed the young woman's fingers while patting her head.

"It's time for me to leave now granny; I am coming back to see you soon. Stay safe" The girl kissed the old woman's forehead and came out of the house; she held a basket in one hand. Armion followed her soundlessly; he escaped himself with the aid of the shadows of the surrounding bushes. Suddenly, the girl turned back, startled by Armion's unexpected sight.

"You" she exclaimed out loud.

"Yes, it's me" Armion stood in front of her.

"The bird got fixed its wing and flew back to his home, and it said to me pass the message to you." Armions eyes sparkled with a colourful smile.

The girl raised her eyebrows and shook her head to escape his enchanting eyes. But Armion peeped inside her face.

"I waited for you many days, but you didn't come," he said calmly.

The girl drew a few steps backwards and turned around.

"I didn't make any promise to you," she said firmly.

"A promise," Armion repeated with a bright chuckle.

"Is this your house?" he questioned.

"No, I frequently visit here to take care of the Granny because she is aged, and there's nobody to care for her."

"Why you do so?" he questioned again after a few moments of gazing at her.

"Well, I would like to lend a hand who needs any aid," she explained unhurriedly.

"What's inside that? It looks heavy," He asked while glancing at her basket.

"It's some food for a woman who's expecting a baby, she lives nearby And some sweets for her little kids." The girl replied humbly.

"What a beautiful angel," he whispered.

"Who?" She questioned back.

"It's you, no one else," Armion replied with glittering eyes.

"Why do you do so? he asked, getting a few steps closer to her; their eyes met for a split second. She gazed at him with a muted mouth, then shifted her head away from his sight.

"Look, you are questioning too much; I'm getting late; let me leave now."

"please answer me, don't leave," Armion murmured and glanced at her pleadingly.

"I want to satisfy myself by healing others," she responded hurriedly to move her steps. But Armion stood in front of her way and halted her again.

"Can you heal me too," he asked kindly.

"What do you mean" the girl asked in a confused voice.

"Please tell me; Your name, I was much waited to know it."

The girl gave a shocked look, wide-eyed.

"Or else I will call you angel," Armion added.

"I'm getting; late ; let me go," she implored again.

"You are heeding people and animals; please have mercy on me; let me know about you; I'm abandoned," he whispered, and his limbs directly stood closely behind her, and his lips slightly touched her ears. She shivered, but her whole body kept drowning in unknown emotions.

"Will I be able to leave if I tell you my name?" she turned her face back.

"Yes, of course," he stared at her.

"I am Arianna," she said softly while looking down.

"beautiful," he muttered in a secret tone.

Arianna moved swiftly away from him. "I'm leaving," she hurriedly ran away.

"I'm waiting for you every day near the creek," he shouted aloud. But Arianna hastily flees out of him without giving a second look.

Armion found it quite unsettled in his mind when he returned to the castle. He had been thinking for a long time and had denied speaking with Hatra and Hatop. He had his supper alone inside his room. Hatop seemed to be relieved after ravaging Armion's garden. Armion's tears, vexed attitude and dissatisfied spirit consoled Hatop. He searched for his inner peace by disheartening Armion. Majorly, Armion's victories and happiness agitated Hatop; he never committed to watching his younger son's talents. Hatop never participated in Armion sword performances; only Hatra cheered for him. But Hatop never hesitates to waste his time on behalf of Joser; most of the evenings, he spent time with Joser before Gaika's arrival. He encouraged Joser, and they shared a deep bond as a father and son. Yet Hatop's whole manners reacted differently from Armion; he craved to grab the absolute honour he possessed as the father of the kingdom's most renowned and brilliant Crown prince, Thebeslon. When some royal relatives criticise Armion purely because of his jealousy, Hatop always joins their side and blames his youngest son. He never confronted behalf of Armion. Laicha comfort Armion all the time. She recognised the Armion's guiltless heart and the pathetic discrimination situations he coped with inside the mansion. Hence, Laicha always cared for the crown prince as her child.

Armion combated with himself for nameless charming emotions. Though his heart aches at viewing his naked garden, he quickly forgets it by remembering Arianna. He felt her like an angel who whispered some unsung magical spell into his ears. Arianna's charming appearance and her kind soul enchanted the crown prince immensely. Day by day, Armion is pursuing her. Therefore, each day, he waited near the riverside for Arianna. But she didn't appear. Armion got frustrated with his tiresome, painful emotions.

Nevertheless, he didn't give up his efforts to meet her again. On another gloomy evening, Armion unexpectedly visited the forest river. His eyes whole shined, and his throbbing heart elated with her sight. She sat calmly under the oak tree, gazing at the forest river, lonely. Armion hid noiselessly and carefully watched her. Arianna slowly wiped her tears and sighed deeply. Finally, Armion showed himself in front of her.

"Arianna," he opened up.

"Oh! You" Arianna, got shocked and stood in a flash.

"I'm so glad to see you here, Arianna because you made me to wait uncountable days," he said arrogantly.

"I didn't promise you about my arrival," Arianna mumbled in a frightened voice.

"It's not about the word; its promise remarked in your eyes" Armion slowly approaches her. Arianna looked down anxiously.

"May be you are ignoring me for my raggy old attire and wretched appearance, aren't you Arianna?"

She raised her head suddenly with his sarcastic tone.

"No, brother, please understand me. I'm not condemning; honestly, I'm afraid to talk with strangers," Arianna replied in a broken voice.

"Am I stranger for you, why do you feel like that?"

He peeked into her face.

"I'm really not knowing about you brother" Arianna stepped backwards confusedly.

"Can you trust me, Arianna? Armion stopped his words for a while and stared at her beautiful face.

"If you can't trust me, you can walk away, and if you don't, you may stay." Armion said firmly. But Arianna didn't move her legs; instead of running out of him, she ceased her legs and looked at his face.

"who are you brother?" She questioned.

"someone is searching your shadow," Armion whispered after a few seconds. Arianna straight looked into his eyes. Then, she silently sat under the oak tree, and Armion leaned against the tree trunk.

"Well, I'm an isolated slave in here but I secretly got escaped and I'm from kingdom Spavitar I'm finding my way back to home I was born as an orphan, I am lonely and poor, I want to fly out from here." He explained while gazing at the blue sky. Arianna quickly stood up and came close to him.

"Oh, brother beware from prince Joser goons, if they spotted you they might surely kill you, they are so cruel and dangerous." she said worriedly.

"Are you afraid to see I am dying, Arianna?" He asked, holding her hand. Arianna slightly twirled her head shyly.

"Arianna I'm starving do you have something to eat?" He asked softly.

"Oh yes, I plucked some berries for my granny" She hurriedly took them out of the basket and stretched them to Armion.

"Thanks, how nice you are," he presented a thankful smile while grabbing the berries. Then, started to eat the berries happily.

"This is so good Arianna," he exclaimed.

"Where do you live, brother?" She asked.

"I have no permanent place to live Arianna, I roam inside the woods. I can sleep anywhere I am comfortable. Most of the time, I slept on the top of the trees," he admitted. Arianna looked at him pitifully.

"I can bring you some food each evening if you like," she said calmly. Armion glanced at her gratefully.

"I have no words to thanks to you Arianna, I appreciated your whole sympathy about me," Armion responded in a thrilling voice.

After that, they met near the river each day and every evening. Arianna brought the hot porridge and bread for him. Armion repeatedly thanked her while enjoying her delicious food. They spent numerous unforgettable evenings together while sharing their emotions. Armion brought a bunch of daisies to her when he met her.

"You are more beautiful than these daisies," he whispered to her. Arianna covered her face shyly. Armion grabbed her hands and leaned on to her slowly as Arianna sensed the warmth of his every breath. She slightly shut her eyes. Armion's one finger ran through her eyebrows.

"Aren't you afraid, Arianna, to serve food to a man like me If we might get caught they will kill both of us," he asked.

"I'm not afraid," she mumbled.

"Why?"

"I don't know" Arianna quickly turned around. Armion grasped her shoulders softly and turned her back to his side.

"You don't even my name," Armion murmured.

"Maybe I have known it from ages," she answered secretly.

"I have nothing to give you Arianna, I have no money, no gold; I'm not wealthy. My clothes are worn out, and I'm homeless. Indeed I'm a filthy impoverished slave. Honestly, I'm not aware how long my life will be survived." Armion touched her soft, smooth face, and Arianna abruptly placed her two fingers on his lips and stopped him.

"You have everything I want," her words expelled from her trembling lips.

"What am I having?" He lifted her chin delicately.

"I'm captured inside your soul, It's a quiet dazed spellbind, so I am," Arianna faltered.

"Oh, I'm so sorry" She rapidly shook her head and turned around, covering her face with both hands. Armion slowly leaned and grabbed her smoothly by her waist; his lips played around her neck and ceased close to her ear.

"What do you want to say? Please tell me, Arianna, cure me," he whispered. Armion slowly twirled her to his side, his hands wrapped around her shoulders; their eyes met. Arianna watched the shadow of her inside his enchanting eyes.

"I love you," she mumbled. A shiny sparkle burst out of Armion's lips. He felt he was fluttering between the blue sky and beyond the moon.

"I love you too, Arianna" he snatched her lips. Arianna hides her face inside his broad shoulders. They spent a few days enclosed with their enticing romantic hearts. The riverside and the woods seemed familiar with them and their charming moments. Then, one day, Arianna sat on his lap under the oak tree's shade. Armion's lips wandered around her neck.

"You are stunning both inwardly and outwardly; your beauty can attract even a royal prince, don't ruin your life because of this broken soul," he muttered.

"No," she cried.

"It doesn't matter if you leave me out of your life, but my soul will chase for you forever; I wanted to be with you in this momentum. I have no dreams about the future." She slowly commenced crying. The tears ran through her eyes.

"You don't love me, do you?" she questioned with tears. Armion patted her wet cheeks sadly.

"No Arianna" He kissed her madly.

"I was in love with you from the very first day I spotted you, yet I can't let your life drown in this endless war," he sighed.

"I can endure it if you are with me," she murmured while concealing inside his warm chest.

"I'm leaving this kingdom soon, Arianna. I'm pleased if you can come with me," he admitted. Arianna silently started to sob.

"I can't be left alone my grandparents they are too old, they will die alone there's no one to take care of them. They raised me up, I can't come with you I'm sorry it's my responsibility to look after my grandparents."

She kissed his forehead; he sensed the warmth of her unstoppable tears.

"But," she halted.

"I will be waiting for you every day until I'm free to elope with you and whole myself, my soul dedicated to you always" She nuzzled his face slightly and stared at him with watery eyes. Armion watched her with pitiful eyes. His heart yelled in pain because of her honesty and innocence.

"Your eyes so vivid, Arianna, it's crystal clear, it remembers me someone" he paused his words and sighed woefully.

"Arianna, prince Joser's goons hanging around the woods, I can't stay like this anymore. It's not safe, so I have to drive my way back to Kingdom Spavitar as soon as possible," he whispered heavy-heartedly.

"I might not be able to see you for a long time, hereafter."

He added. Arianna embraced him tightly and lamented.

"Will you wait for me, Arianna until I arrange all the things to take you to my own place. Our own world," he whispered while kissing her forehead and sucking her tears from his lips.

"I can wait even more than another hundred years, I promised," Arianna snuggled to him. They spent the whole evening, and Arianna mourned immensely. Armion wiped her tears while he kissed her thoroughly. Then, finally, he walked back to the castle bearing his twinging heart. Her innocent eyes and charming face haunted him each second. Arianna revisited the riverside many days to search for his shadows; she wept alone, on behalf of her first love. She desperately dreamed about his warmth and memories tangled with him. Arianna felt it hard to revive her heart and entire spirit without him. She sunk into the centre of deep grief and couldn't drag herself out of it. Yet all her soul has been smitten with that continuous attachment. They are both imprisoned inside the chain of emotions.

"It's not your fingers touching him. Your sentiments grab him. Though your fingers released him, he is inside you.

"You started it, my dear; now you ended it. But there is no difference between that beginning and end until you defeat yourself."

Mother Atunura whispered to her.

CHAPTER 10

Armion's mind commenced to blame himself; he didn't want to delude her. Yet he feared she might frighten him if he revealed the perfect truth. He was craving to sense her pure love. He entwined with her soul along with her beauty together. Her virtuous heart enthralled him more and more to be with herself. He forgot his reality and even his royal status; he wanted to further carry out this false because he loved her. He wandered about the next step; indeed, he didn't wish to lie to her hereafter. Armion pondered during many sleepless nights. While his natural breath of life sought her to reappear again in front of him, he struggled with memories. He abandoned her world; his deep heart criticised him for lying to Arianna. Armion fought alone, twirling around his sword. He tried to expel his guilt but became weary with his pleading heart to meet her. Eventually, his brain prevented him from disguising himself and entrapping her inside that big play. He kissed the daisy flowers to recall her,

"You are my golden daisy flower, Arianna," he whispered to himself. At night, he gazed at the sky full of stars

"I don't want to break her heart. I want to stay with her whole throughout life, Arianna be my Queen, we are made for each other" he whispered to the quiet night.

Armion consumed many weeks inside his chamber. Then, finally, one morning, Queen Hatra visited to meet him.

"Armion, my dear son, why you seem stuck inside here all the time, and you denied having supper with us," she complained and walked towards him.

"You all denied me from the very beginning; what's wrong if I repeat it," he mumbled secretly, then moved his eyes away from her sight.

"What?" Hatra asked confusedly.

Armion shook his head.

"I wonder about your question mother," he snarled.

"It's all over now Armion, you are my son and for god's sake forget all these little disputes. Joser would never ever behave like this he talks pleasantly every time. Please don't hurt your father Armion he is too worried." Hatra patted his head.

"If it so you have to console him not me mother" Armion gave a furious glare at her.

"I ordered to rebuild your garden as your wish," Hatra admitted kindly.

"Nobody wants to rebuild my wounded, fractured soul," he sighed frustratedly.

"Armion, please." Hatra grasped both of his hands.

"I have no wishes, mother; all of you are free to recreate it according to your intention," he yelled.

"Forgive me, son," Hatra implored.

"I got hurt mother" Armion sat on the bed and sighed frustratedly.

"I know about you, my dear son; I'm your mother. I won't let it happen again, I promise to you. So please believe me." Hatra sat next to him.

"I only respect true promises." Armion stood up and walked away. But Hatra drags one arm to halt him.

"I 'm an uninvited visitor to here, mother, so no need to be troubled about my emotions because it's totally invaluable to all of you," he shouted.

"You are wrong, son," Hatra opened up in a broken voice.

"I was destined to be killed inside your womb yet, somehow I got gifted with breath. I hate this worthless life, and I'm fed up with ill-treatment,." he yelled.

Hatra released his hand and started to lament; Armion slowly came close to her sadly. He loved his mother from his deep heart because he had a delusional fear that he was incapable of surviving without her. He wrongly thought that Hatra was the only person who sheltered him. He believed she was taking part in a great bond with him. However, Hatra pretended to all the others that she loved Armion more than Joser. Hence, Armion is habitually trapped inside Hatra's love. He never wanted to hurt her. Hatra's tears stir up his pain again. He silently blamed himself when he noticed her sad eyes.

He quietly knelt beside Hatra.

"I didn't want to make you cry mother, I'm still disappointed about all these forgive me," he whispered bitterly. He kept his head on her lap while Hatra sobbed silently.

"Forgive me, mother; it's all my fault," he said woefully, wiping Hatra's tears.

"Do you know Armion, how much I struggle to raise you, How much I suffered because of you, I got tormented, yet I gave birth to you, and I love you bottom of my heart more than ever. You became my whole world. I secured you, fought for you from the onset you reside in my womb." Hatra spoke between the tears.

"I didn't want to make you cry mother, but I'm still disappointed" he said downheartedly.

Hatra sighed miserably, and her fingers ran through Armion's hair.

"I can understand you my son but there's no point to hide yourself alone to relieve your grief," she whispered to him while glancing at his innocent eyes.

"I'm searching for my contentment throughout this pain, mother. Though it is hard, someday I'll succeeded," he answered softly.

"Never mind, let's forget all these matters, Armion; we have a particular function today," Hatra said with a shined face.

"Ok what's now mother?" Armion questioned tiredly.

Then he slowly hid his face again on Hatra's lap.

"Today, we have Thebeslon dancing festival; the whole kingdom gathered for the ceremony. So Armion, you must come with me for this," she said firmly.

"Why me, mother, you and father can participate in all these as usual" Armion inquired irritated.

"He refuse, to go and it's your responsibility Armion as the crown prince you cannot reject all these events."

Hatra shouted. Armion swiftly raised and moved away from her.

"please leave me alone, mother. I'm so fed up with this dramatic life dance," he mumbled.

"Why you are bothering me Armion, why you are reacting so rudely I am your mother" Hatra cried.

"Ok, mother, I'll be attending to it with you; my head is terribly aching now; let me rest for a few moments," he pleaded.

Hatra gave a contented glimpse and then quickly walked outside.

....

It was the most momentous day for the Thebeslon people. They all assembled around the place where the festival took place. Everybody looked at the dancing stage, which seemed to be perfectly fine. The spring breeze quietly blows all over, carrying the fragrance of the blooming flowers.

Arianna sat with a sad face while Yesmin, her grandmother, decorated her hair.

"Please granny decorate it only from daisies," she implored.

"My dear, this is your very first dancing show; you are the only person capable of carrying our dance traditions. Therefore, you should appear on the stage more attractively than others." Yesmin admitted.

"She is gorgeous and graceful, no one can beat her beauty and her dancing talent Yesmin. She is my pride. Queen Hatra and Prince Armion arrived here. So the festival will be start soon" Saina Arianna's grandfather said delightedly.

"My dear, show your all skills in front of the royal guests" Yesmin kissed Arianna's face. She nodded slightly, stared at Yesmin, and then waited silently until her turn.

Armion sat next to the Hatra during the whole ceremony and was a constant nuisance for himself. His heart pounded incredulously; if Arianna spotted him in this royal attire, what would happen, he thought quietly. He couldn't concentrate his mind while watching the show; hence, he warily waited until the show's end. Meanwhile, the music started. Arianna entered the floor according to the rhythm. The crowd cheered out loud. Armion raised his head unexpectedly "Arianna," he mumbled. He was entirely numb with sudden joy. Her dance, her absolute beauty, dazzled him. Each step lifted him above heaven. It was an endless alluring combined with remarkable intoxication. Armion felt her as a fairy who appeared in this world. Her simply designed long floral dress enhanced her pure natural beauty. His eyes shimmered when he noticed the daisies she bears on her long, glossy hair, which swung side to side.

"Arianna, you are still living with my memories," he thought silently. Armion surrendered under his emotions; he was obsessed with each dance step, although he roamed between their memories. Her spellbinding sight revived his eyes again; therefore, he sat like a statue, utterly charmed by that. Hatra enjoyed it immensely. Each one appreciated Arianna's' magnificent and spirited performance. At the show's end, Queen Hatra stepped onto the stage and admired Arianna. Saina and Yesmin embrace each other merrily.

Arianna was named the dancing Queen of 'Kingdom Thebeslon. Crown Prince Armion was invited to present the elegant tiara to the new Thebeslon Dancing Queen.

Armion attended on the stage, holding his thudding heart; he tried to control his paralysed fingers. Finally, he tried to move his immobilised legs. The crowd applaud cheerfully. Arianna looked downward nervously; she had never met the royals before; thus, she felt simply awkward facing the crown prince.

Armion came close to her; slowly, his fingers touched her forehead and went through her long hair. Arianna kept her eyes shut to get rid of the anxiety. Suddenly, she sensed his warmth, breath, touch, and mighty arms wandering throughout; at that moment, she realised it was familiar to herself. Then, she raised her face on the spur of the moment; their eyes met in a flash. Arianna was speechless.

"You," she expelled through her trembling lips. Her whole body shuddered with fear.

"Yes, it's all me Arianna, I'm the crown prince Armion."

He whispered to her ears. And it was his most pleasing voice. Arianna forcefully moved her frozen legs, then stepped forward and bent to honour Queen Hatra and the Crown prince. Meanwhile, she glanced at the handsome crown prince again, watching her with his winsome smile and charming eyes; she felt her whole surroundings spinning. People cheered out loud again and again. Arianna didn't sense she was remarking on one of the most eventful moments in her life when she was renowned as the dancing queen of Thebeslon and about the most prestigious crown she was holding. She positioned herself on the stage, resembling a statue. Afterwards, she dragged her legs among the daydreams.

"I made love with the crown prince," she mumbled unconsciously. She was gifted with numerous flower bunches. But her ears were numb; she overlooked the loud applause.

"Oh god, mother Atunura, what I have done," she said secretly.

Arianna got down from the stage; she wanted to escape his sparkling eyes. She quickly ran from the crowd and didn't even want to share the joy of victory with her grandparents. But, she forgot the whole world. Arianna recalled their particular moments, how he expelled his love, and how his warm touch and lips ran throughout her. She walked rapidly, holding her long dress in one hand, towards the colossal pinewood surrounding the festival ground. She ran between the pine trees; the flower bunch she bore, on the one hand, dropped with her speed. The flowers spread everywhere. She abruptly paused near the huge pine tree and held it tightly, leaning on the pine trunk beside it.

Arianna panted and closed her to save herself from his romantic haunted memories. She sat under the pine tree and gasped; she slowly hid her face inside her bended knees and sobbed.

"What I have done, it's all my fault, oh please save me god mother Atunura," Arianna repeatedly mumbled while crying alone.

"Arianna," his most familiar kind voice outstretched quite close to her ears. Arianna raised her head, stunned.

Her eyes tried to catch his sight in between the tears.

He was wearing elegant, ritzy royal attire. His sharp, almond-shaped blue eyes covered a crescent of moon eyebrows. His angular cheekbones showed a dimple on his cheek; his smile emerged with it enamoured her.

He gazed at her with shimmering eyes resembling blue crystals inwrought in a milky pool. Prince Armion carried an imperious nose and sloppy brownish hair gathered neatly backwards. His bold shoulders were part of his burly physique. An exquisite scent swirled around from his nifty clothes. He stared at her with a delightful heart, and his light brownish stubble glimmered with dim sun-rays. Arianna remarked on his entire fascinating gesture with mesmerised emotions. The shadows of a poor, miserable person who showed up to her with old raggy clothes and messy hair stuck her in some unknown remembrance. Prince Armion hesitantly approached her," Arianna," he opened up.

Arianna swiftly stood and walked a few steps backwards; she was about to run again.

But Armion seized her inside his strong arms at once.

"Don't run Arianna," he whispered. Arianna felt embarrassed; hence, she shifted slightly down her face to avoid his eyes. However, she shivered when she sensed his breath close to her, and her lips trembled with his warm touch.

"Arianna are you afraid of me?" he questioned kindly.

"Forgive me, your highness; it's all because of my stupidity" she stammered.

"No, Arianna, I should apologise to you; honestly, I didn't want to lie. I was about to reveal this whole truth, yet unexpectedly our destiny played an interesting part among us." Arianna opened her eyes; he was staring at her with bright blue eyes. His entire appearance hypnotised her to trap inside him more and more endlessly. She was speechless for a few seconds. Then, she hurriedly released herself from his mighty arms.

Arianna moved backwards, creating a distance between them.

"Forgive me, Your Highness, I could not recognise you; I behaved so foolishly I was so.. Silly... And she spoke anxiously, and her eyes filled with tears. Armion slowly approached her; he wrapped one hand around her waist and kept herself quite attached to him, then placed one finger on her trembling rose petals.

"You are my golden daisy flower, aren't you?" he muttered secretly.

His finger danced around her lips and red cheeks.

His lips touched her forehead,

"I yearned to be with you every day, each second of my life. Will you be my princess, Arianna? Could you stay with me forever? He asked in a hushed tone.

"Your highness," Arianna stoned. Her heart pounded with unknown fear.

"Believe me, Arianna, Prince Armion, madly in love with you. Don't leave me, please," he pleaded. Arianna gazed at him with enlarged eyes. She quickly struggled to release herself from him, then moved a few steps away. Her heart beats rapidly. Armion watches her with loveable eyes and stretches his hand towards her.

"Arianna," he mumbled

"Arianna, please hold my hand," he implored.

Arianna watched his eyes with eyes full of tears; then, she ran as fast as she could while wiping her tears.

"Arianna," Armion called her out loud.

"I'm waiting for you every day near the forest creek."

His voice vibrated throughout the lonely pinewood for a few seconds. Armion stood alone; the dusk veiled the lonely pine trees, blotting her shadows far away from his sight.

Arianna stopped herself in front of her small cottage.

Saina and Yesmin were troubled about her sudden disappearance in between the ceremony. They were waiting for her doubtfully. Distressed Yesmin grabbed her.

"Where were you my child?" She screamed impatiently.

"I'm sorry, granny, I'm not feeling well."

Arianna answered quietly and locked her room.

She rested her body over the closed door and gasped for breath. Then, she slowly sat on the floor.

"What am I supposed to do now" she mumbled.

"Prince Armion, Why you... how all these things happened only for myself. No no I must halt this"

She murmured to herself.

Arianna spent many days snuggled on her bed. She was thinking alone. Eventually, she became ill and stayed at home for a few weeks. Though her body weakened with sickness, her mind roamed among the whole past with Prince Armion. She combated to cease her irrepressible sentiments. Yesmin worried about her most adorable granddaughter; she blamed Saina for overtiring Arianna to win the crown. Arianna kept herself whole, thunderstruck by this unpredicted revelation of her secret lover. His amazing smile, captivating blue eyes, and warm lips tingled each muscle. She moaned along with her deserted soul. Her heart tore pathetically.

"Your highness, I am simply tangled in your pure heart. Your enormous affection. But I can't be your princess and you deserve better, forgive me," she thought desperately. Arianna was cured slowly; however, she began her daily routine. She refused to return to the forest creek and denied the wood either. Finally, though her whole heart pleaded to see him for a split moment, she quit her soul to end everything forever.

Meanwhile, Armion waited for her each day beside the oak tree; he was guilty because he lied about his true identity to Arianna and miserably repented about sudden circumstances. He sat under the oak tree to see, seeking her reflection; he turned up his ears even for a rustling sound of leaves that mistook him for her footsteps.

The time flew by, and Arianna's grandmother fell too sick of a sudden. Hence, she spent her entire day heeding her.

One cloudy evening, Arianna was walking alone on the footpath attached to the woods. She carried a basket full of herbs she collected to treat her unwell grandmother.

The sound of a galloping horse passed her slowly, and the horse halted its move right in the middle, blocking her without warning. Prince Armion got off the horse, and after a while, Arianna spotted his weary eyes opposing her. She looked downward while holding her basket tightly.

"Arianna," she heard his heartening call after some time.

She lifted her face tentatively.

"Why are you ignoring me Arianna?, I was expecting you,

What do you want by punishing me so terribly?"

He grasped her from the shoulders and shook with distress.

"I have already explained to you Arianna, I'm truly loving you, I'm not playing around you, please do believe me Arianna, I want you to my life."

Arianna shut her eyes to cease her hidden tears.

"I know it, your highness," she sobbed.

"Then why you denied meeting me? Why you behaved like this?, answer me, I can't hold this anymore."

Arianna sniffled; Armion released her shoulders and turned the other side impatiently.

"Forgive me your highness I'm not disrespecting you. I'm a worthless poor girl. I'm not eligible to be your Queen. Don't get ruin yourself by twisting with me."

Armion quickly turned back to her side and touched her wetted cheeks softly,

"You are wrong Arianna, you are much worthy to me; I'm stuck inside your heart I want only you." Arianna stared at him; she had forgotten about her surroundings; they were the most charming words she had heard throughout her entire lifetime. Yet something pricked her mind again; she struggled to avoid it silently, then assembled her courage.

"There's a vast distance between ourselves your highness, I'm merely a tiny candle, though you feel my shine it's not visible among the bright, sunny sky. You deserve better." She let out with trembling lips.

"No, Arianna that tiny candle can only shine my soul, I'm seeking for that, let me hold it please." Armion's slightly pressed his forehead on her eyebrows.

"I loved that anonymous, unknown slave, I felt he was much similar to myself. He is lonely and wretched. Though it was you, I am unconditionally dazzled in that magical dilemma. I'm in love with that miserable soul. It's not you your highness. I can't find him from you. You are much more prestigious and overpowered than him." she said between the tears. Armion was startled by her words.

He glanced at her and grabbed her tears with his lips.

"Forgive me your highness," she repeated.

"It's me Arianna, I am still here with you, though you honoured me as the crown prince I'm that miserable soul who is chasing for your heart, so don't leave me Arianna"

But Arianna slowly stepped behind and released his arms hanging around her.

"Forget me forever your highness, I beg your pardon."

She turned backwards.

"I can't forget you, Arianna, I would never ever do so. I will be waiting for you every day near the forest river, I will remember you every second in my life. You are always welcomed to meet me whenever you changed your mind."

His eyes kept quietly stuck on her with each word.

Then he slowly reached a few steps closer,

"Arianna hold my hand," he implored.

"Walk away your highness," Arianna gasped mournfully.

Then she wiped her tears and moved a few steps away to escape his sight.

"Let yourself out of me and let me walk in my own path, I am not capable to grab your hand. So walkaway prince Armion." she cried.

He returned to the horse with a muted mouth while Arianna held the basket alone. She was gazing at the sky; she heard his horse galloping, then quietly turned around.

His fading shadow shined in her blotted eyes,

"I wanted you to get yourself free from my ill fate,

Do not ever step in to my gloomy world. Though I'm living in a hell you will stay in my soul forever." She lamented.

CHAPTER 11

There's a crumbling house on an isolated mountain in the middle of the kingdom, Thebeslon. It is an aged and shabby stand with peeling walls. The low cracked roof is set as a crooked tree with falling leaves. It is perpetually trying to hide away from the grumpy wind. The black cinder, twisted with gloomy, ruinous shadows, masked the upper walls. The rainwater dripped along with the stained patched bricks from the leaked upward. The musty smell unfurled all over. The fractured furniture decorated the inside with the dust fouled up the floor. The fragmented, huge, woody doors dangled from the hinges. The cobwebs surrounded the shattered ceiling. Though it is a remarked symbol of an indigent, it has the last remnants of some ancient opulently luxury—the other half of the house placed with dropped partition. Hence, the bitty space is vacant to be used by the owner.

The house's front yard seemed to be couthy with some flower beds surrounded by daisies of numerous colours. The butterflies wandered around them. A small window of the house was kept open until dusk, and a young woman stood beside her with eyes strapped with a gigantic azure sky. The sky is fathomless, sketched with clouds, stars, the sun and even the moon. It created an outline of sunshine from dawn and was patterned with the heavenly body during the night. Though it's a delusional reflection framed in our own eyes, the expectations are continually remarked on in that fallacy. The untied white clouds travel with the breeze with the joy of being unconfined. It is a marvellous gift of endurance for vanquishing the hypnotising illusion of existence. Yet, sometimes, the rain tumbles down from the weeping sky. The shower pleased the thirsty earth from the solemn clouds of dark, big and static teardrops. It's a shadow of a heart veiled with endless vows and desires.

The girl beside the window sighed, then gazed at the golden daisy flower she held in her palm.

She kissed it, then lightly wiped her large black eyes, which seemed wetted. So she is Arianna, the pretty dancing Queen of Kingdom Thebeslon. Her bow-shaped eyebrows inclined somewhat as she stared at something.

Her eyelashes of radiant black blinked once slowly. Her heart-shaped pink lips are rose petals and appear captivating with an elegant nose. Arianna resembles a fairy who stepped down from heaven. Her well-shaped body is a carved statue shined with glossy skin. Her wavy hair towards the knee was slightly brown, a robe of dawn twisted with sunrise. Her eyes sparkled when it was bright, and each day, she stood to seek her sun rays like a sunflower blooming.

A few steps behind her, an old-fashioned rusty armchair, almost half-broken, made a noisy sound while rocking. It was born a middle-aged woman with saggy-torn attire. Who looks filthy with thick, entangled, curly hair. Her face seemed rowdy, with reddish eyes and messy, uncombed hair for ages. Her thin body down with her limbs appeared as cold icicles stretched out from her long oversized gown. The woman screamed loudly and then laughed. A malodorous smell spread all over her mouth. She struggled to flee, yet her hands and legs were tightly fastened to the chair with some cloth stripes. She glared at Arianna, then screeched like a beast and twirled her eyeballs weirdly while gazing at the roof. Arianna slowly reached beside the woman with an old wet towel, softly wiped her face and rubbed her legs.

"Water, give me water," the woman shouted.

Arianna quickly gave her some water, but suddenly, the woman threw away the cup, smashed it into pieces, and bawled aloud.

"You are a witch. I hate you; let me go. This is not water. It's poison; let me go, release me," she cried out.

"Mother, listen to me. I'm afraid I want to protect you because you are not well. You are sick." Arianna pleaded while patting the woman's pale cheeks. The woman scowled at Arianna and laughed strangely.

"Mother, please don't be angry with me stay calm I want to keep you safe until you will become better. I want you stop from endangering your life. I love you so much."

Arianna bent towards the woman and patted her head kindly. The woman groaned and kicked Arianna harshly from the one foot she secretly loosened while struggling. Though Arianna lost her balance, she pressed her arms on the floor and ceased falling herself. The woman sneered at her and laughed out loud.

"Mother," Arianna hesitantly came close to the woman, sat beside her, and delicately grasped her fingers. The woman shook her head and then roughly grabbed Arianna by her throat. Arianna gasped. The woman frowned and groaned.

"You are the curse of my life. You ruined me,"

She shouted while showing her dirty, ugly teeth. After a few seconds, she groaned and pushed away Arianna hard. Arianna sat on the floor and began to sob. The woman muttered the exact words numerous times and suddenly fell into sleep.

Arianna wiped her tears slowly.

"I'm sorry, mother, forgive me," she whispered.

....

Arianna is the daughter of Luma. Kingdom Thebeslon possesses an inheritance of dance traditions renowned as iconic for their feature. Saina Arianna's grandfather belonged to this generation of dancing. Hence, Saina and his family represented this unique art of Thebeslon. Yesmin, Arianna's grandmother, was crowned as the dancing queen of the kingdom. Yesmin's s family is also owned by this generation. Indeed, they were born to carry out this style of dance. Saina and Yesmin have four children: two daughters and two sons. Luma is their eldest daughter and thoroughly rejects being part of this family and their dance traditions. Her arrogant, self-centred behaviour seeks something beyond her state. She neither bothered about others.

Luma habitually disregarded others' feelings by demanding herself. Her awful temper hit her quickly when her siblings or parents criticised her. Hence, Saina and Yesmin had to cope with Lumas ' exasperated mood, whatever the circumstances. Luma had endless quarrels with her sister and brothers. Because she believed that her entire family should always obey her commands. Luma neglected all household duties and fought with Yesmin. Yesmin, their mother, always worried about Luma and their impoverishment.

She had to accept that Saina's and her dance skills could not meet their daily needs. Saina consumed most of his time hanging around with men. His ears got stuffed with Yesmin's continual speeches. Yesmin got mad with the heavy burden of her children and the insufficiency and hopelessness. So, she pursued a way to escape from this restricted life of misery.

Each year, Thebeslon has a splendid dancing festival in the springtime kingdom. Saina and Yesmin get hold of the initiative for this. Yesmin, the time applause of the crowd was not only for her excellent dance ability but also for her luring body and gifted, stunning, bewitched semblance. As soon as Yesmin starts to dance, the poet writes sweet exploratory words with inexhaustible emotions smitten with sensual insane. Yesmin's toes nimbly move throughout the stage. Sometimes, she is a colourful serpentine. Indeed, a queen of beauteous and enticement. People were elated with the enormous, fanciful, ecstatic emotions aroused by Yesmin. Because she covertly grabs out all the most eminent men's sight. The Yesmin's amorous kinesics almost always defeats Saina's energetic performance.

After a yearly dancing festival, numerous flaring stories ran around about Yesmin and some famous, wealthy, handsome men in the village. Saina kept himself quiet about all the things. Yesmin used to blame him uninterruptedly. She disgraced him in front of the children, showing off his inabilities. Many wealthy men visited their cottage each season. Yesmin's naked body was hidden in the ocean of desires while gold coins and jewellery filled her necessities. Prosperity filled the house. Their children laughed joyously with satisfied tummies. They dressed nicely, similar to other children who belong to affluent families. Saina used to leave the house when Yesmin kept busy with some new lover.

But he cannot bear the insulting smiles and talks of the village. So he quit all his deeds and walked away from his mates. He consumed his time inside the isolated old shed close to his cottage. He stewed with rum from the dawn tonight. His half-opened eyes remained reddish every time. His ears pretended deaf for the Yesmin's erotic moaning throw away from her bed. Her room, each time, was kept shut. So nobody bothers her charming fantasy with her significant person. Saina slept inside his dingy shed silently, but sometimes, he wandered into Yesmin's chamber when the door was not shut. Yesmin was sleeping after a heavy romantic night. The dawn has vanished with rowdy sun-rays. Yet her eyes were exhausted. He stared at Yesmin's gleaming body while lustrous reddish eyes flared in sudden desires. He soundlessly dragged his foot beside her. Though his body waved side to side, Saina leaned over the bed and began to kiss her impatiently. Yesmin opened her eyes with an unexpected rough touch, then tried to shade her naked body hurriedly from the robe and yelled.

"You are stinky, useless idiot don't touch me. Get out of my sight drunkard" She growled and pushed him down harshly. Saina grinned, stood up, and attempted to arrest her in his arms strenuously. But Yesmin quickly pulled him away rudely.

"Let me sleep, moron, I am too tired," she screamed, kicked him out of the room, and closed the door loudly. Saina sat beside the door heavy-heartedly and thumped it out loud. He gritted his teeth with a wrecking mind, yet he was a disvalue coin for her.

After a few days, Yesmin surprisingly became visible inside Saina's old shed. It was a cold, windy autumn night; Saina stared at her half-closed eyes. Finally, Yesmin removed the robe around her body, and her charming pink toes, step by step, came close to him. Saina thought he was dreaming, but he healed madly and deeply in that miraculous instant.

"You are so beautiful," he whispered while his whole breath and trembling lips twined with her gorgeous body.

Yesmin slept the whole night on his chest. Saina watched her face the entire night; his fingers ran through her cheeks and long hair. Finally, he sighed alone with his sore heart.

After a few days, Yesmin was found sick and tired. Her bright eyes struggled with some unknown fear. Nevertheless, she purposefully ignored Saina's sight.

Her new lover didn't spot others for some extended period. Though Yesmin tried to hide something from Saina, he observed her. When Saina accidentally visited her chamber, she could not keep that secret. Saina was shocked when he noticed her grown belly.

"Yesmin," he shouted.

"This is our child, you know it didn't you?" Yesmin faltered.

Saina came closer to her and grabbed her hair.

"I'm not a dumbass Yesmin though I'm performing my part perfectly to match it. Because that is my fate, and it's my consent regarding your freedom to chase for your fulfilment," he said.

"I am... I don't know I am terribly guilty," she halted. Her fainted voice tries to gather words.

"It's not yours," Yesmin confessed while sobbing.

Saina screamed and pulled his hair madly. Then, he released Yesmin and turned back to step out.

"I can kill it if you want," she said slowly.

Saina turned back. His eyes got enlarged with anger.

"Do you think this innocent creature should pay all our sins by halting his breath?" he groaned.

"What am I supposed to do or else I will kill myself" Yesmin hollered.

Saina grabbed Yesmin from her shoulders,

"I knew I screwed up; you ruined your life by being in love with me; your beauty and your talents can enchant a king, not an idiot like me. But it happened; it's our destiny. I could not accomplish your dream of luxurious life; hence I granted absolute liberty for you to go after it. Because you always denied our simple life." he uttered.

"I hate whole this poverty it's torturing me so I sold my body and it's all because of your negligence," Yesmin wailed.

"You only valued the coins and forgot the bonds, but don't let this poor innocent soul inside your womb to pay out these debts. You cannot kill him under my roof" he threatened.

"I will be his father, Yesmin; let me raise him as my own child let him breath peacefully. Though people has named me as a moron I am happy to accept it because I love you Yesmin so how can I hate this child. I'm not a most prestigious lord and I can't be a god yet I'll keep myself as that shithead" he said calmly. Yesmin wept for a long time desperately. Saina quietly walked away.

A few months later, a deep silence filled their sphere. Yesmin gave birth to their youngest son. Luma quarrelled with her mother about their newest family member. As she was completing her eighteenth year, she had numerous disputes. But soon after the new visitors' arrival, each person made love with their younger brother named Samuel. While Yesmin entered her habitual life, Luma took care of Samuel. He grows leisurely with his brothers and sisters, yet his round face and short, stumpy body do not match his siblings; nobody questions it. Nevertheless, Samuel's outer image tormented Saina because it is the mirror image of one of the wealthy merchant of a nearby village.

He paid several visits to Yesmin throughout the last year. Saina smoked many nights alone in his shed; he shivered in the cold wringing inside him; wild flames burnt his whole forlorn spirit. He tried to pause his mind to compare the appearance of his youngest when it was found difficult; he finished his rum pots alone. However, when Samuel came to cuddle with him, Saina blamed himself for his evil thoughts the following day. He embraced Samuel and began to tickle his little tummy. Soon after, all Samule's sparkling chuckles satisfied Saina's wounded heart.

Time flies, turning Luma into a charming young woman. Her outward form is much more similar to Saina's than Yesmin's. Hence, she looks innocent and calm. Luma holds Saina's tan skin complexion and soft black eyes with thick eyebrows. Her slim body, sharp nose, curly hair, and captivating smile made her notable to others. Though many young men were attracted to Luma, neither yearned to love following her arrogant behaviour and nasty rumours around their family. They were satisfied with her outer image. When she danced, each step stole their eyes. Luma carries no awareness about affection between men and women. Because she has never been familiar with emotional relationships. Luma knew Yesmin and Saina had an extraordinary life. Many men visited Yesmin to sense her body. Luma secretly watched everything happening in her mother's room through the half-shut window; she recognised it as a contract rather than the bond of love between most men and women. She realised each person who visited Yesmin held a reputable family outwardly. Luma decided to use that bond to reach her secret plans instead of believing those complicated attachments and twiddling with romance. She was waiting for someone better, opulent, and worth a bundle.

Yesmin and Saina do not exhibit the emotions of love, yet Yesmin endlessly makes Saina ashamed in front of the Luma. Hence, Luma never showed her honour to men. Besides all, Luma has her dreams about the future. Luma desired to carry on her life as the most famous and wealthiest woman. Thus, she hates her family's lower status; she is impatient to change her life design.

Somehow, one destined night, Luma performed at the Thebeslon dance festival. A particular person attended the show with other royal guests. He is not another lord Ramses from the other kingdom named Yunas. Who's the elder brother of the King of Yunas. He is the sole owner of a lot of assets and coins. He is handsome, fair, and decent-looking; he talks slowly and calmly. He would never shout at others. Everybody appreciates his humbleness. Ramses's empathic heart always tends to help others. He enjoyed a respectful lifestyle, and it seemed to be relatively peaceful. Ramses is extensively entangled in Luma's captivating dance. He memorised each step by himself. Her entire gesture haunted his eyes profoundly; he fell in love with Luma at first sight. Yet, unfortunately, he might have never known about the unsound, puzzling catastrophe he is inviting to his feet.

Hence, he arrived at Saina's house, bearing enormous expectations of Luma.

Yesmin's life is inverted by the rhythm of the time. Gradually, she became unfit to dance on the stage. Her arms and limbs vaguely shift on the scene, rarely enthralling the audience. Instead of following the rhythm, her ageing body shivered. Numerous wrinkles covered up her face, along with her magnetic contour. Her long, thick, wavy hair turned grey and dried. Mostly, it resembled the overused broom head. Her luring, gorgeous body appeared as a drooping cloak. Besides, her stunning face with sparkly eyes looked weary with dark circles. The lips resembled flower petals now dried and peeling. Her entire beauteous has decided to leave her. Her bed often comforted to play untold acts of love, remained quiet because nobody visited to taste her wretched, doddering body frame. Indeed, an aged, disfigured body isn't inviting them for intimacy; it only shows impermanence's pathetic transformation. Eventually, Yesmin grabs her life in the way of the opposite. She starts to worship several gods. Every night, a god visited her dreams. Therefore, she was able to talk with God. The divinity made her dreams more audible and visible. Unfortunately, no one in her house was lucky enough to meet God except Yesmin. She believed she had obtained all the blessings from God, and this mighty divinity had chosen her for a specific reason.

All her lifestyle changed with this unexpected call of the invisible God. She made a particular place in her house to worship God. No one was allowed to get inside it except Yesmin. She never let Saina touch her body; though he was the only man who wanted to have a romance with her at present, Yesmin rejected him. Yesmin blamed Saina for trying to kiss her most sacred body, which was merely dedicated to Immortal divinity. Each week, Yesmin changed her routines according to God. She began to wear white attire, which resembled the pureness of her unspoiled soul. Her room was filled with numerous white flowers. Each day, she lit candles for Godhead while worshipping. Sometimes, she spent extended time with that God in her sacred space. Gradually, her neighbours became keen to learn about her new transformation. Hence, many of them paid for several visits to her house. Little by little, one came to Yesmin to receive blessings from the unknown supreme being. Yet the Yesmin is the unique identification of the most precious divinity. Successively, Yesmin made herself wonderous, stepping into another higher standard. She governed the whole house. Everybody has agreed to her because they fear the nameless supreme power veiled around Yesmin.

Saina kept himself silent as usual. Each month, more and more people gathered around her sacred room. Broken, shattered, helpless human souls bent down, pleading for some aid from the unseeable celestial being. Their overwhelming lives intertwined with decrepit hopes open the way for Yesmin to hide inside the speckles robe of the supreme being. The past secretly recognised Yesmin as the village whore. She was immensely decried for her impermissible role previously. Yet the moment gifted her the most prestigious position. Many women used to insult her and now honoured her by kneeling beside the "mother of god." Unfortunately, the divine being is nowhere, but he saved Yesmin.

Nevertheless, the presence of lord Ramses diverts the entire atmosphere. Yesmin starts to shed tears of happiness now that she knows the future is much better than it was. She thanked God for rewarding her with such a magnificent prize; thus, she convinced Luma to romance with Ramses. Luma seems much more attracted to Ramses's outward appearance. He is handsome and rich. Yet his extraordinary decent behaviour and silent manners disappointed her.

On the other hand, Luma is often enthusiastic about talkative, joyful men. She enjoyed the dirty jokes rather than the loveable honey words. Yesmin's unstoppable sermons troubled her mind. Luma doesn't want to change herself on behalf of Ramses, but she can adjust it for a short period until she succeeds in her target. But her whole mind tangled; indeed, she hated his innocent, kind nature.

"He looks like a saint rather than the tough guy," she frowned.

"Never mind, I can transfer this valuable prize to your sister though she is still young. I am happy about it because she might surely have a prosperous future. You are free to choose your own path" Yesmin grinned. Luma was shocked by her mother's surprising words. She hates her sister because her sister looks pretty and fair. After all, she was more captivated by men than Luma. Hence, it bursts her anger and jealousy; consequently, Luma pretends to love Ramses, following her mother's instructions. Honestly, she has neither emotions nor affection. However, the Ramses is a sack of gold for her. Besides, she is waiting to join as a member of the renowned royal family. So, somehow, she was determined to emerge from her hidden desires only to accomplish her triumph. Meanwhile, Yesmin pulls her rope to carry the entire family more and more upper state using Luma. She was striving to pile up unlimited coins to maintain their flourishment of life.

One evening, Ramses and Luma met with each other.

Luma seized his hand and glanced at him with her large, lustrous eyes. But Ramses turned his face shyly because it was the first time he had touched the girl. They stood lonely under the shade of the big willow tree. The evening got shadowy bit by bit. The stormy grey clouds plumped around the drowning sun. The wind howls, letting Luma's long, thin gown shake vaguely. Luma leaned on to Ramses; her charming fingers miraculously ran through his face. They both were gazing at each other

"Ramses, do you love me?" Luma leaned her body towards him slowly; her steaming lips ran through his neck and halted on his lips. Luma glanced at him with half-open eyes. Ramses felt all her touch and voice intoxicated invitation for his chasmic soul. Slowly, both of his hands tied around her slim waist. The thunder rumbled. Soon, the rain started, yet their flaming bodies could not sense it. The water dripped from Luma's drenched gown. Her shining figure sighted Ramses through her thin attire, tightly attached to her body with water. He was unable to shift his eyes away from it.

"Ramses, I feel cold," Luma whispered and snuggled upon his neck. Then they began to kiss each other contemporary to the rhythm of the rain; though heavy rain tumbled down, they never bothered about the grumbling sky. After a few minutes, the rain reduces its strength and begins to moan

"Ramses, take me home," Luma pleaded to him secretly. Ramses held her by both his arms and carried her among the drizzle. Luma stared at his face while both her hands rested around his neck. They slowly reached the Saina's house. Ramses's heart pounded; hence, he became restless.

"Don't be afraid; take me inside my room. I feel exhausted," Luma mumbled. The house remained quiet; Luma jumped down from his arms when they entered her room. Luma dragged Ramses inside quickly, and she quickly locked the door. Ramses stared at her hesitantly; he was amused with unknown awkwardness. His entire clothes are soaked. Luma slowly reached to him and stood behind.

"So it's only you and me. We are all alone," she whispered, squeezing her cheeks to Ramses's neck, her hands wrapped around him. Then her trembling lips touched his face while her fingers drew unseen patterns on his chest, her attractive glossy body remarkably noted in Ramses's eyes through the tiny candlelight glinting up the space.

"Ramses, I am shivering my clothes are too wet and too tight can you help me to loosen them" Luma implored in a hushed voice, then closed her eyes; after a few seconds, she felt Ramses's heavy, warm breaths wandering around her shoulders, and his fingers impatiently ran through her gown then around her glimmering naked skin. Finally, Luma blew out the tiny candlelight's in her room and smiled at the darkness.

Ramses eyes are blotted in unknown disastrous pitch black, yet he is unaware of escaping.

CHAPTER 12

The rain paused, but the cloudy grey sky appeased the lonely night. Luma's soft moaning touched the Yesmin's ears. She sighed with relief. Because the Luma has followed all her instructions, it is proved by bringing Lord Ramses into her space. Beforehand, Yesmin commanded the rest of the children to leave another neighbour's home to spend the night. She needed to give perfect freedom for Ramses and Luma's very first act of love. Yesmin's eyes sparkled with triumph. She confirmed to herself that Ramses would never leave Luma now. Yesmin silently sneaked into the sacred room to devote more time to her god. Because she needed to grant wholehearted gratitude to her supreme being, she thoroughly trusted god sent this mostly rich, privileged man to Luma. Hence, Yesmin worshipped the god for many hours.

Meanwhile, Saina spent his time alone in his small room. He saw Luma return home with an unknown guest. His heart felt numb with pain, but he could not expel his anger. So Saina pondered alone with watery eyes while little Samuel plumped on his tummy. He was sleeping so peacefully. Saina patted Samuel's hair.

"Poor child," he mumbled.

"I saw only your outward beauty, Yesmin, not your inside dark. I wanted to win you. So, chased for you until I accomplished my goal to make you mine. I didn't give up. Everybody praised me I am succeeded. Though you had so many admirers, you chose me I was the hero of everyone in that colourful past. But presently I am the loser. Because you made me abandoned unexpectedly." Though Saina's broken, sad words unfolded, nobody appeared to listen.

As time passed, Ramses never missed a single day to visit Luma. He had never experienced this kind of love. However, he was new to this subject.

Therefore, he was quickly imprisoned in that puzzle. But, though he drowned inside the vast, mystifying dark ocean, his quench didn't fill up.

On the contrary, the salty water enhances his thirst day by day. His limbs made him drive beside the Luma's bed to content his scary appetency. Some days, Luma pulled him away from his shoulders and laughed out loud. But his burning eyes trapped with her disrobed charming feminine outline beauty. It's not affection but merely lust. Though their hearts did not meet, Ramses felt they were bound unconditionally.

He never got on that he was gilding on terrible phantasm.

Ramses's family got enraged after knowing about Luma. So they forced him to get away from this wrong turn. His mother implored him kindly and wept beside him to change his decisions. But Ramses denied breaking the promises he made in the name of Luma. He pursued Luma. Likewise, he is isolated in a desert without knowing his eyes knotted with mirage. Hence, he disregarded all the others' judgements about Luma and her family. Ramses eventually achieved his victory and got married to Luma. Soon after their secret marriage, they moved to Kingdom Yunas.

Yesmin threatened her other children never to speak about Luma's marriage and Lord Ramses. When neighbours questioned about Luma, Yesmin kept herself with a muted mouth. Thus, they believed that Luma had fled out secretly with someone unknown since nobody had spotted the shadows of Lord Ramses, who made visits with the moonlight. Yesmin worried about the lousy gossip connected with her awful past. She was mainly afraid it would spoil her whole image if Ramses became aware of those horrible rumours. Consequently, she got much relief after Luma's marriage. She wished that they would never often become visible to Kingdom Thebeslon.

Soon after the marriage, Luma removed her mask. She began to control Ramses. Her arrogant attitude astonished him for the first time. Frankly, Ramses is an innocent, kind-hearted person. He speaks slowly and not in a loud voice. He is courageous and cares for Luma. His extreme patience, bound with quiet manners, wrongly manipulated Luma to take all powers in her arms. Her superior mind incessantly attempted to grab all his money under her. She was so keen to know about all his assets. Luma didn't sense Ramses's emotions. She never bothers to hear his talk. During their conversations, she pretended to be listening, but honestly, she was acting. Though the Ramses family didn't accept their relationship, they welcomed them to the mansion. They never disrespect Luma. Everyone kindly treats her. Firstly, Luma was startled by the unusual behaviour of these royals.

Then, she blindly thought they were treated because she was a much more important character than others.

Therefore, she expected all others to bow their heads on her behalf. She quarrelled with maids even for a small mistake. One day, she slapped a new maid for accidentally spoiling her elegant dress during tea time. The poor girl ran back to the kitchen, wiping her tears. Most of the servants were blamed by Luma, even for tiny mistakes. Ramses's mother, who knew a kind-hearted lady, was shocked by Luma's disgraceful behaviour. But she kept herself quiet, letting Luma adjust to the new environment. Hence, She thought that Luma would change with time. Luma ignored her mother-in-law. She chatted with her while holding a sarcastic smile on her lips. When Ramses's mother acknowledged the mansion and royal life principles, Luma got mad at her. Her upper lip curled in disdain. Because she denied listening to others' advice, she hates to be criticised by others. Eventually, she began to struggle with her mother-in-law. Then, with Ramses's sisters. The entire atmosphere of the mansion diverts into unpleasant situations. Constant fights took place, as Luma felt entitled. She believed the world would revolve around her. She sought validation for her introverted self-centred action. Her mind persuades her that she is perfectly normal and righteous; others should agree.

Some days, when things got worse, she locked her door and spent the whole day inside her room. She refused to be joined by others to have supper. Ramses has endless troubles with Luma's reckless behaviour. He mistakenly thought Luma was sad about the sudden separation from her family. He bought new jewellery to satisfy her. Many times, he took her to fabulous royal functions. Luma was dressed in glorious attire and appeared as the palace queen. But her restless mind wasn't content with all these. She was yearning to become the most authoritative person in the Ramses house and every-thing. She considered Ramses as his bonded servant rather than the husband.

Most of the time, she condemned Ramses for minor reasons. Sometimes, she makes herself laugh at him. Day by day, Ramses got exhausted with his life with Luma.

Luma's merciless behaviour disappointed him immensely. Luma never pays attention to understanding his inner core. He ponders many nights, sitting on their bed while Luma sleeps peacefully. Ramses rested both arms on his head to relieve his torturing mind. Luma's slightly robed body glimmers with the moonlight. Yet It didn't elate his broken heart. He could not find genuine affection inside her eyes, merely their physical bodies attached to satisfy their lust. It healed Ramses just for that moment. But afterwards, his heavyhearted soul began to crush with unknown fear. Gradually, after his marriage, he had limited conversations with his family. After returning to the mansion, he had to console Luma and solve all the unnecessary problems she had created throughout the day. Sometimes, he had to negotiate with his parents and siblings on her behalf. Hence, It made him more and more isolated from his family. He was shattered when he spotted his parents' sad faces. He felt like everyone was sympathetically looking at him. Each day, he struggled to overcome his sufferings. But it was not as easy as he thought? He doesn't like to make Luma unhappy. He regarded Luma as his responsibility, considering Luma and himself as one spirit. Ramses never hides anything from her. But he hasn't known the darkness shading him around. He hardly sensed that Luma was transforming himself into another gesture to fulfil her desires. Sometimes, he behaved like a puppet of her. She took the decision beforehand without his consent and never bothered about his permission. If he opened up to something against her, Luma jumped at him like a wild tigress and argued with him for many hours. But Ramses utterly reject these awful situations, tempting to reward Luma with expensive gifts. Unfortunately, when an innocent creature got trapped in some spider cobwebs, it was hard to find a way to escape it. It is trapped purely for the intriguing patterns of cobwebs. The web concealed it inside and sucked his entire energy; hence it could not fly out from the day. Gradually, its tiring, exhausted frame becomes the meal of the unknown cruel spider. Even Ramses was unable to realise this horrible truth. Though he remembered he was rather late.

One year passed with all these unverified circumstances. Luma got pregnant unexpectedly. Indeed, it was the most unpleasant accidental incident she had faced. But she tried to hide away her hopeless emotions from the others. Ramses's joyful soul got some new expectations. He thought this would change his whole life and even Luma's. His wretched heart blindly trapped him again so that Luma would positively make herself with her motherly hood. He was never aware that Luma secretly worried about the situation. Firstly, Luma was shocked when she realised some innocent visitors had resided in her womb. She spent many days with unusual quietness. Luma never thinks about how she is going to change as a mother. Though She had seen Yesmin face this thing numerous times, she felt so confused.

When Luma got older, she and her elder brothers had to look after the younger ones. Yesmin spent her entire day sleeping after an awakening night with her romantic visitors. Luma and others carried their lives the way they wanted to be. There's no one to teach them what they should do or shouldn't. Saina kept himself stewing up with rum. They used to cook something for themselves when they felt hungry. Yesmin never let herself be bothered by those kinds of matters. Nobody wasn't allowed to enter her room during the daytime while sleeping. If they did so, they got kicked outside. Each day, they had good food to eat, and they dressed nicely. Yesmin's cupboard never gets empty with coins. Luma never knows the absolute truth about becoming a mother. Soon after each delivery, Yesmin settled the newborn with someone else to regain her habitual life. Hence, Luma did not recognise the love, care, and responsibility the mother should have held herself. Luma wished to wipe out this nuisance from her body, yet it wasn't accessible inside this mansion. Ramses kept his eye directly towards her, much lovingly. Luma got weary with his overflowing affection.

"Coward," she mumbled to herself. Day by day, Luma got ill. She vomited the whole day and couldn't eat anything. Luma lay on the bed while maids massaged her feet. She cursed the one who was inside her womb. Her body pains ideally increased her hatred. When she realised she was bearing Ramses ' child, she hated it more and more. She worried. Likewise, she had loosened all the things. Luma planned to grab a significant portion from Ramses and turn her life into another way. But this child destroyed her plans.

"What a curse, It ruined me."

"This is not a child, simply a nuisance," she whispered while lying on the bed shattered with a sick body. Many weeks later, she understood that she had no choice but to accept this nuisance. However, she eventually decided to divert her plans to another path.

Even though Luma spent her whole day with a weakened body and sickness, it aroused her anger incessantly. Therefore, Everybody has faced her bad-tempered, intolerable deeds again. She began to make arguments with others around the clock. Finally, she laments while sitting on the Ramses's lap. Luma sobbed, her watery eyes resting on his shoulders. Her tears wetted his shirt. He patted her head softly. Much kindly. Ramses didn't want to hurt her and their child. So he consoled her. His fingers smoothly ran through her hair, and his eyes filled the whole affection. But neither divert Luma's stony heart to meet Ramses's inner core. It was just a few minutes of dramatic schedule for her.

Luma made plenty of arguments with her mother-in-law; hence, more tears filled her eyes before Ramses only to remark on her innocence. Finally, she cuddled Ramses while sobbing madly. At last, it made him ride away back to Yesmin to make her mind more peaceful until the delivery. After that, Yesmin took on the responsibility of taking care of her. Ramses money quickly transformed Yesmin's old shanty into a sizeable spacious roof. Because he was constantly worried about Luma's comfort. Luma spent her whole days on the bed, troubled by all her body aches. Sometimes, She waddled like a duck holding her big belly. Samuel always stayed beside her for aid when Yesmin was not present. Luma counted the days to get a release from this unwanted, heavy burden.

One gloomy morning, Luma screeched with unbearable pain. Her horrific voice incised the air. Finally, an older woman happily handled Luma's most precious gift of life, the ultimate reward of her and Ramses's bond.

"No, no, I don't want it. Get her away," Luma screamed madly. The real pain veiling her body annoyed her unconditionally—nevertheless, a newborn who should fore-mostly be welcomed by the mother. But unfortunately, little Arianna got rejected. Is it tolerable? Nobody knows the agony of that tragic injustice circumstances.

Yesmin kissed Arianna while carrying her smoothly. Luma drifts off to sleep. Arianna cried the whole night. She was yearning to cuddle up inside her mother's warmth. Yet her sound never disturbed Luma's rest. Yesmin and Saina have to look after Arianna except when Luma feeds her. Luma never bothers to touch that innocent child, even while sucking up some milk from her breast. Instead of that, Luma gazed at her daughter without any emotions.

Arianna shakes her tiny hands and limbs to grab her mother's attention, yet it is so hard with Luma holding her dark heart. Ramses cuddled Arianna with enormous love, and joyous tears fell from his eyes.

"My daughter," he murmured and kissed Arianna's head.

"I will bring this whole world beneath to you because you are my sweet little daughter," he confirmed. Uncountable hopes twisted with acceptance and rejection whirled around Arianna, yet she never knew how her fate would guide her throughout this unpredictable life journey.

Arianna grows slowly, and Yesmin and Saina do most of her duties. Meanwhile, Luma kept herself more leisurely. Samuel used to play with her. When Arianna turned two years old, Ramses drew them back to Kingdom Yunas. Luma redesigned herself. Her shadows of darkness and cruelty again started to show up. She didn't let Ramses's mother touch Arianna. Besides, she threatened Arianna to ignore her grandmother.

Hence, the poor child used to hide and get away when she spotted Ramses's mother. All this maltreatment made Ramses's mother so miserable. She constantly worried about her son. She knew that Luma would never devote herself to Ramses, and all the considerable separation Luma had created between Ramses and his siblings shattered her heart. Gradually, she became ill and unhealthy. She lay on her bed with an endless sore heart.

Ramses rarely visited to meet his mother because he feared Luma's worthless quarrels. Ramses's life became more and more perplexed and heavy with each day. Things didn't change even after Arianna's arrival. Ramses constantly suffered from an intolerably tormented destiny. He and Luma fought until midnight. Their unresolved troubles haunted the entire mansion. Arianna wakes up often because of the enormous noise made by her parents. She closed her little ears and silently crept under the bed to sleep. Arianna felt frightened by these fights. She wanted to see her parents live happily with her. Yet it was hard to know because they habitually used to make wars. After each battle, Luma kept herself inside her chamber. She scolded little Arianna if she disturbed Luma. Most of the time, Arianna spent time with her two maids, who attended to her instead of Luma. Ramses's dispirited mind changes his routines. He used to return to the mansion quite late sometimes. He didn't return until midnight. Ramses ' mother secretly watched her son's odd behaviour. One night, she spotted him entering the mansion, and it was almost dawn. He stumbled forward, grabbed his servant's arm, and leaned on him; therefore, his servant had to guide him to his chamber. She wept desperately. Her whole heart ripped into pieces when she understood that her mostly kind, innocent son had wasted his life. Then, one morning, after following a massive fight with Luma, Ramses went out. He did and didn't return home. Luma waited anxiously with Arianna and finally went to sleep. Ramses returned to the mansion after midnight. He walked awkwardly and held the wall to escape from falling over with Reddish eyes. He slowly reached his mother's room. His body wavered side to side.

"Mother," he faltered.

"Ramses," she woke up confusedly. Ramses fell down and raised, grasping the big door at the entrance. He hauled his body close to her. The mother tried to stand up, but her frail body and illness made it difficult for her. Ramses tumbled down beside the bed. Then, he hardly placed his head on the edge of her bed. His head pressed tightly inside her body, yet his tormented mind sought her unlimited love.

"Mother," he whispered.

"My poor Ramses, my son," she began to sob.

She patted his head softly. Ramses sensed her pure warmth of love. After ages, he felt much more peaceful and secure near her.

"My eyes, my desires, trapped me. Mother, I can't find me. I am desperately alone," he started to sob. This sick, older, loveable mother is unable to bear her son's pathetic situation. His grief tortured her more than the Ramses. She knew how she tried to understand Luma. She always treated her kindly. She took Luma's side most of the time and even neglected her children to cover up for Luma. Because she utterly wanted to see the joyous of Ramses.

Hence, she sacrificed whatever she could do on its behalf. But Luma never changed herself. Luma's disheartening sarcastic words tear her heart. Eventually, she realised that Luma married Ramses purely for some other reasons. Luma's cruel and disrespectful manners frustrated herself pull down her well-being. Ramses falls to sleep after a while. The woman keeps patting his head. Ramses woke up confusedly at dawn, and his mother's cold hand halted on his head. Her powerless body seemed to be resting close to him. Her eyes remained shut, and her natural warmth became frozen cold. Ramses screamed and banged his head on the wall. His loud wailing echoes all around, yet Luma slept peacefully beside Arianna.

After the Ramses's mother's unexpected departure, the mansion remained muted. Each person blamed Ramses and even Luma. Ramses was ignored by his relatives and even by his family. His father refused to speak with him and Luma. They are convinced that Luma's awful behaviour destroyed their whole family and the complete serenity of the mansion. Luma repeatedly began to argue with Ramses because her egomaniac mind never accepted this guilt; hence, she needed to transfer it to him. Therefore, She blamed him for his reckless shaming actions in taking his mother's life. Ramses burst out angrily and hollered while shaking Luma strenuously from her shoulders.

"You killed my mother, you killed her, I lost her, I lost her," He repeated.

Arianna sprinted towards Luma and hid inside her, crying. Luma yelled at Ramses

"Are you insane? You are making this poor child afraid."

Ramses groaned and jumped over to her, but suddenly, he noticed Arianna's tearful eyes. She was snuggled inside Luma, her body shivering with fear. Ramses paused himself and tumbled down on the chair. He began to cry like a child.

"My mother, I lose her love I'm nobody now I'm alone there's no one for me in this world." He mumbled to himself.

Luma was found unable to cope with this sudden tragedy. Hence, she decided to go back to Kingdom Thebeslon with Arianna. She didn't want to share the Ramses's grief or understand his woeful heart. Neither soothing words didn't spill out of her mouth to comfort him. She packed her stuff precisely and then moved out of the mansion. One rainy night, Luma stepped in front of the Yesmin's door. She was crying out loud, cuddling her little daughter. Then, keep weeping the whole night. Saina and Samuel look after Arianna. The poor girl looked at their faces with confused eyes. Samuel tried to make her laugh. But she hides inside Saina and closes her ears. Her parents' endless arguments terrified her perpetually.

"My poor child," Saina sighed sorrowfully.

Luma blamed Yesmin for destroying her life and letting herself be married to Ramses. She said it's a mansion full of lunatics. She confirmed she has no idea how to deal with those low-graded, shameful royals. It was hard to get to know why Luma hated her marriage. Ramses's empathy, endurance and calmness twisted with self-restraint behaviour indeed, execrated by Luma. The rowdy, blazing red sun cannot be soothing with the soft wind. Likewise, the violent, stormy hail and silent forest river never meant each other. However, Ramses wanted to ride their boat throughout their entire life. Arianna's innocent eyes recall him all the time. It tore him. However, his wounded heart never relented. Hence, he decided to drive back to Thebeslon to talk with Luma. He is determined to solve everything and start a new life with Luma for Arianna's sake. Ramses and Luma agreed to live together again after a long conversation. Ramses accepted all the guilt to console Luma. He built a grand house on the top of the mountain of Thebeslon. He gave some significant portions of coins to Yesmin to satisfy Luma. Luma's brothers and sisters got all the benefits from Ramses. Luma's sister married, and others carried their lives much more smoothly because of Ramses. He helped whenever they asked for it. The coins, gifts, and other valuables always filled their houses with the aid of the Luma's compassionate emotions.

The villagers knew little about Luma's marriage, but Yesmin kept hiding that top secret. She never mentioned Arianna's father to others. On the other hand, the neighbours didn't become familiar with Lord Ramses because he is from another remote kingdom. They thought the man Luma ran away secretly had kicked her out with a child. Eventually, she trapped some big fish with her mother's help and returned to the Kingdom using his power of money. This rumour is established around their lives, but nobody wants to change or recreate it. The people used to laugh unnoticeably when they spotted poor

Arianna. Luma seemed to be kinder and more peaceful with Ramses. She treated him with overflowing affection. They had numerous romantic moments. Ramses blindly thought that his whole dark time was over. He is unaware and fooled by Luma's false love. Once again, he was digging his hole by blindly trusting Luma. The most valuable belongings owned by Ramses, including gold coins, eventually got the authority under the Luma's hands. But Ramses desperately believed Luma would always be his most trusted life partner.

Meanwhile, Luma fell ill suddenly. She had to lie on the bed for many days with a frail body. Saina took Arianna to their place while Ramses heeded Luma. Luma got massively weakened with sickness. Hence, Ramses stayed beside her all the time. He feeds her and cleans her body without the aid of a maid. For many days, he kept sleepless until she recovered completely. Luma appeared to be calm after the illness. Ramses proved his enormous love and commitment towards Luma; hence, she would realise it more than before. But Luma considers his whole process his responsibility. Thus, she does not show any gratitude for it. But for some reason, Luma kept her mouth shut. She hasn't had any struggles with him so far.

"Ramses, I 'm saving some money for our daughter so she will hold a prosperous, bright future" she whispered to him. Ramses kissed her forehead lovingly. Luma kept her head on his naked chest and began to kiss him. Their body rhythms met with each other somehow. Nevertheless, their souls had vast distances—the ruthless spider weaving its web again to capture its prey of guiltless heart.

Chapter 13

A few months passed, and Luma was able to pile up a massive sack of wealth by winning Ramses's heart again. Unfortunately, her perfidious affection misleads Ramses. After Luma had succeeded in her game, she dropped her mask. The battle starts again. Whenever Luma sighted him, she started up her wars. She was angry and resentful if he granted some coins to the needy. Hence, she condemned him.

Luma was bewailed for her freedom, which slipped away from her due to marrying Ramses. According to Luma, Ramses has ruined her. There is no ending to her disputes. One morning, there was a massive argument between them. Luma tried to kill herself by jumping over the deep stream nearby. Luckily, Ramses grasped her tightly from her one arm and pulled her back out.

Honestly, Luma performed a dramatic dance to frighten Ramses. His fearful face pleased her. His tortured eyes elated her deeply.

The tree, quivering with stormy wind. But the heartless wind captured all its leaves and flowers. However, this strong tree tried to get up somehow. The leaves slowly fly away with the whirling wind. Though Ramses felt his desolate, hopeless life revolves in the same circle, he could not escape it. Arianna's innocent smile drew him back. He kissed her rosy cheeks heavy-heartedly.

One sorrowful blue midnight, Luma kicked out Ramses. She cursed him and confirmed she didn't want to live with him. Besides, she threatened him that she would destroy her life if he wanted to carry their bond further. Ramses has no choice. However, he gathered his entire might to give a glimpse at his little daughter. Then he breathed mournfully, wiping his unstoppable tears. He couldn't kiss her because the poor girl was sleeping. She might never know that this might be their last farewell beforehand, the departure destined for ages. Ramses sobbed alone and then walked out of the house. He stood in the thick mist, looking desperately. While wandering around with grey eyes, his pockets remained empty. Lord Ramses dragged his feet and then halted after a few seconds. Then gave an anguished cry. His eyes blurred in the hefty dark. Thus, he pulled his hair vaguely. He sat under the huge tree which sheltered their first meeting. The sky groaned. It started to lament with Ramses. He shivered in the cold with wet clothes. He is all alone, abandoned in pitchy darkness. There's no Luma, or maybe that love, warmth and promises have been left away from them. The time has passed. Yet this unexplained catastrophe baffled him. Glowing memories of attachments radiant as the scintillating sun were unearthly quiet. Yet the moment of the colourless rainbow haunts him. Hence, he drowned in the bizarre dreams of the past, frozen by life's horrendous uncertainty.

The night flew out after the morning sun-rays arrived. Ramses woke up. He was thunderstruck by the remembrance of the last night. However, he convinced him all that was a scary nightmare. He was still under the tree, trembling with cold, wet clothes. His head is bursting with pain. He rose and tried to move his legs.

"Arianna," he mumbled. Ramses directed his steps back to the Luma's place. Afterwards, he hides near the bush. He was waiting until Arianna was visible. Then, he heard some loud noises inside the house. It might be Luma's brothers and family. But he kept himself quiet.

After some time, Arianna appeared out of the house. Ramses silently moved nearby her, and Arianna began to play alone. However, nobody seemed to be—The maid the Ramses brought to look after Arianna has been sent back home by Luma. The reason was that she was loyal to Ramses rather than the Luma. Ramses came close to Arianna and quickly grabbed her tightly.

"Come with me, Arianna," he whispered.

"Father" Arianna exclaimed out loud.

"please don't shout, my dear come with me. We have to go big journey"

"But father, I want mother to come with us too. So three of us can go together. I want both of you to stay with me" Arianna suddenly stopped her words.

"Mother, please come. We are going," she shouted aloud before Ramses paused her. Then, in a spur moment, Luma and others ran towards Arianna.

"How dare you" Luma scowled, glancing at Ramses and screaming.

She quickly grabs Arianna.

"Luma, please listen to me. If you want to kick me off, I am happy with that. You can keep all the money as your wish. But please give me my daughter because I want her to be with me. So You can carry your life peacefully." he pleaded. Luma smirked; Ramses appeared as a pauper rather than an affluent royal lord. All his rich garments soak with mud. The sweat ran through his messy hair.

"Mind your words dumbhead all your money possess to Arianna. I have nothing to do with it It's all for the sake of my daughter."

Ramses grinned and laughed sarcastically, peeking into Luma's eyes. Then, he dragged Arianna vigorously to him.

"Arianna let's go," he shouted.

"He is insane," Luma said out loud. Arianna began to cry.

Luma's elder brother Hugo pulled Ramses from the arm swiftly.

Meanwhile, Saina quickly stepped in to release Arianna from the Ramses. Luma kept sobbing, leaning toward Yesmin. Subsequently, Hugo grasped Ramses by the neck. Ramses yelled while struggling. Hugo kicked him fiercely. Ramses dropped down and then grunted with pain. The blood dripped out from his wounded lips.

"Father" Arianna screamed. Then, she closed her eyes with fear. Samuel hastily took Arianna into his arms and moved away.

"No, please don't take my Arianna, Let me kiss her for the last time Please I beg you" Ramses cried while trying to stand up from his powerless limbs.

"Get lost, moron" Luma's younger brother, Seth, kicked him again. Ramses lose his balance once more. He began to sob while hauling over the floor.

"Why?" he murmured.

Saina kept watching the entire scene, but neither word spilt out of his mouth. Though he knew the Ramses was guiltless, he didn't want to save him. It was his long-term habit never to take action against the unacceptable misdemeanour. He was somewhat concerned about slipping away secretly from those awful circumstances. Then hide in his sphere, letting him forget them all. But, as a responsible father, he never warned his children to quit their nasty attitude.

Meanwhile, Yesmin wiped Luma's unstoppable tears. But Yesmin's eyes neither exhibit any sympathy. She never tried to encourage her daughter to protect her husband and family. However, her eyes glitter when she remembered the coins and other valuables Luma had sneaked from Ramses. She considers this catastrophe another fortune or a gift from her unknown God.

"Terrific," Yesmin mumbled throughout the event.

Ramses draws his helpless soul out of the property built on his own. Indeed, Hugo and Seth throw him out. Ramses's heart ripped with agony more than his painful body; consequently, he strayed alone between the woods. Sometimes, he tumbles on the muddy streams. Then, it moved again with tottering limbs while the whole body was sheathing with mud and sweaty blood. He was senseless about his entire surroundings.

Nonetheless, his profound intellect realised that he had been trapped by wolves. Eventually, he became aware that he was still alive, and somehow, he was lying beneath his mother's grave. He sobbed on a cold morning, pressing his head tightly towards the tomb.

"I can't find me, mother, you better take to me your hands, it would be much more peaceful to me," he faltered with numb lips. Suddenly, one warm arm grabbed him from his shoulders.

"Son, I am here with you."

A kind, affectionate word touched Ramse's ears miraculously.

"The darkness of past never be changed but this moment I am holding you so let's make this moment to shine the future Ramses. Get up my son."

Ramses's father took him back to the mansion.

....

Luma and Arianna returned to Yesmin's house. Because Luma found it uneasy to look after Arianna, she refused to stay alone in her residence. Luma blended fictitious stories related to Ramses. Therefore, she proved her sinless purity to all the spectators. Saina kept himself pondering inside his chamber, content with rum. Yesmin was elated when Luma handled a significant portion of the treasure snatched by Ramses. Luma thought she could stay with her family leisurely hereafter; hence, she did not hesitate to fulfil them with money. Hugo and Seth were pleased about their involvement in expelling Ramses from the Kingdom of Thebeslon.

Each person is shrouded in their egotistical logic. Meanwhile, Arianna played alone with her dolls, never knowing the harshness of life without her father's security and affection. But she has to struggle with her life under the guidance of one greedy, devious, insensible mother. Arianna's life changed rapidly. Her beautiful eyes became a pool of tears. She got beaten by Luma many times for no reason. Luma threatened her never to talk or recall about Ramses. Luma burnt all the goods belonging to Ramses, which she saw as worthless. Some prized furniture and ornaments got Hugo and Seth's helpful hand as they pulled them to their homes for more safety. There was a portrait hanging on the wall. When Luma spotted it, she tore the picture into two parts. It was the portrait drawn during the function held at the Ramses mansion. It remained a beautiful family image. Luma carried Arianna while Ramses stood close to them, smiling brightly. She burnt part of the portrait in which Ramses appears. Afterwards, she secretly hides the rest of the piece. Somehow, the blood-sucking leeches were never conscious of the warmth they touched. They were neither sensible to enwrap around that charming endearment. Besides, they would instead attach solely to the taste of blood. Hence, their voracious appetite seemed to be never satisfied.

It is tiring to believe why Luma hates Ramses particularly. Maybe after accomplishing her goal, she considered him a part of rubbish. Perhaps all his recollections call her mind repeatedly about her evilness. It is curious why Luma kept Arianna to herself because she never committed to a perfect, loveable mother. On the contrary, Luma does not greet Arianna once as if she were her child. Instead of that, she perceived her as a personal asset she possessed.

However, the gossip about Luma's split marriage ran over the village. Hence, Luma played an act to exhibit her endurance as a devoted wife. She unfolded her sorrows to prove her righteousness while cursing her ill fate. Which tends her to agonise throughout an extended period on behalf of her family. She regretted the past miserable life she had spent with that horrible mansion. Luma creates a new story to blame Ramses and his mother each day. Her eyes filled with tears when she remembered how she had spent her long days locking her room alone. After being repeatedly condemned and humiliated by the egomaniac royals. Eventually, Luma confirms Ramses is a drunkard fool who has run after the whores before marrying Luma. There-fore, he continually engages with his habitual life even after the birth of little Arianna.

Furthermore, she said all her family members are following these cheap behaviours. Hence, she needed to build up Arianna in an excellent, decent way. So firstly, she left that filthy royal mansion and then the Ramses. Thus, with all her immense efforts, she performed absolutely for the sake of her most loving child. In fact, to spare themselves from that reckless cheap Ram-ses. He resembled himself as the absolute puppet of his disgraceful mother, who held a shady character. Luma wept in front of her relatives, patting Ari-anna's rosy cheeks. Besides, she uses her daughter to divert others' sympathy towards her and remake herself as the most virtuous and courageous mother. However, she rudely governed Arianna. Therefore, she constantly appeared as an authorised mother and desired to keep Arianna beneath herself. So she blamed the poor girl all over. Sometimes, when Luma got angry, she hit Ari-anna with whatever she grabbed in her hand. Then pushed her away. Hence, Arianna used to spend time with Saina or Yesmin with bowed-down eyes. Luma raised Arianna entirely because she knew she needed someone's aid when she got old.

Even though Arianna is still young, she looks more graceful and pretty than the other girls. Each night, Luma keeps staring at her. She touched Ari-anna's rosy lips and glossy skin.

"She will be the most gorgeous out of everyone,

So your future might be more colourful than mine," Luma smirks.

"My daughter, you would be a priceless gift for me after your father." Her thirst to please her indefinite intentions enhances day by day. Her tunnel-vi-sioned mind never hesitates to vend her daughters' soul to achieve her ex-pectations. Luma wanted to be attached to Arianna while taking control of her hands.

"When you grow up, I will show your mostly great beloved royal father how I raised you nicely without him," Luma thought silently. Luma never shows any patience with Arianna. When she started to cry, Luma used to whip her badly.

"Arianna, you have to respect me, and you must always follow my commands," she confirmed. Eventually, the poor girl habituated to hiding her emotions. So she thought, spilling out her words as an action to get punished by her mother.

"Arianna, you have no right to talk over to me. I'm the eldest. You must obey my commands and respect me," Luma ordered. Although Luma followed rudely, sometimes she kissed Arianna and bribed her with good food and toys. Because she needed to vanish all her loveable memories related to Ramses and cease herself. Thoroughly, Arianna must only twist with Luma.

"Arianna, you are my everything. I committed my whole life to you," she whispered while glancing at Arianna's sparkling eyes. Consequently, she persuaded Arianna that Ramses had left them and returned to his place. Furthermore, she said that he would never love them. Luma introduced Ramses as a shameless character abundant with misdeeds. Hugo and Seth invariably comfort Arianna. Luma told her these two good-hearted uncles would love her more than her father. However, Arianna's immature mind trusted her mother's fantasy tales. Yet she felt it was pretty hard to accept why her most loveable father abandoned her alone like this. She touched her earrings to remember him. It was a gift she received from his father and an attractive necklace. Unfortunately, her mother took the chain out of her and hid it for more security. She assumed that Arianna was relatively small to bear that valued necklace. Yet after a few months, Arianna saw her mother was wearing that necklace. However, she kept her mouth silent without asking questions. Soon, Arianna's earrings got exchanged with Hugo's' younger daughter. Arianna miserably hold those cheap, unattractive earrings belonging to her cousin and sighed woefully. Each day, Arianna lost her self-confidence. Profoundly, her backbone was broken up by her own mother. Thus, she loses her power to speak for her own sake. Fear, grief together, and loneliness misguided her. Then, she appeared quiet and highly humble in her mannered behaviour. Her lips were closed tightly. She always got shook when she heard the Luma's voice.

The neighbours used to ask Arianna frequent questions about her father, but she was speechless.

She remembered Ramses each night. She wished he would come back again. But it was merely a dream. Arianna recalled the days that Ramses used to cuddle all through the night. Arianna used to sleep on his broad chest. Therefore, she grasped her pillow tightly. At midnight every day, she saw he was visible in her dreams. He embraced her and kissed her forehead. Arianna placed her head on his chest, touching his slightly grown beard, but in the morning, she woke up suddenly, and there were no Ramses. Instead, she found herself holding her pillow. Some days, She watched secretly how Uncle Hugo played with her daughter. Her laugh and giggles shattered Arianna's little heart. She yearned to return to her father and spend each second with him. Yet one gloomy shadow wandered around her.

"Why did he leave me? Am I as bad as mother says?"

She mumbled to herself.

Slowly, Luma revived her life back. She decided to enjoy her life and her youth. She is wealthy enough to pursue whatever she needs. Most of the time, Yesmin cared for Arianna. Luma used to spend her days and sometimes nights with her friends. However, she does not hesitate to neglect her responsibilities as a mother. Some days, Arianna waited many hours until Luma returned. She sat on the log near the gate and gazed at the small path directed to Yesmin's house.

Nevertheless, Luma never worried about it. When she arrived back, she knitted bountiful lies to make herself perfect. Yesmin fed Arianna, and she used to sleep beside her. In the morning, Arianna played with Samuel. One day, both of them walked inside the woods. Arianna chased after the butterfly. She believed that the butterfly could find the father for her.

"Little butterfly, show me the way to my fathers' home," she whispered to the thick, dark woods. Unfortunately, neither Samuel nor the butterfly got sighted in her little eyes. Instead, she got frightened by fearful noises and massive trunks of large trees.

"Samuel!" She screamed loudly.

But no one came in front of her. Arianna began to cry and closed her eyes. Then, unexpectedly, she heard a kind voice.

"My child, hold my hand."

Arianna opened up her eyes. Then she saw a beautiful lady standing in front of her. She was wearing shining green attire. On her one hand, there was a bouquet of blossoms. Arianna stared at her with surprised eyes.

"Who are you?" she asked from the unknown gesture.

The lady calmly reached close to Arianna and sensed a floral scent. It soothes her unconditionally. However, the little girl holds the lady's ' hand.

"Are you a fairy?" she asked again.

The lady smiled, and then they walked near the forest creek. She sat under the giant oak tree and laid Arianna on her lap.

"I'm your breath may be your entirety I govern this whole universe. I am the power of nature or else Goddess Atunura."

"Fairy God Atunura," Arianna chuckles.

She touched the face of the goddess. Her bewitching smile and empathic eyes enchanted her. A little girl slowly falls asleep. She heard the beautiful song of Mother Nature in between her dreams.

"My child, your destiny is fixed; hence you have to cope with it. You are eligible to find out the deep truth throughout the suffering. So explore the place between dark and light unless this endless agony will chase after you forever."

Mother Atunura's words stretched around the atmosphere. The Oaktree sways slightly to show their humble gratitude. The creek flows in sweeping meanders.

Arianna slept peacefully with the warmth of Mother Nature. A light smile decorated her face. Maybe that butterfly has found the route to go back to her father.

....

Samuel looked everywhere for Arianna. He walked deep inside the forest. Still, Samuel was unable to find even her shadow. He called out her name many times. Then, he desperately sat on the fallen tree trunk beside him.

"What will I do now?" he said anxiously, pulling his curly hair. Meanwhile, Luma arrived back home. She was waiting for Arianna. Yesmin was praying for her most important God inside her sacred room. Suddenly, Samuel ran towards Luma and panted.

"Arianna," he faltered.

"Why?" Luma queries a frightening voice.

"I took her inside the woods, but now she is nowhere. I couldn't find her."

"Oh, what have you done is this way you take care of her?" Luma began to yell, shaking Vaguely Samuel from his shoulders.

"My Arianna where are you?" Luma bawled while lamenting.

Saina, Yesmin's entire neighbourhood, gathered around. Luma blamed Yesmin harshly for neglecting Arianna. While others keep themselves busy inside the woods to search for Arianna, Luma beats Samuel. Afterwards, she began to lament immensely, rolling over the ground. Yesmin tried to console her, but Luma sternly pushed away from her mother, letting that old woman fall down. Luckily, Samuel got hold of Yesmin. Luma's magnificent drama occurred until the Saina reached the house, holding little sleeping angel Arianna in his arms.

But Luma was enraged instead of being happy when she saw Arianna. She pulled her vigorously out of Saina's hand and slapped the poor girl.

"What the hell have you been?" she groaned.

Soon after, she beat her incessantly, and the poor girl shouted in pain while crying. Saina, Yesmin and Samuel had to be involved in a massive struggle to release Arianna from the annoyed Luma.

After a few days, Luma shifted back to her routine. The gossip ran through the village about Luma and another married man. Meanwhile, Luma's sister came back to Yesmin for her childbirth. Yesmin asked for another portion of Luma's money. It makes her irritated, and she begins to quarrel with everyone. However, the house again got filled with Luma's ongoing fights. Luma even fought with her in-laws. And often got condemned. Eventually, they all began to criticise her. The house is filled with the arguments of Luma and Yesmin. Sometimes, Yesmin walked out and stayed at Hugo's home. Seth and Hugo had to console their most good-hearted mother from their evil sister. Yesmin secretly persuaded Arianna to tell Luma to drive back to Ramses. Then, she thoroughly forced Arianna to do so. However, when these disastrous words are out of Arianna's, Luma is infuriated with Yesmin. They had massive quarrels. Luma threatens Yesmin that she will take her life away if she forces her to be settled with Ramses. But after the involvement of Seth and Hugo, the Luma ceased herself. Day by day, Luma felt that she was losing herself. However, this is not the life she desires after splitting with Ramses. She was yearning to sense her independence and youth, after all. But was unable to understand the total bareness that veiled around her.

Meanwhile, Arianna spent her time with Luma's sister. Arianna massaged her swollen feet with her tiny hands. She was so curious about the baby inside her tummy.

At the same time, Luma fluttered her wings alone with her lover. She is aware that her family ignores her totally. Therefore, Luma chose to turn a new chapter of her life. She began to make numerous promises, binding her hands with the man named Wilson. He is older than Luma and is the father of three kids. Suddenly, his wife appeared before the Saina's house and cursed Luma for ruining her family. But as usual, Saina kept himself quiet manner. Yet Hugo and Seth fought for their most precious dignity and family status with Luma. They all directly accused Luma of being liable for this disaster. Yesmin began to sob because of losing her considerably valued reputation. Eventually, Wilson agreed to leave his family in the name of his love for Luma.

Wilson and Luma shifted to Luma's house, which was built by Ramses. Wilson's heart never changed. Even his elder daughter grabbed him from his hands to halt him. Instead, he snarled at his wife, weeping close to him. He gathered all his belongings and stepped out without looking at his household.

Luma's captivating eyes and beautiful gestures enthralled him more than his ageing wife. Who was incapable of enchanting him with her unshapely figure and tired face. Because she gradually loses her charming appearance after each childbirth. The poor woman watched his fading shadows among the evening dusk. Wilson stepped quickly to free his eyes from his wife's unpleasant sight. Yet he could not recall the deep heart and devotion she had made throughout their journey. She sobbed with wrenching sadness while holding their little son in her hands.

However, Luma and Wilson started their most precious new life in the big house built by Ramses. Luma took Arianna with them. Wilson showed his wholehearted, warm love towards Arianna. Meanwhile, Luma forced Arianna to respect Wilson as her own father. When Arianna seems hesitant, Luma threatens her to do so. Hence, Arianna used to call him father. Wilson's unbelievable kindness surprised Arianna at first. Though he is quick-tempered, she mistakenly thought her new stepfather would love her most. At night, Arianna cried constantly. She needs Luma to sleep with her. But Wilson got mad at her and pushed her inside her room to sleep alone. But Arianna slowly sneaks out to Luma at midnight to cuddle with her. One day, Arianna awoke at dawn and slept beneath Luma's bed. Thus, the poor girl silently raised her head and looked for Luma. The warm tears fell down from her and wetted the cold floor. Luma and Wilson, sleeping peacefully, embrace each other. Arianna wiped her tears and quietly walked back to her space.

"Father left me he would never come back to fetch me, and mother loves the Wilson more than me. So I'm all alone."

Arianna began to sob, letting her isolated soul rest in her noteless tears.

CHAPTER 14

A few months passed unhurriedly. Luma and Wilson are found to be fantasising about their world. Arianna used to spend her long days playing with her toys. But, honestly, she didn't receive any new toys after the Ramses's separation. Most of the toys seemed overused and broken, but no one bothered. Every day, Arianna realised that Wilson was not truly sympathetic and tender as he showed up. Some days, he commanded Arianna to do specific chores. When she was unfit to complete his orders, he got irritated.

"You cannot do any single thing such a brainless girl" he often humiliated her. After one year, Arianna visited the older adult who resembled himself as the tutor. Wilson took her every day for learning. Everybody gazed at Arianna awkwardly. Other children whispered some secrets to each other, glancing at Arianna, but she remained quiet. Sometimes, they laughed at her for no reason and ignored her. Hence, she was unable to make any friends at school. Her mouth shut when the school teacher asked the questions even though she knew the answers. Therefore, the teacher got annoyed with her.

Gradually, she loses her confidence. Sometime later, neighbours began to query about her father, and she introduced Wilson. But when she noticed their sarcastic smile, she was confused totally. Eventually, the people thought that Luma knitting great lies related to Arianna's fatherhood. Hence, they began to believe that Arianna was a child of an unknown father. Thus, nobody wants to treat her as a royal daughter.

"Even Luma may never have had any idea about her true father." People made various gossip related to an innocent girl. Therefore, she got disgraced in the village without a limit. Indeed, she has to pay off herself because of her mother's awful misdeeds. Sometimes, Wilson used to speak softly, holding a colourful smile. After rewarding her with sweets, he implored her to sit on his lap. Arianna obeyed him all the time with frightening eyes. While she was seated, he began to touch her shining little body. He tightly squeezed her thighs, then her tummy, and pinched her tiny tits. Though it was painful, Arianna was incapable of resisting him.

"You will be the most stunning beauty out of this entire kingdom, just like your most renowned grandmother," he snarled, and then his fingers ran through her silky hair. And subsequently halted on her little bum. Then he pressed her bum more forcefully than the thighs. Arianna remained speechless, though the tears burst out of her eyes.

"You are hurting me. It's painful," Arianna complained.

"How can I hurt you, my little daughter?" Wilson smirked.

Arianna quickly escaped from him and ran towards Luma.

She drags Luma's long gown to cover and hide herself inside it.

"What are you doing here? Arianna let me leave alone. Will you please go and play" Luma yelled. Arianna slowly moved her little toes to her room. She crept under her bed, closed her eyes, and began crying. But nobody seemed to be listening to it. Wilson became reckless regarding Arianna as he was clearly aware of her vulnerability. Thus, Wilson was delighted to grab all the advantages. He never senses the same emotions relevant to Arianna; likewise, her daughter sits on his lap. Instead of overflowing love spilling out on behalf of his own blood, his whole mind veiled out with blind lust beside Arianna. Finally, however, Luma decided to send Arianna back to the Yesmin. She thought she needed some freedom to be with Wilson.

"My dear Arianna, you better stay with your grandmother because she is missing you so much," she uttered and kissed Arianna delicately. So the following day, Saina and Samuel took her back to Yesmin. However, Arianna sighed with relief, wrapping her hands around the Yesmin's waist.

Luma bounded with Wilson more affectionately than the Ramses. She found her own contentment inside his rowdy and arrogant manners. Profoundly compared to Ramses, Wilson is not calm and decent. His eyes not ever obeyed him beside the charming females. He used to tell dirty jokes to them. His immodest personality and playful acts seemed to be totally irresponsible. But Luma was immensely attracted to his hot-blooded nature. He sipped his rum pot, and his lips impatiently roamed through Luma's bare trunk.

Wilson overpowered her more, and many times, he bawled at her. His dirty mouth limitlessly insults her. But she listened to them all with tearful eyes and repeatedly pleaded for him to stay with her. Wilson's rude attitude and short, stout, unpleasant appearance more satisfied her than the handsome, well-mannered Ramses.

Saina and Yesmin were delighted after Arianna's arrival.

Arianna went to learn from a village tutor with Samuel. She watched the stars at night while sitting on Saina's lap. His fascinating folk stories thrilled her heart, letting her laugh aloud after a long time. Samuel plucked a bunch of wildflowers for Arianna every day, then braided her long hair decorated with flowers. Yesmin cared for her granddaughter more than her own children. Arianna chased for the birds sitting on Saina's shoulders. He began to teach her their dance traditions, which neither of his children had learnt. Absolutely, Arianna was born to dance. All her dance talents overjoyed Yesmin, bringing up her bright memories of the past. Eventually, as time passed, Arianna healed Saina's wounded heart. His eyes shine when he hears her soft voice. But when the night arrived, Arianna placed her head on the pillow, thinking about Ramses, her beloved father. She met him every day in her dreams. Though he was so far away, Arianna felt he was so attached to her. But when the morning arrived, she realised it was only an illusion.

Luma and Wilson were spending their infinite romantic days. Luma got frenzied with exhilaration. She didn't let Wilson take her eyes away for a single minute. Meanwhile, in that mansion, Ramses alone, rambled inside his chamber. He was bearing Arianna's little frock on his one hand, kissed it several times, and then wiped his sleepless, sore eyes. He was expecting his death rather than his life. The agony tortured him, and he felt his whole spirit pierced. Ramses hit his head on the wall with a wrecking heart. He was so incapable totally of the suffering of losing his own child, entire wealth and honour. Yet he was only betrayed and cheated. All insults and grief relieved him as a prize for letting himself be loved by a heartless woman. Seth and Hugo gave a warm welcome to Wilson. They gradually enjoyed his smutty jokes; Wilson became the favourite of all except Arianna. Luma's family praised him greatly. His inappropriate talk and personality comfort them more than Ramses. When they realised that they had built all their lives with the aid of Ramses, it destroyed their ego and the entire nobility. Hence, they were delighted to wipe him from their whole life. Therefore, they insulted Ramses and humiliated his humbleness.

Arianna grows with the time day by day. She becomes more graceful and attracted. She spends a lot of time with Samuel. They roamed around the woods and creeks and played together. Arianna felt Samuel was his own brother rather than her uncle. However, Samuel seemed to be a few years older than her. Luma visited to meet Arianna for a few days. Yesmin queries for some coins from Luma because they had a lot of needs that needed to be fully filled. Some days, Arianna had to stay with Seth's wife to look after her children. Luma has told her to help her uncles whenever they need any help. Hence, Seth's wife used to order her to do all her household chores.

Arianna swept their floor and then cleaned the dirty dishes. Afterwards, she bathed their kids while her aunt gossiped with neighbours. Arianna faced the same situation when she went to Hugo's home. But Arianna endured this ill-treatment and happily helped them. One morning, Hugo's wife bought some cottage cheese. Arianna came to their home that day because Yesmin visited to see her younger daughter. Arianna completed many duties commanded by her aunt. However, Arianna got some leftover food for lunch. Though starving, she felt shy and afraid to ask for more food from her aunt. But when she was cleaning her kitchen unexpectedly, she glimpsed the cheese. Arianna slowly took it in her hand and sensed its' tempting smell. Her tummy rumbled with hunger. Yesmin never spent her coins on these kinds of food. Hence, she usually cooked ordinary, low-cost meals.

Arianna remembered her childhood, the days spent in her father's mansion. Each day, she sat to eat. The great platters filled with luscious food decorated the grand table. Ramses's mother used to put some significant portions of cheese on her plate. And the maid keeps her glass of milk beside her.

"Arianna, my love, if you want to grow up fast, you have to eat these all and drink your milk," she uttered in a kind voice, slightly touching her face. Arianna quickly wiped her wet cheeks before her aunt got noticed. Then she sneaked some small portion and hid it inside the pocket.

She knew even though she worked for her aunt from morning to night, she would never treat her with these kinds of food. Therefore, Arianna's frustrated mind did not feel any regret about her actions of snatching some cheese. Arianna thought about moving out, but suddenly, her aunt appeared before her.

"Did you finish the work, my dear" she questioned and yawned loudly? She slept almost two hours leisurely.

"Yes, aunt, I'm not feeling much well. May I leave" she asked back.

"Of course, my dear, but don't forget to come and see me again, my sweetheart," she embraced Arianna.

Arianna slowly slipped away and walked back home. She looked around suspiciously. But nobody noticed her eyes. Hence, she comfortably sat on the log and sighed with relief. Afterwards, she began to taste a treasured piece of cheese.

"What are you doing?" Arianna was shocked by the rough voice. The cheese fell down when she jerked. Arianna stood at once. Then She looked down with frightened eyes, wiping her sweaty forehead slowly. Samuel spotted the piece of cheese on the ground.

"Where did you get it? Did someone give yourself? He queries.

Arianna was speechless.

"Oh, did you sneak it?" Arianna looked away, her eyes filled with tears. She started to sob.

"I am starving," she mumbled.

"How did you get it?"

"I found it while cleaning uncle Hugo's house, so I only took a tiny piece." Arianna stammered.

"Did aunt give it to you? Or you steal it, aren't you?"

"No, on took it by my own I didn't tell her."

Samuel stared at her with a grumpy face.

"I won't do It again. Please, I promised you. please don't tell it to the aunt and or granny," Arianna pleaded.

Samuel took a deep breath and observed her face. Then, without warning, his mind got veiled with some peculiar feelings. He came close to Arianna and grabbed her arms forcefully.

"Ok, I won't tell anyone. It's a secret between the two of us."
he whispered.

"So what you can give to me for protecting your secret"

Arianna peered at his face confusedly.

"What do you want Samuel?" She mumbled hesitantly.

"Come with me," he said, pulling her hand vaguely.

"To where?" She asked again with a doubtful mind.

Samuel took her to Saina's chamber. The old shack was placed close to the edge of the backyard, shady and covered. Samuel took her inside the Saina's room. He pushed her inside hard and watched around cautiously. Then closed the door. Samuel knew Saina and Yesmin would never be returned back before evening.

"What are you doing Samuel?"

Samuel unhurriedly reached to her and seized her from the shoulders.

"Don't be afraid, you silly girl, we are going play some secret game," he grinned.

Arianna stared at him. His sudden, awkward behaviour left her dazed and confused.

"Look Arianna it's a different game I have watched it many days throughout the mother's broken window. She had lot of friends previously. I mean before your birth."

"Did granny have friends?"

"Of course, she had many wealthy friends who used to come here frequently, and they did some specific game with her. And they brought a lot of gifts to us."

"Oh, I never have heard about such kind of thing, Samuel."

"Even your mother is aware of it, Arianna, sometimes both of us used to watch it secretly," he said in a hushed voice.

"I wonder what you speak about, Samuel."

"Ok, you have to close your eyes now"

"Why would I close my eyes Samuel?."

"Stop your all questions Arianna. Do as, what I'm saying to you," Samuel said madly.

"Ok I will do."

Arianna shut her eyes.

"What are going to do, Samuel?"

"Arianna, you promised to me if you don't agree to play this, I will tell your secret to aunt," he muttered in a threatening sound.

Arianna pondered silently.

"If mother got to know about stealing cheese from Uncle Hugo's home, she would beat me definitely. Grandma, Grandpa, Uncle Hugo and even aunt might wrongly have a thought about me as a bad girl. No, no I can't; let it happen to me"

"Do you hear me, Arianna? First, you have to stretch on the bed to begin our game," Samuel shouted.

However, eventually, Arianna decided to agree with Samuel. She lay on the Saina's bed. Samuel slowly came and sat beside her.

"Ok, then close your eyes once more and stay calm. You cannot speak up until I say finish if you did so you will be the loser."

Arianna shut her eyes tightly and obeyed him.

He touched Arianna's breast and began to fondle her entire body.

Indeed, Samuel didn't have any clear idea about what he was doing, but he desired to imitate certain things he had watched since he was a small child.

"Is it over now, I feel awkward Samuel?" Arianna asked after a few minutes.

"Can you recall what I said to you, Arianna if you break the rules again, I will surely make you as the loser."

Samuel was still touching her young body. He sensed some strange feelings that he had never felt before.

"Oh, You are so delicate, Arianna," he murmured.

"Samuel can you please finish this game" Arianna shouted once again.

"Ok you are not listening to me so I won the game today, you are the loser" Samuel grinned.

"So what should I supposed to do after that"

Samuel leaned over to her petite body and peeked at her face.

"You have to come with me to play this game once again."

"Oh dear, I have to keep my mouth shut next time."

"Alright, you Silly girl, we should leave now" he stood up.

"Don't ever tell me like that, you silly grumpy Samuel" Arianna pushed him angrily and turned around to move out.

"Arianna," Samuel halted her in a flash and drew her back to his side.

"What's now."

Arianna looked at him irritated.

"You have to promise to me Arianna to never ever spill a words about this to anyone if you do so I"

Samuel stopped his words and peered at her face.

"No, no, I promised you, Samuel. I will keep whole this as a secret forever," Arianna confirmed.

"Ok, end of, our new game we both agreed to protect our secrets," Samuel announced with a bright smile.

After that, Samuel played this game with Arianna for many days when they got alone. He got addicted to the strange feeling of thrill while touching her. Hence, his immature desires aroused each moment; therefore, he couldn't stop himself. Some unknown pleasure tempted him to sense her body moreover. He remembered the brightly blooming flower when he saw her lying on the bed.

Poor Arianna, who spent her life as a helpless, unprotected child, never knew the harsh truth of all these awful circumstances around her. Though Yesmin cared and loved her, she could not make any deep bond with her. On the other hand, Yesmin never presented herself as a mother. Her children grew up according to their own agendas, which seemed to be neither bothered by Yesmin. Hence, Yesmin raised Arianna, likewise, she is adopting some attractive pets. She loved her without acknowledging the danger. Honestly, Yesmin is not aware of the risk.

On the other hand, Yesmin regrets ruining Arianna's innocent life. Her unforgiving, deep heart blamed herself for all the catastrophes. As she is aware, Luma would never bother Arianna. Yesmin worried about Arianna's future and what would happen after her and Saina's deaths.

"I wish if I can stay more years until you grow up but I'm afraid that, I'm getting older and the death is getting pretty close to me each second" she sighed bitterly while gazing at Arianna, who sleeps quietly closer to her.

However, her devastating soul needs some rest to spare herself from that awful guilt and uncertainty.

Thus, she chased god and implored the supreme being to make Arianna's bright and colourful future. She invariably thought that would protect her mostly affectionate granddaughter.

Arianna reached her ninth birthday. Luma frequently visited to see Arianna. Wilson always tried to show his false affection toward her. He only needed to make her sit on his lap, but Arianna escaped from his hands quickly. Arianna agreed with Samuel to play his game whenever they got isolated. Even though she did not wish to play it, she was afraid of breaking promises. Saina grew old day by day. He kept dozing off all day, sitting on the log. Yesmin was routinely weakened, and Arianna had to help with most household chores. Samuel received much aid from his secret father. A short, stout, fair-skinned, bald-haired man constantly meets up with Samuel. He was a famous merchant of Thebeslon. Ultimately, Samuel joined him. Then, he commenced travelling around the kingdom to sell the goods with his secret, most opulent father. He used to bring many gifts to his family when he returned home.

But he never stopped his unpleasant play with Arianna. Even though he realised the exact profound truth of all of it. He didn't want to halt it. Returning home, he dragged Arianna to isolated, hidden places to play with her. One gloomy evening forced Arianna repeatedly to come with him. Yesmin was sleeping as she had been unwell during the past few days. Arianna was lying on the bed, tears dripping down her face. Soon, she began to sob. Samuel ceased his hands.

"Why Arianna" Samuel asked kindly.

"Will you stop this, please, Samuel? I am fed up with all these."

"I thought you were enjoying our game, Arianna"

"No, I never ever enjoyed it, Samuel, and not anymore," Arianna lamented.

She raised hurriedly and wiped her tears.

"I'm not hurting you Arianna and I'm not harming you. I want to touch you only. Please let me do so you are absolutely aware how much I like you" he came close to her and placed his hands on her shoulders.

"No,"

"Why do you want to touch me Samuel, so far you are performing this awkward game only with me and each day you threatened me to not tell it anybody."

Arianna shrugged her shoulders and walked away.

"look, Arianna, what I have brought to you."

He slowly took a necklace and a piece of cottage cheese and showed them to her.

Arianna turned to the other side to escape from his eyes.

"I don't want these, Samuel, and I'm not craving to eat cottage cheese anymore, never ever," she said in a broken voice.

"Arianna I did want to hurt you and we are not doing any kind of wrong deed"

"I don't care whether it is right or wrong you started it, and you did never want to finish it every day you won and I became the loser. I can't be that loser anymore. Please don't do this with me Samuel"

"Ok then let's change the rules you can win I will become the winner and I am not going to touch you. We can play oppositely."

He halted his words and raised her chin.

"you can win it all the time."

"Don't ever try to touch me, Samuel"

Arianna pushed him away harshly and ran away.

Samuel chased her and grasped her by her arm.

"Arianna," he shouted out loud.

"Please do leave me alone Samuel I beg you, I promise to you. I will never tell anyone about this secret. Let me go please," Arianna sobbed. Samuel released his hands with shocked eyes.

For many days, Arianna didn't talk with Samuel. She ignored him. Samuel decided to start his journey again. Arianna didn't show herself to say goodbye to him, so he sighed sadly and drew his legs. However, He didn't return back to Thebeslon for a long time. The seasons passed, letting Arianna grow up peacefully. Arianna carried on her ordinary life. Sometimes, her eyes seemed to wet slightly. She quickly wiped it out and began to massage Yesmin's paining limbs. When Yesmin began snoring, Arianna moved her legs out of the house. She walked along the path. And turned to the way ahead of the woods. She wondered inside the wood. Her deep heart was seeking someplace that was hidden in her childhood memories. Finally, she reached that creek and sat down under the oak shade. Arianna gazed at the stream and listened to its murmuring sound. Shortly, she commenced weeping, beating the voice of the water.

"My dear"

Arianna raised her head with that kind of call.

"Goddess Atunura," she mumbled.

"Mother," Arianna stood up and ran towards her. The goddess wore a shiny indigo dress, her lengthy hair assembled with blue roses. She was carrying a bucket of lavender.

"I was much awaited to see, you mother."

Arianna cuddles her. Arianna sensed the infinite love overflowing through Mother Nature.

"Why all these tears, my dear."

"I want to drift away from this gloomy sadness, mother. I am tired enough with it, I cannot hold it anymore. All I am alone."

"Forget the joy, my dear. Then you won't meet the misery, all the sorrows last until the smile. If you can halt yourself chasing for exultant all this suffering be vanquished."

"How would I do it mother? It is impossible."

"The dusk stays until the dawn, the cold would survive until the warmth. When you are living in this entity you are only dreaming but once you are awakened you can descry the soul."

"I frustrated with the struggles sometimes it's a horrendous nightmare," Arianna sighed.

"You may sense the outer world parallel to the desires inside you, so my dear tear down the desires then you will be capable to reject the illusion."

"Mother, please take me with you I want to be with you whole time"

"It's too early Arianna you have so far to walk and I can see someone is waiting for you."

Arianna gazed at the sparkling eyes of the goddess, and suddenly, all the shadows vanished with the fading sun rays.

CHAPTER 15

L ife revolves around each moment. Maybe it is a conjuring trick, a dream, a delusion of hopes and expectations you created by giving specific power. Struggles to make them a reality while searching to end them. Unfortunately, this dream has no end until you conceive the truth. The truth will bring you the agony of absolute reality. It will wound you. The agony is the only reflection of deeper understanding. Until then, your thoughts bound with emotions are unstoppable. The emotions bloom with patterns that die within a split second, creating another bundle. Thus, the present remains the familiar reward of history, and the future is the mysterious gift of the present. There's no pause in mind abundant in thoughts, and it is wearisome to find the roots. Yet only the persistence of emotions that govern an individual is visible evidence. The whole world remarked inside the eyes fluctuates with the contrast. Hence, each creature struggles for equivalence. They yearn to light up the darkness to feel the magnificent blessing of the living instead of agony. Thus, each soul chases what they desire rather than what they receive.

Arianna reached her youth and became extraordinary primarily because of her beauty, yet very little is known about her tender heart—Yesmin, who grew older and unwell each season. Arianna always comforts her. Yesmin waited for Samuel, who hadn't visited them for a long time. Poverty veiled them around constantly; however, Luma handled only a few coins for Arianna's sake. She blamed Seth, Hugo, and the others for neglecting Saina and Yesmin. Eventually, Arianna commenced teaching dancing to little kids. She courageously earned some coins to heed her poor grandparents. Arianna had to work hard every day. She woke up early and helped Yesmin with all the household chores.

Some days, she visited Luma when Wilson was not around. Yesmin always recalled Samuel and expected him to come home. But Arianna secretly satisfied his long-term absence and carried out her habitual lifestyle with re-lief. However, She tried to find her inner peace by helping others. She walked inside the woods many days, then relaxed quietly under the oak tree for a few minutes. The murmuring sound of the creek healed her utterly. She became familiar with her loneliness. In whatever way, everything remained calm until she met that unexpected visitor. That young man suddenly appeared in her sight and ceased her heart for a while. She found some strange familiarity in his enchanting blue eyes. Though he seemed messy with his old raggy clothes, Arianna was captivated by his charming smile. His words with overflowing kindness elated her unconditionally. His warm breath thumped her wounded heart. But somehow, she tried to escape from him. Indeed, she yearns to flee from her bottom heart, immensely wandering around that unknown man. Hence, Arianna drew her legs forcibly away from the creek. Many times, she hid near the bush and watched him.

"He is waiting for me," she said to herself.

Arianna tried to halt her emotions to drive him out of her mind. But again, unexpectedly, he appeared in front of her. He admired her. His sympathetic words touched her heart more than her ears.

"Angel, am I an angel? Why did he introduce me so?" Arianna questioned herself and pondered alone about her wretched life. Yet the whole joyous found to be so far from her. She has seen the people laugh and spend their moments with much completion. But for herself, it may be far away.

"I am still seeking, and I am expecting something which does not belong to me," she thought miserably.

"Or else I am attached to his sympathetic words. Why I can't get away from it" she blamed, alone. Without any notice, that unknown gesture haunts all over each minute. Arianna became anxious about herself. Eventually, she seemed irritated about her unrestrained emotions. However, her abandoned mind made her insensible about the outer world. One night after dinner, Ari-anna was washing some dishes. However, her mind ran through the memo-ries. His dazzling blue eyes disturb her. She fastened her eyes in a flash to avoid those images. But suddenly her hand slipped and broke some dishes. Yesmin hurriedly came to the kitchen with that cracking sound.

"My dear, did you get hurt?" Yesmin asked anxiously.

"I'm sorry, granny, it's all my mistake. I interrupted your sleep."
Arianna replied worriedly.

"Go and sleep, my dear. You must be tired because you are working the whole day without a rest" Yesmin came closer and patted Arianna's head.

"No, granny, please don't be sad. I am fine."
Yesmin sighed regretfully.

"You have to pay all the debts of sins though you are not liable for any," Yesmin sniffles.

"No, granny, I am happy to stay with you and grandpa."
Arianna carefully aids Yesmin in sitting on an old wooden chair beside them. Yesmin gazed at Arianna downheartedly. Arianna sat on the floor beneath Yesmin and then kept her head on her lap.

"Oh granny, I have a terrible headache these days. I wonder when I will be able to be cured." Arianna whispered.

Yesmin began to rub Arianna's forehead. Arianna peacefully shut her eyes. Yesmin's smooth touch relieved her greatly. Arianna wanted to end her inner struggles. Besides, she had to battle more and more to conceal herself from the outer world. She didn't want to make others visible her transformation, though. But each day, she eventually got fed up arguing against her heart each moment. However, that young man's spellbinding gesture followed her unstoppably at every moment.

"My dear, why do you try to cease your emotions let it flow. Feel it you ought to be sensed it whatever the consequences. Unbound yourself, Arianna."

The voice of Mother Atunura whispered to her ears. Arianna opened her eyes, letting morning sun rays sneak inside her. She sighed and woke up silently.

"I will meet him up because I don't want to halt this anymore I am so exhausted," she confirmed.

Nevertheless, Arianna made uncountable visits to the woods and sat under the oak tree for many hours, but she was not alone. Her entire soul mutedly twisted with that unknown, mysterious blue eyes.

"I am caught inside some magical spell."
Arianna mumbled, staring at him.

"Me too," he said, peering into her eyeshadows.

They were stretching on the floor, gazing at the blue sky. The Oak leaves danced with the humming pitch of the soft breeze.

"So what are we supposed to do now, she asked in a hushed tone. Once again, Armion leaned over to her.

"Would you come to my tree house?"

"I can't."

"Why?"

"Are you afraid of me?"

"No"

"I know you still feel like I am a stranger,

didn't you Arianna?"

"You are wrong it is not like that. I didn't even ask your name, but each day I came to meet you without questioning." Arianna raised her head, peeking at him.

He sighed.

"I am currently imprisoned inside you; I can't escape from it," Arianna said softly, lying on his chest.

"If it so I am pleased," he smiled.

"Would you like to visit my tree house to watch the stars at night?" he asked secretly.

"At night," Arianna repeated.

"Don't worry, and I will come to get you at your house."

Arianna gasped with widened eyes.

"But what will happen if someone might spot us."

"Why do you bother about others, Arianna it's only you and me."

"Ok, I have to leave now," Arianna said, standing up.

He grasped her hand, dragging her to sit beside him.

"I will come to take you tonight. So be ready to go when everyone drops into sleep, Armion murmured.

Arianna chuckled, then released herself from him and ran away,

"Arianna, you can't break this promise," he shouted aloud. His deep voice wandered through the woods.

Arianna returned to the home and locked the door in her chamber. She breathed vaguely. Then, she slowly walked close to the mirror. Arianna smiled at the mirror.

"Why I am so delighted," she spoke to herself and shut her eyes for a split second.

When the night arrived, Arianna tried to stop her pounding heart. But, instead, she felt entirely jumbled with some wonderous surprise. However, Arianna secretly stepped out when Yesmin and Saina set off to deep sleep. But in a flash, she got arrested by someone's strong arms. Arianna struggled in fear.

"Don't shout it's me, Arianna," he whispered to her ears.

Arianna nodded and wrapped her arms around his neck, cuddling him. He lifted her slowly and carried her out.

After a while, he approached where he had settled his horse. Armion aided her to sit, and he drove it hurriedly.

"Is this your horse?" Arianna questioned confusedly.

"This is not the time for inquiry, hold me tight, or else you can lose your balance," Armion commanded.

"Nobody to save you if you fell down," he smirks.

"I feel bit scary," she murmured.

"Then close your eyes, Arianna."

Arianna holds him tightly and shuts her eyes. Then, after some time, he stopped the horse.

"I'm not going to open my eyes,"

"Never mind, you better stay like that," he twinkled. Then he calmly stepped down and set his foot towards Arianna.

"Ok, now slowly clap on my back. I'm going to take to my palace," Armion said while enclosing her arms around his neck.

"A palace, I wonder about your castle," she smiled.

Armion climbed to the top of his treehouse carefully. Arianna bundled up her hands and wrapped them around his neck while her legs twisted around his waist. A small lamp lit the place. Armion climbed to the top of the tree without haste. Later, They both lay down leisurely and stared at each other.

"Who are you? If you are slave how did you get a horse?"

Her finger ran through his eyebrows, nose and lips.

"I am lonely and miserable same as you, and we are seeking some shelter from ourselves, Arianna."

"But I'm afraid," she raised and covered her face with both palms.

"Why do you afraid of the night."

"I am not afraid of the night except the gloomy darkness, one day, that darkness stole away my father from me forever, this dark reminds me of his warmth and how he cuddles me" Arianna ceased her words and began to sob. Armion kissed her and thoroughly seized her inside him, showing his enormous love.

"Look, the stars are shining, Arianna. He said in a hushed tone; they can drift away that gloomy darkness."

"Listen to me, Arianna; I walked alone among the woods many nights. I have visited many mysterious places all alone. But I sensed nothing in there except that horrendous false delusion created in our mind." He stopped his words to kiss her wet cheeks.

"Then I began to pursue actual truth, which is invisible in that fallacy."

"I know you are fearless and brave, unlike me," Arianna whispered.

"No, I'm not Arianna. I am afraid the gloomy nightmares appear in most of my dreams; they are halting my breath, letting my muscles freeze and immobilise, and gradually, I will become powerless. So I suffer whole through the night, But still, I can't escape from them," he sighed. Arianna stroked his face, and her fingers moved along his neck. Then, unexpectedly, she noticed a necklace dangling down.

"What is this?" she asked suspiciously, glancing at the shining Tanzanite.

"It's a special gift from my grandmother," he chuckled.

Arianna touched it and peeked at his face again.

"Who are you?" she mumbled.

"You may find it someday, I am after you every day of life and even after the death. You are mine, Arianna"

"I don't want to know, but I am wondering. I want to sense this exultation forever, and I fear losing it," Arianna whispered while placing her head on his shoulder.

"I feel so scared I can't be separated from you I am so desperate. Please don't do anything harmful," she wiped her tears.

"I am not Arianna nothing can harm me,"

Arianna straightly looked at him.

"As you have mentioned, you are a stranger to Thebeslon, and I wonder why prince Joser treats his servants so sympathetically, yet I have heard many bad stories about him."

"Are you doing some secret mission?"

Armion smirks.

"Maybe I will do some mission for the sake of the whole kingdom, but however it's too early"

"It's not a joke prince Joser is so cruel he is not like prince Armion," Arianna cried.

"What do you know about prince Armion Arianna? Have you met him or talked with him?."

"No," Arianna nodded.

"I have never met him, but my grandpa and grandma and each person in the kingdom praise his kindness. They said he is very much unlike the other royals."

"If it so I think he would be delighted to hear this all" Armion smiled. His finger roamed around her rosy lips.

"What else do you know about him, Arianna? I would like to listen to those all stories whole this night."

"Not much, but my granny said that he will end up in poverty and recreate the golden period of the Kingdom Thebeslon." So do you believe Prince Armion can achieve his goal, Arianna?"

"Of course, he possesses a good heart; therefore, he has all the blessings to accomplish his dreams," Arianna replied with sparkling eyes. Armion stared at her speechlessly.

Then he began to kiss her again while arresting her inside him.

"So tell me, Arianna do you grant your blessings to him when he becomes King."

"Yes, I wished him good luck every day," Arianna murmured.

"So what if he wants to meet you, and he might inquire from you what do you desired to have? I mean any dreams that you wish to fulfil. He is such a mighty and prestigious king who rules the entire kingdom" Armion paused his words while glimpsing at her eyes.

"The king can do anything," he added.

"Oh I don't think he will bother about the dreams of a worthless poor girl like me," Arianna laughed.

"Why? Do you say you are worthless you are so precious to him."

"What do you tell?" Arianna queried.

"I mean you are so precious to me," he whispered.

"So answer my question, Arianna."

"I will implore him for you to grant freedom and stay with me forever" Arianna smiled.

"Are you sure?" Armion asked.

"I don't remember anything that I want to see your happiness; that is my dream," she sighed.

Armion stared at her.

"Those are the most beloved words I have heard." They stared at each other for a few seconds. Then, Arianna suddenly raised her head.

"Look, we didn't watch the stars," she reminded me.

"I am no more interested in watching other stars, Arianna because I am holding the most prized gem on my hands."

"I know it will spark my gloomy nightmares," he added.

"I feel sleepy." Arianna yawned.

"I want to sleep on your chest," she mumbled.

"I used plump on my fathers' chest ages ago when I was small, and it was so cosy I the slept whole night."

Armion chuckled and lay down, letting her stretch on his broad chest. He patted her lovingly until she fell into a deep sleep.

"How would I let you know about my exact truth, Arianna? Of course, I am not aware of your reaction, but I will solve this whole puzzle someday and you will be mine forever," he thought, silently touching her beautiful face.

The gloaming robe shifted away with morning sunbeams.

"Oh, my God, I have to leave now."

Arianna stood up anxiously.

"Why so hurry, Arianna" Armion rubbed his sleepy eyes.

I must go before granny wakes. Otherwise, It would be a disaster," she shouted.

"Oh my God, I cannot raise my body it's all paralysed," Armion cried.

"What happened?" Arianna came close to him hurriedly.

"A big whale slept on my chest," he muttered with a bright smile.

"Are you hurt?" She attempted to raise him, grasping his arm. But Armion instantly tugged her hand, and she fell on him.

"What have you done" Arianna screamed.

Armion embraced her." What have you done to me? Please don't leave."

He quickly tried to grab her lips. But Arianna hastily pushed him with a smile and moved away.

"I am getting late," she sighed. Then she drew back her steps towards Armion and hugged him tightly.

"Let me drive you back to your home. Please don't go alone," he said, tightening his head on her silky hair and kissing it.

"I don't want to endanger your life, so let me go alone."

"If I have to leave you someday do you get angry with me Arianna" he inquired while turning her face to his side.

"No, I would never ever," she confirmed.

"Why you should hate me if such circumstance happened between us."

"I know that you will disappear someday like my father," she sighed.

"But I respect your affectionate towards; there's no hatred, not even closer. I am not craving to seize you for the sake of mine. You are free to leave me any time on behalf of your success"

"I am devoted to you, Arianna," he snatches both her hands.

"Thanks for loving me whole these moments will be unforgettable memories to me," she kissed his hands while staring at him.

"It is, you, Arianna, you brought this wholehearted love to me ; you don't need to be gratitude for me. You are the one who heals me. You are like a colourful rainbow suddenly became visible in my life. I will always heal whenever you beside me."

Arianna kissed his forehead.

"I will come back soon near the forest creek wait for me," she whispered.

"I am waiting for you every day, Arianna."

"Let me leave now before somebody gets noticed us."

Armion pulled her again from her hand.

"Just hold my hand, Arianna," he pleaded.

Arianna kissed his hand, quickly peeped out of the treehouse, and then looked around cautiously. Only the white mist covered the entire woods. Arianna slowly gets down from the treehouse. She walked fast in the woods. Arianna secretly crept inside the house and panted. She found Yesmin and Saina still sleeping.

She sat down on the old wooden chair, recalling whole memories.

"He loves me, he admired me. he waits for me," she whispered.

"Mother Atunura, he loves me, and I am much precious to him am I?" she smiled alone. Then, she stood up and twirled around merrily.

"My dear, why did you wake up so early? You should have some rest." Yesmin yawned, pulling her messy hair.

"I am fine; granny simply woke up early today" Arianna looked down shyly. Yesmin hauled her shaky limbs towards Arianna.

"Wait granny I will ready the tea" Arianna helped Yesmin sit on the chair.

"It's a beautiful morning, my dear, and you seemed to be so cheerful" Yesmin held Arianna's hand.

"Oh, it's nothing, granny, that I saw some sunflowers blooming up in my garden."

"You are more than beautiful than sunflower. My dear do you know I am begging to God to secure my life until the time that I can lend your hand to someone who holds a good heart. Then only I can join my death peacefully. Otherwise, you will alone," Yesmin sobbed.

"Oh granny"

Arianna quickly grabs Yesmin's hands.

"You will have a long life granny don't worry."

Arianna wiped Yesmin's tears.

"I made a mistake, my dear. We created all these troubles for you. I separated your father from you. Now everyone owns their blissful lives but only you are holding all these distress. You were born as a princess in that mansion, but we utterly ruined you" Yesmin thought silently. She was unaware of how to run away from her guilt.

....

Armion came back to the palace. He set off his horse and walked inside the castle. Hatra noticed Armion, who was walking towards his chamber. She woke up early and suddenly thought about having some fresh air outside. However, she accidentally sighted Armion. Hatra was stunned by his appearance. He was wearing some simple clothes similar to those of an ordinary person. So Hatra made herself hide from his eyes. She waited in the small passage behind the rocky arch near Armion's room. Hatra paused her steps until Armion shut his door.

"What on earth he is doing much earlier in the morning? It seemed that he hasn't spent his night in his room," Hatra mumbled suspiciously. She spent a few minutes and then walked back to the garden confusedly. Hatra kept thinking about Armion; she didn't even notice Hatop sitting beside her.

"What's the issue dear?" Hatop asked.

Hatra shook with the unexpected voice and beamed.

"Glad to see you, Hatop, so early this morning," she smiled.

"It's nothing. I saw Armion, and I assumed he was not in his room last night."

"If it so, no wonder he is roaming throughout the jungle. Your mother accustomed that unusual habit to him. Therefore she is responsible for all these nuisances. So don't bother me with these worthless matters," He said roughly.

"Oh, I didn't bother you, Hatop, and this is not a worthless matter; it's about our son Armion. And please do remember he is the future king of the kingdom.

So if we neglect him, we might lose our dignity and authority." Hatra glared at him madly and walked back to the castle. In the evening, Hatra went to Armion's chamber, holding a dish decorated with his favourite sweets. She stretched it towards Armion with a pleasant smile.

"I made whole this to you my son" Hatra kissed his head lovingly.

"Thanks for your delicious dish," he replied.

"You looks tired my son are you doing well" she questioned kindly.

"I am fine and all good mother," he grinned.

." Armion." Hatra raised her voice and presented a short glimpse at him.

"You are reaching your right age, Armion. Why don't you think about set-
tling your life? As a crown prince, you should marry a perfect princess."

Armion chuckled.

"Don't take this all as a joke Armion" Hatra frowned.

"I am not after the affluent royal princesses' mother I am concerned about
a soul who can twisted with me wholeheartedly."

"What are you saying Armion?"

"What do you know about love mother?"

Hatra sighed.

"What a magnificent question, my son; as you know, I have sacrificed my
entire life to you I raised you in between endless troubles. I gave birth to you,
and you became my entire world and my only hope. That is my sole evidence
for my awareness of love. And that is my story of love."

Hatra looked at Armion with eyes full of tears.

"I have heard it many times throughout the ages" Armion looked down.

"I can talk endlessly about my endurance as a mother of you."

"Endless talks means endless hopes mother; endless talks tells the nature
of endless attachments. Endless laughter or endless tears it all simply attachments. It is the sole evidence for being trapped in this illusion." Armion stared
out from the balcony.

"Maybe," Hatra said.

"So what is your plan about forthcoming years' Armion."

"Simply, I am not planning my future mother, I have nothing to hunt
There's' nothing existing physically according to my awareness So I have no
battle to possess a physical values. Yet everything remained in our thoughts.
we chase for the things to satisfy our mind. Hence all those victories we
gained are merely contenting our mind. Still we deeply stick with that phan-
tom and attempt to secure it until the end."

"Armion, you have a responsibility in your hands. You should be conscious
of each simple aspect relevant to you. You cannot behave recklessly."

"I know about myself, mother, and I am not doing anything harmful"

"But" he paused.

Hatra wrinkles her forehead.

"What?"

"I am not desired marry any elegant princess' mother. So don't force me to do so. I wish to marry a simple girl with a big heart. I want to give my hand someone who is isolated and rejected I want to see her smile instead of tears. And I am desired to change someone's' pathetic, life to a mostly successful"

"Armion" Hatra exclaimed.

"That is my ultimate wish, mother and I would not ever change it," Armion confirmed, gazing at Hatra.

CHAPTER 16

Queen Hatra think about the Armion the whole night. The sleep was unable to meet her eyes. Lord Hatop didn't worry or bother her thoughts; he slept peacefully and snored loudly. Hatra silently got down from the bed and stepped towards the balcony. She gazed at the dark night. The moon ceased its shine, covered by an unknown cloud beside. However, the stilly night welcomed her mutedly. The Autumn breeze joined with the rustling sound of the falling leaves. Hatra shut her eyes and breathed. Suddenly, a black shadow stood in front of her,

"You must visit me with Hatop. He will bring you to my place because he cannot deny my command. You have only to remind him about the journey in the morning" The shadow groaned and disappeared. Hatra wiped her eyes, stared at the dark for a while and sighed.

"Armion, you are shifting yourself further, unusual to me daily. Your words imply to me that I should tie my knot strongly. Otherwise, all my efforts might be destroyed."

She muttered to herself. Early the following day, Hatra woke up with the first raised Sun rays.

"Hatop," Hatra shook his shoulders. Hatop opened his eyes confusedly.

"We must get ready for that journey," Hatra whispered.

Hatop rubbed his eyes and looked around.

"Orana, she is waiting,,, the cave," he stammered, gazing at Hatra.

After some time, they secretly escaped from the castle. Hatop rode his horse among the dark, hidden route in a gloomy, thick wood. Giant trees bounded together and stood beside them with their crowded green roofs of crowns. The large vines entangled around their mighty trunks. They rode further inside the path, built up with queer darkness. Finally, the way ended near the small lake surrounded by reddish-brown bushes. Though the water was not blue, it seemed grey and black. Beside the lake, a rock shelter path opened to a pitchy dark. Both of them got down from the horse. Hatop tied the horse to the tree trunk nearby, and then he held Queen Hatra's hand and slowly raised their steps inside the den. They walked forward and waited beside a gigantic stone wall. Suddenly, the wall opened, letting them inside another narrow, shadowy pathway. They led furthermore, and numerous bright red candles were lit at the end. They halted again on the floor covered with white sand and looked around. The remaining area was filled with blue water, which miraculously shone. The roof is surrounded by red edgy crystal knobs, letting Some crystals swell and stretch beyond the water. The entire passage was a half-curving area that glittered with red and blue. At the end of the path, a dark shadow was facing an enormous, shiny, reddish crystal rock. She was silently standing between the other two lengthy, ruddy crystals. The entire hallway was lighted with blazing red.

"Orana" Hatra exclaimed. The dark shadow turned around, holding a long, slender, glistening black stick in one of her hands. A sparkling giant fiery black viper coiled around her shaft, with the eyes shimmering in bright orange. Another one seemed to be twined throughout her waist. It hissed violently with great open-mouthed eyes; simultaneously, its tiny eyes appeared as red crystals. A slender necklace like numerous black vipers curled all over her arms. She patted them with her long fingers with sharp, bright black nails. But they hissed furiously with endless anger. Eventually, She came forward with a bent head covered with a black veil. Though she was standing on the water, neither her legs touched it. Indeed, she didn't walk. But float on it. Finally, however, her shadowy gesture paused, and a small distance rested between them.

"Your Majesty," A woman with a gritty voice uttered to Hatra. She is slim and is wearing a thick black gown that shines slightly. She raised her head. Her auburn, curly, tangled hair unfolded to the knee and became visible between the long black veil. However, Her quiet, mysterious look enhanced her sharply pointed chin and long neck. She owns a stubborn face with cold cheeks visibly shined and pale, thin lips. Her bushy, sickle-formed black eyebrows met her blazing Rubicon serpentine eyes. It was hard to notice a tiny smile on her pale, annoying lips, yet sometimes she laughed out loud like the rumbling thunder of a gale.

"I was expecting your visit, Queen Hatra" Orana smirks.

"I believe your expectation can resolve my issues, Orana."

Orana turned around and lifted her stick.

"Go ahead, Queen Hatra," she commanded.

"Armion is changing each day; therefore, I am afraid that he might release our all bonds."

"If it is so, we all might need to trap him with my enchanting spell." Orana laughed.

"Orana, this is not a joke. He must do whatever we desire to do. He must respect and obey ourselves"," Hatop opened.

"You never believed in me, Lord Hatop aren't you? and currently, you chase after my powers of black."

"I believe your dream Orana. You guided me so far."

"So," Hatop whispered.

"Armion behaved differently in his childhood, so I could not trust his capacities somehow, everything changed unexpectedly," He expressed silently.

"You all would never trust him, and his soul might never be twisted with all of us because we are different." Orana turned around and looked straight at them.

"Why do you mean by different?" Hatra questioned.

"We are the souls governed by the black vipers, but prince Armion is a pure soul who belongs to nature. However, he was born at a highly auspicious time; hence he had the enormous fortune to become a ruler of the whole Henaten. But..." she stopped her words.

"What?" Hatop asked.

"The opposing force of vipers will cease him for an extended period," Hatop beamed.

"If so, what about prince Joser?" he queries with glittery eyes.

"Well, he is fortunate to become a member of a royalty; nonetheless, he is not strong enough to become an emperor. Though he is soul energy by the vipers, he is less powerful than prince Armion. He is not living with nature. The nature denied powering his soul because it's not vivid. Joser walks ahead, but he will only touch with falsity. Eventually he will be stuck inside his it. Armion is stepping behind to seek the actuality."

Hatop sighed with the Orana's' reply.

"Lord Hatop, when you have a heart filled with hatred, greed, and delusion, you will ultimately become a victim of suffering. The vipers enchant you by healing your pain. Then your soul will bring rebirth incessantly to fulfil the role governed by the world of black vipers. That is indeed a wheel of the existence of life. The vipers show you the taste of the promises that belong to the upcoming. Though it is a fallacy, it will survive in your mind as realistic. Sooner they will abandon you all inside that mysterious hallucination." Orana patted the snakes, hissing while speaking.

"Joser," Hatop whispered.

"Prince Armions soul denied these three poisons; hence, the vipers couldn't attach him. Only their negative power drew him back. But the energy of nature drives him continually until he meets his final destination. The power of equanimity will make him a governor of his own soul. Therefore, he is eligible to become the emperor of Henaten."

"Orana, I cannot let the bird soar as it wishes because I possess it. I brought it up, slaughtering my life. Therefore, I need to bind it. He indebted to me forever," Hatra shouted out.

Orana wrinkles her forehead. The vipers began to twirl their heads with enclosed fearful maws. Meanwhile, they hissed uninterruptedly.

"Slow down, your majesty. You will make my babies frightening," Orana scowled. She turned back and moved away from them.

"Queen Hatra, you are seeing yourself through the mirror, but it hasn't been wiped for ages. Try to uncover you. Discover about your mind because you are incomplete. Your spirit remains fragmented up to that time. You will be the victim of dark expiration with this imperfect life. You must not expect victory from this competition. This is merely to acknowledge your failure. You can meet your rescue by realising your fault. Hence, wipe your mirror for the freedom of your soul. Simply because this process will purely catch each person on a monotonous ride"

Orana smiled, looking upward.

"Orana, we should protect our future. Only Armion is capable of it. We need to have a mighty spell to conceal him only with us" Hatop announced.

"Why are you so worried about the future, Lord Hatop?"

"We should chase for our future, Orana, before you lose it."

Orana laughed out loud, shaking her whole body.

"You begin your journey wandering about the end, but it is tragic to see that you cannot recall it in the middle of your path. However, you try to survive throughout. But you will gain nothing. Isn't it terrific, lord Hatop.?"

"Probably I wait to respond to your riddles Orana," he said. Hatra shook her head,

"Orana, I can live my life peacefully if Armion is attached to us. I am yearning for my contentment."

"Queen Hatra, you suffered because you have loosened the bliss of your soul. You are attached only with your physique, not with your deep heart. Profoundly you have killed your spirit?. You live in your life grabbing your emotions which arose according to each situation."

"What am I supposed to do? I am bonded to the whole of these. It's an obligation to secure my family" Hatra murmured.

"The bright illumination of the sun fools you convinced there is no darkness exists, but shortly after the sun is gone, the dusk appears and implies you there is no shining afterwards. Unfortunately, each second it trapped misleads you about this fantasy. Alas, It drags you away from the liberation."

"I want to die peacefully Orana, I want see my son Joser similarly successful like Armion. But if Armion overpowered than Joser, it would agonise himself. He might have spent his whole life under the commands of Armion, that is not fair" Hatop groaned.

The vipers hissed out furiously.

"This is a world full of injustice, but while cutting your flesh by your hands, you all suspects a devoted soul of nature. You all would never spot your image through the mirror. You rejected your heart; hence you all are burning with grief."

"Orana, I beg you, please help us resolve this confusion. We want to have a clear and bright future," Hatra implored.

"The future you are talking about its mere a mystery, Queen Hatra. We are all trapped in an illusion. No future in front of you It is only an imaginary picture of your mind. Nevertheless, I am responsible for standing by you," Orana sighed.

"Though we are Ovigons, we are part of universe. My spells will halt and destroy everything for a while, but nature will find another door to accomplish its agenda. Mother nature can divert but not us. We are trapped in our dark silhouette unconditionally. Hence the liberation is far away from us."

Afterwards, she raised her shaft upward, and the vipers began to hiss violently with their shining eyes. The entire atmosphere turned to red with rumbling terrific sounds. The floor they were standing on began to shake. The water rises upward with a giant ripple. It lifted Orana upward. Suddenly, the fire appeared from crystals. Orana turned into a gigantic black viper. Who carries large, orange, blazing eyes. It whistled with a thunderous noise and had a blood-watering mouth with sharp teeth. Hatop quickly moved backwards, and Hatra grasped him tightly with a frightening face. The viper hissed continuously and twirled its large head instantly. A strong wind blew around, and, at that moment, the water had changed into an enormous ocean with tides. The vast flames encircled the water. The blood spilt out of the vipers' mouths, transforming the blue water into red. Hatra shut her eyes and hid her head inside the Hatop while his arms enclosed her strenuously. Thick smoke circled the viper immediately, transforming it into numerous black vipers. They are not gigantic but comparatively small. Their incessant, violent, hissing noise filled the air, allowing Queen Hatra to close her ears with both palms. Simultaneously, she gasped with soaking sweat.

"Release the power of Ovigons for sake of the vipers; we all are waiting to trap the soul of nature. Arrest him under the power of the evil. Black vipers are allowed to let out the energy and seized the soul inside the dark."

Orana's voice echoed through the sphere. Subsequently, the glistening black small crystal dropped down beneath the Hatop. Slowly, the entire atmosphere changed as the previous. Each thing vanished. Yet Orana didn't appear as visibly. Only her voice spoke to them. Hatra looked all over cautiously.

"What happened, all vanished suddenly," Hatra whispered to Hatop and wiped her eyes.

"Take the stone of black and hide it inside the wall of the castle," Orana's voice grunted out loud. Hatra shivered and moved backwards.

"If someone touches the hidden stone will be cursed."

"You may leave now immediately," Orana yelled.

They raised their steps rapidly to move out of the den.

"Wait," Hatop stopped confusedly.

"Remember, I am responsible only for what I have announced but not what you have heard," Orana uttered.

They bow their heads and hurriedly escape back to the castle.

....

Arianna quickly walked near the creek. She suspiciously looked throughout while walking. Finally, she spotted him waiting for her, sitting on a rock, the water slightly lapped over his feet.

"Sorry, I was late, did you wait long time?"

She came close to him.

"Of course, you made me stay a long time. Therefore, I can't accept your apologies. Armion stood up and walked towards her.

"I was teaching dancing to some kids, and I didn't realise the time," she said, slowly gazing down.

"That is not an excuse for your fault, Arianna," he smirks.

"You should face my punishment." Armion came nearby to her and dragged vaguely from her arm.

But she snuggled inside his chest, slowly raised her face, and peeked into his sparkling eyes.

"I would accept your punishment. Please punish me," Arianna murmured.

"Let me create you through my fingers" Armion touched her rosy cheeks.

"So create me you are eligible to do so." She kissed his fingers.

Armion carried her slowly, walked back to the creek, and kept her on the same rock he sat on until her arrival.

"Arianna, now you have to stay here. Don't shift away."

He footed back, staring at her. Then, he placed his hands on the clay.

"Look at me and hold your smile Arianna" he said.

While Arianna sat still, his magical fingers tied with the clay. Armion snatched her beauty through his visions.

She was wearing a yellow gown. Her long, silky hair rested on her lap. Her gorgeous face and soft, rosy lips glazed with radiant sunbeams. Her dazzling eyes are a divine invitation to himself. Indeed, her overflowing image of beauteous halted Armion's breath for seconds.

"My golden daisy flower," he whispered to himself.

The creek flows calmly while the green mountains brighten with daylight. Though the wind howls unsoundly, Butterflies hang out around in the time flowers twist with bees. Little birds hopped on the grasslands. Arianna gazed at him, her eyes charmed by his whole handsome gesture. His enticing eyes and bewitching smile enthralled her. Yet even though Arianna wished to cease unrestrained thoughts, she was imprisoned in that fantasy.

"I am stunned in this magic," she thought silently.

After a time, Armion walked back to her. When Arianna was about to open her lips, he placed one finger on them and stopped her.

"Arianna, my fingers are yearning to sense you furthermore," he whispered while leaning over to her.

"They are allowed to sense me." She lay on that flat rock, letting her long hair slip into the water. His fingertips played around her face, eyebrows and along her neck.

She closed her eyes to feel his warm breath. Then the fingers remarked their presence around her slim waist. Then, it ended the journey close to her thumping heart. Arianna felt his body leaning towards her moreover. She gasped when his lips rambled all over her neck and deep. Arianna opened her eyes to meet his.

"My soul has fallen in love with you my princess. I searched for you across the whole kingdom and beyond the Henaten," he mumbled.

"Am I?" she said slowly.

"You are like a frightened deer yet my entire spirit pined with you," he murmured, calmly kissing her.

"I belong to you. Please don't leave me."

Arianna wrapped inside Armion, her hands crossed over his neck.

"I would never ever leave you, Arianna, unless you left before me, death cannot apart us because I am seeking for your soul."

"What I give back to you forever belonged to you."

"If it so," his lips snatched hers.

"What I have to lose out on? I have nothing yet everything belongs to you."

"However," she paused.

"What" he peeks at her eyes with tears.

"Without you I am nothing, I can't find me I am nobody." She embraced him tightly.

"Then, don't leave me, Arianna, whatever the circumstances, hold my hand eternally with me."

"I will until I have to release you for your fortune."

"No, you have to stay with me if I entered in front of you in some other unexpected gesture."

"What do you mean?" She asked.

"What you see through your eyes maybe not be the reality," he sighed.

"I know I see a dream while opening my eyes, but reality waited until I close it."

"Then close your eyes and grasp the reality."

"I can't since I am bonded with that dream. Profoundly I am trapped in it. I can't save myself because there is nobody like me there."

"That's because it is a dream, Arianna."

"I am smitten with that dream; therefore, I cannot escape."

"Close your eyes to realise about the actual truth, then only you will be able to find it," he said softly.

"I would love to stay in my dream; therefore, I want to keep my eyes open. So please don't ever try to appear in front of me differently because it might hurt me a lot," Arianna whispered while cuddling him.

"I am entirely desperate and strays throughout the unknown end of this puzzle. Let me solve it, Arianna.."

"No need to solve it for my sake as I am desired to tangle it together with that unknown end." Arianna looked at him with teary eyes. Armion sighed and stared at her with all bewilderment.

....

Arianna returned back to home late in the evening. The dusk slightly arrived around. It was strange that she heard both Saina and Yesmin chatting with someone. Arianna walked in suspiciously.

"My dear, you were so late today. We waited for you," Yesmin exclaimed when she spotted Arianna.

But it was not only Yesmin. Arianna suddenly glimpsed the sight of another person.

Then, she ceased her legs and stood like a statue.

"Samuel," she uttered with shivering lips.

"How are you Arianna?" Samuel asked softly.

Arianna gave a light smile without looking at him straight.

"My dear, look at you, all your hair and clothes are wet, what happened? Are you alright?" Yesmin queries worriedly and comes close to her.

"No granny, I am just slipped down" she stammered.

Arianna turned her head with embarrassment to get rid of the Samuel's eyes. As he watched her doubtfully.

"Go and change your clothes, my dear, before you catch a cold. I will make some hot tea for you," Yemin said kindly. Arianna quickly escaped and shut the door of her room. She sighed bitterly and tumbled on her bed with a muddled mind.

"Why did he come back?" she questioned herself. Arianna spent the whole night alone inside the room and didn't come outside. She told Yesmin that she had a bad headache and wanted to sleep. Honestly, she needed to omit to confront Samuel. But Samuel waited patiently until he could chat with her again.

But the next day, early morning, Arianna prepared breakfast in the kitchen. Yesmin could not wake up because of her sore feet; hence, she rested on the bed. Arianna turned around, holding the Yesmin's tea. She was about to raise her steps to Yesmin's room. Suddenly, she gasped at the unexpected sight of Samuel, who was directly staring at her close to the entrance. Arianna halted. Her heart pounded with distress. He came closer to her gradually and stood right opposite her face. Then he grabbed the tea in her hand and slurped it.

"It's tasty as usual, you know Arianna, how much I missed your tea and food," He said in a charming voice.

Arianna smiled while keeping her head looking at the floor. Her whole body trembled. Meanwhile, Samuel placed his three fingers on her chin and lifted it upward vaguely. Their eyes met with each other.

"You are ignoring me aren't you Arianna?" He asked roughly.

"No, I am not feeling well," she faltered.

"Really, I am so sorry to hear about your sudden illness," he scowled.

"Where have you been last evening and with whom?"

"I was teaching to my students."

"You are lying, Arianna," he groaned, peering into her face.

"Why are you mad at me Samuel?"

Arianna stepped back, distressed. His rowdy face with reddish eyes made her more frightened.

"Of course, I am mad because I am worried about you," he admitted angrily.

"I have to work Samuel I have to fulfil my responsibilities," Arianna replied slowly.

"Then come with me Arianna I came here to fetch all of you to my place I am a successful merchant now I can look after both my parents and you. I have enough money so you don't need to work and suffer anymore." Samuel touched her face.

Arianna quickly removed his hand from her face.

"You can't refuse me like this Arianna I heed you when you were a baby and raised you up, how easily you have forgotten those past days. That's not fair Arianna" He glanced at her face sadly.

"If it so why you are behaving like a so ruthlessly Samuel?"

"No, I am not. See what I have brought you. So many gifts, jewellery, clothes and many things. I bought it all only for you. Not anyone else."

"I am not interested in gifts, Samuel; I am only desired about my inner peace."

"You can live as you wish. If you come with me, Arianna, you, me and my parents can have a luxurious life. There is no one to disturb if we can move out of Thebeslon."

"No, Samuel, I desired to live here," Arianna said firmly. Samuel squeezed his eyes and gave a suspicious glance at her.

"Are there any special reason for that Arianna?"

She shook her head and looked down. Samuel reached for her and slowly walked around her.

"You are becoming so beautiful daily, Arianna. Please come with me. Believe me I can give you a superior life Indeed you can live like a queen."

Arianna gleamed and raised her head.

"I am not chasing for a superior life, Samuel, and I am not yearning to become a queen. On the contrary, I am rather satisfied with my simple life. Though it is hard, I accept it happily." she paused and moved a few steps behind

"Samuel you should not appreciate about my physical appearance because you are ought to be my uncle. I respect you always if you do so" Samuel laughed out loud.

"How silly you are Arianna, you have never known how much I remembered you during this long time. Honestly I didn't meet anyone like you I missed you so much"

"But I never missed you Samuel and I never wished to see you I wanted to wipe your whole memory from my entire life." Her fainted voice pierced his heart.

"I didn't do any harm to you, Arianna. As you remember, it was just we played a game. I didn't do anything wrong to yourself, not even closer," he confirmed.

"Really, is that all merely game for you, but that memory of those dark past torturing me. I am suffocating. As a child, I have so neglected, and nobody for me. That is the actual truth."

"Forgive me, Arianna," he sighed.

"How can you ask for forgiveness? You were already older than me, Samuel. You were aware of that wrong. Now you act like a saint."

"Of course, let's forget this all past. I can bring you a bright future. Come with me Arianna I am always here for you" he placed his hands on her shoulders.

Arianna shrugged her shoulders frustratedly and moved away.

"I am not interested to have a bright future Samuel, please do behave in decent manner." she snarled.

"Yes, you were absolutely right, my dear. I am a no-good person. This is because I was born in an indecent family, And my birth happened most unacceptably. So how would you suppose I should behave like a reputable man" he laughed a few seconds, then gradually came towards her. He grabbed her chin and swiftly turned her face to his side.

"Don't worry, Arianna, I know someday will arrive soon that you agree with me. That day you will need me moreover than you reject me. Hence please don't ever hesitate to accept my kindness" Arianna pushed his hand away and moved quickly.

CHAPTER 17

Samuel drove back after a few days. He visited his brothers and sister's home with a handful of goods. Therefore, he was admired by everyone. He gave some money to Yesmin and Saina, but Arianna stayed inside her room and never came to see him. However, he kept the big box full of presents before Arianna's door. Soon after he had gone, Arianna returned all the gifts to Seth and Hugo's daughters. Yesmin wasn't surprised by Arianna's behaviour because she knew Arianna held quite simple manners. A few days passed one evening, and Arianna returned home with a gloomy face. She cried the whole night secretly.

"I don't know that I will be able to see you again," she mumbled to herself with an agonising heart.

"Your sculpture is almost complete, Arianna, and it was the most artistic creation I have ever done. I kept it in my own secret location. Someday I will take you to there and that day would be the most precious day of ours."

Arianna remembered the words that he said. She felt the warmth of his loving lips, which touched her forehead.

She spent many days lonely beside the creek. Her soul desperately sought his shadow. Her entire spirit yearns to repeatedly be trapped around his warm-hearted gesture. Eventually, she used to make up her mind to carry on her isolated life. One day, she sat beside Saina

"Grandfather, I am ready to fulfil your wish. If you consent, I would like to participate in the Thebeslon dancing festival." Arianna admitted softly.

Saina's eyes began to gleam with her words.

"My dear that's fantastic news to hear, I am sure you can bring our pride of dance," he exclaimed happily. Arianna started to do her practice daily. Intensely, she worked hard to forget his image, which was constantly veiled around her eyes.

"It's all past. Why am I crying? I should be thankful to you for making my miserable life much radiant during that small interval. Therefore I am owed to you. But all this pain because of the bond I shared with you, and I am fear of losing it." she thought silently.

Nevertheless, she worked hard until the festival, but her entire world unexpectedly collapsed when she sighted him. Instead of that simple ordinary man, he has transformed into the kingdom's crown prince. Arianna struggled to get out of her mind from this surprising storm.

"This might be the puzzle you wanted to solve, but I felt I am stuck among that maze, prince Armion," she mumbled. After that, Arianna wept alone on numerous nights.

"I have to close my eyes now to end this dream, now I am aware of that actuality, your highness but, I released you while loving you because you are suitable for better, not me. Though I am stuck with your whole heart, you have to stop solving this puzzle," Arianna confirmed to herself before falling asleep. As she shut her eyes mother, Atunura appeared in front of her,

"Look, my dear, I brought you a beautiful flower," she whispered. Arianna stretched her hands to hold that blossom. It was gorgeous, with shimmering pink blossoms and golden petals, besides the unbelievable scent unfurling throughout the sphere.

"This is the most beautiful and fragrance flower I have seen," Arianna said happily. She held it tightly and took it towards her face to sense its fragrance while closing her eyes. But suddenly, the flower vanished. Arianna opened her eyes and wondered what had happened.

"Mother the flower is gone," she shouted.

"My dear, the world exists until you see through the whole this body along with sound, sense and taste trapping, you in a fallacy. Once, you will be fooled by the bright shining and then the pitchy dark will trick you again. Whole this dream will trap you until you discover the place between the bright and the dark. Then you are eligible to unleash from the entire delirium"

"What I have to do, mother."

"Your mind seeking for thoughts for wars. The whole mind tricked you throughout the life. Eventually, it destroys you while making a distance between you and the freedom."

"I want to discover myself but?"

"The insatiable mind full of the thoughts of unrestrained never grasp the beauty of the blossom Everything is under by the power of nature. It is the superiority of all."

"I want to see the exhilaration of people around me it pleased me rather than chasing for my own satisfaction, mother."

"That is why you are accepted by nature, my dear."

Mother Atunura hold Arianna's hand.

"Do you want that flower, Arianna" she questioned?

"Yes, mother," Arianna said with a sparkling smile.

"Then don't grasp it solidly my dear see it likewise there is no flower in front of your eyes. Sense it's scent and touch it likewise there is nothing feel. Realise illusion instead of holding it down. Deeply sense the flower likewise the way of silent sky sensing it. The earth gave birth to thousands of blossoms. Though all the flowers plucked out permanently earth would never blame anyone. Hence Endure it and accept the rhythm of this swing Untie your soul my dear"

Mother Atunura's image vanished away, and Arianna abruptly woke up. She wiped her eyes and jumped out of bed. She heard Yesmin whimpering in pain. Who spends the entire day in bed because the sickness worsens each day. Arianna quickly walked into Yesmin.

A few weeks after the dance festival, Yesmin became extremely ill. She was unable to walk even for a few steps. Arianna heeded her carefully. Sometimes, Luma visited to help Arianna. But she didn't forget to make arguments between Seth and Hugo. Yesmin's trunk got wasted gradually as she refused to eat. Arianna made some delicious soup and fed it to her kindly. Yesmin cried, always holding Arianna's fingers. Gradually, she loses her voice.

She lay on the mattress, burning with the insufferable aching. Her entire trunk looked like a skeleton. Her hairless head slightly dropped down while she widened her toothless mouth. Her face was desperately pointed at the roof the whole day, and her eyes were half-shut. They are not as sparkling and lustrous as they were in the past days. Instead, a foul smell hung around her. Arianna bathed and cleaned her and removed her wet, dirty garments. It is harsh to believe the transformation of the lively, glamorous, and adorable gesture of Yesmin into an aged ugly, wretched woman.

No devotees seemed to be around her, but the flies frequently stayed with her. Nobody entered her awfully smelled chamber except Saina and Arianna. Her wrinkled skin stuck to her torso. Saina sat beside her woefully and murmured some words while holding her hand. It resembled a dried stick. Her magical legs moved throughout the stage and rested parallel, on the bed. There were no poets to elaborate on her stunning beauty. Yet solely, her unbearable sound of agonising body spanned everywhere. Sometimes, she shrieked out loud. That sound is much more terrific than her lustful, attractive dance. She yearned for her extinction more than death was expecting her. Her most honourable, unknown God seemed to be nowhere. Unfortunately, he didn't want to be visible in her dreams. The sacred room built for God had been closed after her illness. Maybe God cannot rescue her from these catastrophic circumstances; hence, he might be abandoned. One night, Yesmin shouted out. Arianna tried to relax Yesmin while massaging her feet. Her face and swollen eyes appeared weary after many sleepless nights with Yesmin. In a flash, Yesmin gasped simultaneously, clenching Arianna's hand firmly. Her eyes were straight, peeking at Arianna. While attempting to say something undisclosed, her eyes desperately pleaded for mercy.

"Granny," Arianna whispered and patted Yesmin's head slowly. The tears ran through her cheeks. Yesmin stared at Arianna, but her eyes only saw Ramses's dejected image. Yesmin sees Ramses sitting beside her instead of Arianna. Hence, she yelled out loud and dragged her hand back. She wished to remember God, but some gloomy darkness surrounded her. Because of the vast distance, God cannot reach her. Suddenly, Yesmins began to shudder, and she raised her hands upward. She spotted some dark shadows pulling her. They showed her whole past life tales. Yesmin screeched. Her entire soul was praying for forgiveness for her mysterious terror. Gradually, she became quiet. Her eyes seemed to be enlarged, and her mouth was widening. Her heart didn't sound. Her entire powerless body lay on the mattress horrendously. And it is not the most beautiful and glorious past, Thebeslon dance queen, but someone else trapped and beaten by themselves. Probably, she had halted her story until another beginning. Poor Arianna wailed beside her loving grandmother's deathbed.

Seth and Hugo took part in arranging their mother's funerals. Though they never appeared inside Yesmin's room, they decided to do it perfectly as an honour to their mother. Luma cried round the clock, sitting permanently next to Yesmin's corpse. Luma's sister and both wives of Seth and Hugo joined with Luma intermittently. But Arianna kept herself inside the kitchen, preparing to serve all the tea and meals to the people who expressed their misery wholeheartedly. She sobbed quietly while busily engaging with her chores. Saina gazed at Yesmin insensibly, neither word expelled nor tears visible in his eyes. He stayed resembling a statue beside her corpse. The people who visited Yesmin's funeral secretly talked about her awful past. Some who came as followers of Yesmin's nameless God honoured her for the sake of their supreme being. They brought flowers to cover the Yesmin's corpse. Yesmin's wish was to enclose her dead body with freshly bloomed flowers. She told Seth and Hugo about these a long time ago. Yesmin was so attached to her body all the time. She was immensely proud of the charming appearance she inherited. Hence, she heeded her body more cautiously. She spent quite a long time in front of the mirror from a young age, watching herself repeatedly. Yesmin was impressed by her great outlook and was elated to hear all her honey words from admirers. Hence, she believed her most precious body should be decorated with blossoms even after death.

But those blossoms faded shortly after they were placed inside her coffin. Therefore, Seth and Hugo ordered their children to fetch flowers continuously. So they peeked all around to find flowers. It was strange to glimpse Yesmin's awfully aged, wasted, disfigured, frightful, lifeless trunk lying among the pretty, attractive blooms. One evening, when the sun went down, Yesmin's body was hidden inside the six-foot hole in the earth. Luma screamed,

"Let me go with my mother, please, release me. I want to be with my mother," she wailed uninterruptedly. Wilson struggled to hold her while she was weeping noisily. Arianna stayed mutedly watching all these. She wiped her tears secretly. Seth and Hugo's wives fainted many times with unbearable grief. Hence, the neighbours got busy helping them each time. At the end of the event, everybody drove back home. Only Saina and Arianna were left alone. They stood beside Yesmin's grave. After a while, Arianna' came toward Saina.

"Grandfather, let's go home. Granny must be sleeping peacefully," she said in a broken voice. Arianna dragged the old man and walked back home. Days passed, and Arianna carried out her routine while looking after Saina. He sat in the front yard and stared at the road. But didn't speak with anyone, not even with Arianna. He sometimes roamed around the village and used to stay his nights beside the Yesmin's burial.

"She is alone in there, so how can I stay here without her?" Saina murmured to himself. He hung all over, mumbling and talking only to him. Sometimes, he laughed, and many times, sobbed. Arianna had to guide him back home whenever he did not return. People said Saina had gone out of sense after the Yesmin's death. One dreary morning of the cold winter, Saina's seemed to have fallen on the floor near the front door. His lifeless trunk, cold as the ice, was lying silently. Perhaps he thought it was his responsibility to join Yesmin's journey. Arianna's wailing faded with the snowstorm until the dark arrived.

....

Arianna became lonely at home. She wept immensely, remembering her loving grandparents. Samuel never attended any funerals and did not mention himself to his family. However, Seth and Hugo repeatedly invite Arianna to live with their families. But Arianna neither showed her any consent to them. Indeed, Arianna does not desire to be their servant. Finally, Luma decided to bring Arianna to her place. Soon, Arianna shifted to Luma's home along with the spring sunrise. All woods are prepared to wear their gowns of emerald, green. The shrubs with pretty flowers twinkled their eyes. The bright sun gradually authorised to drift away from the frozen breeze. Though the birds skipped over the greenery fields, they chirped jovially with the humming bees. Arianna received a warm welcome from Luma after a specific period. Luma greeted her daughter, making all the comfort. Wilson showed Arianna his kind attitude, yet everything lasted a few weeks. Eventually, Arianna had to work from morning to night. She cooked and washed all the dirty pots while Luma slept until noon. Arianna cleaned up the house and swept the floor.

Then She filled water in the buckets. After all, She walked the stream close to wash her clothes.

Meanwhile, Luma kept herself busy gossiping about her friendly villagers. However, as a tradition, she fought with Wilson during the night. Sometimes, Luma got beaten, and she kept crying until midnight. Arianna introduced Wilson as her father according to Luma's commands. Though she hardly agreed with Luma, she silently worried about it. Sometimes, Wilson walked away when following after the massive quarrels. He returned at midnight with halfway shut eyes and dragged his legs unsteadily. Yet sometimes, his mates brought him back home when he drank heavily. Arianna had to wake up to open the door for him. At the same time, Luma is stuck in a deep sleep. Frightened Arianna hides inside her room after his return.

And in the morning, they began to fight again. It is hard to believe in the serenity they have achieved by satisfying their selfish desires. Wilson's kind manner towards Arianna turned over with the time. He started to criticise her on every point. When he spotted her, his mind was unstoppably hanging around the memories of his own children he abandoned on behalf of the Luma. It sensed him more deeply when his ears caught the Arianna's introduction of him as the father. It reminded him each day of all his past misdeeds and about the current distressed life he is carrying out. Arianna's face reminded him of his elder daughter, who was the same age.

"I am sheltering someone not holding my blood," he whispered alone. Wilson secretly repented about the blissful life he left away. Moreover, all the memories of his past family tortured him each second. Hence, He was yearning to hide himself from that unbearable pain.

Arianna's life seemed more jumbled after she arrived back in Luma. She constantly wept when she recalled the last moments spent with her grandparents. Wilson used to rebuke her for each household chore. He persistently complained about the meals Arianna prepared. One day, Wilson threw his tea in front of her. He scolded her harshly for each thing.

"I have never seen such a brainless girl who ruins my life." He was recurrently irritated with Arianna for no reason. He kept his empty teacups and half-eaten plates in front of her.

"Wash these all you dozy mindless girl," he scowled.

Arianna completed all his tasks silently. Arianna's vulnerable situation and extreme innocence triggered Wilson to release his whole guilty bonded agitation by overpowering her. Some mornings after Wilson left, Arianna walked to the stream near the house. Which is quiet and calm; hence, she gets some relief from her tormenting life. The trees greeted her, standing alone. They hold their head wreaths while the thick mist scatters throughout. Though the fresh green saplings chase for the sunbeams, morning dew overlays her pretty feet. The soft breeze tingled all over her. Arianna slowly placed her pail and began to wash the clothes. She sat bending forward on the flat rock and scrubbed the dirty linens. Some rustling sound hung around. Arianna twirled her eyes all over the place, then gradually increased her speed to wash hurriedly, but the tears flowed parallel to her hands. Suddenly, she stopped and covered her eyes to stop the unstoppable tears. Yet all in vain, she began to sob.

"These eyes do not deserve tears Arianna," a familiar voice touched her ears.

"Your Highness," she quickly raised up and stepped backwards. Armion came close to her. Arianna turned her head down frighteningly.

"Your tears too weighted for this beautiful morning. Look around Arianna's the atmosphere following their rhythm They expelled the gloomy twilight. It allows the sun's rays to bring warmth to frozen dawn. It can heal the sore heart absolutely" He said in a hushed voice. Arianna wiped her eyes while trying to escape from his charming gesture.

"Why you can't catch a glimpse of the tiny glow through your gloomy night, Arianna?" He questioned. Arianna closed her eyes. Her entire spirit was sensing his warm breath.

"Because my eyes are sinned, your Highness therefore I am not eligible to touch that light," she whispered in a faint sound.

"Any questions about my presence here, I am delighted to know?" he peeks at her face, and their eyes meet.

"I am so glad I have no queries about your presence but I must admit this is a pleasant morning to chase for the spring blossoms, your highness,"

"Hmm," Armion beamed.

"But as you aware I am chasing for the one and only special golden daisy bloom. It is the most precious, incredibly stunning one I have ever recognised."

Arianna gazed at him. Then she slowly stepped behind, yet Armion moved forward with her. Arianna' had to pause her legs against the tree trunk right back to her. Armion concealed her inside his arms.

"I am quite close to that flower Arianna, I am pleasing to embrace it warmly. I want to hide it out to make it forever mine. I know how much it is worth to me. I want to feel the fragrance of it which most sensual and sacred. Touch it without hurting the soft petals. Secure it in my soul. Would you allow me to pluck it for me Arianna, I am much waited until"

"Your highness, unfortunately the flower is bred in the mud so nobody can reach it."

"So what? I am not bothered about the mud."

"Beware your highness, never let yourself be crummy forget that worthless bloom because you deserve better."

Armion sighed heavily.

"What do you sense about my love Arianna?"

"How do I admit to you? Please do tell me a way to unfold my heart to you?"

"Your highness, you ought to be a king in this kingdom. therefore you should understand about the duty you carry."

Armion smirks.

"A king would bear his authority for a certain period, for a particular territory or for a specific planet. All those power survived for a short time, it is impermanent."

"But," he paused.

"I am desired to be the king of my soul." Armion touched Arianna's face.

"After bonding with your eyes, I have chosen the route to seek your soul furthermore to hold with mine."

"I am so repenting about my eyes for letting bond you; hence, forgive me, your highness."

"Believe me Arianna, without you, I am nowhere. You hold my breath."

"If you are gripping one path tightly, you, will be burnt out your highness. You might be wearied struggling with that devotion."

"I want to ruin the dream before the demise to cease the appearance of life, Arianna."

"Then find your Serenity living with the absence your highness."

"You cannot meet the serenity in isolation. This fantasy never halts until you combat. It battles. It is a conflict with our hearts twisted with thoughts. You cannot kill it either have to watch it. Then only you will reach for victory. So I am waiting for you, Arianna."

"Why? you, wait for me. You are capable of walk alone without me your highness?"

"How should I explain to you Arianna, with your presence

my life is much easier we can seek the freedom to vanquish the departure from life. It is the beam among the glow and gloom."

"I am exhausted with life, your highness; hence I am much desired about the end, so I don't need to halt it," Arianna said downheartedly.

"If you chase for life, you will meet the death, expect the expiration, before-hand then you can sense the life Arianna."

"Death is merely an event which faces it but it would bring sorrow and desperation to who lives" Arianna tried to get released from his arms.

"Then hold my hand to find the eternal truth with me" He seized her inside him again.

"Beware, your highness, humans, died without accomplishing the reason of their arrival. Never let it happen to you"

"Then hold my hand to be the part of the nature. I am waiting for you and your soul."

"It is impossible to defeat the future, your highness. Release the hand and untie yourself."

"Arianna, the rhythm of nature has no edge, ripples of ocean never vanishes. Can you halt this hysteric breeze. They are immortal. We both have to seek for it."

"Yet this human life-changing with the time, your highness, but the nature proceeds the same manners."

"You need to awake from your dream Arianna, then you will snatch the life to seek the actual truth."

"My eyes are sore, your, highness. So I feel much relief living with dream."

"Then look through from my eyes, Arianna."

"If it so I need to confess, your highness."

"What?"

"I have fallen in love with your eyes from the moment you came in front of me."

"Go ahead," Armion whispered.

"I am trying to leave you every moment, but believe me, I am defeated because" she faltered and sobbed.

"Tell me about it." Armion's lips wandered around her tears.

"You broke my heart because I loved that simple sight, but suddenly you became visible. Though he was someone, You proved to me he is you I was following you and your soul. Because you brought a wonderful memories to me. Now I am desired to leave you. But I am struggling because you have become my shadow. Explain to me, your highness, how to leave my shadow."

"Then let it that shadow to twisted, with your soul Arianna."

"No, your highness, It is impossible. I see my whole divinity in your face It is only you and you gave me so much affection. You are my hope henceforth I bow to you always. Please don't ask for my consent."

"Arianna," Armion exclaimed loudly.

"Please, your highness, don't take my shadow away from me."

"I can't hold your hand forget me forever."

"Release me, your highness, and Forget me, then release yourself from me."

"The forest creek never ceases Arianna. It will flow through the years maybe the beyond."

"You are talking about continuity because there is an extinction, but you are stepping back your highness."

"Of course, I am not desired to win. I try to destroy myself hidden in my soul. That is my war, Arianna. I am not chasing expectations. Because I am seeking for the absolute reality."

Armion put his hands down. Arianna moved near the stream and quickly grabbed the pail with clothes.

"I am waiting for you near the forest creek," he muttered slowly.

"Tear down what you require, then you can reject the dream your highness."

"I am attempting to realise the dream, Arianna before the rejection," Armion approached her.

"Someday, you will hold my hand to join my voyage, so I am waiting until then," he confirmed. Arianna stared at him and sighed. "Forgive me, your highness. Though the memories became a pain I would love to hold that past except the beyond." She rushed back home.

CHAPTER 18

Arianna moved quickly and stopped holding the kitchen door. Then she slowly locked the door and breathed for a few seconds, but his whole image sauntered over her mind.

"No, I should halt my heart and listen to my brain. This is not a normal person. He is the kingdom's crown prince, but who am I?" she mumbled. Then, she began to do her regular work. She worked even after she had completed all her chores. Thoroughly, she needed to forget Prince Armion; however, all her thoughts looked around only for himself. She feels that he is casting some spells around all sides. However, it freaked her out when she sensed some unwavering magnetic power forcing her to return to his cherished arms. It was such a horrendous, persuasive incantation. He visited her dreams to enclose her in his soul. Arianna woke up at midnight and panted. She was imploring her heart to avoid him. Ultimately, She became frustrated about her thirst, begging for his enormous love. It directed her to become infuriated with her own restless mind. Thus, she purposefully neglected herself and worked round the clock. Luma spends her days in bed because of some unknown illness. For some reason, Wilson presented as being elated. They had peaceful conversations in their chamber instead of constant wars. Arianna sighed with relief when got heard their bright chuckles. She even got stunned when Wilson started to treat her kindly. Instead of endless insults, he appreciated Arianna for caring for Luma. But this whole calming atmosphere did not last for long. Everything changed one afternoon when Luma returned home, leaning on another woman. She looked weak and pale; Arianna took her to the bed with a doubtful mind. She got worried about Luma's sickness. Unfortunately, Wilson had gone out. Arianna sat beside the Luma with a scary face.

"Mother are you feeling better, I wonder why father is getting late today? Have a rest mother I will make some hot soup for you." she fondled Luma's head with love.

"Arianna"

"Yes, mother"

Luma grabbed Arianna's hand tightly.

"No need to make any soup, listen to me. Don't tell anything about me to Wilson. Don't ever let his ears catch that I stepped out today after he left."

"Why mother?"

"That is not important to you, Arianna. Do as I say to you. Now go to your room and close the door," Luma commanded. Arianna stared at her with a baffled mind.

"Now get lost Arianna, are you deaf?" Luma groaned.

Arianna nodded with shocking eyes, then shifted out hurriedly. She came inside her room and sat on her bed.

"What on earth is going on?" she said anxiously.

Then sighed desperately and lay on the bed. Soon, she fell asleep. Arianna woke up suddenly in the middle of the night. She heard someone banging at the front door loudly. Arianna snuggled inside the bed hesitantly, but she heard Wilson's grumpy noise after a few seconds.

"You witch open the door," he growled.

Arianna jumped over the bed and ran to open the door.

She stepped back fearfully when she sighted Wilson.

His sweaty hair sticks to his just as his messy clothes. He frowned while bending to hold the wall. Then, he tried to stand, but his tottering body wavered from side to side. His eyes were whole red and blazing with unbearable outrage.

Arianna slowly kept the lamp on the table and dragged her limbs backwards.

"Father," she mumbled.

"Where is she? Where is that evil witch?" Wilson yelled out.

Wilson came close to Arianna in a flash and grabbed her long hair. Arianna screamed.

"Mother," Luma woke up and tried to rise up feebly.

"What is going on, Wilson?" Luma jumped among them and tried to free Arianna from his rowdy arms.

"You bloody witch, you destroyed my blood again" He stomped angrily inside the house.

"Why did you keep telling lies to me
all the time?"

"Wilson, we can't have any kids," Luma said calmly.

"I was much expecting to have my own one under this roof," Wilson hollered.

"You already have three kids of your own, Wilson."

"But I left them all because of your bloody evil witch, and then you repeatedly destroyed my blood resided in your womb and fooled me with your fictitious stories every time but not hereafter." he peered at Luma's face and grinned madly. Luma implored,

"Wilson, please understand I can't our have own kid under this circumstance."

"What circumstances are you talking about? it's simply because of your wickedness. It is only your ruthless heart."

"Wilson, please listen to me. You would never know how much pain I am bearing. Look, Arianna is reaching her age to be getting married. So how can I carry another child? It might be a shame to Arianna."

"A shame," Wilson repeated the word sarcastically.

"You were born under the shield of one of the shameless families and your daughter too. So what do you suppose that filthy girl should be married by a prince" Wilson laughed.

"Wilson, you better get some sleep now. You are too drunk."

"You screw up my whole life, and your evil daughter brought another curse. How can I sleep? You both ruined me."

"Mind your tongue, Wilson," Luma shouted.

"You bloody witch wait and watch how I will dig your grave today, I will end you."

"No, please don't," Arianna shouted, shivering.

Wilson leapt furiously, pulled out Luma's hair, and repeatedly smacked her face. Then, finally, he snarled, lifted up his one leg and vaguely hit her waist. Luma cried out and fell over the floor. For the moment, She is whimpering with agony. Wilson bent and placed his one leg right on her neck. Then, he began to press it deeply by his feet. He was holding both Luma's hands strenuously. Luma struggled to get relief.

"Wilson please," Luma pleaded.

"No, please don't kill my mother" Arianna jumped and tried to set free Luma. But Wilson pushed her away.

"No," Arianna screamed while standing up again. She pushed Wilson's leg with all her might. However, Wilson lost his balance and fell over the floor. He thumped the floor with his hand. Yet Wilson could not get up with his boozed head; therefore, he lay on the floor and groaned. Luma murmured unconsciously while her eyes remained closed. She coughed continually.

"Mother," Arianna fondled Luma and kept her head on her lap. Then, she lamented, patting Luma's face.

....

Luma opened her eyes and looked around. Her body was aching terribly. She has no strength to raise up because of her spinning head.

"Mother, how do you feel now?" Arianna questioned with frightful eyes.

"Where is Wilson?"

"I don't know, mother. You were unconscious, so I took you back to the bed. Then I stayed beside you until now. But he seemed to be nowhere.

"Maybe he has gone," Luma whispered.

"Why did you do so? mother."

"What?" Luma wrinkled her forehead.

"Why did you do that horrible thing?"

"Oh! You don't have to worry about it Arianna."

"You passed your whole sins to suffocate that guiltless child mother."

"I made it not to happen because of you Arianna."

"Because of me, you did all these," Arianna exclaimed loudly.

"Yes, I don't want to disgrace you?"

"What a disgrace mother?"

"Think wisely Arianna you are reaching your age to prepare your marriage this I made my self-commitment for the sake of you. You are too old have your own brother or sister." Luma said harshly.

"You never devoted yourself mother, not ever for someone or anything and not even for me. You invariably followed for the sake of you."

"Mind your words Arianna."

"If you handed over that baby right after giving the birth, I will raise him in my hands. I will never let him abandon like me. But that wretched soul paid all the debts of sins of others. Therefore he was brutally punished."

"Enough, Arianna," Luma said in anger. Her lips twitched, and she was trying hard to control herself.

"Look, Arianna, I have only quite limited coins now. We are becoming poor and poor each day. I cannot put this whole burden over to Wilson. Specially about you. As you are aware he is not happy to take all these responsibility."

"Mother, I can look after myself, don't bother. I am happy to stay alone in granny's' house," Arianna sighed.

"Hugo is remaking your granny's' house as a gift for his daughter whose getting married shortly. You have no place to go, Arianna."

Arianna looked down sadly.

"If it so," she whispered.

Luma touches Arianna's fingers with love.

"Look, my dear, you are the most beautiful girl out of this kingdom. You can enchant men. Many wealthy men ask for your hand if you are giving your consent. Why don't you think about it, Arianna? You can easily win the heart of most of the affluent and prestigious men. And it will end up our all sorrows."

"You may be bidding my temporary trunk mother for your all prosperous future. aren't you?" Arianna mumbled downheartedly.

"I am trying to find your fortune, Arianna. Think wisely."

"I have seen many eyes wandering around me with overflowing lust. It solely an invitation or a longing for a greedy night but not to have a hand in my soul."

Arianna said slowly, then she paused, her mouth recalling something.

"But except him, he is still waiting for me" her heart mutedly screamed.

"Think about your future Arianna, you can have a blissful life." Luma admitted.

"You are much worried about the future mother. Whole your vanity struggling to protect the time ahead. Hence you will capture endless misery and ultimately you end up with exhausted. You would never realise the life mother yet you are living with it."

"Forget your foolish thoughts, Arianna, Please try to understand the truth I am explaining to you," Luma expelled anxiously.

"Though I am attempting to grasp the truth, I can only see the falsity close to me. That means I possess only the lies. The truth remains unseemly. Nothing but we can only sense the untruth inside us."

"Think from your brain Arianna don't listen to your heart, It always trapped you."

"No mother, I want to stand against my brain and listen to my heart."

"You are completely lost, Arianna. I am fed up with you," Luma sighed desperately.

"From the day I belonged to myself, I was expecting many things. Thus I made myself stronger to freeze my agony. It doesn't remark I am not broken-hearted. Only I am making it sturdy, in a certain demarcation."

Arianna ceased her aching soul with trembling lips.

"Do you know this mother?" She faltered.

"My heart made a note up to the time that I am belongs to mine. I am powerless and incompetent. Therefore I wish for my end inwardly till my actual death."

Arianna wiped her wet face and moved out. Luma shook hopelessly.

Wilson stayed out of home for several days. Luma waited impatiently, stuck inside the room. Once he returned, Luma put all her efforts into grabbing his attention again. But Wilson ignored her while resting in a separate room. He doesn't even face Arianna but leaves home at dawn before others usually wake up. He occasionally arrived at midnight, swaying his woozy head. Luma kept herself waiting for him, and they fought until the following morning. Poor Arianna couldn't sleep because of their noisy debates. Luma wept whole through the night after getting beaten by Wilson. So, on the whole, this unpleasant dilemma scares Arianna immensely. She hesitated, horrified, whenever she had to step among them to save Luma from Wilson's fearful attacks. Each day, Arianna's life became an arduous journey. She had to halt her dance teaching, and all these awful settings pushed her to spend her whole days only as Luma's maid. Arianna pondered with an empty, frustrated soul.

One early morning, Arianna woke up earlier. She strayed out of the house, and her limbs moved on the way to the woods. Arianna sighed heavy-heartedly with her unchangeable, colourless life. However, her footsteps magically brought her close to the forest creek. The oak tree stood alone, the same as in the past days. As she peeped around cautiously. Only the soundless forest sighted to her weary eyes, together with drizzly mist, muffled the treetops. Though the creek flows calmly while greeting her, She looks down with a faded face. Her eyes split into tears. Arianna drew her weak legs and turned back to go. But in a flash, she was yanked by some unknown strong arm. Her slender body vigorously strikes some broad chest.

"Looking for someone" Armion's gentle voice touched her ears. Arianna stared at him with a rising heartbeat. Then, while swaddling one hand around Arianna's waist, Armion's fingertips rolled her chin linear to his eyes.

"Read my eyes Arianna then you will find the thing you are wandering through," he whispered. Arianna shut her eyes to sense his warm breath again and again. Armion's finger unhurriedly sauntered around her eyebrows and touched her long eyelashes.

"Prince Armion," she uttered with trembling lips.

"I want to punish you Arianna, for forgetting me for a long time."

"Am I?" she mumbled.

Armion tightened both hands around her waist slowly, allowing her body to squeeze into him. It enclosed the distance between them.

"Every morning, I was much awaiting to see you. But you totally forgot me and put me under such a terrible pain. I was breathless. You did all this to me Arianna."

She gazed at him for a few seconds, enchanted by his kind eyes.

"If it so forgive me, Prince Armion," she stammered.

He placed his cold finger on her lips.

"Shhh"

"You have to call me Armion hereafter."

"Oh, it is impossible for me, your highness," she said hesitantly.

"You have to accept my punishment, Arianna."

"But, beforehand, give me your shoulder to shed my tears hidden in my sore eyes."

"My shoulder only allows for your smiles, Arianna."

"So then, Armion," Arianna muttered in a hushed voice and looked down shyly.

"Oh, say it more loudly, Arianna, I didn't hear that," he whispered and smiled. She peeks at him, enchanted by his whole gesture. While their eyes meet each other, Arianna closes her eyes with excitement. She felt his warm breath more closely. Then his fingers ran through her forehead and halted on her reddish cheeks. And again, those fingers wandered through her long neck and hair. Eventually, it stopped on her trembling lips, gifting the most eventful sensation. Once more, his lips hung around her eyes. Arianna cuddled at him, wrapping her arms around his neck. Her entire heart implored to enclose in this warmth. Suddenly, Armion lifted her into his arms and carried her under the oak tree. He made her lie down on green grass. The muted forest blessed them to expel their own hidden emotions to each other. Arianna's lips greeted him along with her pounding heart. Armion's halfway shut eyes were dunked in her whole beauteous, letting his lips sneak. Arianna could only be concerned about how smoothly he joined with concealed desires. It simply obsessed her further to be captured inside his warm affection. Thus, she flew over the moon. Her eyes sparkled after a long time. Arianna chuckled and snuggled up to him more and more to invade her senses. After a while, Armion raised up and kissed Arianna's forehead delicately.

"You are forgiven, my princess. I love you so much," he murmured.

"Armion, I am ready to accept your all punishments forever," she mumbled, rubbing his dark stubble cheeks.

....

Armion's appearance totally enlivened Arianna's life. She lay aside whole, her desolation twisting her fingers with him. She gathered wildflowers while listening to the sound of the hummingbirds. Unexpectedly, she sighted the glowing surroundings around her. She was stunned by those profound, coloured, scintillating visions. She placed her head on his shoulders and folded inside, seeking his warmth like a small rabbit who shivers in stormy winter.

One of his kind looks delighted her entire spirit once again. They sat under the oak tree, and Armion listened to her hourly talks. Arianna chuckled loudly when his impatient lips and fingertips tickled around her neck. They often climbed the mountain tops among the drizzle to watch the bright rainbow stretch over the sky. Arianna danced, twirling round and round, holding his hand. Her long braided hair decorated with daisies moves according to each step. Armion cherished her and made herself much more precious to him. He gradually healed her fractured heart with his boundless love. Arianna was yearning to grab his most divine tender hearted affection to fill up the hollow ponds of her existing life circle.

Arianna keeps smiling every day with sparkling eyes.

Meanwhile, Wilson and Luma carried out their habitual style with endless wars. Wilson visited Luma's house occasionally and got invisible for a few weeks. Hence, Luma is outraged by his peculiar behaviour. She was keen to find out the reasons for the Wilson's absence. Thus, Luma was trying to alleviate her befuddled mind thoroughly. Yet she grew more and more despondent. After the quarrel with Luma, Wilson kept wandering whole around. He recalled the memories of his past family somehow. His legs drew him back to this former house. Though he abandoned them for an extended period, he received a warm welcome from his previous wife. When he spotted his grown children, he could not escape the guilt. He was terribly ashamed of himself. However, he has no courage to cope with that regretful emotions. Hence, his whole mind is replaced with hatred toward Luma. He believed that Luma ruined him. So, he visited Luma to quench his thirst for revenge. He was much satisfied to hear Lumas lamenting with pain after getting beaten by him. Then, he drives back to his family to seek peace and love. Wilson's previous wife, Maggie, gave him full respect, yet he could not read the agony hidden in her spirit. He never recognised exasperation concealed in her pale face. Wilson did not know about the awful life struggles she confronted after his separation.

Though she accepted him for the sake of her grown children, it didn't content her wounded heart. Maggie barely looked at the roof while Wilson panted on her disrobed breast. He left her midway on their journey, though he returned; unfortunately, her desires were nowhere. Hence, she sighed with a desolated mind along with her numb trunk. Wilson wanted to revive himself completely between Maggies' absolute calmness and extreme obedience. It exhilarated him, moreover. Yet her emotionless resemblance with misery eyes pricked his heart repeatedly.

Nevertheless, Wilson remains a visitor to his home because he cannot rebuild the bonds he broke to accomplish his selfish desires. His children only seek their mother's consent profoundly. They respect only their mother, even in front of the Wilson. So, he felt that he had gradually turned into an unvalued coin in the house. He loses his mind because of the unpleasant circumstances. Eventually, Luma's captivating image began to haunt him, letting him boil over with rage. One rainy evening, Wilson went back to Luma's place. He was watching outside from the kitchen window, shivering with chilling cold. Suddenly, he saw Arianna returning, drenched in the rain. Her gown, tightly attached to her body, showed her all the rhythms of beauty. Wilson was stunned by Arianna's unexpected appearance. He stared at her secretly. Arianna bent down and began to wipe herself with a dried cloth. She leisurely did it without being aware of Wilson.

Her glossy skin was shined with the water, and her gorgeous bosom was more notable through the dripping wet. She lifted her gown bit upward and slowly rubbed. Afterwards, she rises up and shakes her long hair as it flows down like a wavy shower among her slim waist. Wilson forgot his breath, and his eyes kept sticking to her. Arianna turned back to enter at once, and Wilson quickly moved inside. He went to his room. Those exceptional, attractive visions gleamed beside his reckless heart. He endlessly seeks to grab that sense. While his entire sentiments restlessly attempt to abolish whole fences. Sadly, he was utterly burned, not with fury but over spilling lust.

Lumas was thrilled about Wilson's unexpected stay at her place for many days. He waited pretty patiently, quitting all arguments with Luma. Since he was roaming around Arianna, his behaviour diverted to the opposite. Wilson secretly watched Arianna, treating her more sympathetically by aiding her with household chores. When he accidentally cut his finger, Arianna cared for him, showing her entire good heart. Wilson felt much joy while her long, charming hands heeded his small wound; it absolutely drove away from his pain. He sensed the warmth of her fingers and touch, his nose tickled with the floral fragrance unfurled throughout her. Wilson's eyes neither observed her, yet it was swallowing her greedily. He felt she was much more radiant and bubblier than in past days, her rosy lips embellished with a bewitching smile. That day evening, Wilson brought some sweets and stretched them towards Arianna.

"What is this father?" Arianna asked surprisedly.

"This is some sweets for you, my dear," he replied generously.

"Thanks, I will give this to mother. She would love to eat sweets better than myself." Arianna smiled and carried them to Luma. Wilson gazed at her in despair, twitching his lips angrily. Then, one morning, Wilson stepped inside the kitchen and peeked vigilantly. He heard Luma's snoring loudly, herself wrapped inside a large robe.

He stood right behind Arianna, who was making tea alone. He slowly kept his hand on her shoulder. Arianna gasped in fear and turned around with an unexpected touch.

"My dear, it's me." Wilson grinned. Though Arianna gave him a light smile, she became confused about his sudden peculiar attitude. Finally, however, she offered him his tea. But Wilson grabs the teacup, deliberately letting himself touch her fingers. Arianna quickly pulled her hand and stared at him with widened eyes. Wilson kept treating her with his own mysterious smile. While Arianna was busy with other duties, Wilson sipped his tea and merely drank her natural beauty through his eyes. Arianna, who bathed in the morning, the tiny water dots sprinkled on her face resembling bloom, showered with morning dew. She dressed pleasingly, her lengthy hair wavers dancing on her sweetly curvy hips. Wilson neither felt the warmth of the hot tea, yet her charming gesture melted him utterly.

Wilson was unfit to concentrate his mind; hence, he walked outside. He wanted to cease his soaring fire. Though he emptied a few rum pots, it didn't satisfy his quench. Only his eyes yearned for Arianna's vision. He returned in the night, crept inside his room, and pretended to be sleeping. Luma was afraid to talk to him; therefore, she patiently stayed without dispute. Because she wished to remain with him for the rest of her life. Wilson sat on the bed. Sleep did not even come to meet his eyes. He secretly walked close to the

Arianna's chamber and slowly pushed the old door. As the door unfastened, he stepped inside bit by bit.

Arianna was sleeping, and the moonlight entered the room from the window directly in front of Arianna's bed. Wilson stood beside the bed. She lays on her bed, her entire body visible to his eyes with the unfurled moonbeams. Her halfway exposed bosoms and the forelimb shined throughout her thin nightgown. Wilson breathed heavily, yet he could not take his eyes off her. Maybe she is not a human being or some gorgeous angel dropped down to earth. Wilson closed his eyes hastily and tried to cease his burning thoughts. He quickly stepped out and lay on his bed. He remembered Maggie staring at the ceiling. She lay down on the bed, which resembles a heavy wooden log. It neither shifted unless someone pushed it because it was completely numb and powerless. Indeed, Wilson has executed her emotions before the end. Her face veiled with agony stood the mirror image of Wilson's odious character. Thus, it tortured him eternally. Though he recalled the memory of Luma, her real intimacy awakened his wrath. His deep mind wandered between hatred and guilt. But Arianna, her unique beauty bonded with complete innocence, abandoned him somewhere beyond the earth. Wilson cried out, burning with unbearable hunger like the violent tiger, then scowled at the gloaming.

CHAPTER 19

A few days passed silently. Wilson stays with Luma and does not return to Maggie. One misty morning, Arianna woke up tiredly. Though she felt a little bit unwell, she completed all her duties. Afterwards, she went to meet Armion. They spent the whole afternoon sitting under the shady oak tree. Arianna rested her head on his chest while his fingers ran between her hair. She felt much more peaceful under his shadow. He kissed her forehead before letting her back home. The next day, dawn arrived with heavy rain. Wilson sighed, glancing at the rainfall over to simmered down the atmosphere. But the raindrops were unfit to eliminate the flames firing inside Wilson. He loitered on the Arianna's doorstep like a wolf lurking around for its prey.

End of the rain, the evening appeared mournful as heavy grey clouds enshrouded the sky. Wilson covertly stepped out, ignoring the weeping sky. Arianna was sick and feebly tiring; some bad headache ruined her day. She lay on her bed. Hence, Luma has to cook meals and engage with Arianna's chores without help. End of the day, Luma stretched on her armchair with drowsy eyes. Wilson's sudden vanish agitated her badly. The house remained quiet when night arrived, and Arianna fell asleep early. But at midnight, she woke up by a rowdy touch. Arianna freaked out with unknown fear. She spotted some black shadow standing close to her bed. Suddenly, the shadow leaned over to her body and began to kiss her forcibly. Arianna jumped out of bed and ran outside.

"Mother" she screamed to Luma. But that black shadow chased after her and then grabbed her arm. Arianna was startled when her eyes quickly recognised that black shadow.

"Father," she mumbled with shock.

Her stepfather, Wilson, appeared in front of her. His eyes were reddish and squeezed with bursting desire, and his wasted body jiggled from side to side. Wilson seized her with all his might. Arianna struggled to get released from his prison. Then he drew her briskly close to him.

"Listen to me my dear you have never known how much pain I am bearing because of you. Have mercy on me. Let me touch you. If you can stay calm nobody will be aware about our secret," he whispered.

"No, let me go, please," she implored.

But Wilson attempts to unfasten her dress wildly. Arianna struggled repeatedly and tried to push him away. Then, at last, Wilson peeped inside her face.

"Arianna, I will give you whatever you expect, my dear, I will make your life more comfortable. Let me feel you. Your mother will never get know about us. I promise to you. We can build our own place." he said in a hushed voice, the time trying to snatch her lips.

"No, get away from me, please" Arianna strenuously pushed his face.

Wilson rolled his eyes weirdly and grinned.

"You are going to make a big mistake. You will have to face the dreadful consequences of rejecting me Arianna,. You may never know how bad I am," he threatened harshly. Then his palm enclosed Arianna's mouth, not allowing her to make any noise. Arianna fought with him to get free in whatever way.

At last, Wilson struck her. As She tumbled below feebly, he turned her upward and flattened her body parallel to the floor with his brawny arms. Though she tried to escape, his heavy trunk bent over to her. Arianna sobbed with fear, but her mouth still paused with Wilson's palm. He nibbled her violently while his one hand moved through her dress. However, Arianna shouted aloud during the split second she was free from Wilson's wild arms. In a flash, Luma came. She was shocked. Indeed, Luma gaped at Wilson, yet she couldn't believe her own eyes.

"No"

Luma hollered and pulled out Wilson, and then she began to slap him continuously.

"How dare you, Wilson? Are you insane?" Luma yelled. Wilson stood up, touched his face, and grumbled. Then he started to laugh out loud like a madman. Luma stared at him with blazing eyes. She twirled her eyes, then again leapt towards Wilson and slapped across his face. Arianna dragged herself to the nearby corner and then started to lament. Wilson booted away Luma roughly, letting her collapse on the floor. Luma cried with pain. Meanwhile, Wilson again approached Arianna.

"Bloody whore what do you think about yourself? You didn't allow me to touch you. You should have learnt from your grandmother about all this art. I thought she would have taught you whole lessons before her death."

"Hold your tongue, Wilson," Luma groaned while trying to raise her body. Meanwhile, Wilson bent down, grabbed Arianna's chin and slapped her.

"You might be waiting for a prestigious money bag like your mother. Beware, oh, better keep me a space after he left you. Because I am much more capable of quenching the thirst of all of you rather than those fat cats," he laughed. And again, he bent to Arianna and quaked her face vaguely while snarling and kicking her by his leg. Arianna cried out loud.

"Get lost, Wilson leave her alone," Luma yelled out. She dragged her powerless legs close to Arianna, wringing with unbearable agony. Finally, she stood up as her limbs shook side to side.

"You are such a bastard Wilson. Get out of my sight," Luma screamed.

"I am out from your life mad witch none of the commands is needed for that," Wilson raised his voice.

"I know you are already with that past mistress. You betrayed me"
Luma yelled while pulling from his neck.

"Yes I went back to my own roof. That is where I belong. I want to leave you forever. Hide out your princess from me. Because as you aware I am too dangerous and insane. I will destroy her likewise you teared my whole life." he growled in a husky sound.

"Get lost, you bastard" Luma grasped his shirt and pushed him out of the house. She closed the door with all her force.

The thunder burst out, trembling the everlasting spheres. The trees wobble to escape from the thunderous grey clouds. The chilly wind circles up and down to wipe out Arianna's endless tears. Who wept, isolated in a dark corner. Yet, at the same time, everything haunted her and entered as a horrendous nightmare. Luma came closer to Arianna and sat opposite her. Arianna raised her head, awaiting Luma's sympathetic words and loveable touch. Yet Luma glanced at her doubtingly.

"From the day you resided my womb I suspected I would gain nothing from you. But I accepted you because there's no way to deny. Though I hope to have my own life you were became my burden." Luma glared.

"Mother," Arianna mumbled.

"I am not finished, listen to me carefully from the day you stepped here. Wilson changed a lot. He began to hate me. I lost my entire happiness. It's all because of you, Arianna You used your beauty and your charming tricks to enchant him. You made him come after you." Luma leaned forward, staring at Arianna's eyes.

"No, mother, I would not ever," Arianna sobbed.

"You ruined my life Arianna. He left me totally because of you. You were a curse to me Arianna. You carried only your born bad luck nothing else." Luma shouted angrily.

"No mother believe me. I have not once realised all these. If I do I will leave this house before him. I always respected Wilson as my own father. I have no wish to destroy your life. Not for a moment. I want to see your happiness." Arianna touches Luma's hand. But Luma dragged it back irritably and stood up.

"Go to your room Arianna, get out from my sight. If you want to stay with me, don't be visible in front of my eyes," Luma announced with infuriating eyes. Arianna slowly raised up and hauled her aching body to her space along with her wretched heart. Luma watched her for a minute and shifted to the room.

She locked the door and dropped down to the bed. Luma felt her entire body was paralysed. She began to pull her hair while bawling. Yet it only vibrated through the walls. The storm started to howl around its terrifying sound. Nonetheless, It ceased the Luma's unforgivable iniquitous wailing.

A few days passed, and Arianna decided to accept her own pathetic and indecisive battle. She wiped her tears and engaged with her daily duties. Luma didn't appear outside for many days. Though Arianna kept her food on the stool beside Luma's locked door, she refused to eat. Luma kept herself stretching horizontally along with the armchair. Sometimes, she gazed at the roof and kept thinking it was hard for her eyes to catch some sleep. Hence, Luma hung around her own isolated world. She lamented continually, and at times, she began to cry out, tugging her own hair violently. Afterwards, Luma giggles alone. Even though Arianna felt hesitant to talk with Luma, she sat beside Luma's door, expecting her mother's image. All her mind was almost wholly overturned because of this unexpected nasty situation.

One midnight, the sky came into sight with the new moon. Luma stood up from the chair and began to hoot.

She hooted whole throughout the night, tearing her clothes. Suddenly, she unlocked the door and ran out.

"Mother," Arianna cried out, stunned by Luma's terribly messy outlook. Luma paused her steps and twirled her head around unusually, laughing.

"Ramases, Ramses, where is he?" she murmured incessantly. Then, she leapt outside the house in a flash and ran. She hooted without stopping and wandered around the ground. Arianna chased after her. It was almost dawn; hence, neighbours gathered at their place. Arianna struggled to calm down Luma, but it was all in vain. So eventually, with the help, they took Luma forcibly inside the home. But she fought with everyone and began to throw the stuff around her. She broke whatever she grabbed by her arms and giggled.

At last, they tied her to the armchair. Yet she never halts herself. Instead, she keeps on struggling restlessly for a long time.

"Ramses, Ramses," she murmured again, then fell asleep. Arianna sobbed silently, patting Luma's legs.

Meanwhile, In the kingdom of Yunas, lord Ramses was sitting beside the fire and enjoying the evening tea in his cosy palace. His youngest son sat on his lap while the elder daughter wrapped her arms around his neck. Lord Ramses had a blissful life with his most loving life partner. Who sat next to him.

"My dear, you looked gorgeous, as every day." Ramses kissed his wife's hand and smiled. She gleamed back at him. A shiny pearl necklace fastened around her neck.

"Father, I want to have my birthday gift soon," his daughter pleaded. While the maids serving the cookies and honey cakes, Ramses chuckled.

"You already have plenty of gifts, my sweetheart. There are months more to have your birthday," the girl who looked pretty as her mother gave a bright smile. She was beautifully dressed, and her eyes remained sparkling each moment delightedly. Ramses stared at her carefully, and suddenly, all the memories about Arianna flashed through his mind. He sighed woefully. He felt something pricking his deep heart.

"Arianna, I haven't seen you for ages. You might be a charming young lady now," he thought silently.

Though he desired to see Arianna, he never moved his steps back to Thebelon. Maybe he did not want to involve himself back in that awful crisis. Hence, he denied it all. And even Arianna. Though he knows he has abandoned her among the wolves, he does not attempt to save her. Instead of that, he replaced his life with peaceful attachments. Currently, he is much keener to hold those bonds than Arianna.

"Luma snatched my whole money and wealth, so Arianna can have a good life with Luma in the house I built." he thought blindly.

"Arianna might be much more attached to Luma rather than me. She must have forgotten me surely," Ramses consoled himself many times with numerous justifications. Then he smiled at Arianna's childhood portrait in his secret closet.

....

Everybody in the village came to know about the Luma's craziness. So they started to introduce her as a "madwoman."

However, Arianna had to look after her mother cautiously. She spent many nights without sleep. Her pale face with weary eyes remarked her distress of suffering and agony. Yet nobody shows her any empathy except a bit of mercy towards her. On the other hand, many women exhibit wholehearted compassion and call her "poor girl" outwardly.

Nevertheless, they firmly believed that Arianna's birth brought these entire tragedies to Luma and the rest of her family. However, the misfortune she carried is the sole reason for all catastrophes. The people quietly renowned Arianna as the most ill-fated girl. Something more unethical would become admissible to the barbaric inhumanity who avoids the bitter truth.

Armion waited for Arianna for many days. Ultimately, he became anxious about her sudden vanish. Afterwards, he wandered around her surroundings to catch up with her slight reflection. Arianna looks through the window while Luma dozing off. Her memories tangled with the daisies' quivers coupled with a soft breeze. Then she drew a breath while gazing at the sky thoughtfully.

She repeatedly convinced herself to draw out herself from Prince Armion's shoulders. Though the future is a mystery, she agrees with her present dolorous and repetitive life circle.

One moonless night, Luma was stretched on her armchair, snoring loudly. Arianna stood beside the window, wearied and with a pale face, to sense the light fragrance of blooming jasmines during the dusk. The chilly wind touched her cheeks, recalling her warm, loveable kiss. Arianna shut the window, wiping tears from her hand. She sat down on the floor and hid her eyes between the bended knees. She raised her head with the sudden tapping sound.

"Arianna, it's me, Armion Open the door."

"Armion," Arianna, distractedly, uttered a slow sound and hastily opened the door.

"Your highness, you are not supposed to be here. Please leave," Arianna murmured with trembling lips.

"Why are you trying to pull me out after ignoring me for an extended period? Is it reasonable to treat me like this, Arianna?

He asked in an annoyed voice.

Arianna turned away from his sight and took a deep breath.

"Forget me your highness, I am not the one for you. As I have told you deserve better. Please leave," Arianna uttered in a broken tone.

"How can you tell that so easily, Arianna?" he dragged her vaguely to his side. Then, hold her tightly from her shoulders while pressing her body over the wall next to them. Then peeked at her face with infuriating eyes.

"You better kill myself, Arianna. But don't play with my emotions. I am not a person who's chasing for better rewards. I listened only my heart and what I perceived as right. Nobody can challenge with my choice. I want to stay with you forever."

Arianna was speechless, and soon, her eyes kept staring at him, and she burst into tears. She covered her face, allowing her soft trunk to slide against the wall. She sat on the ground while sobbing silently.

"Forgive me your highness, because I have no choice. I have to look after my mother. She is sick and people said she has gone mad. They called her mad woman."

"Arianna" Armion came close to her.

"Listen to me carefully, prince Armion, this is my life and, I am indebted to you for choosing me to gift your enormous heart. But I can't be your queen. My misfortune will ruin you forever. So I beg you to walk away your highness."

Armion raised her upward by his arms and wiped the tears. Her tiring face with swollen pink eyes seized him. He cuddled her inside him and kissed her forehead. Arianna felt her own serene wrapping in his warmth but quickly stepped back.

"Walk away, Armion," she whispered and turned around.

"No Arianna, I am walking with you. Expel your sorrows with me I have here to listen to you."

Armion pulled her hand softly and turned herself to face him directly. He peeped into her. His vivid eyes were filled with compassion and tender humanity.

"My father left me when I was a small child. My mother never be proud by giving birth to me. Though I was abandoned as an orphan nobody properly addressed me like that. They blamed I am the one who carried all this misfortune. But I would never blame them for splitting my whole life into pieces."

"Arianna, you are not misfortune, you possess a golden heart. Yet it so unvalued among the ruthless wicked souls."

"My mother cursed me Armion, that my beauty stole her eternal love away from her because Wilson my stepfather tried to destroy me right next to her eyes. They never cried for me. Neither spare a single second behalf of me. Nobody wipe my tears. Nobody listen to my wailing. I suffered alone from that intolerable agony."

"Whole these grief and dismay, is a part of part of this dream Arianna. There is joy hidden inside the agony. Sometimes exhilaration can be ended with the desperation."

"people exhibit their mercy. The women kept their leftover meals in front of the door. They throw away their raggy old clothing to me. They believe I am extremely poor and incapable to fulfil my requirements. They condemned me about my ill luck while their men and sons hanging around my house. They are yearning to satisfy their desires showing the handful of coins. They are asking my price. They said my grandmother much enjoyed these coins rather than the dancing so I am too perfectly inherited to carry out her tradition."

"All these words pierced my heart Arianna, I am boiling. They are unseeing the reality. I am wish for the day that I can rip their souls to expel that gloom."

"They express no value, neither dignity towards me. But only asking me to sell my body for the sake of my life and their lust."

"Arianna, I am here for you I can save you from this all misfortune. Come with me."

"No Armion, you are not destined to join with my pathetic life. You will gain nothing. As a future king of this kingdom, don't ruin your life behalf of me, We cannot walk so far."

"No, that's not true Arianna we will, I can only seek my triumph with you." Armion holds both her hands.

"What brings you here Armion, that royal palace would never ever accept me, why you after me?"

Armion drew her back, attached to him. Then, as their eyes gazed at each other, Arianna instantly turned around.

"No, wait, Arianna."

He forcibly enclosed her body to stick inside of his shoulders. His hands fastened throughout her waist.

"Listen to me Arianna, I am after your soul and solely with your heart and your emotions. Whole your selflessness. It is much worth to me. I am aware of that our bodies are not permanent. Hence I love your soul more than all. Believe me I want to seek the place between the dark and the light. But not alone, only with you. Join with me Arianna though is not easy we can be the part of the nature. We can end this dilemma. There is no uncertainty remains in rhythm of nature."

Arianna sighed.

"We are not same your highness, the bond you are making with me not a reward. You will only get disgraced"

"We are in under the same circumstances Arianna, though I have born in a royal mansion. I too suffered. I was about to slaughter however I was gifted with my breath. I too rejected. And those gloomy shades haunting around me."

"If it so, think twice before you leap this muddy swamp, Your Highness," she whispered, releasing herself from him. She walked a few steps ahead and turned back. Armion stretches his hand towards her.

"Would you hold my hand Arianna, for the sake of our souls. I will be here with you forever and ever. Do not turn back I am chasing after you."

"Walk away Armion, your love will be forever sacred in my heart. No one can reach my soul except you."

"What if I don't."

"Then I would run away from you. You may not be able to see me forever."

"Why do you want to punish me like this?"

"We created whole this pain because we pursue for happiness. We chained with each other. And It is the easiest road to hunt that joy. But there is a misery in the bottom. You have to shed more tears with that long lasting bond."

"Arianna, please listen to me."

"Your highness, don't visit to this doorstep again."

Arianna moved swiftly moved inside, and the door slammed loudly. Armion stood alone. Her silent sobbing sound touched his ears.

The moon is pouring shades of love
made vows to blooming Jasmines.
Sunshine touches the morning mist,
I am enchanted by an elated breeze.
Arianna, my princess, take my hand.

I breathe in cold tears,
I am owed to loneliness,
never let it be gloomy,
Armion walks away from me.

Flowers are abundant in this life jungle.
We can fly over the mountains.
Sharing tears and laughter.
Smiles can defeat sorrows.

My shoulder is for your rest.
Arianna, my princess, take my hand.

I am isolated in dessert, willing to end in burning rays.
I am owed to sand drops.
Never let it be gone.
Armion walks away from me.

I am seeing your soul,
My hand awaited to vanish your raindrops.
You are the reason for my being.
We can run among the golden stars.
Arianna, my princess, take my hand.

I am surrendering in deep blue.
I am owed to silent thunder.
Never consent to be bright with light.
My hand is frozen and numb.
Armion walks away from me.

Arianna watched outside the window and saw Armion's shadows disappear with the midnight dark. She sighed woefully.

CHAPTER 20

Hatop steps swiftly, muttering alone to himself. The thumping sound of his heavy footsteps vibrates the wall.

Suddenly, the door opened with the sight of Queen Hatra.

"What on earth were you being doing?" Hatop asked roughly.

Hatra slowly stretched on a cosy chair and beamed.

"Calm down, Hatop,"

"Are you insane, Hatra? Do you know about that nasty girl Armion caught up?

Hatra sighed." I knew about it some time ago."

"Why you kept yourself silence Hatra. Why are you tolerating his unacceptable decision. She is poor girl related to awful family. Our son is the future king. What an embarrassment."

"Forget about the embarrassment, Hatop. That is not worth it." Hatra grinned while Hatop wrinkled his forehead.

"I wonder what you are talking about, Hatra. As I have arranged everything with the King of Kingdom Temos about his one and only daughter for Armion."

Hatra raised up.

"Oh, I have heard much about the crown princess of Kingdom Temos. She is beautiful, intelligent, talented and powerful." Hatra uttered with a gloomy face.

"Temos is one of the prosperous Kingdom in Henaten. They are wealthy and strong. Therefore we can gain lot of benefits through this connection. As I have heard this princess is well disciplined and generous. She is good-natured, and I think she is a good choice for Armion." Hatop said thoughtfully.

"What an impressive elaboration about the princess Lord Hatop. I believe she would be really proud about herself."

She smiled scornfully.

"She is the greatest princess out of the Henaten," Hatra exclaimed loudly. Hatop squeezed his eyes with Hatra's sarcastic sound.

"Would you explain me what is in your mind Hatra?"

Hatra gave a light smile and moved near the closest. She poured a glass of wine and turned back to Hatop.

"We don't prefer another royal diva to this palace Hatop."

"What?"

"Yes, I will be the Queen who rules this mansion, though Armion crowned as a King. He would have to obey only my commands. I am his mother and the most important person of his life not anyone else."

Hatra sipped the wine calmly.

"Armion should not be married by a royal princess Hatop. Thoroughly this palace needs someone who can dance following my rhythm. Someone innocent, someone with great obedience and a vulnerable person, simply like an orphan. Moreover, a simple girl has a little more upgraded than a maid."

"Why do you expect that type of choice Hatra can she capable to cope up with the highest states as a Queen.?"

Hatra laughed out loud.

"Oh Hatop she is not gaining any higher standard."

"I will be the Queen forever. When Armion became the ruler this poor girl is barely a person who has dedicated herself to satisfy Armion. To heed him and raise his kids. She will never try to use her power to overcome us. Furthermore, nobody will recognise her as a Queen or she will neither received any dignity because of her horrible background. Hence we can easily keep her in that low state."

Hatra finished her glass and placed it on the table.

"Is it possible, Hatra she will understand all these shortly after the marriage."

"Hatop I am the one who is extensively knows Armion. He loves Arianna madly. It is purely because she is innocent, selfless and good natured. Look Hatop she is spending a pathetic life. And we blessed her with all these luxurious royal phantasy."

"So then, but remember this, Gaika never listened to us, Hatra. Though she owned equivalent status to Arianna. She always behaved arrogant manner. Gaika never respect any royals not even us and she even controlled Joser for her sake."

"Hatop this girl is a totally opposite of Gaika. She will believe me and I will be her most wonderful mother. I would never present myself as a mother in law. Arianna would be my beloved daughter who can only listen to myself and I will govern her." Hatra beamed slyly and draped around his neck.

"So think my charming Lord Hatop if Armion got married to that royal princess can she fulfil my requirements?"

"I wonder how thoughtful you are, my Queen," he whispered.

"These royalties drowned in their own ego. They are powerful. So better we choose someone resistless with a broken, paralysed soul. Hence I totally agreed with you, Hatra," Hatop sneered.

"Princess of kingdom Temos might stand as an obstacle when she stepped into Thebeslon. Her authority will create a huge separation among us. And Armion will be more powerful; therefore, we would never control him. It will be a challenge to yourself, even Joser and Gaika too. However, I am not desired to let him get free so easily. I want to pull the string while the kite soars up to the sky. According to the predictions the day when he becomes the Emperor to the whole Henaten we should be privileged as his creators." Hatra confirmed.

"That day, Joser also must earn all the benefits as Armion's brother though he was unable to hold the crown we should secure his future. Therefore, he ought to be advantaged and honoured equally to Armion," Hatop uttered.

"That is my one and only wish, Hatop; I want to see Joser's success," Hatra sighed.

"If it so, this Thebeslon dancing Queen Arianna is the perfect match," Hatop's arms tangled around Hatra.

"Think Hatop, this is a good opportunity to win Armion's heart back. We have to exhibit all our jovially blessings regarding him and Arianna." Hatra said delightfully.

"Of course," Hatop confirmed.

"No, there will be no two queens in this castle except Queen Hatra. Long live the queen," Hatop shouted with a colourful smile.

"Oh, Hatop stop making fun of this" Hatra tapped him slightly, laughing happily.

....

Arianna spent her days caring for Luma, who became more aggressive daily. However, Arianna kept watching her mother all the time. She fed Luma and bathed her. Many stayed many nights sleepless beside her loving mother. Luma's sister did not step into their house, and Seth and Hugo didn't mention their presence. Though they obtained many benefits from Ramses's money sneaked by Luma, they were convinced that Arianna should carry out this isolated struggle.

Meanwhile, Armion made himself busy with his sword. He engaged himself with sword practice round the clock. It was so hard to release his mind away from Arianna. Armion gazed at the sky surrounded by stars in his treehouse. Yet, each moment, all the memories smitten with Arianna flashed into his eyes. Eventually, he wandered inside the forest and climbed the mountain tops while spending a lonely stretching out on the flattened peaks. He sighed sadly. He could not sense the beauty encircled him since his deserted soul wept mutedly.

One midnight, Luma woke up suddenly. She twirled her head weirdly and grinned. She spotted Arianna, who was napping beneath her armchair.

"Witch," Luma scowled. Then she raised up silently and stepped out of the house. The darkness veiled all over, and Luma strayed forward, mindlessly giggling to dark shades invisible in her cold heart.

Luma roamed among the woods.

"Ramses, Ramses, where is he?" she murmured. Yet the dark woods were found gruelling to reply to her questions. Luma yelled out wildly, pulling her curly hair. The rowdy wind rolled out through the woods since the sky grumbled, gathered with heavy clouds. Luma commenced wailing. But unexpectedly, the sky began to tumble with restless, uncontrolled raindrops. Neither wanted to listen to her outcry; hence, Luma sat tiredly under a tree. Her old gown was soaked with mud, and she shivered in the cold.

"Ramses, Ramses save me," her trembling lips uttered. The storm arrested the entire night until dawn reached. As Luma woke up, she seemed to be searching for a way to return home. Hence, she turns to roam alone with her staggering, feeble trunk. Her scrawny body was covered with mud and dirt. The eyes that popped out in her gaunt face enhanced her horrifying sight. It is not enthralling like her past youth, simply terrific like a haunting gesture of an awakening corpse. She dragged her legs towards the river, murmuring to herself. The river ran among the stones out of control, overflowing mercilessly after a violent thunderstorm. Luma stepped onto the slippery rock and chortled at the raucous, wild, heartless river.

"Ramses, Ramses save me," her pleading voice echoed in the atmosphere and faded away. The mist wrapped close to the river unhurriedly.

Arianna suddenly opened her eyes and then looked around. It was almost morning. The sun was already showing out.

"My God," she cried out as she spotted the Luma's empty armchair. Arianna stood with a shocked mind, then wandered all over the house. However, Her entire heart began to shudder when she could not find Luma inside the home. She ran out of the garden.

"Mother, where are you?" she yelled. But no sign of Luma existed except muddy grounds soaked with rainwater. Arianna closed her face and panted. Then abruptly, she flew and ran around the roads, calling for Luma. Arianna walked all over the neighbourhood, yet no sight of Luma existed. Yet, ultimately, she came to know people gathered beside the river. Thus, she drove herself carelessly. The people stared at her with frightful eyes. It may be sympathetic, sad, and startled; however, she moved forward with shaking limbs. One woman came close to her and dragged her by the hand. As Arianna stretched ahead, people stepped back to allow herself to move. Arianna tugged her shivering body and halted beside Luma, lying on the sand. Her powerless corpse rested along while her worn, raggy gown covered it slightly. Moreover, It looked extremely fearful, with halfway shut jaws and enlarged eyes. Arianna sat slowly beside and waited with blotted eyes while someone covered the corpse with a long robe.

"Why mother, Why you left me alone so soon. I wanted to you more than you needed me. But you never realised it. Not ever." She whispered.

Though her eyes were emptied with tears, she sat beside it until the sun disappeared. Then she began to sob. Suddenly, she lifted the robe away and hugged Luma. Then, She started to weep out loud.

Though this dream creates an endless voyage, we hang within until we destroy our individuality. What we possess resides inside, though it is unseen. The outward seemed to be unvalued beside the end. The tears hold the smiles while the dark is concealed in the glow. The untouched nature, the whole universe, invites the selfless souls devoted to being huddled with its rhythm of momentum. The breeze never halts, the ocean waves never hold back, yet the weary humans gather their tombs till they close out their dream.

Arianna sat upon the window. She felt that each day, time passed too slowly. Thus, she wept silently to eliminate her long, isolated days. Luma was buried next to Saina and Yesmin with the aid of the neighbours. Arianna received their genuine compassion and sympathy only for a few days. Afterwards, neither one remembered her. She became lonely in that deserted old house. Arianna quickly shut the window to pull her eyes out of the dark night. However, her unrestrained emotions wandered among the dreary past. In her childhood, her father was invisible one dark night. Arianna slightly pats her cheek to sense his last touch. Though he was far from her, she felt he was still beside her. Maybe it might be a part of this tormenting nightmare. Saina, Yesmin, and Luma were unseen in the dark. Yet solely Arianna stands beyond the gloaming. They seek something existing to please their physique for a moment, but they are all gone when it is out of their presence. They stuck behind the darkest because their souls stood unrevealed. Though it remains a mystifying phenomenon, the verity is bound with it.

Arianna sighed bitterly. Neither of Luma's siblings attended on behalf of their sister. Seth and Hugo never showed up themselves. Now, they are carrying their lives like one of the wealthiest and most decent families in Thebeslon. Hence, their mad sister, Luma, was barely ashamed of their family's reputation. Thus, they rejected all their relationships with Luma. Wilson never appeared as he moved far remote in Thebeslon with his family. So each person chased for their own rest, though it was hard to touch it. Arianna snuggled on the bed and tried to shut her eyes stiffly while the unbearable misery veiled her soul. She shrinks with fear; hence, sleep does not catch up with her eyes.

"Armion," she muttered among the tears.

Armion locked his door and sat beside the fire. Though the room keeps warming, his pale face is numb and cold. Suddenly, someone tapped the door.

"Armion, my dear son, we want to have a word with you?"

Hatra spoke up. When the door opened, Hatra and Hatop walked in. Armion sat on his bed with sad eyes.

"What is the problem, Armion? You never showed up even for supper," Hatra questioned gently.

Armion nodded.

"Were you being sick Armion?" Hatra asked again.

"If you have any problems, we can discuss them, Armion. We are your parents," Hatop said kindly.

"We apologise my son. We hurt yourself" Hatop came close to Armion and warmly kept his hands on Armion's shoulders.

"Oh it's not an issue with you. I am not twisted with the past," Armion raised his voice.

"Then what is the issue my dear" Hatra asked anxiously.

Armion breathed and wrinkled his lips.

"I am in love," he whispered.

"And I want to marry her."

"but," Hatra interrupted.

"Wait, mother, let me finish. She is not a princess. A poor simple girl. Though she neither possesses any higher status, she holds true a heart. Which I am yearning for; thus, I am deeply stuck with her. If I am not able to marry her, I will stay forever alone." he said firmly.

"If it so, what do you expect? Why are you trying to neglect us? We always wanted to be with you," Hatop said tenderly.

"It doesn't mean I have disobeyed you. On the contrary, I would rather respect both of you as my parents. But, nevertheless, I am not pleading for your permission, and I would never ever change my decision" he looked away downheartedly.

"I am glad to hear that you are talking about your marriage my son. It is such a pleasant surprise for me. Isn't it Hatop?" Hatra turns out to Hatop delightedly.

"Of course," Hatop confirmed.

Armion gave a glance at them with a startling face.

"I must admit, Armion. What you have believed about us it was totally misjudgement. You will get our whole blessings, son," Hatop smiled politely.

"We wish to see the success and happiness of both you and Joser, and that is my one and only hope," Hatra peers to Armion.

"My dear, we always stand by you, we trust you more than everyone."

"I am sorry, mother. I have never thought you would understand my emotions."

"As a family, we have to be together, son. So you can do anything as your wish. We never bother you," Hatop said thoughtfully.

"Armion, we will bring Arianna to the castle, and I will command the maids to get ready the carriage."

"How do you know her mother?" He asked surprisedly.

"I can sense your heart, my son. It means I understand herself without a doubt," Hatra replied softly.

"Now, we can arrange your grand wedding, and it was my most awaited dream, isn't it, Hatop" Hatra looked at Hatop with sparkling eyes.

"Of course as your pleasure my queen," Hatop beamed.

....

Arianna sat leaning towards the wall on the corner, staring at Luma's empty armchair. She hid her face on her bent legs and sobbed silently. The whole atmosphere was remarkably muted. She realised that it was hard to accept this silence anymore. Yet it was unable to relieve her agony. She cannot get rid of all her worries. Suddenly she shakes with the unexpected thud on the door. Someone repeatedly bangs the door hard.

"Arianna, open the door" She stood up abruptly with that familiar sound. Then she snuggled inside the dark corner, shivering.

"Arianna, I know you are there, so open the door before I break," a harsh, threatening voice filled her ears.

"Samuel," she let out fear and gasped. Finally, however, she dragged her frozen limbs close the door. Samuel repeatedly shouted, then shaken the door. Finally, Arianna unlocked the door and stepped behind. Samuel quickly came inside and closed the door.

"What on earth were you doing Arianna? Didn't you hear me" he frowned madly.

Arianna looked down and stood against the wall. Samuel slowly came towards her and held her chin.

"How are you Arianna?" he said in a hushed tone.

Arianna turned her face to oppose him.

"It seems you are still ignoring me, Arianna" Samuel grinned while peering into her face.

"Ok, now get ready to go with me," he commanded.

Arianna looked at him with shocked eyes.

"No," she said out loud.

"Why?" he vaguely grasped her.

"I want to stay here, Samuel. Leave me alone," Arianna cried.

"There is no one for you Arianna, so it's my responsibility to look after you."

"I can look after myself, Samuel. You don't need to bother."

"I don't want any arguments with you. You Must come with me" Samuel pulled her and seized her inside his arms.

"Don't touch me, Samuel. Take off your filthy hands," Arianna said madly.

Samuel chuckled.

"This is not the first time I touched you, my dear," he said furiously and grasped her throat.

"You never know, Arianna, how much you are indebted to me. Whenever your mother neglected you, I cared for you. Sometimes you slept on my chest. You can't forget me, Arianna, and even I can't release you."

Arianna began to sob.

"What do you want Samuel?"

"I want you, Arianna."

"You are my uncle Samuel, why you behave like this?"

"When we leave Thebeslon, no one will know that secret. So we can build our own world peacefully."

"You are insane, Samuel; you are totally insane," Arianna tried to get free from his mighty arms.

"You were right I am insane, and I will be more insane if you didn't agree with me" He arrested her strenuously inside him.

"I cannot come with you. And I am not ready to satisfy your vulgarity. You should be ashamed of yourself."

Arianna screamed.

"You don't know me Arianna, I can be more evil than you believed. So please think wisely and come with me."

"If you want, you can kill me, Samuel, and succeed in your wish over my dead body. I am much awaited to my death."

Samuel clenched his teeth and slapped her face.

"You can't die so soon," he groaned.

Arianna slouched against the wall and whimpered.

Samuel pulled her again, and Arianna struggled.

"Mother Atunura," she whispered.

Samuel lifted his arm to hit her, but Arianna pushed him with all her force on the spur moment. However, his foot was accidentally caught in the rug, and he stumbled. Samuel moaned and tried to get up again. But Arianna unfastened the door instantly and flew outside. She ran as fast as she could. It was almost dark all over. Arianna wept silently, never knowing the actual end of this miserable life. Suddenly, she sensed all her eyes caught in some gloom. Arianna panted feebly. Then she glimpses the slight glint of something swiftly approaching her. Some bright shadow vaguely ran towards her, yet her eyes slowly shut in the pitch of black.

CHAPTER 21

A rmion gazed at Arianna worriedly, who was sleeping silently. He touched her innocent face, which looked pale. Her entire frail appearance aggravated his sadness.

"What happened to you my Arianna?" he mumbled.

"Armion" Hatra came close to him.

"She is weak and broken down with her mother's unexpected death. Give her some time Armion. She needs to be recovered from that tragic past" Hatra patted his head softly.

"I can't see her like this, mother."

"Everything would be fine, Armion, be patient."

"I don't know how much I should have to thank you, mother, for understanding me and taking care of Arianna."

Armion hugged Hatra.

"I want to see your happiness, my son; that is my ultimate wish" Hatra kissed Armion's head.

Arianna opened her eyes after hours. She looked around with her eyes full of aches. Still, slight gloom wandered throughout her.

"How are you Arianna?" Armion embraced her.

"You made me so scared, Arianna. At that moment you fell over on my hands. And you didn't open your eyes so I." He stopped his words sadly.

"What?" Arianna murmured confusedly.

"What happened to me, Armion? Where am I?

"You are in the castle, my darling, with us," Hatra appeared.

"Mother," Armion smiled.

Hatra sat beside Arianna and held her hand.

"How are you my daughter?" Hatra asked kindly.

"Your Majesty," Arianna stammered.

"No, my daughter, you should call me a mother hereafter."

Hatra said warmly. Arianna quickly turned her eyes to Armion. He saw the bewildered look on her face,

"Arianna, my parents gave their consent to me to marry you," he uttered.

"What? Can it be" she whispered.

"Of course, we grant whole our blessings for you two," Hatra exclaimed.

"Look, my daughter, I am arranging everything for a grand wedding ceremony, so you must rest adequately. She admitted happily and came close to Arianna.

"You are gorgeous my dear and I am so impatient to see you as a beautiful bride of my son," Hatra said with a bright smile and touched Arianna's face.

"Your Majesty, I have no words to describe your kindness. And I am owed to you for your entire sympathy and good heart towards me," Arianna said with eyes full of tears.

"No no my dear, I don't want to see you cry. Please don't cry." Hatra consoled her, wiping the tears.

"Armion, my son, I have a lot of work to do during a; short period; therefore, would you like to join me?." Hatra smiled, gazing at him.

"Yes, mother," Armion quickly agreed.

"Arianna get some sleep Betty will look after you, If you need something let her know" Armion kissed her hand

and moved out with Hatra.

"Mother" Armion stopped near the door.

"Yes, my son" Hatra turned back to him.

"I have never known you hold such a big heart; hence I feel so proud of being your son. I love you very much, mother." Hatra stared at Armion for a few seconds speechlessly and opened up.

"You have never known how much I loved you, my son. I committed my whole life to raise you up. Do not ever leave me Armion. Stay with me until my last breath. I have nothing without you my son." Hatra tried to stop her tears.

"No mother, I would never ever leave you. I promise to you" Hatra kissed his forehead and smiled.

After a few days, Arianna recovered completely, and the whole mansion came to be ready for the grand royal wedding of Prince Armion. Queen Hatra became extremely busy with the preparations. She wandered through the castle while Lord Hatop relaxed with a bottle of wine.

He spent his life as usual without bothering with any matter. Then, the day before the wedding, Armion and Arianna walked along the sea beach.

"Armion, I confronted lot of awful incidents past days. It hurt me a lot, terrifying me like a bad nightmare. I want to tell you about all these. I am so helpless and incapable of forgetting them," Arianna sobbed.

Armion placed his finger on her mouth to cease her words, and then his warm lips slowly ran through her eyes along with her wet cheeks. Arianna closed her eyes to grab his warm breath. Her head rested on his chest while both arms hung around his shoulders.

"I want to see only your smile, Arianna, not your tears. We cannot change that gloomy past, so let it flow away with this breeze. Let's start our new life with colourful hopes." They spend a few minutes letting their eyes meet each other. Then they slowly stepped onto the beach, twisting their hands. They had a bunch of talks, fantasising about their upcoming life. However, their dreams were high and soared far beyond the horizon. Yet, the sun was almost halfway sunken in the dark ocean. The clouds unhurriedly captured the red sky. The dark enclosed the dazzling ivory sea ripples, never letting them reach their dreams. The dreams abandoned with the absence of light. However, the ocean enfolds the waves hesitantly. Thus, their wishes are bound by the drowning sun, never knowing about the evil cave of darkness concealed deep inside.

....

The next day morning, sunbeams shine through the Armion's eyes. His bright, handsome, attractive image captured others' attention. Arianna thought that she was flying over a fairy tale. Hatra heartily welcomed all the guests. When she spotted Arianna's appearance, she shouted happily.

"Look everyone, the God gifted me a most charming daughter to care my beloved son. My Armion, the crown prince of kingdom Thebeslon. Arianna is my own loving daughter. I would never consider her as daughter in law because I represent myself, as her loving mother."

The visitors greeted the new couple and praised Queen Hatra. Arianna looked around with sparkling eyes. Hatra's extraordinary, kind words surrendered her in a momentary hallucination. Eventually, poor Arianna was eligible to touch the unique, genuine relationship between the mother and daughter.

The whole kingdom was delighted with the announcement of Prince Armion's grand royal wedding. People have become so keen to learn about it. His dedicated, charismatic nature made him quite famous at a very young age in the kingdom. Armion's unfeigned broad smile and his gracious, warm heart pleased the people well. Hence, they expected their future king, Armion, to fulfil their bountiful dreams and bring real prosperity to Thebeslon with his skilled, excellent leadership. Even though Prince Joser was good-looking and powerful, Armion's vivid, kind eyes and peaceful gestures stood first in their bottom heart.

A thousand daisies decorated the castle. Numerous notable royal guests accompanied the function. Each person was stunned by the enchanting sight of the bride, dressed in a gorgeous, brocaded gown. It was dazzling and exquisite, fitting to her attractive slim body. The valuable, magnificent, lavish jewellery ornamented her long neck, ears and hands. Queen Hatra made all these a special gift for Arianna. Gaika watched around, looking slightly miffed. Her heart secretly fussed with countless logic. Frankly, her wedding dress and jewellery were not impressive and elegant compared to Arianna's. Besides, she was not warmly welcomed by the palace. Their wedding was celebrated, most likely as an ordinary function rather than a splendid royal occasion. Foremostly, Gaika greeted Arianna cordially because of Arianna's pitiful status, and her nasty family stories majorly contented herself. She was worried about the terrible circumstances she would have to cope with if Armion married a reputable royal princess. Thus, throughout the extended period, she ardently convinced Hatra that a high self-esteemed princess might create multiple issues for innocent and soft-hearted Armion. She calls him" my little brother." However, when she heard about Arianna and Armions secret love, it elated her greatly. But, all those reasons brought her joy turned into an unknown bitterness. Because Arianna is enormously prettier than Gaika. Hence, she was immensely praised by almost all visitors. This disappointment made Gaika sulky and disheartened. Then, slowly, she realised that someday, this beautiful Thebeslon dancer would be eminently crowned as the prestigious queen of King Armion. Gaika tightened her lips while staring at Arianna. But she neither forgets to promote her warm wishes to her little brother and sister.

"My dear sister-in-law, I wish you eternal success and joy." She politely hugged Arianna. Then she turned at Armion

"Oh, my little brother" She warmly greeted him.

"You may have a wonderful journey of life with entire prosperity," Gaika uttered with overflowing kindness.

Afterwards, she walked a little distance away from the couple and stared at them, secretly giving a sour look to Armion. But Armion never noticed it.

"This coward made total catastrophe to Joser. If he was not born, Joser would be the most renowned King in Thebeslon. And I am his glorious queen. But now I will have to suffer throughout my life, losing my reputation in front of this filthy girl. Such a disgraceful misjudgement of destiny." Gaika mumbled to herself with furrowing eyebrows, then gritted her teeth. She scowled at Arianna quietly as her face reddened and her eyes fired angrily.

Luma's brothers and sisters were stunned when they saw Arianna as the future king's adorable bride.

That entire royal grand wedding startled them deeply. However, Seth, Hugo, and their wives admitted their heart full wishes to Arianna and embraced her with love. The cold tears streamed from their evil eyes. They regret it mainly because they failed to take advantage of their royally combined niece. The long-distance they sustained through the past tragic period Arianna faced alone had flattened whole bonds between them and her.

Ahead of time, Arianna's presence made them irritated. Their eyes filled with jealousy always hung around her since she was a kid. While their children undergo a complex, poor and ordinary life, Arianna is fortunate to possess a wonderful, luxurious childhood as the daughter of lord Ramses. However, her all-wealthy status sharpened their misery. Therefore, their total heartache was ultimately resolved when Ramses got permanently expelled from her life. They satisfied their atrocious minds by dropping her down to an ill fate solely created with their aid. Unfortunately, this entire sequenced story progressed unexpectedly, startling their wicked, monstrous souls. They breathed rapidly while the envious fires raged out from their red-blooded eyes. The Ovigons coiled inside their craving spirits with hatred and resentment and were delighted.

The ordinary people in Thebeslon rumoured plenteous amounts of tales related to Arianna. The elderly men recollect their memorable stories linked to Yesmin and Luma. The middle-aged women are impatient with their unmarried young daughters and covertly worried about their bad luck. Therefore, they fraudulently connected that history to Arianna and criticised her for using her flirtatious nature to trap the poor crown prince. They bragged about their unspoiled, well-mannered daughters while knitting mountains of untrue gossip to one guiltless, kind-hearted girl. Because it utterly pleased their cruel insight.

Meanwhile, the young men who tried to twist with her purely to satisfy their lusty desires renamed Arianna, similar to the perfect gold digger. They confirmed that she is more talented than her grandmother. Besides, they show off their very own intelligence, which helped them secure their remarkable virgin souls from that cheap girl. At the same time, queen Hatra was highly appreciated by her old maids solely for her immeasurable humility, sensibility and boundless love towards her son. They said it totally exhibited her exceptional enormous heart. The noblewomen in the kingdom honoured Queen Hatra because of her humble, down-to-earth attitude. However, they exaggerated that Queen Hatra showed her selfless manner by letting her most noticeable, highly reputed son marry an ordinary woman from a low-class family instead of a royal princess. Neither remembered Queen Hatra's nasty past stories and the tragic death of their legendary king Amenmose because of Hatra's misdeeds. However, they scrubbed queens' stained, grubby, blackened robes with all their might and blamed a sinless virgin for her speckless white robe. Profoundly, the colour white is not illuminated, radiant, or enchanting. But crafty art's colourful, glowy patterns shine foremost and are absolutely eye-catching.

Seth and Hugo muted their lips for not dribbling a word about Lord Ramses. They were gratified to hear the fancy rumours hanging around the kingdom. Most of it thrilled them except for some, So they precisely drew a veil over the Arianna's true identity. They wished to cease herself being honoured about her own inherited royal blood. Alternatively, they spread other fake talks about the ill luck she carries. They said it badly affects Luma and the rest of the family. While unrolling the embellished stories throughout everyone, they confirmed that her horrible misfortune would destroy the palace. But Arianna is unaware of all their barbaric minds as she is utterly fulfilled with her most loving soulmate. She politely thanked everyone who greeted her. Armion could not escape his eyes from her gorgeous smile, and all her innocence and humble attitude touched his heart. It seemed to be everyone cheering them wholeheartedly for a joyous, blissful life. However, they walked among the crowd, twisting their fingers.

....

Armion leads the way to Arianna's room. As he opened the door, she slowly footed in. The royal maid greeted them obediently and arranged some hot tea.

"Your highness, let me know if you need something," she told Arianna respectfully.

"Thank you so much." Arianna replied.

As the maid moved out, slamming the door soundlessly, Arianna walked inside the room and rolled her eyes timidly. It was a cosy, grand, luxurious spare sizeable and more attractive than her tiny old room. The room seemed quiet and peaceful. The long windows with neat curtains allow the dainty sun rays to brighten it. Several transparent, slender, open-mouthed vases are abundantly ornate with freshly bloomed daisies. Their various radiant colours were enriching and marvellous. Besides, a pleasant fragrance unfurled through the air. The broad bed covers the rich ivory colour sheets and a comfortable, nicely pleated, ruddy panel with a golden border. The large pillows leisurely encircled around. Frankly, Arianna has never seen such an opulent, lavishly decorated room. The stupendous view of this gigantic royal castle had dazed her during the past few days; presently, it baffled her mind. Eventually, she became desperate when she realised the vast distance between herself and Armion. She looked down to get rid of the fearful thoughts that suddenly shot into her head about her upcoming new life. Because she has neither awareness nor prepared herself as a royal princess.

Armion came close to her, and his arm wrapped around her waist. Arianna leaned to his shoulder while he peeked through her scary eyes. Then his finger ran through her long neck and nose and waited on her fearful eyes.

"Arianna, what I possess it's all yours. And there is no difference between this all materialistic world and yourself, all these materials solely created to comfort this ruining trunk nothing else," he whispered. Arianna gave a light smile.

"How you read my mind Armion."

"Because it's mine," he chuckled, and his fingers ran around her glossy hair. Then, he silently removed all the gorgeous white roses her hair held.

"What are you doing Armion?" she asked.

"Wait, these roses are not perfectly matching you, Arianna," he answered.

"Of course, these roses are eligible for royal diva not for a poor low girl like me." she uttered in a stilly voice.

"No you are absolutely wrong my dear I mean you are more attractive and much precious than these roses."

As he stood behind her, his arms enclosed her shoulders, and he gathered her hair while kissing her neck.

"It's not true, Armion. I am scared," she whispered.

"Why" he turned her to him.

"Listen, my dear, even though these roses are rich and elegant, carries all dignity unfortunately it hold sharp rowdy thorns. It can prick and hurt. Honestly it carries a beauty outwardly but inside it remains heartless. The self-image of vanity is worthless to me. But this golden daisy possess to me truly beautiful in both in and out. So you are a gift for me Arianna."

Armion placed his lips on both her eyebrows with enormous love. While Arianna stared at him sparklingly, he grabbed the daisies nearby. He unhurriedly decorates her hair with bright, dazzling daisies.

"Now it looks perfect," he said gleefully. Arianna touched her hair and giggled. And again, his hands wander around her. He slowly unfastened all the jewellery she wore.

"What are you doing? Armion." she queried with a frightened face.

"Don't worry, my dear. I am only taking out this jewellery."

Armion whispered and smirked while Arianna turned away and closed her face shyly. He removed the necklace, bangles and even her earrings.

"Now it's simply you, my charming, innocent princess, I love this simplicity snatched my heart forever," he said happily. Arianna's arms swiftly hang around his neck. But soon, he lifted her up.

"Armion put me down, please," she shouted, laughing.

"No, I have a request; I will put you down only if you agree."

"What's now, Armion?"

"You have to come with me to go forest creek."

"Now" Arianna exclaimed.

"Yes," he grinned.

"Armion, it's almost the evening."

"Yes my dear, the evening is still young and we can come back before the dusk."

Arianna nodded to say yes, and Armion twirled around while carrying her. Arianna fondled him with shining eyes.

....

Armion rides his horse carefully to the woods as Arianna holds him frighteningly. Then she closed her eyes and wrapped his back more tightly.

"Arianna, don't be so afraid, as a princess you should be brave. Remember you have to learn a lot," he said.

"No, never not me."

"Open your eyes unless I will pinch you," he laughed.

"Don't be so rude, Armion. You are too bad," she complained. Then, she closed her eyes and remembered the night she spent with him in the treehouse.

"But now everything has changed. I am with you forever."

she thought silently with her joyful heart.

Armion got down first and carried her out in his arms as they reached the place. He carried her under the shady oak tree and stretched her on the carpet of green grass. But Arianna kept her eyes shut and held her smile.

"Open your eyes, princess, or get ready," he stopped.

"What?" she asked in a secret tone.

"I am going to tickle you," he said aloud, inclined over to her as his fingers moved vaguely around her. Arianna laughed without stopping.

"Please don't Armion," she pleaded among the laughs.

After a while, Armion lay down beside her and sighed with a smile. While relaxing on his chest, Arianna looked all over. The wildflowers sway with their breath and cheer the recently wedded couple. As the birds began to skip on the grass, whistling their tunes, the leaves whirled in the eddies of wind. The creek sounded like a gentle and peaceful song. Then, it runs over the curved rocks dispersed, which neither hassles the rhythm. They followed their melody together, recreating an extraordinary beauty to the whole atmosphere.

"I wish my father was here today," Arianna uttered.

"Oh, I totally forgot about it, my dear," Armion said.

"Arianna, who is your father may I know his name? Is he live in Thebeslon?" He questioned anxiously.

"It is so complicated Armion, my mother never wanted to talk about him. She cursed him often. She said he fled out from us because of his execrable character. Even my grandparents and my uncles found disgraced to talk about him. They all hate him. My mother warned me not to spill any word about him. She was scared all his awful matters might spoiled my life."

Arianna cast a wistful glance at the sky.

"But there is something that I couldn't forget him."

"What is that, Arianna?"

"He sensed his love though I shared a very short time with him. I slept on his chest cuddling inside his warmth. He gave me everything what I wish. He was my father and still he is whatever others say about him."

"Maybe we can find him out, Arianna."

"I don't want to be cursed by my mother's soul Armion. I promised her to forget him forever."

"But," Arianna sighed.

"What?" Her gloomy face stuck between his palms.

"Each night, when I am on my bed, I wait to meet him secretly. Simply in my dreams. I was yearning to wrap inside his warm breath. But he never showed up to me. He is far away from me."

"Whole this life remains as a dramatic imagination Arianna from the entrance and end. We carry our miseries together with smiles in that dream until our last breath. But merely we are acting in this drama. So let it leave and enjoy. Because all of us have announced our farewell someday to the roles, we play in this acting. So do not ever have faith in this dream. Never be shattered by it."

She grasped his fingers while bearing a thin beam on her lips.

"Oh, come on my dear, we have to grant our gratitude to this woods and this oak tree for protecting our secrets of love" He pulled her up.

"Thank you all," he shouted out.

"Goddess of nature mother Atunura may grant your kind blessings for our new journey," Arianna mumbled, starting at his glimmering eyes of hope.

"And now we have to salute the creek" he smiled.

"But how," she said.

Armion swiftly dragged her towards the creek, and soon, they began to splash water on each other. They played until the dark warned them to return back. As their elated echo unfurled all over the woods.

CHAPTER 22

Armion rode back to the palace, and they caught in a drizzle suddenly fell. Arianna huddled in his warmth along the route as they returned, the dusk surrounding the way. The stilly night heartily welcomed them. Armion grasped Arianna's hand.

"Arianna"

"Yes," Arianna stammered with trembling lips, and her long dress was almost slightly wet.

"Come on. I will carry you" Armion smiled with his glistened eyes.

"No, Armion, I feel awkward if somebody might spot us," She said hesitantly.

"Oh, come on, Arianna, this is my palace, so I am the crown prince," he said and peeped into her eyes.

"The crown prince commands you to obey or else accept his sweet punishment."

Armion dragged her vaguely, allowing his arms to fasten around her waist. He captured her inside his warming breath. While he was staring at her face, her eyelids flickered. She leaned backwards, letting the fingers enclose his neck.

"I cannot obey you, your highness."

"Because," she halted.

"What?" he bent forward and whispered.

"Because I am not afraid of your punishments," she chuckled. Armion grinned.

"Just wait and watch. You never know this crown prince Armion."

Then instantly, one arm gathered around her back, and his other grabbed her bended knees.

"No Armion," Arianna cried, looking all over.

But Armion quickly began to climb the steps holding her.

"Am I heavy?" she asked secretly.

"Hmm, much heavier than the large whale," he laughed.

"Armion, you are too bad" She frowned at him and pinched his arm.

"Oh, don't pinch me Arianna, I will put you down," He shouted.

Arianna raised her eyes fearfully.

"Oh don't worry my dear I am holding you forever and you will never fall over from my arms," he uttered.

Armion brought her in front of the room. Her joyous giggles broke the silence of the atmosphere. As he opened the door, Arianna was startled by the entire appearance inside.

Innumerable flower petals covered the floor. The shine of the several burning candles already lights up the gloom. Arianna closed her eyelids to sense the charming resilience of fresh flowers. The fragrance of blossoms and the gratifying aromatic scent of candles contemporaneously unfurled all over the place. The dinner lay on a fascinated, decorated desk in the middle of the space. Many platters were served around, and indeed, they were ambrosial. A few steps behind in the corner, a log fire was burning. It warmed up the whole chamber. Beside the fire, The large bed seems enchanting with the numerous designs of flower petals scattered throughout the panels. Arianna forgot her breath and looked at Armion with great eyes.

"It's all my greetings for us from my mother," he said, wrapping his fingers around her waist.

"See how much she loves you," he smiled, staring at her.

"The whole mansion welcomes you, my love," Armion said, kissing her hand.

"I feel like I am dreaming Armion I am still amazed and it hard to believe all these."

"We are all stuck in a dream Arianna however you have to sense before you close the eyes. This swinging life going up and down. Therefore you are ought to turned away from that awful past and accept this gift of fabulous moments."

"All the moments I spent with you are a sole reward for me," she mumbled.

"Come on, I have to show you something," Armion pulled her while opening the large wide window. It directed to the long, expansive terrace. The small pots of Jasmines, lavender and daisies created a pleasant sight.

"I love to grow flowers," Armion said, touching the Jasmines.

"The presence and the fragrance blotted out my miseries," he sighed.

"What miseries, Armion; why were you sad in this gigantic castle?" Arianna touched his face.

"It's not the time to talk about that Arianna, anyway, forget them all."

Arianna embraced him, and their eyes met with each other.

"Look, Arianna look at that tiny star shining alone," he pointed. Arianna raised her head.

"I used to look at the sky most nights; it holds some mysterious star patterns. This boundless sky is incredibly fascinating. Just look it carefully to glimpse the beauty."

He stood right behind her and said calmly, leaning towards her ears. Then, while both arms encircled her belly, he rested his chin on her shoulder. Arianna giggled when her neck got tickled by his warm breath. His lips restlessly wandered throughout it to then snatched her rosy cheeks.

"Armion," she whispered, with halfway shut eyes. Then, slowly, he grabbed her lips. Arianna entangled with him and seized inside him deeply.

The soft glow of the moon wholly lit up the sky much fulgently. But unfortunately, the tiny beam of the star is rarely presentable among the splendent moon.

"Armion"

"Hmm"

"The star you pointed to me doesn't look remarkable when it comes up with this bright moon. It is completely not much shiny and notable. So why are you after that?" she turned towards him. He smiled while arresting her again inside him once more. His lips roamed all over her softly and gently. He patted her face.

"It's because I am in love with that little star. But only my eyes catch up with its light. Simply only to me. And it shines behalf of myself. That star pleased me over and above. It is my one and only wishes. And I know It will utterly heal my soul," he murmured, staring at her sparkling eyes.

"If it so," Arianna whispered.

"You are the most precious gift I have ever received, Armion. Thank you so much for your unlimited love."

"Ok, then there is a way you to show your gratitude for me, Arianna," he said.

"What?" Arianna wrinkled her forehead.

"Well, teach me how to dance."

Arianna chuckled softly.

"Teach you to dance now," she said surprisedly.

"Yes, shall we?"

"But why do you want to learn dance?"

"Look, I have already learned a lot of things. But now I am married to Thebeslon dancing queen so that you can be my tutor very simple."

"Yes, it seems to be very simple and quite interesting," she grinned.

"But, there is a rule."

"A rule," she repeated.

"Listen carefully, hereafter, you are eligible to teach dance only for me, and you are strictly not allowed to dance in front of others except me."

"Oh that's too harsh Armion isn't it?" Arianna wrapped her arms around his shoulders.

"No not at all, so will you agree with my command?" he questioned.

"Well, it shows up your jealousy but I, feel bit tired" She quickly released her arms and turned backwards.

"Ok, accept my command or else obey my punishment. This time, it would be rowdier."

Armion drew her back and arrested her inside him.

"You are taller than me," Arianna tried to get released.

"Then you can step on my toes."

"I feel cold, Armion" she turned around.

"Then embrace me more closely, Arianna," he whispered, tugging her hastily towards him. She smiled gratefully and stepped on his toes. At the same time, his arm rang around her waist. Arianna tangled her fingers with him. They danced slowly with the rhythm of the cold breeze.

"You lied to me Armion, aren't you?"

"I never lied, Arianna."

"You know how to dance more precisely, and frankly, you don't need any lessons."

"Oh perhaps I was secretly watching your quite a long time and eventually became an expert of that" He chuckled.

"How interesting" she smiled and nodded. Armion grabbed her hand and twirled her into his arms.

"It's only you and me, Arianna, alone," he whispered. She stared at him with glistening eyes, and an enchanting smile crossed her face.

"So then," she uttered secretly. Armion stopped him for a second and watched her effulgently. Arianna trembled in the chilly wind and unfolded in his arms. As her wavy hair locks his face, she lifts her hand to shift it away. But Armion slowly grasped it onto him and laid it on his shoulder. Then he gently gathered her wavy hair behind her ear. Arianna twinkled her eyes.

"I only followed your steps, Arianna, but I want to invade your beauty completely to bring our souls together. So I am delighted to make this moment unforgettable," he mumbled.

Some uncontrollable emotions tingle them in each step. But Arianna let him control the rhythm of their movements. There was no force to hold them back while pursuing their bliss of promises. Armion drew her close to his chest, and her arms encircled around his neck.

"I want to see your shine of beauty," he whispered.

Arianna set her head onto his shoulders, and he halted his steps. Then she lifted her head as her halfway shut eyes stared into him.

"I am all yours," she said secretly. Then Armion leaned forward and placed his lips on her. He slowly wrapped his arms around her neck and held her tightly. Arianna felt the burning warmth while smitten with his partly opened eyes glimmering with some unknown desires. His lips insanely passed all over her neck and deeply arrested her arousing sentiments. Arianna shut her eyelids and stretched on his arms. He lifted her delicately and carried her inside. Then, he laid her on the bed more gently than he held a flower. Arianna's long wedding gown unhurriedly dropped from his fingers without distressing the rose petals beneath. The candles could hardly glow with the soft wind, which blissfully invited the inner chamber. Armion's lips sensed her entire pure body and attracted her to be enwrapped with him. He healed her more calmly and peacefully. His magnetic persuasive superiority overflowed deep inside her and cured her unconditionally. While his lips murmured her name a thousand moments, they drowned in their paradise. Her all beauteous breast emblems, the white swans squeezed under his blazing broad chest. Her own sudden gushed ulterior desires stuck with that delight. Her silky lips signed various patterns around his tireless body. While Armion was resting on her, his deep, indulged sighs fluttered in her heart. He nuzzled her face, and his winsome smile abandoned her in mountainous love. It was a perpetual gift of moment relief to be concealed with their virgin life rhythms. Armion kissed her incessantly, and then she slowly fell asleep on his chest.

"Sleep tight, my so love," he whispered and slowly drew the warm panel to cover her unveiled beautiful body. His eyes kept watching her, and then his fingers smoothly ran through her wavy hair and pinkish cheeks.

While they are holding contentment with their new journey, a dark shadow is covertly watching them. The eyes of the dark shadow were red, and it became more horrible when that flaming dark heart sighted Armion's enormous love for Arianna. All Arianna's happy waves of laughter raise her heart's pace. A fire of envy blew out from her blazing eyes while gazing at their romance. She groaned soundlessly and grasped her black gown tightly to control herself. And she is no one else, the loving mother of Prince Armion. Queen Hatra crept under the shady large bush opposite Armion's chamber. However, that location made an excellent place for her to watch her newly married son.

Queen Hatra tried to close her eyelids as she spotted Armion kissing Arianna because she sensed all that view pricking her eyes. Though Armion showed up, his boundless love for Arianna Hatra received endless criticism from Hatop. He constantly nags Hatra, blames her, and many times disgraces her. Neither romance nor adorable words are present in their relationship. Armion holds Arianna in his arms, but Hatra gets slapped and kicked out by Hatop. During the first meeting, Hatop was impatient about knowing her body instead of recognising her heart. Hatra's nudity, her physical outline over, thrills him apart from her isolated heart. Hatop's lips never spill his warm, charming, loveable sentiments. Yet she was hardly bitten by his rowdy, wild lips. Hatra was amazed by her son's warm attitude and how calmly he touched Arianna's whole soul. He was much more passionate about her emotions rather than her body. His affection, together with his kindness, was overflowing around Arianna. And it was profoundly mind-boggling.

"Could he be the son of that cruel stony-hearted man?" she whispered slowly. She closed her ears when listening to Armion's enchanting phrases of "I love you" was painful. Those words Hatop have never uttered in their past love story. Hatra wrinkled her forehead angrily when she sighted how serenely Armion embraced Arianna. Indeed, his soft fingers neither harassed the flower petals surrounding her. But Hatop vigorously ripped Hatra's gown, and his fingers desirously ran through her. At the same time, his red eyes flamed with limitless lust. Hatop utterly pursued after the physical excitement fairly. Hatra played her part as the prayer to the reflection of his superficial bond. Hatop never bothers about her after he contents himself neither of his lips trouble to kiss her delicately as Armion does with Arianna. But Hatop only worried about his smoking pipe and halfway emptied rum pot. It pleased him more than everything. After giving a slight peek to Hatra, he swiftly moved away. It was the end for him until he sat with her for another meeting.

Hatra's entire body tensed. She begrudged Arianna's fortunate stroke of luck.

"Even though she was born under the poverty roof she is greatly fortunate than me. I am the most renowned royal queen of Thebeslon but my destiny punished me harshly. I wonder what's her eligibility to possess his wholehearted love. Neither commitment she is holding behalf of him. I got tortured, slapped and cursed while carrying him in my womb. I was condemned and completely agonised while raising him up. Now he is the future king of the kingdom and she is about to become the queen. They are all happy and fulfilled but only my life is halfway ruined. Neither praised me for my devotedness. Though I dedicated my whole youth for Hatop but I gained nothing behalf of my sacred love I gave only to him. I grieved my whole life alone and they are rewarded with a blissful future. Can it let happen?" Hatra thought silently and clenched her fist.

"It is unacceptable," she mumbled.

"I must obtain justification for myself and I should fight for it," Hatra says to herself with glistening eyes. Then, suddenly. A hissing sound touches her ears.

"Orana," Hatra whispered with a tiny smile.

As she raised her head, a black viper appeared before her. It curled, and its eyes sparkled in red. It hissed violently, showing its sharp fangs. Hatra grinned.

"I know you are happy to offer me your blessings, Orana."

"Of course, Queen Hatra, you might be a chase for another goal to discover your contentment," Orana's voice came out.

"I am seeking my harmony and I am eligible for it," Hatra exclaimed.

"It's you queen Hatra. You fight simply with you, not with outward. You are bearing your peace already though it unseen and remains hidden from you until you destroy yourself."

"No," Hatra muttered.

"You can keep up running I am pleased with it all your efforts which revive my soul. It nourished me for far beyond and this chain proceeds without a halt. So I am with you eternally." Orana laughed.

"I want to satisfy myself."

"There is no gaining until you are aware of nature's rhythm, yet we both have to get away from it. You should learn to cry in the misery and laugh among the joy. And Fight for yourself to seek the desire because all desires you seek pleasures me, and it's my survival. Don't ever forget your desire. Chase for it senses it as much as you could."

"But"

"What?" Hatra raised her brows.

"Don't ever forget the agony follows you."

"No, I want to demolish all this suffering."

"Only nature knows the secret to smiling between both pain and elation. To bear it the same way and to be immortal. I am vulnerable among the power of nature, but you are the one who promotes my life, so I must follow you as long as you hold me. I am your desire. Grab me and hold me tight, Queen Hatra I am your hatred and your fear maybe your envy or your exhilaration. I am your prestigious image who governs you. Stay with me, Queen Hatra."

Hatra smirked.

"As long as you protect me, Orana."

"We ought to be together in this fantasy and remark its continuation, queen Hatra. Therefore, let me take hold of your soul more hardly and deeply."

Hatra nodded and closed her eyes. The black viper vaguely jumped, coiled around her, and vanished quickly. Then she turned and gave a glance at Armion's chamber. Her eyes shined with red, and she scowled. Then she moved her legs back to the castle while the clouds hid the moon.

....

Armion suddenly wakes up after a few hours' past midnight, and the dawn is not even ready to reach yet.

He rubbed his eyes and stared at Arianna, sleeping calmly beside him. He slanted to her and kissed her cheeks and then her lips. Arianna opened her eyes.

"Armion, are you awake, why didn't you call me up?"

Her arms tied up around him.

"I was watching you," he bit her ear and whispered.

"Why aren't you sleepy?" she asked, and her fingers wandered through his hair.

"You look more beautiful when you are sleeping so I found difficult to shuteye."

"Really" she chuckled.

"Yes, it was quite enjoyable rather than snooze," he winked.

"So," she kissed his lips and nuzzled his neck.

"I feel pity to wake you up" he snatched her lips again.

"Armion"

"Hmm"

"I am starving."

"Me too, shall we eat something?" he raised, looking around. Then, he slowly wrapped Arianna from the robe and lifted her into his arms. Arianna snuggled to him with a bright smile. Then, secretly gazed at his charming outline. His strong arms, broad chest, and attractive face with glowing eyes tickle her. She felt butterflies fluttering on her belly once again.

"What are you looking at, princess?" he asked, holding his smile.

"I wish I could lay my eyes on you every second," she replied with a bright chuckle.

Armion made Arianna sit on his lap.

"I wonder all these food platters waited for us along time," he muttered, feeding her slowly.

"I wish if I could fly out from this kingdom with you Armion."

"Why?"

"Then I can keep you all the time beside me, and we can have an ordinary life. Only you and me," she mumbled.

"I need you to become that normal person I met before but" she paused.

"But I am the crown prince," he peeked into her face.

"And I am with you each moment I promised to you."

"I know," she sighed.

"Arianna, I cannot leave this kingdom, this mansion and these responsibilities on my hands. And specially I cannot leave my mother alone here. Because she underwent a so many sorrows to made me up."

"I can understand Armion," she said calmly.

"Why don't you like this luxurious life, Arianna? You are the future queen in this castle."

"I would prefer to have a normal life with you. I want to be a typical wife rather than a princess" Arianna rested on his shoulder.

"I want to cook meals for you and grow flowers, and then I wish," she said, stopping her mouth and covering her face with both palms.

"What? what else? Tell me I am so keen to hear your dreams, Arianna" he removed her palms and held them warmly, peeking inside her eyes.

"I want to have a son, and it is my most precious dream to become the mother of your children. I am yearning to hear lot of childish giggles around us."

"How many may I know" he snuggled to her and kissed her eyes."

"It's a secret, Armion, but I want a son. A strong man who holds your blue eyes and this good heart" She kept her palm on his chest and beamed. He will possess your wavy hair, dimple whole this charming image, this bewitching smile" Her finger roamed over his face.

"And then," she looked up, thinking.

"What else" he whispered.

"Somebody like a white lotus who carries compassion and peace to heal the entire Henatan. Likewise the fragrance of the blue water Lilly unfurled each corner and everywhere. Somebody smart and exactly similar to you physically and mentally."

"What a wonderful wish" he began to kiss her with overspilling love. Ariannas giggled, her hands roamed through his neck, and she touched his necklace.

"Tanzanite," she clenched the pendant dangling down.

"Yes, Tanzanite is waiting for our journey, and it symbolises the blessings from my loving grandmother," he said thoughtfully.

"It's amazing" she patted his face.

"I have to fulfil my grandmother's dreams and rebuild whole this kingdom. Will you help me, Arianna," he asked directly, looking at her.

She nodded and kissed his head.

"The goddess Atunura, mother nature, may you grant your blessings to fulfil my life and duties. I believe you and your whole energy govern this entire earth. You gifted our lives holds our breath, and I am honoured and indebted to you for securing our souls," Arianna murmured, shutting her eyes. Yet suddenly, a terrific noise shattered her unexpectedly. It's the shrieking sound of a poor animal from far away woods. That old wailing frightened Arianna, and she shuddered with fear.

"What is that, Armion? It's so scary?" she hid inside his chest.

"Hmm, an innocent doe might be captured by a wild beast."

"No," Arianna shook.

"It's always routinely happening in the dark woods Arianna, you don't need to be scared" he embraced her.

"Even-though that doe is harmless and innocent it has more enemies, all cruelty governs this planet Arianna, once who is innocuous and guiltless easily destroyed by the heartless. This is the bitter truth of every single thing."

"That is so ruthless Armion," Arianna said in a broken voice.

"Let's get some sleep my love we have to visit some special place tomorrow."

"A special place," she repeated.

"What is that?" she twirled her eyes.

"It's a secret" he carried her back to the bed.

"I am all surprised and impatient to visit your secret place" Arianna smiled and lay on his chest. Armion cuddled her warmly inside his arms.

CHAPTER 23

Armion rode the horse along the road among the thick woods. Arianna was holding him tightly.

"Armion," she whispered. Unfortunately, she cannot see the outer because her eyes are covered with a cloth strap.

"Armion, are we close to the place?" She asked impatiently.

"Not yet, stay calm," he said in a firm tone.

"Oh, no I am tired Armion," she sighed. After some time, Armion halted the horse. He helped Arianna to get down.

"Now hold my hand Arianna, and walk with me."

"How, I cannot see anything Armion."

"If you can trust me you can follow my steps with blind eyes."
he said.

"And I am forever holding your hand until the end," he added.

"Yes, I will follow you," she agreed. So Armion began to walk, and Arianna stepped after him while their hands twisted together. They walked between the small footpath, and suddenly Armion stopped.

"Why," Arianna asked confusedly.

"We cannot walk furthermore, Arianna," he whispered to her ear and swiftly carried her into his arms.

"Armion," Arianna mumbled, enclosing her hands around his neck. He nuzzled her.

"Listen, hold me tight," he murmured.

"hmm"

She chuckled. Armion entered a shady path and began to climb along the long steps.

"Where are we going?" she asked.

"It's a surprise," he answered. Then, after some time, he paused his legs and kept Arianna down. Finally, Armion slowly removed the cloth strap, and Arianna opened her eyes.

"Oh my god, Is this heaven?" she stunned. Arianna looked around. It is a large cave, and the ground beside them seems like a pool of water. When she looked upward, a big hole was sighted. The sun-rays drop through it, and the rock surface is shrouded with greenery, plants and trees. They popped out of the hole, seeking the sun-rays. The vines holding a bunch of flowers coiled around the trunks. Numerous flower petals have fallen from the blooms decorating the water. The tiny water ripples shine together with the rainbow colour petals. Arianna stepped in front, and she widened her eyes. Something familiar was in the middle of the pool on the flat rock.

"The statue," she gasped.

"Armion, I can't believe my eyes" She grabbed his arm and embraced him. Arianna's statue glimmered among the blue water, and it looked more radiant with the dainty sun rays. Butterflies flew throughout. The water dripped down along the rocky surfaces around. The murmuring sound of water cuddles with the soft wind. The tree vines kissed the blue specks of water. Yet her statue was silently placed in the middle, resembling herself as an angel. Armion's magical fingers magnificently have remarked all her beauty on it.

"Armion, I have no words to explain how am I feeling" She stopped her words and stared at him with enormous gratitude.

"Arianna, this is the most special place for you and me. The nature holds our secrets and our bond. So whole this place is a true verdict for it. The nature ought to protect our souls until we become the part of its rhythm," he said.

"If so, I hope to seek it with you forever and ever."

"And I have something more," he smiled.

"What"

"I need your hand."

Arianna stretched her hand, and an elegant ring was placed on her one finger.

"Armion, it's beautiful," she mumbled and touched. He kissed her fingers delicately.

"This ring is a symbol of our love" and maybe a divine gift for someone who carries a golden heart." He uttered with sparkling eyes.

"So the gift should be gifted to succeed a true hope because it's blessed," Arianna whispered. Armion kissed her forehead, and Arianna cuddled him. The slight drizzle fell down, and the statue looked more captivating with the tiny raindrops. The whole picture seized in Mitra's eyes and slowly blotted out. She woke up and looked all over. Mother Atunura appeared in front of her.

"I am twisted to the dream, but it's over," she sighed.

"No, now it's just the beginning of the dream Mitra."

"Then it would be the fallacy."

"Touch it, my dear, sense it the, release it."

"I want to end it mother."

"You cannot end it unless you touch it but don't grab it."

"I don't want to be a part of that fallacy."

"Then Don't try to get out of it but don't get drowned. Realise it."

"I am confused mother."

"All acknowledgement starts with the confusion. We made reasons and those reasons will become our life."

"What is life mother?"

"It is a bundle of comparisons, we enchanted to it and those comparisons fooled us. We hold it firmly and deeply because we hesitate to get free of them. We think it's precious and important. But there's is nothing exists."

"There is no sense in life," Mitra sighed.

"There's no sense unless you destroy the creator Mitra."

"Who is the creator, mother?"

"You my dear it is simply you, because you are the owner."

"But how mother?"

"Be with you solely acknowledge about you without a force if you try hard you are incapable to unchained."

"But, unfortunately the vanity aided the most mistake."

"What do I suppose to do mother?"

"Blaze your heart and watch the flames but don't struggle, princess."

"We are unaware of our beginning and the end, mother, so we are abandoned in this dream. Yet when the breath halt, we have to leave our characters and the drama."

"But the dream continues Mitra, with another identity."

"I have to touch the hope without seizing it," Mitra whispered. Suddenly, a shiny ring dropped on her hands.

"The gift" Mitra shouted.

"The gift is for you, a gift of truth and hope."

Atunura murmured.

"How would I see it?"

"Walk among the visions, Princess Mitra. But unfortunately, this is not the end." Mitra closed her eyes.

Intermission

Until the journey begins with Amazonite..............

ABOUT THE AUTHOR

Santhushee's lifelong dream of becoming a writer began in her childhood amidst the natural beauty of Sri Lanka. Despite completing her MBBS and graduating from Tianjin Medical University in China, her passion for literature and creative writing never wavered. Determined to achieve her ultimate ambition, she embarked on her writing journey with "Tanzanite," marking the remarkable start of her writing career. As we all seek salvation in our enduring journeys, she invites readers to explore and enlighten themselves through the pages of "Tanzanite." Allow your soul to wander through her miraculous imagination.

www.ingramcontent.com/pod-product-compliance
Lightning Source LLC
Chambersburg PA
CBHW072349020726
47506CB00004B/1073